Champagne Book Group

Presents

No Hero Here

By

Faith Cameron

Champagne Book Group
www.champagnebooks.com
Copyright 2019 by Faith Cameron
ISBN 978-1-926681-69-6
Print Release: October 2019
Cover Art by Trisha Fitzgerald
Produced in the United States of America

Champagne Book Group
2373 NE Evergreen Avenue
Albany OR 97321
USA

Dedication

To my grandmother, Betty Cristaldi, and my mother, Lynn White—both guilty parties for giving me my love of romance books.

Chapter One

Somewhere in England, 1784

One.

Two.

Three.

Four.

No, no. Five.

Five highwaymen chased her carriage. *How exciting!*

Rose Witherby braced herself on the worn leather upholstery. Her racing heart fueled the cheeky grin she aimed at her brother, Robert. "I wager the rest of my molasses cookies that it's the bandit Silver Hawk. Just think of it! England's most charming criminal is intent on robbing us this day. We're so fortunate."

"Fortunate?" Robert fired his pistol into the crush of thieves. "Don't tell me you've fallen for all those outlandish tales of unparalleled good looks and exceptional manners? Bloody hell, Rose! I'm sorry to burst your bubble of high expectations, but there is nothing romantic about dying at the hands of common criminals."

"Rubbish. We're not going to die. Silver Hawk spares every life. He assaults with kind words and a heroic deposition. Robbing the rich to give to the poor, and the like." She clapped her hands together. "In fact, while we're enjoying the lively farce of being shot at, we should make ready our baubles." She dove for her bag, digging through the contents.

"Make ready our baubles? Dear God. Rose." Robert ducked as a piece of wood exploded overhead. "Listen to yourself! Do you hear those loud popping sounds? They're called gunshots. We are being attacked by real bullets, by men who doubtless have more than the acquisition of 'baubles' on their mind."

"Really? What else could highwaymen clamor for?"

He put down his weapon to give her a baleful stare. "Did you leave your wits behind in Virginia? I know you've been under a great deal of stress lately, what with your arranged marriage to a perfect stranger, but really, this innocent act of yours is beyond the pale. You know what criminals want with a woman."

"I know what English soldiers want," she said in a voice gone flat. "But Silver Hawk—"

"Is not the man out there shooting at us!" Robert scrubbed a hand over his face. "This robbery is not a farce, Rose. It's not staged. Our situation is dire, and I think you know that, no matter how much you pretend otherwise."

She cleared her throat, not caring for the grim tone in her brother's voice, or the tension filling the air between them. Her excitement fizzled. "All right, Robert. What shall we do?"

"What *can* we do is more the question. I'm afraid our options are limited." Lurching forward, he stuck his head out the window, looking ahead and backward. A sinister grin appeared as a bullet found lodging in the carriage frame. "Rose, I have an idea."

The small hairs on the back of her neck rose to attention at that grin. "I know I'm not going to like it, but let's hear it anyway." A bullet zinged past her ear and landed in the wood behind her head. "Time is of the essence."

"Right." He pointed in the direction the carriage was going. "Just up ahead there is a bend in the road and a grove of trees. When we round it, I will push you out of the carriage where you will run like mad into the grove and hide until I come for you." He grabbed her wrists, hauling her to a standing position. "Are you clear?"

"Clear as a wall!" She screeched, twisting to pull her wrists free.

He pushed her to the door of the carriage, standing behind her, so she had no retreat.

"Are you mad, Robert? The fall will kill me! Then the highwaymen will kill you! And if you're dead, who will come for me?"

Nonplussed, he looked at her. "If you're dead then you won't have to worry about highwaymen or marrying that duke. And I can die the hero for solving both your problems."

Rose gaped at the man she called brother. "I was wrong. You're not only an idiot but a morbid one at that. I thought mother and father raised you better."

They were about to go around the corner. She could see the grove of trees up ahead.

He leaned his head close. "Trust me."

She gulped, her heart thumping frantically against her ribs. "Just promise me one thing?"

"What?"

Rose took a deep breath. "Promise me, you won't scream 'God

save King George' as you toss me out. I don't want that to be the last thing I hear—oh!"

Interrupting her plea, he kicked the door open with his booted foot and pushed her out of the carriage. The battle cry used when they were children—and doing something their parents would later punish them for—had become a jest between them. While sailing through the air, she couldn't help but be pleased life would end with her having the last word.

The feeling didn't last long. Rose hit the ground hard and rolled several feet through the dirt. Her right ankle exploded in pain. Gasping, she pushed herself up onto her uninjured foot. The world tilted for a moment, as dizziness came and went. She vowed vengeance on her brother if they ever crossed paths again.

Galloping hooves rattled the earth around her. Picking up her dusty and torn skirts, she abandoned thoughts of revenge and limped her way into the grove of trees, shrinking into the shrubbery as the band of highwaymen rounded the corner in pursuit of her brother.

The sound of their chase dwindled, along with her fears of being discovered by rough men suffering from a lack of decency. She closed her eyes to rest her aching head, as a voice shouted in the distance, "God save King George!"

So the battle begins.

~ * ~

For what seemed like hours but was probably much less, rest eluded her. A nagging worry for Robert's safety surged to the forefront of Rose's mind. She forced herself up, only to wheeze as a bolt of pain raced up her leg.

"Drat!" She would be no help to Robert in this condition. Perhaps now was an excellent time to pray for a miracle. Or a fairy godmother. "Either would be a blessing at this point."

Except fairytales were make-believe rubbish. And the only miracles in life were those a man or woman performed with their own two hands. God did not listen to prayers uttered by mortals. The war with England seemed to have taught every American she knew that lesson.

Lifting her leg, she flexed the damaged foot, rotating the ankle around in a circle. No bone extended through the skin, but the area was rapidly growing. Bending, Rose ripped a piece of her tattered skirt and wrapped the fabric around the swelling joint, fastening it with a double knot.

Now for a weapon!

A few feet away, under a bed of dried, brittle leaves, lay a long tree branch with a jagged point on one end. It would serve as both an excellent staff to lean on and a nimble weapon to bash on a highwayman's head.

Perfect!

Emerging from the shrubbery, she followed the tracks produced by the carriage and herd of horses, limping and leaning on the staff, nursing a pounding headache.

An hour passed before evidence of a great battle appeared on the open highway. All around were splatters and trails of crimson red. The smell of gunpowder still permeated the air. She stared at the carnage thankful she hadn't eaten anything at luncheon. The mincemeat pie Robert tried to force down her throat would have joined the gory scene.

She had more experience with British soldiers than highwaymen, but this crew of miscreants were a bloodthirsty lot. Highwaymen were thieves. It didn't make sense to kidnap the person you intended to rob. Unless kidnapping in itself was the reason. And there could only be one purpose for that—ransom.

But who in their right minds would try to haggle payment over her brother?

More likely the highwaymen will be offering her precious coin to take back their prisoner before the night expired.

Rose bent, closely examining the ground. There were two separate paths. The carriage had taken off in one direction. The other trail was marked by a small stampede of horses. Wonderful. Hoof prints and carriage marks told her nothing. Out of all the courses she studied in school, why was tracking dimwitted men not offered among needlepoint and cooking classes? The least Robert could have done was left a note. Something along the lines of:

Dear Rose,

I'm off fighting bad guys. Hope I didn't kill you throwing you out of a racing carriage. Please fend for yourself for dinner.

All my love, Robert

P.S. Bet you wished you ate that mincemeat pie now.

Spying a small boulder beside the road, Rose collapsed on top of it. As much as it pained her to think it, there was no alternative but to assume he was either captured or injured and would not coming back for her any time soon. She shivered, glancing up at the sky. The sun's descent toward the horizon had begun some time ago. It was not a calming thought to be a lone female at night in a strange country—even if one had a staff.

Tears stung her eyes. Self-pity was never an emotion she indulged in, but damn it, what was she supposed to do now? She sagged forward on the rock, telling herself she had gotten out of worse jams than this before.

If only the duke hadn't decided to take her father's offer to heart.

But *oh no*, Sebastian Graham, the Twelfth Duke of something-or-other, had insisted she come to join him at his estate in England and live with him for the rest of her days as his duchess.

The man must be a toad to look upon if he wishes for the daughter of a man he doesn't know. Ugly and old.

A twig snapped behind her, followed immediately by another.

Was there any worse fate on a woman than to have an old duke plant his seed in your womb and declare it a joyous occasion? He's not going to give a fig if I die in childbirth. Oh no. He'll have his heir and freedom back in—

A gloved hand closed over her mouth.

A deep male voice whispered into her ear, "Stand and slowly turn, love. I've been looking for you."

Chapter Two

Rose stood and turned as the deep male voice commanded. Her brows furrowed. *What oddity was this?* In the few minutes she sat indulging her imagination, a black tree planted itself and grew roots. Her gaze lifted, ascending the tree trunk, noting a thickly corded neck and chiseled, lean jaw. A snug-fitting black mask covered the rest of his face. Over the top of the disguise was an abundance of black hair. Her gaze became ensnared by a pair of vibrant, deep brown eyes drinking in their fill, looking her over from top to bottom.

"You wouldn't by chance be the highwayman called Silver Hawk, would you?"

The mysterious eyes widened. "My lady, have I threatened you before?"

"No." She adjusted the grip on her staff, ignoring the burst of excitement she felt. "This is my first time in England, yet a girl can scarcely travel the dismal streets of London without hearing your name spill from female lips."

He grinned, displaying an even row of pearly, white teeth. "I hope you heard all good things about me."

"Indeed." Rose took a step back, to better look at the famous thief. "Most of them were hoping to be robbed by you this very day." She smiled at the rogue. "I dare say they'll be disappointed."

"The night is young, and I yet full of energy. Who knows what will happen?" The man winked.

A bubble of laughter spilled from her mouth. *What cheek!* Charming and handsome as the devil. A dangerous combination; one she ought to fear.

She lifted her chin. "Well, what now, Silver Hawk? This is my first experience with a highwayman. Do you demand coin or my virtue?"

His eyes bulged from underneath his mask. "Good God, you're bold! Are you by chance American?"

"I am, but that shouldn't signify in a robbery."

"Ah," he raised his hand, "but it does matter, if the robber does not intend to rob his victim but use the victim to blackmail a certain duke."

"I see." She grinned, unable to dredge up an ounce of worry over this potentially dangerous situation. Indeed, the notion of delaying her impending marriage was a cause for celebration.

The thief's firm lips pressed together into a grimace. "Usually, the victim in these types of circumstances begins to panic or make some attempt to escape. My lady, forgive me, but you seem rather thrilled you're about to be kidnapped. Perhaps you do not understand the danger I am placing you in?"

"Utter nonsense." Wiping the smile off her face, she adopted a serious expression, jabbing a balled fist into her hip. "Any sensible victim should realize the first thing they ought to do in these types of situations is to stay calm. I am merely following common sense."

Silver Hawk crossed his arms over his chest. "This is a lovely fairytale. Tell me, what is the second thing a victim ought to do— presumably if the victim has any common sense?" He raised a brow at that, apparently in doubt that she had any sense in her head, common or otherwise.

"Well." She nibbled her bottom lip, thinking things through. "I suppose the second thing to do would be to inquire if you mean me harm." She pierced him with a hard look. "Do you intend me harm, Mr. Hawk?"

"I haven't decided. I'd rather hear more about this virtue you were offering."

"You'll find your victim to have less value if you intend to steal away her virtue."

"A point well made." He bowed. "Bravo for having enough *common sense* to remind me of that. My lusty thoughts could have cost me a king's ransom." He smirked.

"Are all highwaymen this impudent or are you singular among your kind?"

He stepped closer, forcing her head back. Brown eyes scrutinized her face, causing heat to bloom into life on her cheeks. In fact, the whole man emanated heat like a volcano. Perspiration dotted her forehead. Dampness clung to the insides of her thighs. Parched lips begged for moisture. Having none to offer, she licked her lips with a tongue made of sand.

Her attention drifted to Silver Hawk's mouth. Wet, firm and tempting as the apple from Eden. Wonderful. A forbidden fruit dangling in front of her water-deprived face.

Silver Hawk lifted a delicious corner of his mouth. "I cannot decide if you are looking at my lips with wonder or morbid fascination. As I am a singular man amongst thieves, I fear I am forced to conclude the latter."

His face filled her vision. Did that mean? Could it be? Was he going against the rumors?

"They say you are a thief of honor, sir. You take only from those who can afford to lose. And you would never cause injury or harm to a woman."

Warm breath blew over her face as delicate as a summer breeze. "There is no dishonor in asking for a kiss from a beautiful young woman." His masked face withdrew. "The dishonor lies in taking what a lady does not offer of free will." He watched her, a bold invitation emerging from fathomless eyes.

This highwayman was dangerous. The power he wielded was a heady potion, wrapping her senses in an intoxicating spell. Tension, pleasure, apprehension—all battled for consideration. It was madness to entertain the silent request.

"Kiss me." The husky demand slipped from a loose tongue, but she did not call back the words. Breathless, she waited for the thief's reaction.

Thin lips curved upward. "Is this the request of a victim possessing common sense?" Steel crept its way into his voice as he said, "Because I must confess, at this point, I would disagree with my victim's assessment of their state of mind." He seized her shoulders, his jaw locking, nostrils flaring. "I am a highwayman, little fool! Not a romantic figure or whatever else a woman's mind may conjure." He gave her body a jarring shake. "You pay heed to bold words spoken by brazen women who should fear a man intent on robbing them. Why would you favor their carelessness?"

Mortified, she felt her cheeks grow warm. "Must I tell you?"

"Yes!"

"Very well." She breathed deep, her diaphragm struggling to expand beneath the heavy weight of his hands upon her shoulders. "I wanted to understand why so many women would wager their lives for the smallest chance to receive a kiss from your lips."

"They are fools, a title you may boast of having for desiring what other women may not have." He removed his hands, clenching them into fists at his side, turning his back to her.

Rose caught his arm when he moved to walk away, swinging his accusing glare back toward her. "You mistake intent, sir," she murmured, earning her another scowl. "A year ago, I was made an unwilling spectator while soldiers assaulted two of my dearest friends."

The lines around his mouth eased.

"I've only known violence from men, but women still demand what I have learned to fear. And I do not wish to live in fear." She held his eagle-eyed stare with more bravado than her wobbly knees could claim. "If you live by a code of honor that states you must ask consent instead of seizing what is not yours, then I must conclude you are the proper man to seek a kiss from."

Silver Hawk's posture melted from stiff anger into something else. The harshness of his lips mellowed into a soft smile. "I may have passed judgment on you too rashly," he stepped with exaggerated care closer to her, "and perhaps you are right. I am singular among my kind because I will never force a woman beneath me for baser pleasures." He bent his head, his mouth hovering above her own. "But I am still dangerous. And I am still a threat...to *you*." He cupped her face, brushing the pad of his thumb across her bottom lip with strokes to match a feather.

Her blood sang with need, rushing to the juncture of her thighs, pounding the area with visceral need. She gasped in wordless surrender as male lips closed with infinite care upon hers, molding and plaint. Strong arms the size of oak branches encircled her waist, pulling her close against a warm, hard male body.

She waited for the old fear to come rushing back, for the panic to settle into her chest. This man was a masked giant. A young maid with an ounce of sense would be terrified right now. But here she was, not only asking for his kisses but responding to them as well. Feeling proud of herself, she dared to touch a hand to his chest.

He growled low in his throat.

She liked that noise. It gave her a heady rush of power she'd never felt before. Intoxicated by this new awareness, she parted her lips when the tip of a tongue sought entrance, tracing the closed seam to her mouth...and her world exploded when Silver Hawk deepened the kiss.

Her legs dared give out. How wretched to be one of those swooning women when kissed by a man, hanging in his arms like a limp rag doll. *Intolerable*.

Rose wrapped her arms around his thick neck.

Intolerable or not, there was no harm in admitting she was injured and resting her bad ankle. It was a necessary evil to cling to this highwayman's brawny shoulders to spare herself more pain. Except now she was hurting in an entirely new location, one due north of her aching ankle.

Pinning her to his body, his tongue thrusting in and out of her mouth in erotic play, adding fuel to the massive inferno engulfing her in scorching flames.

Perhaps there existed another side to the marriage bed after all. One that spoke of longing and needs, and maybe, even love. She allowed her tongue to rub against his. The answering rumble in his chest told her he favored this bold behavior—at least in this. She kept kissing him, dangling down the front of his sculpted body, marveling at the strength of his embrace, and the touch of something else. In days past, such contact would have sent her fleeing in fear.

But this was different. Their bodies touching in intimate places fired her blood, replacing old terrors.

Silver Hawk tore his mouth away.

She opened her eyes to half-mast. Her brain was fuzzy, and a delicious lethargy was stealing over her entire body.

The highwayman's eyes were a scarce inch away from her own. She marveled at the color change. When first they met, she thought his eyes the same shade as chocolate. Now they appeared as warm maple syrup, a molten core dripping with sweetness.

"Little one," he said, lowering her feet back to the ground, "you should not look at a man in such a way if you wish to keep your innocence."

"Why? Because my husband would want it so?" Frankly, she didn't care what her future husband wanted. It was her body.

He frowned. "Because your chastity is your gift to give, and I—an unworthy highwayman—am not fit to accept such a priceless treasure."

Rose melted inside, her annoyance with him drifting away. When a man held your innocence in such high regard, one could forgive an intended insult. "I fear my betrothed may not be a man fit to receive it either. Do you know of him? The Duke of Dorchester?"

His face shuttered, losing its warmth. "I know His Grace all too well. It's why I picked you for ransom. The man could stand to lose a coin or two."

Her stomach clenched. "Is the man I am to marry so terrible?"

Silver Hawk stepped away, putting distance between them. "I heard tales of his escapades before he left for war. He was handsome of face and possessed a charm few ladies could resist. He was your typical rake."

She frowned, yet at the same time, rejoiced. At least the duke didn't sound old enough to be her sire. Robert now owed her money. "You say these things in past tense. Did he not return from war the same?"

"He returned a recluse, wearing a mask at all times." He shrugged. "People say he bears a scar. I've not seen it myself."

A scar?

The highwayman confirmed her worst fears. Rose turned away, lost in grim thoughts of her future, took a step then faltered—forgetting her injured ankle. Quick arms grabbed her before she fell onto the dirt road, pulling her once more against a well-muscled body.

"You're injured," he said, scowling. "Here, let me look."

He lowered her to the ground, but she slapped his hands away when he tried to raise her skirts. "Don't make me bind your hands," he said.

Unimpressed with his temper, she stared him down. "You wouldn't dare."

He reached to his side and held up a whipcord. "You'd be surprised what I can do with this."

Scoffing, she pointed to her abandoned staff laying on the ground. "You'd be surprised what I can do with that."

He reached a hand up to cup her cheek. "I know what a quarterstaff is, little one. I would not be surprised to see one used as a weapon. What does shock my senses is the knowledge you have not used it yet against me."

"The night is young," she recited his earlier words back to him. "And I yet full of energy. Who knows what will happen?" She winked for full measure.

The highwayman threw his head back, roaring in laughter. "Touché, little one. I must admit, you are not what I expected."

"Oh? And what did you expect?"

"I'm not sure." He offered a frank, appreciative stare. "But it was not your beauty or sense of fair play, to be certain. You must have broken many hearts back home in America when your father shipped you off to England for marriage."

She glanced away, wincing. "You cannot break a heart when no man offers his to you for breaking."

He grabbed her chin, forcing her eyes to meet his. "I find it hard to believe no young man fell in love with your beautiful face."

"If you must know," she wrenched her chin away from his grasp, "the truth of the matter is, I broke more heads than hearts when overeager young pups tried to take more than what I was offering. And all I ever offered them was friendship. A thing not wanted by young men. They felt they were entitled to *more*."

"Ah," he said, "I see. And you felt I was taking 'more' when I was hoisting your skirts to examine your ankle."

"Precisely," she said, brightening. "Kissing should not imply you may take other liberties without my consent. I'm glad you understand, Mr. Hawk."

"Very well." He sat, cross-legged, on the dirt road with her. "Miss…" he raised an eyebrow.

"Witherby. Rose Witherby of Virginia."

"Excellent. Miss Rose Witherby of Virginia, may I please have the honor of looking at your bare ankle, to see if it requires medical attention, and nothing more?"

"What more could you do with a woman's bare ankle?"

He sighed. "Don't get saucy, Miss Witherby. Just answer the question."

"Yes, Mr. Hawk. You may examine my ankle. Thank you for asking." It warmed her to have a member of the male gender ask consent instead of taking. If only all gentlemen held a woman's opinion close to heart, the world might prove a safer place.

He inclined his head, accepting her gratitude.

The warmth from her chest traveled north creating a heady feeling. Lord, she could see why the other women were so enthralled with him. He addled the senses using wit and flaunting a pleasing form to ensure a female eye did not go wandering. How dare he be both amusing and perfectly formed!

Inching her skirts up as she dared, she made quick work of discarding her stocking, then removed the makeshift bandage.

He examined her ankle, moving the joint, prodding at the skin with gentle fingers. "Am I hurting you?" he asked.

Squirming uncomfortably, she muttered, "It's rather difficult to say."

He bit his bottom lip, the corners of his mouth twitching sporadically. "I see." He released her foot, changing subjects. "I don't think it's broken, but I would feel better if a doctor were to see you. Come…" he stood, holding his hand out to her.

Rose grabbed it without hesitation, her mind sounding warning bells for such bold behavior as her feet gained solid ground.

A deep furrow creased his forehead. "I say, are you usually so trusting of highwaymen?"

"Actually no. I am usually distrustful of all men."

"Except those rumored by other women to be good kissers."

"You dare patronize me?"

"A common trait among my kind, I fear." His stare intensified to the point where she was forced to take notice. "Yet I would warn, not all of us are simple thieves. There are those amongst us who clamor for more than simple baubles. You shouldn't trust us, or me, for that matter." He repeated his earlier warning, and to the same effect.

"But you're the gentlemen thief," she countered. "They say you do no harm toward women."

"There is a first time for everything, Miss Witherby." Turning, he blew two sharp whistles. A black horse emerged from the cluster of trees, coming to stand beside his master. Silver Hawk rubbed the horse's muzzle affectionately. "Jupiter meet Miss Rose Witherby of Virginia. Miss Witherby, Jupiter."

"You named your horse after a god?"

"No other horse in England can match Jupiter for speed and beauty. I thought it a fitting name. Now," he stepped forward, hearing her breath catch at his sudden nearness. "Do I have your permission to give you a boost onto Jupiter?"

Rose bit her bottom lip. "I don't know. My brother was fighting a large group of highwaymen. I must help him."

"Miss Witherby, I fear your brother's fate will be decided long before you can reach him."

She stiffened. "I don't think I care for your impudence."

He shrugged at her frowning face. "So now I'm an impudent, singular thief who lacks empathy. I rather like that sound of that."

"You may add 'unappealing rogue' to your list of faults too."

His eyes twinkled in merriment, adding to his handsome visage.

She frowned so he wouldn't think her swept away by his charm and disturbing good looks.

He stooped, bringing his eyes level with hers. "Unappealing I'm I?"

Stifling the urge to kiss him, she sighed, "Immensely."

He threw his head back, roaring in laughter.

"Laugh all you like, but I am not leaving without knowledge of my brother." She crossed her arms over her chest, taking a defensive posture. "It speaks poorly of your character to chuckle over another soul's possible demise."

"Life of a highwayman, I fear." His humor at last abated. "I will find your brother, little one, but first I intend to see to your welfare. After all, I cannot ransom a dead bride, or one missing a foot. It'd be a shame not to receive full value for my investment, you see."

"Oh yes. I wouldn't want you to lose precious coin on my account. How will I sleep at night knowing you might not receive full payment for all your troubles?"

"What a delightful victim you make. And how accommodating.

I'm so glad you understand." He winked.

She threw up her hands in disgust. "Talking with you is rather like speaking with the village idiot, leaving one with the same results— a pounding headache, frayed nerves and an intolerable urge to throw something."

"But at least I can kiss. What more would you have of your captor?"

"A silent mouth and desire to concede to my every wish?"

"Utter rubbish. I'm a highwayman, not some housebroken mongrel pup. But I'll get you a kitten to order around if it makes you feel better. For now, we're going to visit a friend of mine. He's a doctor whom I happen to trust explicitly."

"Where will you be taking me after that?"

"We shall stay in his barn overnight, then journey to your new home in the morning."

"But it will only be temporary—this new home, correct?"

The highwayman looked at her in amusement. "Eager to meet your betrothed?"

Rose shook her head. "You mistake intent, Mr. Hawk. I am no more eager to meet my husband than I am to be his duchess. This marriage was an arrangement between our two fathers, made when the English general invading our homeland spared my family's home in exchange for my hand in marriage to his son. Father never asked for my consent."

"Would you have given it had he asked you?"

"Of course not!"

A predatory smile appeared. "Then perhaps we might come to an arrangement, you and me. But first things first—may I assist you up onto Jupiter? I fear our time here on the road must be cut short. I hear horses approaching."

Sure enough, Rose caught the sounds of hooves galloping and voices raised in alarm. She gave a quick nod, wondering why she was giving consent to her own kidnapping. Small wonder Silver Hawk had looked at her in amusement when she prattled on about having common sense. It would appear she traveled to England without an ounce of it.

Latching onto her waist, he tossed Rose up into the air, forcing her to scramble for purchase in the saddle as Silver Hawk mounted from behind. He encircled her waist, eliminating the gap between them.

Her mouth opened to protest his manhandling but realized the necessity of a strong grip seconds later as he launched Jupiter forward through the woods.

The pace was dangerous, given the darkness of the hour and

the uneven ground strewn with rocks and branches, but both horse and rider did not falter. She relaxed into his embrace, a cocoon of safety lulling her senses.

A cocoon of safety lulling her senses? She was being spirited away to a highwayman's lair as a captive! And she found comfort in his arms like a simpleton. And what was that about coming to some arrangement? What kind did highwaymen favor?

She choked on the knot of excitement lodged in her throat, displeased with the rapid thudding in her chest. Was it her imagination, or were the corners of her mouth ascending into a smile?

Chapter Three

But you're the gentleman thief.
They say you do no harm toward women.

Logan Sandhurst, Viscount of Edgewood, looked at his young charge. Her besotted expression worried him, even as he longed to kiss her again. And throttle her. Wanting to kiss a highwayman based on rumor and hearsay? He may lack empathy because he was a man, but at least he had good, old-fashioned common sense. Or used to lay claim to owning some. This was his first kidnapping, and already it wasn't going as planned.

Could he kiss her again while riding in the saddle?

He swore at his stupidity, unable to ignore the feel of her in his arms. God, she was beautiful. Rose's pale skin and dark chestnut hair were enough to stir any man's lust, but her wit and humor…well, he hadn't expected to be so fascinated with her right from the beginning.

He should have known better.

Two years ago, he admired her courage when His Majesty's soldiers landed on her family's plantation along the James River in Virginia. She battled to keep her life with greater skill than many of the young men beneath his command. And he had done nothing but watch the spectacle, forcing himself not to lend aid, believing his cause to hold higher purpose, willing to sacrifice a young woman to its glory.

Now here he was, making the same choices. Putting Rose in harm's way once more to serve his selfish agenda.

No, you fool. You're saving her. Should it matter your plans for her rescue and your vengeance follow the same path?

He shifted his weight in the saddle, uncomfortable with the truth.

Jupiter slowed on his own, and Logan spotted the doctor's small cabin up ahead, having been there many times before.

Rose stirred in his arms. "Is this your doctor's home?"

"It is." Jupiter halted outside the tiny cottage. Dismounting, Logan handed the reins up to Rose.

She accepted them with a teasing smile. "You trust me not to run off when you turn away?"

He smirked. "You are free to try, but I fear Jupiter only moves beneath my command."

Her smile wilted. "A well-trained horse. Pity that."

"Fear not, little one. There are worse fates to befall a young woman than to be kidnapped by a well-meaning highwayman."

"I'm sure I can't think of one." She lifted her chin.

He caught the twinkle in her eyes, belying the disdainful expression on her face. His heart squeezed in a manner never felt before now.

"Rest easy," he told her. "I'll be back in a moment."

Tearing himself away, he approached the front door of the cottage. He rapped three times in quick succession, as per their code, and was gratified to have the door opened at once. A wrinkled, ancient face framed by short, silver hair greeted him.

"Silver Hawk," the doctor said. He looked him up and down, his shrewd gaze taking stock. "A social call this evening? You appear in good health, my friend."

"Indeed, I am, sir, but I have a friend who is in need. She has an injured ankle that warrants your attention. And we require a warm bed for the night if you are agreeable."

"Indeed." He paused. "*She*?"

Logan was thankful for the mask hiding his reddened cheeks. "Yes. *She*." He refused to elaborate and wasn't sure if he could.

"Very well, Silver Hawk. You know where the barn is. Make yourself at home, and I will be out directly to have a look. I'll have the missus prepare a tray of food as well."

Logan bowed his head, then reached for the doctor's hand, dropping a handful of coins into his open palm.

The old man flushed with gratitude. "My wife and I have not the words to express our appreciation."

Logan clapped a hand to his shoulder. "Nor do I desire to hear them spoken. Your care and friendship are blessing enough for a lowly thief such as I."

The doctor drew himself upright. "You are a man of honor, sir, and I'll hear no such talk from you about being a common criminal. You are far from common and a blessing to every family in this county who cannot afford the Duke of Dorchester's high rents."

Embarrassed being the object of such gratitude, Logan nodded. It was the least he could do to help the people against his half-brother. "My friend and I shall await the pleasure of your company." He removed himself and made his way back to Rose, accepting the reins she handed over to him.

"Are we to share a room in his cottage?" she asked.

He shook his head, pointing across the yard. "That small structure over yonder serves as his barn and a place of rest when I need it. It's cozy and warm," he added at her dubious look, "and will serve us well this night."

Guiding Jupiter over to the small barn, he opened the door and walked inside. Releasing the reins, he held up his arms toward the hostage intending to pluck her down but halted when he remembered her words on consent.

"May I—"

Rose fell into his embrace before the question could leave his mouth. Unable to bite back his smile, he stared into eyes the color of summer grass, letting her weight drag down his body until the tips of her toes reached the ground. Her blind trust in him was flattering but disturbing. Most men who called themselves highwaymen were reprobates of the worst sort. They would not hesitate to kill or rape her on sight.

"You may release your hold on me, sir."

Logan blinked, unaware he'd been holding her hips while daydreaming. He snatched his hands away, his face burning. "I'm sorry," he muttered.

She smiled, and he stared transfixed, unable to remember why his mouth was forming apologies.

"Are you truly? Because I am not."

He inhaled sharply. "Miss Witherby, you are too bold."

"I know." She waved a hand. "A fault my father continually laments. But I cannot alter who I am for any man's sake. In fact, I find it distasteful to do so."

His heart constricted, and a strange warmth swept in as welcome as a cooling breeze on a hot day. "I would not ask you to be anything less than who you are," he promised, cupping her face. "But your words please me so, and I find myself on the losing side of an inner battle."

"Inner battle?"

Drawing her close, he whispered, "Aye."

Melting in his arms, cuddling against his chest, she said, "I think I know what you mean."

His nose descended, following a light, floral scent, landing on silky tresses. Lavender. Sweet and earthy. A tribute to her name.

The press of a pert nose against a rib was cause for a smile, and he watched slender shoulders rise with a deep breath, absorbing the feel of twin mounds brushing up against him. Groaning as a deluge of emotion crowded his mind, he fought to find and hold onto some semblance of self-control. Rose's innocence and bold tongue were going to be the death of him. He was the villain here. Not her savior. Not her hero. Not her—

"Does your inner battle have anything to do with an ache between your legs?"

Christ!

Logan's knees buckled. His knees never buckled. "Yes," he croaked, unable to elaborate. Sweat dotted his brow.

"Then I hope you surrender," she whispered, meeting his gaze with unabashed heat. "So I too may find some measure of peace this night."

"Rose…" he groaned, pulling her against his body, an erection wedged against her belly. *Maybe the feel of me will frighten her into silence. Bollocks! This woman does not know the meaning of the word silence. Or decency. Or propriety. Or—*

She wiggled herself more fully against him, fitting her every curve to his.

His thoughts came to a crashing halt. In his arms was soft, willing flesh but there was something else. Something about those emerald eyes that captured his full attention, scattering thoughts into nothingness. Something arresting about the gentle smile bestowed on him. He wasn't worthy of its sentiment. He knew it. He wasn't her hero.

But devil take it!

He crushed his lips to hers in a searing, possessive kiss, branding her as his. She was all he could have wished for and more. Beautiful and sweet, bold and brash. He was drowning, his heart exposed and open. He planned and prepared for this moment for months, once he learned of his brother's plan to marry. But Rose was so much more than he planned on.

Oh God! His brother. Sebastian Graham, Duke of Dorchester. He would crush Rose with his depraved demands. Her innocence would be stripped from her by rough hands and forceful thrusts more designed to cow a woman than bring her pleasure. It chilled Logan's blood to think of this passionate, stubborn woman as his brother's wife.

Ending their heated kiss, he dragged in a ragged breath. He stared in satisfaction down into Rose's heavy-lidded gaze, knowing he was the one to make her wits befuddled. "I am not going to surrender Rose," he said, smiling. "But I promise, you will know peace someday soon, and God willing, I will be the one to provide it to you. But for now," he gently guided her to a bed of fresh hay, helping her sit down, "just rest."

He wondered at the sudden silence, but when she looked up at him, his breath caught. Tenderness flowed in waves from her glowing green eyes.

"Did you mean your words?" she asked.

He blinked, her question not making sense. It was difficult to concentrate when an earnest, adoring expression claimed many of his thoughts. "Mean what?" Good God, the more he stared, the faster he felt himself plunging into free fall. He reached out, desperate to find an anchor to keep himself grounded. His flailing hand whacked into a wooden beam. *Ouch!*

"You promised t-to make love to me, did you not?"

Damn, I'm a bloody, blabbering idiot. "Yes, I suppose I did, and I will, if you consent, but not tonight, Rose. May I call you Rose?" At her nod, he smiled. "Thank you."

"Do you have a given name I may use?"

He thought about that. The risk in telling Rose his Christian name was negligible. "Logan."

She returned his smile. "Thank you…Logan."

The sound of his name being spoken by Rose's soft voice was a heady tonic. A bloody damn intimate one. He squeezed the wooden beam, trying in vain to understand why the entire world was shifting, becoming something new and exciting. Did he make her feel the same way? He longed to ask. Inhaling as much air as he could, he made a decision, releasing the anchor. Freefall it was.

"Silver Hawk!"

A panicked voice sent him spiraling around toward the barn doors, reaching for pistols. The doctor's wife came hurrying toward him.

Eyes wide and frightened, she said, "A village boy came to our cottage. His Grace heads here with a lynch mob. You must leave at once!"

Logan swore, raking a hand through his hair. How had Sebastian tracked him so quickly? And why hadn't Robert derailed his brother? This entire kidnapping was taking a straight shot to hell!

Rose stood, sinking hard fingers into his arm. "You must ride away without me, Logan. I will only slow you down."

He paused before responding. If he were of a mind, he could use Rose as a hostage to draw Sebastian into a lethal duel.

But she might be harmed. With so many guns and men willing

to use them, he could not guarantee her safety.

No.

A surge of protectiveness forced its way into his conscious. "Don't be silly, Rose. We leave together." He moved to ready his stallion, but Rose did not release him.

"Listen to me," she snapped, turning him around with the strength of a man. "His Grace is only after me. If he finds me first, you can make good your escape." She cupped his face, staring hard into his incredulous eyes. "I could not bear to be the woman who brings Silver Hawk to his doom."

"Rose, we can fight our way—"

The doctor's wife cut in, "There isn't time to argue. You must leave now. My husband is at the cottage, waiting for them to delay their search. Please go. The people depend on you so."

"Yes, Logan, go." Rose nudged him away, nodding toward Jupiter. "I will be fine."

Logan set his jaw, his resolve as stone. He snatched Rose's hand, swinging her into his arms. "The victim does not give orders to her abductor!" He brought his head close, his lips a breath away from hers. "I am not leaving you behind, Rose. In fact, I am choosing to bind you to my side for the foreseeable future."

"Thank God." Rose sighed, closing the distance between their faces, kissing his lips with a sweetness that contrasted with her fiery nature.

Logan crushed her to him. They were wasting precious seconds, but he couldn't stop himself from deepening the kiss, branding her with his tongue and mouth, wanting her to remember him. He prayed the night would end with Rose in his arms, and not in his brother's.

Jupiter whinnied, and Logan withdrew, fearing the next few minutes ahead of them. "Jupiter says it's time to go."

Rose opened her mouth, but closed it, only nodding instead.

He thanked God for small blessings. Throwing his charge up into the saddle, he vaulted behind her, gathering the reins. "Hold on to me, little one. I would not see you slip through my grasp if I am occupied defending our escape."

She slid her arms around him, burrowing her head into the valley of his chest. "I will not let go."

He wondered if that was meant figuratively or literally. He grinned, deciding it didn't matter either way.

He nudged Jupiter into motion, and silently his steed left the barn.

But they were already surrounded by a half dozen men on horseback.

His breath froze, and his eyes made contact, even in the inky darkness, with a tall figure, equal in height but not his weight. His half-brother, Sebastian Graham, Duke of Dorchester.

And his brother was aiming for the center of his chest with a pistol primed and loaded.

Damn.

"Silver Hawk," Dorchester called out. "I had thought you might make some desperate attempt to kidnap my bride given our past association." He cocked his pistol. "I would like her back now, please."

Grinding his teeth, Logan considered the options. Put a knife to Rose's throat, using her as a hostage to ensure their safe escape, thrust Jupiter through the close semi-circle made of men and horses and risk a volley of gunfire, or let her go and make a grand fight for the privilege to keep the lady.

Keep Rose? When had the plan changed to include that notion?

His arm tightened around his captive. It was time to fight, or it was time to die. This was the pinnacle he wanted and plotted for. Never mind the timeline had been pushed ahead. It would not alter the outcome. The only difference was the prize at the end. One he never sought but would cherish the rest of his life.

Rose.

Logan glanced aside to the right of Dorchester, making eye contact with another man— Robert Witherby.

Robert held his gaze while casually adjusting the direction of his pistol, pointing it away from him and aiming toward Dorchester.

Logan nodded, beginning to loosen his grip on Rose. "Go back inside the barn, Rose."

"No!" She latched onto his arm, calling out, "Please don't hurt him!"

His arms squeezed her waist in silent warning. "Don't, Rose."

She looked up at him with huge, beseeching eyes. "I cannot stand to see you injured, Logan. Not on my account. If I go with them in peace, you may yet live. Please," she touched a hand to his cheek, "let me go."

He set his mouth; his decision made. "No."

Her eyes widened, but she tightened her arms around him without further argument.

He kissed the top of her head, smiling when Dorchester growled. He gave Jupiter the barest nudge with his knee, and all hell broke loose.

Jupiter reared up on his back legs, spooking the other horses, and while the other men tried to bring their mounts under control, Jupiter sprang into action, launching forward. Unbelievably, gunshots rang out, and Logan wrenched an arm around Rose, making a desperate attempt to protect her from harm. He trusted Jupiter to know his way through the forest, but it was a black night, and even this pace was too reckless for his trusted steed.

The men's voices were not falling as far behind as he would have liked, and Rose was plastered against him, her arms fairly wringing the breath from his lungs. He thought to make some teasing comment to help her relax but abandoned the notion as a gunshot, and a searing pain exploded across his shoulder.

"Logan?" She felt along his back, causing him to cry out. "You've been shot!"

He raised a brow as he continued to guide a racing Jupiter, hoping she would not ask the inevitable question. It never failed to amaze him how many times people asked ridiculous questions in times of tragedy. A house catches fire, and without a doubt, some onlooker will call *what happened?* Or a man gets robbed of his purse, and some poor addled minded fool will ask *are you all right?*

"Yes, Rose. It seems I've taken a bullet in the shoulder."

"But are you all right?"

He flinched, biting his tongue to keep from laughing. "Would you be all right if someone shot you?"

She lifted her head to glare at him, loosening her hold on his body. "Now is not the time for jests! You need to stop."

Jupiter reared suddenly, throwing Rose back against him. Unprepared, they slipped from the saddle together, gravity defying his attempts to remain seated. Instinctively he twisted and curled his body around Rose, so his larger frame would take the brunt of the fall. He hit the ground hard, blackness infringing along the outer rim of his vision.

She landed on top of him with a soft grunt, then jumped up to a standing position, swaying when she shifted her weight from her injured ankle.

Addled from pain, it took him longer than usual to wonder why Rose wasn't looking at him or making a fuss over his injuries. No, her eyes and attention focused on something or someone above his head.

He arched his back, taking in his brother on horseback standing over him, pointing a pistol in his direction. He inched a hand toward his boot, his fingers unerringly finding the knife he kept tucked away for nights such as these.

But Rose stepped between him and his target. "Please, Your

Grace. He is injured. Take me and let him go."

It raised the hairs on Logan's neck to see Dorchester examine her from the top of her dark head to the bottom of her tiny feet. The look in his eyes reminded Logan of a predator looking at his supper. His stomach clenched. "Rose," he hissed. "Move out of the way."

Dorchester lowered his weapon. He urged his horse next to Rose, dismounting before her. "Your heart is too kind, Miss Witherby, to understand this man is a criminal." Dorchester gave him the briefest of glances.

Logan bared his teeth.

Rose glanced at him, her lips forming words he did not wish to hear, before accepting Dorchester's help mounting his horse. *I'm sorry.* She settled into a side riding position, and Dorchester climbed up behind her, wrapping an arm around her waist possessively.

Logan's vision went red.

Yes, Rose would be sorry. The suddenness of his loss burned like acid in his mouth. The taste of love leaking from his broken heart, and the knowledge of what lay ahead in days to come for her if he could not find her in time.

Somehow, he managed to push himself up into a standing position, swaying on his feet. Sebastian once again held his pistol trained on his head.

Rose gasped. "Your Grace, no! Criminal or not, this man has done me no harm. Please," she begged, turning around to plead at his brother. "Please show mercy."

His brother stared at Rose. His posture and facial features relaxed, signaling her pleas had found a willing ear. Dorchester unlocked the hammer, lowering the weapon. "I would not have your first impression of me to be one of violent intent."

Logan gagged.

Dorchester pierced him with a frosty glare. "Yet neither will I be looking over my shoulder for the journey home." He waved a hand, and several men stepped forward, coming out of the night. One of them was Robert. The other was the local constable.

Dorchester acknowledged both men with a nod. "I leave this highwayman to your tender care. Robert, I will escort your sister the rest of the way to my estate. We will see you there."

Logan narrowed his eyes, watching his half-brother leave with Rose. Dorchester's ducal estate was still at least a day's ride from here. No doubt his brother would need an inn for the night, but which one? There were many taverns and inns between here and the manor. His shoulder burned fire, reminding him of his need for medical attention.

He swore every curse ever heard.

Robert sighed once Dorchester was out of earshot. "That was not the ending to the day I planned on. Bloody hell."

The constable looked at Robert in confusion.

Logan immediately stepped forward, punching the man out cold with one solid fist to his jaw. He winced, shaking his good hand. "I did my part. You were supposed to delay Dorchester. What happened?"

"He met me on the road, dispatching the highwaymen you sent to chase us when we were locked in mortal combat." Robert scowled. "That reminds me. Why did you tell your band of merry men to shoot at us? I could see one shot fired into the air, but directly at us? They could have killed Rose, or me!"

Logan blinked to bring his friend's face back into focus. "I gave no such order. That part of the plan they devised on their own. I wondered why you tossed your sister out of a moving carriage. I made several mental notes to wring your neck when I witnessed your careless actions."

Robert drew himself up. "And I had similar plans when I was forced to fire back on your men."

"They are not 'my men!'" Logan snapped. "I claim no kinship to mad criminals. I gave them coin toward one purpose only, but I should have guessed they would prove themselves unworthy of following the simplest of commands."

"You're a good man, Logan," Robert said with quiet dignity. "And you're titled. What need have you to play the part of a highwayman? Surely there are other pursuits worthier of your time. Don't people of your ilk usually lay about drinking and making wagers regarding what poor woman's skirts you'll be under that night?"

Logan scowled. "Dukes do that. I'm a viscount. We spend our days building fortunes so we can tower above those who consider themselves our betters."

"Spoken like a true colonial."

"Bloody hell, Robert. Sod off, will you?"

"Look." Robert clutched Logan's good shoulder, looking him square in the eye. "All I'm saying is there must be a better way to fund your rescue efforts than consorting with men not fit to shine your boots."

Logan removed himself from his friend's grasp. "My title holds no wealth other than what I have made from a few well-placed investments, and those investments take time to amass any kind of fortune. The women and children under my care have needs that are of immediate concern. The rich who suffer my presence lose nothing but a few baubles, easily forgotten. But the young child who benefits from the warm meal at the cost of a stolen piece of jewelry— it is a gift beyond measure."

Robert held up his hands. "All right. You win this argument, but I pray someday you will find a better existence than the one you're living in."

"Save your prayers for your sister," he ground out, "when she finds herself beneath the heel of my brother."

Turning, he placed a foot toward Jupiter when a moment of dizziness overcame him. Long, precious seconds passed but the feeling only grew in intensity. Dragging a hand along his back, pain accosted him when questing fingers found the injury.

Robert gave a low whistle while examining the wound. "Come on, Logan. Let's get you patched up. Then I'll ride after Rose."

Logan swayed on his feet. "I'm coming too."

"Like hell you are!"

He caught Robert's arm, his vision wavering dangerously. He knew he was moments away from passing out. "His estate is too far to ride directly to tonight. He will be seeking shelter somewhere."

"Fine then. We will get you bandaged up and in a safe spot, then I'll start searching."

"Not bloody good enough," Logan slurred, hauling himself onto Jupiter.

Robert took Jupiter's reins before Logan could ride away. "It will have to be, my friend. I'm afraid we have no recourse. I do not believe Dorchester will harm Rose this night. He seemed genuinely alarmed and distressed when he didn't find her in the carriage." He shrugged. "Maybe His Grace is just lonely and looking for companionship these days. Every rake has a change of heart."

Logan was too exhausted to argue further, so he withheld the fact Dorchester was more than a simple libertine. If his half-brother couldn't seduce the object of his desire, more times than Logan could count, Dorchester would take by force what he wanted.

Logan began to pray for young Rose. It seemed an awful thing to want a woman to be submissive, but he needed this brave young woman to survive until he could find her again, and survival to his half-brother, entailed a rather generous amount of compliance.

A trait he feared she was not capable of learning.

Chapter Four

Rose was tired. She had long ago given up the battle to stay erect while riding in the saddle. Her back screamed in agony, making her twisted ankle a pain of little note. Exhausted, she finally surrendered and allowed herself to relax into His Grace. He kept his arm wrapped around her middle, more a courtesy than a vice. Tension hung heavy in the air. Few words passed between them. The darkened countryside had more to say than her knotted tongue, and with more enthusiasm. Crickets chirped, birds sang, and all the while her heart beat in trepidation. Logan commanded far more of her thoughts than the man riding behind her.

Was he all right?

Would he come for her still?

Her stomach growled in reply, reminding her of other pressing concerns.

His Grace roused himself from silence. "There is an inn up ahead, Miss Witherby. We shall stop there for the night and eat. We will reach my home by sundown tomorrow. Perhaps sooner if the fair weather holds."

"I thought you told my brother we would be going directly to your estate! You mentioned no inn to him."

The even rise and fall of his chest stilled. "It was a misdirection. Forgive me, Miss Witherby, but it was necessary." Breath blew hot upon her ear. "I wished this night alone with you."

Oh God. Food was a forgotten necessity as her stomach muscles now stuck fast together in fear. "I may be an ignorant colonial girl, but even I know it is not seemly to spend the night alone with a man without vows exchanged."

He reined in the horse, snorting into her ear. "Seemly? You dare speak that word to me?" He laughed, the sound false and bitter. "Tell me, Miss Witherby, was it *seemly* for my betrothed to look half in love with her abductor?"

The blood drained from her face with his snarled accusation.

He vaulted to the ground, gathering the reins, then raised his head to meet her gaze. Her stomach dropped from the anger burning in those twin orbs.

"I don't know what you're talking about, Your Grace." She put considerable effort into keeping her face neutral, clenching trembling fingers into a fist. It was courting danger to display any weakness to a man. "I showed Silver Hawk compassion and mercy. An emotion I wished you were capable of—even in the smallest of measurement."

Narrowing his eyes, he said, "Did I not show *mercy* and *compassion* when you pleaded with me with tears upon cheek to spare his life?"

"I fear you would not have spared him otherwise."

"You do not know me, Miss Witherby." He waved a hand at his face. The moonlight was scarce, but its silvery light illuminated the one item of note on an otherwise perfectly sculpted image.

True to rumor, His Grace wore a mask. Or at least, half of one. It shielded the right side of his face from view. She had not given his appearance proper consideration, but she did so now in the meager light. His Grace was a full foot and a half taller than her, perhaps even rivaling Silver Hawk's impressive height. Broad shoulders proudly held, lay clothed beneath an expertly cut jacket. Chiseled lips now pursed, straight nose and cold blue eyes —all pointed in her direction.

His Grace met her assessing gaze with a raised chin. "Yes, Miss Witherby. As you have noticed, I bear a disfigurement. But I assure you, I am a man in every other sense of the word."

Her heart tripled its beat at his veiled meaning. She closed her eyes, despising the old fear given new life at his words. "I hold no doubts you are a man, Your Grace, and will behave accordingly."

"I'm certain Silver Hawk plied your ears with words such as 'beast' or 'monster' to describe me. An unfair maneuver to gain your trust. I can only give you my word I am neither of those things. I am a gentleman."

Anger flared within her breast. Her eyes flew open to meet his chilly stare. "A gentleman? Ha! If the conduct of your English soldiers is the measurement of a gentleman than I fear I placed you in too high regard. Indeed, I should have lowered my opinion of your character had I known you thought yourself a *gentleman*."

Silence ensued after her insult, quieting her heart. She went too far. A muscle quivered on the side of Sebastian's cheek. His gaze locked on her face, and she couldn't tell if his expression threatened violence or a verbal lashing. Awareness of her precarious position claimed her senses. Alone in a foreign country, with a stranger whose honor she all but spit on. And no staff to defend her wayward tongue. She was waging a war she wasn't going to win tonight.

Rose sighed, a veritable gust of wind in the tense, thick air. "Your Grace, I am sorry." She glanced aside, no longer brave enough to gauge his reactions. A warm hand closed over hers, causing her to jump. Wide eyes shot up to meet Sebastian's.

"The conduct of English soldiers does not reflect the genteel upbringing of English dukes," he murmured, his gaze miraculously no longer glacial. "A thing I am most eager to show you if you but let me try."

All the fight drained out of her with one forgiving look and delicate touch from her fiancé. She turned her hand, palm up, threading her fingers through his, and squeezed. "I would be grateful for a demonstration of kindness and empathy." A teasing tone colored her voice despite the wariness. "Traits I have yet to witness from any man."

Sebastian brought her hand up to his lips, brushing a light kiss on her skin. "Your remarks stir memories of words spoken by my father." He stepped closer, daring to rest a hand on her knee.

She stilled at his touch, cornered into accepting it for fear of angering him.

"He mentioned your skill using a staff and what fate your friends suffered. I'm sorry my father's men made you a most unfortunate victim. A fate shared by many in times of war. But had my father not landed on your plantation, I would never know your lovely face. Or be blessed to call you my wife."

She forced the corners of her mouth upward in a poor semblance of a smile. "I have not yet given you cause to thank God. You may mistake blessing for tragedy."

He returned her smile, and she relaxed her abused spine in the saddle. A man who found humor in her poor jests couldn't be all that terrible.

"I don't believe I've made a mistake," he said. "You are here with me, not shrinking from my touch as so many other young women have done before you. What's more, you're beautiful." His eyes held hers, sky blue eyes deepening in color. "More beautiful than I hoped for."

She tucked her chin, breaking eye contact, hiding her heated cheeks. "You flatter me with bold words."

The hand resting on her knee, trailed down her leg to grip her foot—her injured foot.

She gasped with pain.

His Grace yanked his hand away, a wounded look replacing his teasing smile. "Forgive me, Miss Witherby. I thought, or rather hoped, you might permit me some small liberty."

She shook her head, scrambling to repair the damage her bark of pain committed. "I'm sorry, Your Grace. It isn't what you think. I hurt my ankle when my brother threw me out of our runaway carriage earlier today."

Both brows shot up. "You are injured? Here, Miss Witherby. Let me see." He lifted the hem of her gown without asking consent, taking her bare foot in hand.

Treating her appendage as though it were a priceless treasure, he examined it. His Grace flattened his lips together. "I fear your ankle is quite swollen and bruised." He paused. "Did you say your brother threw you out of a *moving* carriage?"

She nodded. "Robert felt he was saving me from being a victim of highwaymen."

"I see." His eyes snapped with anger. "I do believe your brother and I shall share words when next we meet. But for now, let's get you to a warm bed and meal." He released her foot, and mounted behind her, urging his horse forward with a touch of his knee. Male arms moved with tentative slowness around her middle, as though not trusting her to issue a reprimand for touching her.

Still intent on mending her unintentional insult, she reclined against his strong chest, hearing his soft gasp when she rested an arm over his. Tightening his hold, bringing her further into his embrace.

"I would welcome both food and a bed with equal fervor," she said as they rode. "Although I fear I could out eat a pig and shock you out of committing yourself in marriage to me."

His head fell back, laughter spilling from his lips. "Beautiful and in possession of a healthy appetite. I think our future children will only benefit from your vices."

Her bout of good humor faded. "You wish children?" She winced. He was a duke—albeit, a scarred duke. Of course, he would want children. It was required of him to have an heir and a spare.

Her breath stilled when warm lips brushed her ear. "Children are the expected result when man and wife share a bed together."

Yes, they were. But she would not greet the prospect of motherhood with open arms and bated breath. If only she could find the courage to tell him of her fears regarding the marriage bed and bearing children, although she suspected her screams and fleeing backside would present equal protest when next he pressed the subject.

It was a strange thought, but she could not help but remember her lack of fear when Silver Hawk pronounced his desire to make love with her. Her body responded with an aching need to the highwayman's proclamation. The thought of sharing the same intimacies with the man behind her left in want of any need—other than the one to flee.

What did her heart know that she did not? From what she could see, His Grace was equally handsome of face. Should not her body respond the same?

Her pulse quickened. There was the smallest chance Silver Hawk planted a seed within her heart—an organ she long feared made of stone in regard to men and the havoc their kind wrought upon her gender.

Love.

How was such a thing possible? She barely knew the rogue, and for all she knew, had faults enough to fill the heavens above her head.

His Grace pointed to a distant light brightening the horizon. "We are almost to our lodging for the night."

She roused herself from depressing thoughts. "A prayer answered at last. I thought God had forsaken me this day."

He chuckled, the sound low and oddly pleasing in her ear. "As I thought myself finally blessed by Him." He stopped the horse once more, gripping her chin, turning her around to face him. The look in his eyes was one she was most familiar with—heavy with lusty intent, a direct gaze hinting at unwanted attention.

She wished the space between their mouths a greater distance apart, but despite her reluctance, she claimed no desire to hurt him with a refusal. She was not immune to the longing in his eyes.

Her eyelids closed, and her chin rose, presenting what he wished for most. She heard his soft gasp.

"You're not afraid of me kissing you?" he asked, wonder in his voice.

Her eyelids lifted, and she searched his incredulous expression. "Should I be?"

Tenderness filled his eyes. "I would not have it so—ever. My God, Rose." He brought their lips together with infinite gentleness.

She held herself still, unsure if she found his touch enjoyable or not. The blood in her veins did not race, nor did her heart hammer. Her body did not ache, searching for more.

Disappointment weighed as a loadstone upon her mind, but shame followed on its heels. It was not Sebastian's fault her body sang for another man. She had been wanton, throwing herself into a highwayman's arms, wanting to know the joys of passion instead of the fear of assault. She dared to give in to desire, and now could enjoy the feel of its absence, and she had no one to blame but herself.

Foolish girl.

His Grace's tongue traced the seam to her closed mouth, seeking further intimacy. She fought the urge to sigh. Refusing him was futile. Soon, he would have legal right to do far more than kiss her. She laid a hand on his clothed chest for balance and parted her lips, wordlessly giving her consent for him to deepen the kiss. His body trembled beneath her hand as his tongue swept inside her mouth. Long, languid strokes seized her attention.

This was pleasurable.

She swayed into him, encouraged to feel a knot of warmth unfurl in her belly. He slanted his mouth over hers, his kiss turning rougher and more demanding. Contracting muscles in his arms dragged her closer to a hard bulge in his breeches. It branded as a hot iron, marking her hip as she sat on the saddle in between his splayed legs.

Tempted, she shyly touched her tongue to his, and the effect on him was immediate. He groaned into her mouth, his hands all at once roaming her figure—up her back, over her hips, sliding up to cup her breasts. He was lost in the same storm that claimed her during Logan's gentle touch. She understood the tempest her betrothed found himself in, but could not join him in its rough, sweeping waves. So she remained his anchor, untouched by his tumultuous storm, accepting his arduous attention in silence.

At length, he ended their kiss, breathing heavy, his hot breath fanning her face. It smelled of spirits, as did his kiss. Not unpleasant, but again, not like Logan. What had he tasted of?

He tasted of freedom and love. Sunshine and summer. Clean, fresh.

All the smells she loved best, in one intoxicating scent, Logan carried around him as one would wear a cloak. Enticing, drawing her in as the sun might draw her outside after a rainy day. And she left him.

No, her mind argued, *you saved him.*

The only balm on an open wound she had to give, but in her heart, she knew on nights such as this, it would not be enough. They might not be together—not ever in this life, but at least Logan lived. And that was all that mattered.

His Grace tilted her drooping chin up, holding it lightly between thumb and forefinger. His expression was so tender, Rose nearly wept for being a heartless wench, unable to return such warm regard.

"Thank you," he murmured, smiling with kindness. "You make

me happy beyond the telling of it."

She forced a smile to her wilted face. "Do I?"

He nodded. "As someday, I hope I make you."

"Your Grace?"

He brushed a thumb across her cheek. "I may wear a mask, but I am not blind, Rose. I was jealous when I first pulled you away from Silver Hawk. I witnessed a shared look between you two rife with tender thoughts and concern for the other. It was obvious an attachment formed in your brief time together. But," he shook his head when she opened her mouth to speak, "you are here, in my arms, making every effort to encourage my affection and attention. Despite not being with the man you wanted. To say nothing of my scarred face." He swallowed, casting his gaze aside. "And I most humbly thank you for your efforts. For not being afraid of me. For allowing my touch. Thank you, Rose."

Guilt was becoming Rose's constant companion on this voyage. It pricked her conscious, nagging and pulling on her iron heart in ways not anticipated. "Your gratitude is misplaced, Your Grace. You are to be my husband, after all. I could hardly refuse you a kiss."

He shifted his weight in the saddle. "And yet I would have more of you."

"Your Grace?"

"Your heart, *Rose*. Your love." He chuckled. "Though for now, I will simply take hearing you say my given name."

She could bend and allow that small intimacy in addition to the kiss. "Very well...Sebastian. Though I must warn you I consider the matter of my heart to be no trifling matter. Love is to be earned, not given away to any fool who goes demanding it."

"You confuse love and trust, darling. Trust must be earned, not love."

She lifted her chin. "I consider those two traits connected in my mind, Sebastian. As they should be to any young woman forced into a marriage union."

"Did you hold Silver Hawk to such high standards, or did his perfect face elevate him above your rules?"

She paled at his anger. "I hold all men to the same measure if they say they love me. Silver Hawk," she added with quiet dignity, "never said he loved me."

"Yet I am certain the man held your heart."

"Fear not, Sebastian. No man of my acquaintance has earned my heart yet."

Scowling, he said, "Part of the marriage vow is agreeing to

love, honor, and obey your husband. I do not have to 'earn' anything."

"Then why are you arguing with me over ownership of my heart? If it is indeed part and parcel of a marriage vow, then you needn't worry about earning it or holding yourself to my high standards. And it shouldn't matter if you think Silver Hawk has it since he is not the man I am marrying." Had her life been her own to live, she would marry neither man. She required no chains about her neck. Being born a woman provided enough shackles to last a lifetime.

His scowl eased. "I hate to admit it, but you're right. I am behaving like a jealous fool when there is no need."

She smiled with false sweetness. "I never said that, Sebastian."

At last, he nudged the horse forward, chuckling. "You possess a clever mind, Rose. I'm not certain if I'm impressed or scared out of my wits."

"No man desires an intelligent wife." She said it as a statement of fact, though not one she believed. It had been told to her by her father many times before. Indeed, had her father carved out the Ten Commandments instead of Moses, her father would have chiseled the line as Commandment Eleven, merely to vex the female gender for all eternity.

Sebastian hugged her to his sturdy frame. "I was only jesting, Rose. I am glad your mind is capable of reason when mine is not. It helps me to see when I am an insufferable cad."

She twisted her head to look at him, the tiniest bit of her ironclad heart softening. "I would not have put so fine a point on it. The day has been long for both of us."

"I am sorry."

"And I forgive you."

She did forgive him for being jealous. He bore a scar and was sensitive about his physical appearance. She could dig deep inside herself and understand those feelings. But there was something about Sebastian she couldn't name. Disquiet ate at her stomach, and she found herself unable to relax against his body as they continued in silence down the empty, dark road.

Chapter Five

Rose breathed a sigh of relief when she arrived at a large establishment named The Fox and the Hound. Accepting Sebastian's help sliding down off the horse, she noted his touch lingered longer than necessary. A growing conflict was building in her mind. It was caught between wanting to run and needing to please. She had no wish to incur Sebastian's wrath, but neither did she want to be his wife. A woman should be able to choose her husband, not have the choice removed from hands by scheming men.

Sebastian smiled into her eyes before turning to tether the horse at a hitching post. With him distracted, she decided to start limping her way into the inn. She made it no more than three steps before finding herself swung into mid-air by a pair of lean arms.

"Rose! What in heaven's name do you think you're doing?"

"Walking?" *Hadn't that been obvious?*

"You're injured. I won't allow you to cause yourself more pain."

"'Tis just a bruise, Sebastian. I've had more than my fair share of them. I am fine."

Chuckling, he shook his head. "You and I do not share the same definition of the word 'fine.'"

"I am not a baby, unable to take a slight pain."

His arms tightened. "No, you are certainly no child."

The husky tone to Sebastian's voice silenced her tongue. The inn's door loomed before her, taking the shape of a mouth of a great beast, ready to swallow her body and soul. Apprehension crawled along her skin as they approached. What would the night bring from this man carrying her now? The comfort of a meal and bed? Or the humiliation of having to satisfy a physical appetite?

Crossing the threshold into a large, well-lit room, he set her in a chair. "I'll be right back."

She glanced around as he left her side to speak with the innkeeper. The other patrons looked back at her in mild curiosity, and for the first time, she realized what her appearance must be after being thrown from a carriage earlier in the day.

Grimacing, she swiveled from their curious stares. A bath would be a welcome sight about now.

"Rose." Sebastian crouched on the balls of his feet in front of her.

She blinked as she took in her first good look of Sebastian Graham. Hair the color of summer wheat fell in short locks over a smooth forehead, piercing blue eyes, his jaw square and lean.

But his mask held her attention most of all.

It was a curious disguise molded to his right side, encompassing the eye and cheekbone, up to his hairline on his right temple. The mask was original and must have been made solely for him. But he was, without a doubt, a very handsome man.

He colored under her regard, and she blushed in kind, realizing her lack of manners. "I'm sorry," she mumbled, looking down.

He tilted her chin up. "No apology is necessary, Rose." He lowered his voice, leaning close. "You looked pleased by what you saw."

Despite her misgivings, she smiled, charmed by his teasing. Her peripheral vision caught the surprised faces of the other patrons gawking in their direction. She ignored them, keeping her gaze steady on Sebastian. "I was not given reason to set my hopes high for a happy marriage. I fear I likened you to Lucifer in my musings."

He touched her cheek. "And now, dare I ask?"

"And now," she fought for the right words, not wanting to lie, "I fear no amount of musing could have prepared me for you."

Blue eyes lit with joy before lids descended, heavy with a deeper emotion she could not be sure of. He kissed her, a softer version than the one before on his horse.

Their unwanted audience gasped.

She twisted away at the sudden, intrusive sound, reddening as she glanced aside to see their shocked faces. "It would seem we interrupted their meals."

Sebastian's gaze cooled as it raked over the motley crew staring back at them. He straightened to his full, imposing height. "Come, Rose. Let us depart before such rude company sours our ravenous appetite."

Her empty stomach clenched hard, worrying what ravenous appetite she would be forced to satisfy. Sebastian gathered her again and led the way up a short stairway to the second floor then down a long hall. At the end of the corridor was a closed door. He whisked it open with a flourish, setting her down.

"Our suite, Rose."

She limped inside the room, staring about her in amazement. It was as spacious and elegantly furnished as any small home or cottage. They were standing in a sitting room with a roaring fire in a brick hearth, and a small, rectangular dining table with six chairs rested in a large alcove across the way. Down a short hall was another door, to what she could only surmise was a bedchamber.

She pivoted to Sebastian, finding him watching her face intently. "I had no notion English inns were so richly appointed."

The corners of his mouth quirked up. "Most inns are not. This used to be a favorite stop of mine when I traveled with more frequency from London to my ducal estate. I asked the owner's permission to build an addition for my personal use."

"How nice of him to agree."

"Being 'nice' had very little to do with it," he said, stepping into the suite, shutting the door. "It was more an investment than I intended to see this done as I envisioned." He looked about with apparent satisfaction glowing in his eyes.

A door opened, and she swiveled her head to see a young man and woman coming from a room down the hall. They both were dressed in gray uniforms and—perhaps it was her imagination—but the pair trembled when presenting themselves in front of their employer. Rather strange of behavior of servants to her way of thinking.

Sebastian acknowledged them both with a curt nod. "Rose, this is your lady's maid, Milly. When I wrote to your father, he said you wouldn't be traveling with any servants, so I went ahead and assigned Milly to you. I hope she meets with your approval."

She gave the nervous young woman an encouraging smile, hoping to put her at ease. "I'm sure Milly and I will get along famously."

Milly's gaze flickered up to her and away. "I have a bath drawn and ready, Your Grace, and your trunks arrived a few hours ago."

Surprised, Rose turned widened eyes toward Sebastian. "You were able to recover my trunks from the carriage? How wonderful! I thought them lost to me forever. Thank you, Sebastian." It was a comfort to know her costly metal undergarment would not go unused.

"Of course, my dear." He nodded at his servants, and they vanished from the suite, closing the door behind them. Opening his arms, he took her once more into his embrace and proceeded to give her another slow, thorough kiss.

She endured his attention, dismayed her body remained cold

and unmoved by his fevered touch.

Ending the kiss, he braced his forehead against hers. "I must go and ensure my stallion is being taken care of before I retire for the evening. Go and enjoy your bath. Dinner and a doctor will arrive here shortly."

Acting on impulse to please, she cupped the masked side of his face. He jerked beneath her hand. "Does my touch cause you pain?" she asked.

"No," he rasped, "I am … unused to …" The column of his throat worked hard. "Excuse me, Rose." He left her alone in their suite as though highwaymen were nipping at his heels.

She shrugged, not knowing what to make of his odd behavior. She, on the other hand, was of a mind to celebrate.

Dinner, a bath, and my beloved chastity belt!

The night was vastly improving in her opinion.

~ * ~

Sebastian gripped the walls of the stall inside the stable until his knuckles went white. *Bloody, bloody, hell.*

The days of being a solitary figure alone in a monstrosity of a stone castle, despised and pitied, were things soon to be a distant memory. He wagered the future and won the most glorious of prizes. The atrocities committed by a young man seeking justice in a cruel, unforgiving world would no longer haunt him or cause pain.

I won.

His father would no doubt be rolling in his grave, his sunken face twisted in rage, for his heir planned on marrying a colonial girl, and the stench of common blood would forever taint all the heirs who followed.

Oh yes, he had gained a great victory over his father. But the asking price for such a risk was not one he could afford. Glowing emerald eyes demanded fair value to balance the scale. A gentle smile drew him in like a siren's song. Marriage to Rose was hastily planned, with vengeance upon his father the only reward he sought.

But here he stood, trembling and full of hope, that a lowly colonial girl could see in him something of worth, something his father never found when looking at him. He had died years ago beneath the harsh abuse, forever falling short of his father's expectations. Until green eyes stared at him and something within his soul breathed life for the first time.

Could love be the siren call his soul heard?

He scoffed. *Love is not real. It's a made-up notion by weak men and women brought up on fairytales. It. Does. Not. Exist.* Not for him. Never him. The great former Duke of Dorchester taught his heir that lesson.

Sebastian pressed his forehead against the rough wood, closing his eyes, cherishing the memory of Rose's lips pressed against his own. Her warmth, her soft body, cradled against the hard planes of his chest.

With knees threatening to give way, he tightened his grip on the stall walls, the only thing keeping him upright, as the memory of her sweet, innocent kisses washed over him. And when she gently cupped his scarred face—

Strength fled, and he sank with a groan. Rose dared to touch what no woman wanted, what every female in London shied away from. What the entire *haut monde* ridiculed him for, forcing his retreat into the country when he much preferred his comfortable townhouse in London.

Good God, it was nearly too much. The life he bargained for now was within his grasp. All he had to do was reach out and take it.

A loving wife. Happy children. Laughter, love, family—he could see it all staring into Rose's green eyes. He could envision his entire life with her by his side.

Sebastian surged to his feet. By God, he would not wait until the morrow to make her his bride. He could wake in the morning and find this all a cruel dream. Or worse yet, Silver Hawk could track them, and he might lose her again to that rogue thief.

No!

Sebastian already possessed the special license purchased from the bishop, all he needed was a vicar to come and perform the ceremony.

Rose would be bound to him. She would be his—forever in this life.

Sebastian stalked out of the stable, nearly slamming into a stable boy leading horses back into the barn for the night. He marched across the yard and burst into the inn. His gaze immediately found the stout innkeeper, talking to his equally proportioned wife. He stomped over to them, causing his wife to flag her hand annoyingly in his direction, before sinking into an unbalanced, sloppy curtsy.

He grimaced in acknowledgment. "Mister Hobbs, please send word to the local vicar that I wish to have him here in one hour to perform a marriage ceremony."

The plump man smacked his lips, greed darkening his small, beady eyes. "That be no small favor, Your Grace. Our village vicar will think it blasphemy to perform such a service in the dark of night."

Sebastian raised an arrogant brow. He removed a generous

amount of coin and pressed it into the innkeeper's outstretched palm. "I am sure you can bring the vicar around, and as a token of my good faith, you have permission to keep the remaining funds."

The innkeeper's wife grinned. "Thank you, Your Grace. And how generous you are."

Sebastian rolled his eyes, turning away. Generosity had little to do with his motives. But let them think what they wished, so long as they procured the vicar. He took the stairs three at a time, rushing down the hall to his set of rooms, the muscles of his face supporting an unnatural facial expression—a grin. He stopped at the closed door, attempting to wrestle his riotous emotions under control, feeling the pounding of his heartbeat as though he were a strutting youth at his first ball.

He was a man of two and thirty and without one ounce of self-control.

The knob twisted beneath his hand, and he entered the sitting room, finding it empty. A splash of water from the washroom caught his attention. *Perfect!*

Creeping inside the bedchamber, he slipped off his mud-caked Hessians and tiptoed in stocking feet to the closed door. Holding his breath, he gripped the doorknob and gave it a slow turn.

The door gave way without a creak. He smothered the urge to laugh, fearing the sound too maniacal when seduction was intended. He pressed his face to the partially opened door, the heart beating within his chest coming to a halt.

Rose's bare back was within reach, as she sat in a copper tub, taking a bath. His eyes greedily took in the sight of her pale, unblemished skin, as she caressed her flesh with soapy bubbles.

Sebastian's blood sang with need.

After splashed water on her back to wash away the suds, she leaned back against the tub, closing her eyes, letting her head roll in languid movements against the rounded rim.

Her expression was peaceful. Innocent.

The innocent always slept in blissful ignorance, when danger loomed nearby, ready to strike. Had he ever known such noble slumber, even in youth? Had there not been a time when dreams and hopes lulled his senses into a false sense of security? Perhaps while his mother yet lived, but she died too long ago to recall such happy times.

He turned from Rose, fearing the beast within himself. She deserved more than to be deflowered before her wedding. He may very well look the part of a monster, but he didn't have to act like one.

He sighed, shutting the door to the vision he could not lose. He could wait until tonight to make Rose his—there was no need to pounce on her during her bath.

A soft female groan caught his attention, and all thoughts of honor and decency flew from his head. Stilling his body, he strained his ears to listen from behind the closed door.

There it was again.

A sigh. A whisper of sound so gentle and soft, he might have missed it. But unfortunately, he did not. Oh God, how he wished he had. It would be so much easier to turn his back and walk away, pretending it was naught but the wind whispering such vile words.

Blood roared in Sebastian's ears, and his heart slammed in his chest. Trembling hands reached out and twisted the doorknob, yanking the door open. He crept forward, his gaze alert for any sign of movement or awareness of his presence.

She moaned, and he stilled, above her.

Rose possessed the loveliest female body he had ever viewed, even in his wild days as a much sought-after bachelor. She combined all the best qualities in every female he had ever admired. Long of limb, a beautiful swan-like neck, full, high breasts with delicate pink nipples, never touched—except by herself.

He watched in fascination as one of her hands came up to caress a breast protruding from the water, whispering the hated name.

Silver Hawk.

Rage consumed Sebastian, blurring his vision with the sudden fierce pounding of his heart. The urge to drag her out of her bath and take her innocence on the hard floor nearly overwhelmed him. It was a savage, base need—one he would have acted on in years past.

But this was different.

He wanted her heart and love, and if he took her now in anger, he would never earn it. She would always fear him and his touch. But worse of all, he would kill that which he loved most about her—her graciousness in accepting him and his scars.

He had to tread carefully. Forget his torn pride and heavy heart. He knew Rose harbored a *tendre* for that scoundrel thief. What woman in England didn't these days? But bloody hell, he was a duke, possessing the power to lay the world at her feet! Was it too much to ask for a little piece of her heart in return for the lavish lifestyle he was affording her?

He sank to his knees behind her, stripping out of his jacket as he descended. Casting it aside, he rolled up the sleeves of his linen shirt above his elbows. He gripped the edge of the tub, bending forward, his lips brushing Rose's ear.

"Greetings, my love."

Her eyes flew open wide. "Oh!" Soapy arms rushed up to cover her chest, as she sank further into the murky water. "Your Grace, you intrude on my bath! Get out at once!"

He crossed his arms on the edge of the tub and rested his chin on them, looking at her beneath lowered lashes. "Is that what you want, Rose? I heard you call out though you spoke too softly to decipher the words."

Her face went up in flames. She refused to meet his eyes. "I have no notion as to what you're alluding, Your Grace."

Liar!

"A name, Rose. If memory serves, you were softly calling out a name. Whose name did you utter with such need dripping from your delicate, sweet voice?"

Her breathing faltered. He set the trap, and it was sprung, catching its victim.

Her head rotated to meet his gaze, and he held it with relish, not missing the rapid flutter at the base of her neck, nor the quick, shallow movements of her chest. She licked her lips. He fought the urge to growl.

"Very well," she breathed. "It was your name I whispered with fevered need, imagining our unclothed bodies intertwined in tangled limbs, straining and moving together as one."

The floor gave way beneath his kneeling form with a savage kick to his stomach.

"I did not want you to think less of me because I craved you with such wanton desire."

Lying, scheming wench! Trying to escape your anger and thus your punishment. Let her feel your heartache as you take her innocence, over and over until she cries for mercy against the pain.

The insidious voice offered wise council. Was he not his father's son? Every woman in the peerage thought so, forever casting him in Henry Graham's shadow. The father knew nothing of honor or decency, why should they expect any different treatment from the son? Scenes flashed before his eyes—debutantes quivering in terror when he approached them to dance, the patronesses of Almack's barring him entry despite his title and wealth, his fiancée shuttering anytime he drew near. He grew into a man unloved by family and deemed unlovable by society. He wished a pox on them all.

Yet not his wife. She was the palest glimmer of light on a dark horizon, the beckoning future he risked all to claim. "I will never think less of you for exploring unfilled needs," he vowed.

Confusion marred the earnest expression in Rose's eyes.

"But unfortunately, darling, you will have to explore your newfound needs…with *me*."

She quivered beneath him as he brought his head forward, searing her soft lips with his, kissing her more roughly than he intended.

But she did not resist him. No, in fact, she parted her mouth beneath his onslaught, accepting his plundering tongue with bold strokes matching his own.

She was heaven. A sweet balm to his tortured, lonely soul and he needed her with a desperation he could not explain.

Her hand ascended to frame his injured cheek, and by God, he leaned into her this time around. And Rose grew bolder still. She tugged his hair, dragging him closer, arching her body up, and slanting her hot, wet mouth over his in complete abandonment.

His self-control shattered. An occurrence unheard of in his life.

Thrusting his arms down into the water, he yanked Rose into his embrace, splashing water on the floor, soaking his clothes. But it did not signify. Ignoring her gaping mouth and frightened eyes, he stalked to the four-poster bed by the fireplace.

"Sebastian," she begged, "please, we are not married yet!"

Bracing a knee on the mattress, he laid her gently on the bed, gazing at her glistening body still wet from her bath. Keeping his attention below her face, he fumbled out of his waistcoat, untied the cravat, and slid out of his shirt.

She gulped; her gaze glued to his chest. "Please, Sebastian. Can we not talk about this first?"

Peeling his breeches and stockings off, he presented himself before his rebellious colonial hellion completely nude, save for one thing—his mask.

Her eyes traveled down the length of his body, stopping at his swelled cock. Body trembling, she inched her legs closer together.

Distaste shoved against his conscience, causing him to falter. He was rushing Rose toward intimacy out of jealousy and fear.

Fear of all things. He wanted to laugh—no, worse. Far worse. Cry. He feared abandonment. He was a duke. A duke, by God! A man of wealth and power, yet here he was, stripped bare and exposed, trembling before a young girl, burning on a cross made by his own hands.

Joining her on the bed, he crooked a finger beneath her chin, urging her to face him, flinching when he met her glassy stare. "We will talk later," he promised. "But right now, I want you more than I've ever wanted anything, Rose." He couldn't stop himself from stroking the delicate skin of her hip while he worked to gain courage, forcing himself to say a word never uttered by him before. "Please?" Humiliation warred with the remnants of pride, burning as acid in his throat. "Will you have me? My darling, please?"

Chapter Six

Will you have me?
My darling, please?

Inside Rose cursed, caught in a bed of her own making. Stupid, foolish girl. Whispering a name she had no business uttering. And now there was no choice but to abandon her gift to a man she did not love—or desire. Logan was the only man to stir her body and heart. But he was not here, nor did she have any reason to believe he would come for her.

Cursing again, she focused on the tender, hopeful eyes staring at her, awaiting a decision she did not want to make. At least Sebastian was giving her a choice. Such thoughtfulness was unexpected, even—dare she think it—touching, but not enough to surrender.

"I'm not ready," she whispered, fighting back the panic. All she could envision were her friends being mauled and thrust against, their cries echoing in her ears. Their fate was now hers, and no amount of adornment could make the marriage bed more attractive.

Sebastian cupped her face, commanding her full attention. "Which is all the more reason why we should not put off what we fear the most," he said. "I am no brute, Rose, but a man. A man with needs, and desires, aching for the warmth of a woman's touch. Don't ask me to delay this pleasure any longer."

"What about me? Do my needs and wants matter so little to you?" She waved a hand toward the closed door. "If all you seek is a woman's willing flesh than go downstairs and have your choice."

He stroked her cheek. "Women fear me. Besides, I want my wife."

Bully for you! I want Logan, and you all but ripped me from his hands!

"I am not your wife yet. Or has this moment been your intent from the start?" At his puzzled look, she clarified, "You purposefully misled my brother, taking us to an inn for the night instead of your home. You never planned to marry me, just a quick tumble in bed. Isn't that right, Your Grace?"

"Good God, Rose—no! No, of course not."

"Then if it is truly my choice, as you suggest, I choose to wait until we are married."

A corner of his mouth quirked up. "An event I am happy to say you will have not long to wait for."

"What?"

"I sent for a vicar before returning to our room. We will be married this very night." His expression softened. "Do you truly fear my touch upon your skin? Or are you perhaps unfairly comparing me to the brute behavior of a few English soldiers?"

She withdrew. "I fear an absence of choice regarding the spreading of my thighs. It was a grievous mistake those soldiers made, but I hope it was one they will never forget. Women are not the weaker gender. We are not delicate things, unable to fight when threatened. Our bite will sting if we choose to bare teeth."

He chuckled in a patronizing manner. "Do my ears deceive me or did my fiancée dare threaten me?"

She lifted her chin. "Yes, I dared to threaten you. Your ears did not deceive. I promise to fight if not given a choice to consent to the marriage bed."

He seized her jaw, yanking it down, holding her in place. "I also dare a great many things," he whispered, bringing her mouth close to his. "Perhaps I might dare to invite your fury in our bed someday. I'm not afraid to taste of it." His eyes clouded at her spark of anger. "That is my *threat* to you."

"Go to the devil," she said, wrenching her chin away.

"I'm curious, my dear. You said you would fight. Surely you didn't mean to fight me with fists—lovely though they are." He raised a brow. "Were you thinking of defending your virtue with staff in hand?"

"Yes, but I am more than proficient at using a sword and pistol as well."

Sebastian stroked the hard line of his jaw with thumb and forefinger. "Swords, eh?" He dropped his hand and grinned. "I admit, Rose. You have me intrigued. Let us test your skill with a sword against mine. If you win our little sparring match, you may choose the day and time of our coupling. But if I win," his grin widened, "prepare yourself to surrender your innocence this very night." He thrust his hand forward. "Do we have an accord?"

She'd be a fool not to agree. She reached for Sebastian's hand, giving it a firm shake. He didn't loosen his grip when she tried to withdraw.

Squeezing her fingers together almost painfully, he said, "Hmm, a very firm grip. Something tells me your boasts may have some weight to them." He released her with a laugh.

"You're a cad," she snapped, shaking out her hand to numb the cramp. "When will I have the pleasure of wiping the smile off your face?"

"Tsk tsk, Rose." He waggled a finger at her. "First things first." The sound of doors closing and opening filled the sudden silence. "I suppose it's just as well our coupling will have to wait. I believe the doctor is here to examine your ankle. Our nuptials will follow, so I best take a quick bath." He rolled up from the bed, striding to the washroom.

Despite her misgivings, her mouth dried at the sight of Sebastian's bare frame. His chest was all hills and valleys, contoured in a way that was vastly different from hers. He was fascinating.

For a moment, she replaced Silver Hawk's masked face with Sebastian's, imagining making love to her husband for the first time. Would he be gentle, or prove himself a base beast, no better than the soldiers who tried to rape her?

~ * ~

Rose stared at herself in the beveled mirror, as Milly finished her hair. Thick tresses were piled high on her head, and the white gown her father spared no expense for was ponderous and cumbersome. Milly settled Sebastian's gift around her neck, securing it into place. It was a lovely necklace, adorned with rubies and diamonds, part of the Dorchester family jewels and expected to be worn by each new duchess at her wedding. It was a tradition, he told her.

The thing was dreadfully heavy, and in combination with her wedding dress, Rose felt restrained and constricted in a way no other limitation could match. It was a lovely prelude to marriage.

A knock rattled the bedchamber door. She surged to her feet in a rush of nerves, hobbling over on wooden legs, and a bandaged ankle, to answer it. Sebastian lounged against the doorway on the other side, looking dashing in his black and white formal attire. Even his mask gave a sort of sensual mystery to the man. To her utter shock, the smile gracing her lips was genuine when she greeted him.

His gaze, in turn, roamed over her. The corners of his mouth climbing to produce a wicked grin. "You look radiant, my dear. I can scarcely believe you are mine." He crooked his elbow, holding it aloft. "Or soon will be. Shall we?"

She placed her hand on his arm, despising the nervous flight of winged insects bouncing around her stomach. It was just as well they hadn't eaten dinner yet.

The vicar and his wife waited for them in the parlor by the fireplace, with Sebastian's valet and her maid making up the rest of the witnesses. She wished Robert could have been present.

The vicar cleared his throat. "Dearly beloved, we are gathered together here in the sight of God, and in the face of this congregation, to join this Man and this Woman in holy matrimony; which is an honorable estate, and therefore is not to be taken in hand, unadvisedly, lightly, or wantonly, to satisfy men's carnal lusts and appetites, like brute beasts that have no understanding, but reverently and in the fear of God; duly considering the causes for which Matrimony was ordained..."

Carnal lusts and appetites.

Rose couldn't stop her gaze from seeking out her husband.

He returned her stare evenly, his demeanor solemn.

She wished he would smile or wink, anything to dispel the sense of gloom immersing her heart and soul. It was frightening to know the law and church agreed Sebastian had the right to do what he wished to her body—short of murder.

"First, it was ordained for the procreation of children..."

Her chest tightened. *The procreation of children. Ha!*

Already her marriage could be counted as blasphemy, a foundation they could not build upon for fear of crumbling dreams. Clouds gathered on her horizon, casting shadows on the unusual nighttime ceremony. Sebastian deserved children, yet the doctor's words rang as loud and clear as they had the day he uttered them. *"The women in this family have not the constitution for bringing babes forth into this world. You mark my words, her daughter will suffer the same fate as her mother, and like her mother before her."*

"Secondly, it was ordained for a remedy against sin and to avoid fornication. Thirdly, it was ordained for the mutual society, help, and comfort, that the one ought to have of the other, both in prosperity and adversity. Into which holy estate these two persons present can now be joined. Therefore, if any man can show any just cause why they may not be lawfully be joined together, let him now speak, or else hereafter forever hold his peace."

Rose held her breath, but her highwayman did not make a dramatic entry. Nor did her brother. No one was coming to save her from becoming a duchess.

"Sebastian Tiberius Graham," the vicar intoned in shaky tones, avoiding Sebastian's ducal glare. "Wilt thou have this woman to be thy wedded wife, to live together after God's ordinance, in the holy estate of matrimony? Wilt thou love her, comfort her, honor, and keep her in sickness and in health; and forsaking all others, keep thee only unto her, so long as ye both shall live?"

Sebastian cupped her face, urging her away from grim thoughts. Calm blue eyes demanded her full attention. "I will."

The whispered response did not soothe Rose's frayed nerves. A massive burn began in the back of her throat, building its way to her eyes. She blinked and fought the moisture, knowing she stood alone on a threshold and feeling so confused.

The vicar swung his head, meeting her eyes, the odious man. "Rose Marie Witherby, wilt thou have this man to thy wedded husband, to live together after God's ordinance in the holy estate of Matrimony? Wilt thou obey him and serve him, love, honor, and keep him in sickness and in health; and, forsaking all others, keep thee only unto him, so long as ye both shall live?"

No! Yes! Must I really obey?

"I will," she answered, though her heart split with indecision.

The vicar extended a shaking hand toward Sebastian's right side, but his unblinking stare had the vicar blanching, and he snatched his hand back.

Sebastian took her right hand himself.

"P-please r-repeat after m-me," the vicar stuttered. "I, Sebastian Graham, take thee Rose Witherby to be my wedded wife, to have and to hold from this day forward, for better for worse, for richer or poorer, in sickness and in health, to love and to cherish, till death us do part, according to God's holy ordinance; and thereto I plight thee my troth."

Sebastian repeated the words in strong, measured tones, squeezing her right hand as he finished.

Surely a man who did not care a fig for her would not stare with rapt attention into her eyes, doing his best to put a young woman more at ease with an arranged marriage.

He winked, further dispelling her sense of gloom.

She repeated her vows, her voice unfaltering.

The vicar gulped. "The ring, please, Your Grace."

Sebastian withdrew a gold band from his jacket pocket. Her mouth came unhinged at the lovely piece, the clusters of rubies and diamonds sparkling and dancing in the candlelight.

He clasped her left hand now, again without the assistance of the vicar, and slid the ring onto the tip of her fourth finger. "With this ring, I thee wed, with my body I thee worship, and with all my worldly goods I thee endow; in the name of the Father, and of the Son, and of the Holy Ghost. Amen." He slid the ring down the length of her finger.

It was heavy, and she flexed her fingers, adjusting to the odd weight. It was a branding of sorts, was it not? Branding the broodmare so all the world will know what man owns her.

She stared at Sebastian's tender expression as her branded finger plummeted back to her side. Whatever else she thought, it mattered little now. She was a wife. A duchess.

The vicar directed them to kneel, and she accepted Sebastian's hand as they knelt as one in front of the shaky knees of the vicar. She caught Sebastian smirk out of the corner of her eye. If she didn't know any better, she would have guessed her husband was taking great enjoyment out of intimidating a man of God. She elbowed him in the ribs as she bowed her head, letting him know her displeasure.

His chest rumbled in response, unrepentant.

"Those whom God hath joined together let no man put asunder, for as much as Sebastian and Rose have consented together in holy wedlock and have given and pledged their troth either to other, and have declared the same by giving and receiving of a ring, I pronounce that they be man and wife together. In the name of the Father, and of the Son, and of the Holy Ghost. Amen."

Sebastian laid a hand beneath her elbow, and together they stood. Her heart pounded, from what exertion she could not name, but as she tilted her head back to accept her husband's kiss, it beat harder still. She was his now. And the life she had known, across an ocean, on a continent two thousand miles removed, was lost to her forever.

~ * ~

After the ceremony, dinner awaited them. Sebastian dismissed his small staff, and they were once more alone. Rose found her heart would not settle into a more sedate pace. She was now a wife—a duchess, no less. And her new husband looked at her with a ravenous appetite.

He tugged out a chair. "Rose?"

A smile of gratitude formed and withered as she noticed his gaze failed to meet her eyes. The skin exposed by the low neckline of the bodice tingled beneath such close regard. "Thank you," she snapped, gaining his attention.

The rogue grinned and winked, before serving her from the several platters present. Lamb and sage sauce, potatoes with mashed turnips, and cheeses. It looked delectable, and she made sure to drag out each bite so dinner would last a good long while.

Sebastian caught on to the game. He yanked her plate away. "It will be dawn before we get to our little contest," he complained, rising.

"Besides, your corset must be about ready to burst at the seams."

She dabbed the corners of her mouth with a cloth napkin, affecting an air of disdain. "Are you calling me a stuffed pig?"

He roared with laughter. "Not at all," he said, reining in his mirth, eyes dancing with mischief. "But corsets can be an unforgiving companion. I prefer my opponents to be at their best."

"Never fear, Your Grace. I shall out fence you regardless of my attire."

He met her eyes with a lecherous grin. "We shall see." He strode past her heading into their bedchamber. "Now then," he called, "where shall the venue be for our unconventional contest of skill and strength?"

She heard the opening and closing of trunks.

He emerged moments later, brandishing two steel rapiers. "I would prefer a more intimate setting," he said, extending a sword, hilt first. "But this suite doesn't offer much by way of space. So," his eyes lighting up, "I know just the place. Follow me."

He led the way, out of their suite and down the stairs, his stride never faltering when the busy tavern paused to watch them make their way out.

If Rose felt more herself, she would have laughed at the absurdity of this situation. A bride in all her wedding finery, following her new husband carrying a sword intent on a duel. It had all the makings of a Shakespearean play.

All that remained missing was the romance. Her mind conjured the handsome face of Silver Hawk, and she swallowed hard. Maybe there was a tiny bit of romance—but an illicit one best forgotten. Whatever else she might wish or yearn for, it mattered naught. Sebastian Graham was now her husband.

And the man she planned on fighting against for freedom from her wedding night.

It was an outlandish contest he agreed to. After all, he had every right to take away her innocence and proclaim her as his. He didn't have to accept terms that might prohibit him from consummating this marriage. But he did, and his act was regrettably worthy of notice. It proved he cared for her.

Sebastian led the way into the stable. He paused after crossing the threshold and looked around the occupied stalls. "It's empty of a human audience, at least," he said, whirling to face her. "There's ample room to allow for freedom of movement. Do you agree?"

"Yes, it will suffice," she replied, uncaring if their fight was public or not. She shifted her weight, raising her sword. "Shall we begin?"

As expected, he eyed her bared ankles when she fisted her skirts in one hand. *"En guard!"* she called, leaping forward. The ruse gave her the element of surprise, but it was an advantage quick to be lost as he rallied with a series of small lunges and thrusts. The attack was basic, testing her skill.

She parried a thrust and whirled, lunging and thrusting, cutting his shoulder. "Touché," she called, smiling at his dubious expression.

"Someone taught you well," he said. "I underestimated you." He settled into a ready stance once again. "Shall we continue?"

She brought her sword up, and he launched into an attack, using greater finesse and fancier footwork, proving he'd been holding back. He was agile and graceful, as well as strong. He cut her dress when she parried a second too late.

"You're also well taught," she said, dancing around Sebastian's attacks. He cut her dress several more times. She returned the favor to his clothes, but neither was drawing blood, a testament to both their skill.

A horse whinnied, snatching Sebastian's attention for a fraction of a second, but it was a second she'd been waiting for. Lunging, she whisked his mask off with a swift flick of her wrist.

He jerked back, mouth agape, staring in amazement at her, all movement and predatory expression removed from his stance. Sebastian stood open and vulnerable before her appraisal, not bothering to hide.

Her heart softened in that moment of vulnerability. "How did it happen?" she murmured. "You appear scarred from fire."

He touched the twisted, melted flesh on his right cheek. The only imperfection marring an otherwise handsome visage. "Tortured for information by Americans during the war." His hand fell to the side. He scrutinized her face. "You do not appear terrified."

"Of my husband? Hardly." She smiled. "I think him quite handsome to look upon."

He eyed her with suspicion. "Truly you are not…afraid? Disgusted by what you see?"

She walked forward until they stood toe-to-toe. Dropping her weapon to cup his face, she said, "Truly I am not afraid or disgusted. I am no fragile Englishwoman, given to fainting spells when overwrought, but an American, born and raised on the frontier. We were never safe from the threat of violence." Her mouth twisting into a grimace. "Indeed, I have seen more than my fair share."

"I'm sorry," he murmured, taking her hands in his, kissing her knuckles. "I'm sure you witnessed much by way of brutal deaths. A thing I wish you never suffered."

She nodded, swallowing the lump of grief as she always did when reminded of the day the English came to her home. It was a tragedy she suffered from daily and feared it always would be.

"And yet," he continued, brushing back a loose strand of her hair, "if my father had not come upon you that day, we would never be standing here together, locked in mortal combat." He chuckled; his eyes warm. "You fight bloody well, my dear. I admit I'm impressed. I had thought your swagger an empty boast, but you rival me for skill. Taking my mask off without a single scratch is no small feat." His eyes sobered. "And your reaction, or lack of one, to my scar is a gift beyond measure."

"The women of your acquaintance sound like complete and utter bores, Your Grace." She grinned. "And it's their misfortune not to have the pleasure of your company."

He stroked her cheek with one finger. "Do you mean that, Rose?"

"I do."

A smiled flashed in response to her swift reply. "I had better warn you," he said, leaning close. "If we continue down this path, I may be professing my love for you before the night is through."

Her heart skipped, out of dread or excitement to the declaration, she did not know or understand. Stranger still, she found herself yearning to know the lay of his heart and what might follow if she opened hers to him.

But he is not Silver Hawk!

Rubbish! Give your husband a chance.

Rubbing her cheek into the palm of his hand, she whispered in a throaty voice, "If I chose not to follow another path? Where then might that take us?"

Black pupils dilated as eyelids descended. "To a place where rules and contests do not apply if you are of like mind."

"You have not won yet, Your Grace."

He chuckled low into in her ear, then stepping back, he yanked on her skirts just below the hips. Her dress and stays fell away, billowing around her feet.

She stared at him in stunned amazement, wearing nothing more than her sheer chemise and silk stockings. Sebastian had cut her dress in such a way where it would fall off with the merest touch!

The rogue!

Still, she couldn't bring herself to be angry at him. Indeed, she was rather impressed.

"Do you concede the battle?" he asked, gathering her into his arms.

Unable to resist him, she shook her head, analyzing the strangeness of his body against her nearly nude frame. The warmth of his hands on her waist, the soft texture of his linen shirt against her chest. The hard bulge pressed against her belly, evidence of his desire. The intimate touch did not frighten her, but neither did it sweep away the hesitation and reluctance.

Sebastian was going to make love to her. Here. Now. The hardening of the body beneath her hands spoke of mounting hunger, curling to pounce at its meal to satisfy an arduous appetite.

She was the sacrificial lamb, caught in the jaws of a ravenous beast.

No! Not a beast but a man. Your husband. Trust him. "If I concede," she whispered, "will you be gentle?"

His blue eyes filled with tenderness and longing. "You have my word, Rose." He stilled her tongue from speaking with an index finger pressed against her lips. "I would have a promise from you as well."

Her brows quirked in lieu of verbal demand for clarification.

His finger dropped. "I do not possess the power to reverse the sun, but I would build a future with a wife without hearing the name Silver Hawk drip from her lips."

Everything inside her stilled. "Sebastian?"

"I heard you," he said, lowering his voice, his gaze intense, "whisper that criminal's name during your bath."

Fear seized her tongue. There was no defense to the truth.

He stroked her cheek with gentle fingers. "You hold the man close to heart, and I understand. You are young, too young to realize he speaks pretty words with a serpent's tongue. I do not fault you for falling victim to his charms. Nor do I fault you for trembling at my touch. I know what you experienced at the hands of English soldiers."

Tears came unbidden as he spoke with kindness and compassion, excusing her shameful behavior and faults. Perhaps it was she who did not deserve him. A twist of fate she would not have gambled on. "I am sorry I hurt you, Sebastian. It was never my intent."

He thumbed away her tears. "I know. I know too, you never wished to be my wife."

She reached for his fingers, catching them in hands that trembled. "Yet here I am."

"Yes. Here you are—with *me*." He withdrew his fingers from

her touch. Clamping down on her shoulders, he wrenched her close. "Promise me you will never repeat that blackguard's name."

She jumped, her heart skipping a beat. "I-I promise."

He stared into her eyes, searching. "Give me a chance, Rose. Open your heart to possibilities. I will make you happy if you can let go of foolish fantasies."

Unshed tears swelled her throat. She could do no more than nod, unable to speak past the knot. The hands on her shoulders softened, tugging her forward into a warm embrace. She accepted Sebastian's comfort, glad he offered it instead of harsh words or worse. Slipping her arms around his torso, she returned his hug in a rare show of affection.

"That's better," he murmured against her hair. "I'm not so terrible a husband, now am I?"

She sniffed, bringing her head up. "No. You are not."

He caressed her cheek with the back of his hand. "Do you know what else your husband is not terrible at?"

She caught the teasing twinkle in his eyes and smiled. "No."

Leaning close to her ear, he whispered, "Making love." He chuckled, a self-depreciating sound. "Though, admittedly, he might be a bit out of practice."

A bit of her fire came back. "How out of practice?" She lowered the neckline of her chemise with a sharp shrug, so it bared a single shoulder.

His soft laughter morphed into silent appreciation as she eased the shift down to her hips, baring breasts. Blue eyes darkened to the color of the James River at night. "Rose," his gaze shot up to hers, "you tease a hungry man. I must warn you; my control is waning."

"Let it go."

He eyed her as though he did not trust her words. "Here? In a stable is where you choose to make the sacrifice?"

"No." She placed a hand over his heart. *Thump. Thump. Thump.* His excitement strengthened her resolve. "This is where I surrender."

"Surrender." He closed his eyes, swallowing hard. "Rose, I will ask one final time. Are you sure?"

No. But aloud, she murmured, "Yes."

His eyelids ascended to reveal a deep, somber shade of blue. "Will you also place trust in me?"

She nodded. "Yes, Sebastian. You have my trust as well."

With eyes glued to the other, he walked her backward until rough wood halted her movements. Large hands framed her hips, sliding around to grip her bottom. "I am not Silver Hawk," he whispered, causing her to flinch.

She opened her mouth to acknowledge this, but he hushed her with his lips upon hers.

He retreated far enough to gain her attention. "Keep your eyes on me as I take you," he whispered, hoisting her by her bottom, urging her legs apart. He wrapped her limbs around his waist, fumbling with his breeches. "I would see my reflection in those emerald eyes, so I know where your thoughts linger as I make you mine."

Her heart leaped into her throat as a soft rounded head pushed against her core. A shot of adrenaline, fueled by panic, lay siege to her thoughts, crippling her desire.

Sebastian paused. "Steady, sweetheart. I shall go slowly."

She nodded; their gazes locked. Each flinch by her was answered with a whispered word of praise. Each gasp of breath her mouth made was caught by his lips, kissing away her fears. He worked his way inch by inch into her tight passage, as well as her heart.

He paused at the moment she felt stretched full enough to break. His kissed her neck. "I'm at your maidenhead, darling. I can go no further without causing pain."

"It's—"

"Your Grace!"

He jerked, cursing aloud, nearly dropping her. He yanked himself out, setting her to her feet, holding her while she steadied herself, blocking the intruder's view.

At her nod, Sebastian let go and stormed out of the dark corner of a stall where they hid. "I am here. Who calls for me?"

"'Tis I, Your Grace." The innkeeper stepped into the meager light of a lantern. "A man is looking for you in the tavern. I thought you might want to know."

Sebastian cursed again. "Thank you. I will be out presently."

The innkeeper gave a raised brow, glancing casually around the stable before taking his leave.

Rose crept out as soon as the stable door shut, clutching the remnants of her dress to her breasts. Her heart skipped with the news the innkeeper gave, with excitement or dread she did not know, but her head grew faint over the possibilities. "Who might seek you out in the middle of the night?" she asked.

Sebastian swung around, eyes flashing. "I have no idea." He marched to her side, stripping out of his jacket, settling it around her bare shoulders. "Come. I will escort you back to our suite before greeting my guest."

"Dressed like this?" She motioned to her shredded silk that once resembled a gown.

"We will take the servants' entrance in the back. No one will see us Come." He whisked her away back to the tavern, guiding her to the desired hallway and up a narrow set of stairs. True to his word, no eyes bore witness to her lack of clothing. He parted ways with her inside their room with a quick kiss on the cheek, slamming the door on his fleeing back.

"Well." Her head still spun with all that occurred within the space of hours. Her life changed with maddening pace no sane person could keep up with. What on earth would spring up next?

She walked into her bedchamber, frowning at the darkness. Why had her maid turned down all the lamps? Did Milly think she would be spending the night in the barn? Grumbling, Rose tiptoed around the room, stripping bare, rummaging through trunks to find a nightdress. Thusly dressed she climbed into bed, snuggling under covers that were strangely warm, without a body or roaring fire to keep them heated.

Her head hit the pillow as her eyes widened, the answer springing from the mind at the same time her body stiffened in awareness.

She was not alone.

Chapter Seven

"Greetings, little one."

"Oh!" She sprang forward, joy crashing through her at the sound of his voice. "I thought you for the afterlife."

"From a gunshot to the shoulder? Hardly cause to make such a journey. My wound has been tended to and will heal in days to come."

The bed shifted, and a warm weight clung to her side against the blankets. Her brain issued a warning she did not wish to heed. "I am glad you are well, Mister Hawk, but you should not be here. Sebastian will be back shortly, I am sure."

"*Mister* Hawk? Have you forgotten my first name so soon?"

Her heart and resolve were melting with alarming speed. What this man could do to her with a single look or quiet word spoken by a deep, expressive voice!

Sebastian held no such power over her, beyond the ability to cause her guilt. But he was still her husband, and she his loyal wife. She would not fail him in this.

She eased Silver Hawk's fingers from her face. "I only seek to establish proper boundaries between us."

"Proper boundaries?" His voice dripped incredulity. "Do my ears deceive, or has common sense found its mark on you at last?"

"I married Sebastian, the contract between my father and Sebastian upheld."

"And the marriage consummated?" An icy edge crept into his tone.

She could not lie. "Not yet. It was interrupted by untimely visitors."

The outline of his broad shoulders relaxed. "Then I offer my gratitude. I am not too late."

She blushed. "Giving me the peace I once yearned for is no longer your responsibility. It is for Sebastian to now provide."

"Rose." Logan leaned down, his brown eyes holding hers with grave sincerity. "Do not trust Dorchester to provide it to you either. He is a wolf in sheep's clothing. It's clear to me he has tried to make you happy, and that's all well and good. But trust me in this, when I tell you it is an act to earn your trust, to make the game more amusing when he rips it away."

She trembled at his words, caught between arguing Sebastian's finer points and believing Silver Hawk. "He caught me already in a lie, his response more than I deserved."

He went still. "Go on."

"I was taking a bath, entertaining fantasies of you, and I whispered your name aloud, and Sebastian overheard."

He swore. "What did he do in revenge?"

She laid a calming hand on his arm. "Nothing. He bade me to make a promise never to utter your name again. That was the end of it."

"Of that, I highly doubt. Rose." He got up off the bed to pace the room. He stopped by her side of the bed, dropping to his knees before her. "Come away with me. Now. Tonight."

She reared back. "As your captive?"

"No! As my…" He paused, the column of his throat working. He forced a cough. "As my wife. Marry me."

Her soul exploded with all manner of exuberant feelings, yet the fragile tether created by Sebastian would not sever so easily. She tempered her response, stuffing her true feelings behind a mask formed by necessity. "Marry a second man I do not know?" She laid a hand over his masked cheek, unable to help herself. "Or whose face I've never seen?"

"The lay of your heart should not be dependent on the revealing of my face."

"Perhaps not, but it does not change my answer in your favor."

"You do not love him."

"No, not yet."

His jaw flexed beneath her hand, tightening. "Look me in the eye and tell me I hold no meaning to you, and I will walk away forever."

Her courage faltered. "Can you whisper such words to me? Look me in the eye and tell me I hold your heart?"

He placed a large hand over hers, still cupping his face. "You hold everything of mine I have of worth. A weight no amount of coin can balance."

Tears slipped from the thin veil of control she clung to, her soul in danger of splitting asunder. "I am already married."

"You stall for time, Rose, and avoid my question. I would have a straight answer."

She forced her lungs to expel the air she'd been holding, knowing she damned her soul to eternal purgatory with her next breath. "For reasons I cannot name, my heart favors you."

A smile split his face. "Love rarely follows where logic leads. An irony only besotted fools would understand."

"Yet I cannot marry you, Logan." She dropped her hand from his face as his smile crumpled. "You cannot know how my decision tortures me, yet it must be so. I spoke vows with Sebastian, and I am honor-bound to uphold them. How could you claim to love me if I turned so easily from promises made?"

He glanced away. "I understand your reasons, little one. You need not explain them further for my sake." His tortured gaze found hers. "I only pray they bring you comfort, in all the long days and nights to come." He stood. "I will trouble you no longer." He pivoted on his heel, preparing to go.

"Wait!" She tossed covers aside and raced to his side. "You once needed me for ransom. I would see my price paid."

His hand shot out, keeping her in place. "There are not enough funds in all of England to match your worth to me."

Her voice lodged in her throat, strangled by grief and unshed tears. They stared at the other in silence, the air tense and heavy. Silver Hawk moved his head a fraction forward, and she shifted without thought, meeting his lips halfway. His kiss was fleeting, tender without passion, and all too brief. His way of saying goodbye.

He left without further words, ducking out an open window, lost to the night. She collapsed on the bed, crying useless tears, as angry voices entered the parlor down the hall. Sitting up, she dashed a hand across her swollen eyes and donned a wrapper, trudging out of her bedchamber, feigning interest in the growing argument to hide her broken heart.

Sebastian and Robert stood face-to-face in a heated argument. She cried out at sight of her brother, glad to see family. She moved to throw herself into Robert's arms, but Sebastian's scowl anchored her feet to the floor, propelling her no further forward. "Robert!" She pasted an overly bright smile on her face.

He responded by stalking forward, embracing her in a bear hug. "Are you all right?" he whispered into her ear, over Sebastian's growl.

She nodded, withdrawing from his arms. "Never better," she said, forcing her feet to move toward Sebastian's side. He locked an arm around her waist, hauling her up against his side. By some miracle she kept her smile in place as she faced her brother. "What do you two argue about at such an hour?"

"A matter I would speak to you privately about," Sebastian said, cutting Robert off.

"Oh, come now, Dorchester, are we not family now? Surely we can settle a minor dispute in a civilized duel."

"Duel? What duel?" She swiveled to her husband, awaiting explanation.

Sebastian rolled his eyes. "Your brother thinks I had my way with you without the exchange of vows and God's blessing." He shrugged. "I tried to tell him, but he refused to listen."

"No, I only wish to hear from my sister's lips." Robert's eyes bore into hers. "Are you well and truly married?"

"Yes, Robert. We are husband and wife."

Robert's gaze held hers a moment longer before swinging back to Sebastian. "I still demand to witness a ceremony in a church before I concede and allow my sister to stay in your care."

"Robert," she wrapped an arm around Sebastian, giving her husband a sheepish smile, "I appreciate your brotherly concern, but your argument comes too late."

"Aye, all that remains is the wedding night." Sebastian lay a gentle hand on her abdomen.

She tensed as Robert laughed out loud.

"What in the hell do you find so amusing, Witherby?"

Her brother wiped tears from his eyes. "She's not seen fit to tell you yet?"

Sebastian frowned. "Tell me what?"

"The family curse, of course." Robert grinned. "Oh, I think you two will have loads to talk about now. My wedding gift to you both." He left them, cackling gleefully to himself as he strode from their suite.

Sebastian immediately rounded on her. "What the devil is he talking about? What curse?"

Oh, her brother was a smooth rogue. She wasn't going to mention it to Sebastian, but now the subject was broached, she had little choice. She was curious to know if her concerns would affect his plans to create a family.

Chapter Eight

"I don't understand."

Rose glanced at her brother. "Pray tell, Robert. What notion can your brain not wrap itself around?"

"That's gratitude for you. How about a 'thank you' for saving you from your wedding night obligations?"

She snorted. "I didn't need your help. If I had truly been against sharing a bed with Sebastian, I would have found a way of avoiding it."

"That's the part I don't understand. Why weren't you avoiding it?"

She offered thanks to the heavens for Sebastian's absence. The carriage ride to her new home would have been unbearable. Fortunately, he chose to ride on his horse after ten minutes of Robert's company. Her husband's temper was short having been denied a wedding night for fear of getting her with child.

"I wasn't avoiding it because I wanted to appease my husband. I owed him that much."

Robert tipped forward, his expression earnest. "You owe him nothing, Rose."

"I hurt him, Robert. I had to make amends. But now thanks to you, he's scared to death of touching me!"

"As I said. You're welcome."

She lapsed into silence, her thoughts straying toward a subject of more concern—Logan. She wanted to talk to someone but feared her only option was Robert. She wasn't that desperate yet. Besides, what would he know of love and heartache? It's not as though he knew the thief, or the man's thoughts, and would probably think her daft for loving a man intent on kidnapping her.

She must be addled. Sebastian was a good man, and all she could do was pine away for a thief. Her heart must have a defect within it, as well as her womanly parts. She had no notion her body could burn from a man's touch until she met Logan. Sebastian tried to ignite her passion but fell short of arousing the same fury.

What was wrong with her?

"Well, would you look at that?"

The wry humor in Robert's voice pulled her attention away from useless woolgathering. "What is it?"

"If I'm not mistaken, I believe the ancient, desolate, pile of rocks we're staring at is your new home."

A feeling of impending doom clogged her throat. Desperate for human contact at that moment, her hand crept out under its own volition to grab Robert's.

Sebastian's ducal estate stood before them.

Perched high upon a hill, a dark blight upon the countryside, a stone creation whose shadow stretched far and wide. Dark clouds overhead heralded a storm, aiding her departure from sanity, along with her brother's maniacal laughter.

She let go of his hand in disgust.

"Oh God, the perfect setting for a loveless marriage," Robert said, reining in his mirth. "Are you still intent on honoring your make-believe debt?"

She did not reply as the carriage rattled forward down the long drive, the castle looming before her as some ghostly specter from the Dark Ages. The sun's light hid behind giant towers and spiraling turrets. Windows both narrow and wide stood dark and empty, yet she felt the weight of eyes upon her face, assessing and judging.

The uncouth American girl to play the part of duchess to the castle's scarred duke. A laughable fate, one born of misery and destined to end the same.

"Look there." Robert pointed out the window.

Sebastian waited with a small army of servants, all lined in a row by a massive, ornate set of doors. The carriage pulled into a courtyard and stopped, Sebastian, springing forward as a footman lowered the steps.

He opened the carriage door himself, smiling as he extended a hand. "Milady, welcome to Dorchester Castle." He peered into her face, tensing. "Rose, what's wrong? You're pale and trembling." He swung an accusing look at her brother.

"Don't look at me," Robert said, putting his hands up. "I'm not the one who chooses to make his home in an eerie castle."

"It's not eerie," Sebastian snapped.

"It is a relic though," Robert countered. "I say, does King Arthur reside nearby? I always wanted a historical figure as a neighbor."

Sebastian's face went red. "You're not living here, Witherby. You're visiting." His gaze slid toward hers, begging for her to step out of the carriage and end his suffering.

She took pity on him. Robert did take a bit of getting used to. Sarcasm was not everyone's cup of tea. "I am fine, Sebastian. The carriage ride made me a little queasy, is all."

Concern furrowed his brow, and guilt ate at her once more over this newest lie.

"Then come into the house, and I shall see you to your room to rest."

She nodded and grabbed his hand, allowing him to assist her out of the carriage and onto solid ground. He swept her away to the row of servants.

"Rose, this is the entirety of my staff." He motioned to an elderly man and woman. They stepped forward; their gazes cast to the ground. "May I present my butler Mr. Harrison and my housekeeper Mrs. Brown."

"It's a pleasure to meet you both." She smiled, hoping to lighten their twin dour expressions. Failing miserably, she addressed Mrs. Brown, as Mr. Harrison drew her husband aside. "Has my maid arrived?"

Mrs. Brown bobbed her head. "Yes, Your Grace. She is settling in now. Shall I ring for her?"

"No, not yet. Thank you." She walked away when Sebastian motioned for her to join him.

Distracted eyes and a thoughtful frown greeted her. "I have a visitor waiting for me in my study, Rose. Why don't you go upstairs and freshen up before dinner? Mrs. Brown can show you the way to your bedchamber."

"I'd like a word with my sister before she disappears," Robert interjected, stepping forward.

Sebastian's lips tightened before he gave a curt nod. "Mrs. Brown," he called, "please show Her Grace and her brother to the salon and bring them some tea." He stepped close, pressing a chaste kiss to Rose's cheek. "I will join you both momentarily."

Nodding, she watched him walk away into the castle. He didn't look pleased by the news he had a visitor.

"Your Grace and Mr. Witherby. Please follow me."

Robert extended his arm, and Rose accepted as they followed Mrs. Brown through the enormous mahogany front doors and into—lavishness.

Looking around the foyer, she gasped. Gleaming luxury

surrounded her. The polished marble floors, the tall, cathedral ceiling with magnificent twinkling chandeliers. And spiraling up one side of the wall was a staircase with an elaborately carved mahogany banister. Sebastian's home may be a pile of rocks on the outside, but nothing could be further from the word 'dilapidated' looking at the home from within its gilded walls. It made her plantation seem paltry at best.

And she was mistress of such grandeur.

She made a face.

"Your Grace," Mrs. Brown called, "please follow me this way." The housekeeper led her and Robert a little further down the hall and into a sitting room papered in gold and cream colors, with matching settees and chairs. "I'll be right back with tea," the housekeeper promised, taking her leave.

Robert went immediately to her side, taking her hand in his. "Rose, I will repeat myself one final time, since you seem hard of hearing and uncommonly hard of head—more than usual," he added at her frown. "You do not owe Sebastian Graham anything in this world. The marriage was an arrangement for a debt owed by our father. I can help you escape if you extend me a little trust."

She was not in the mood to listen to this. It wasn't fair. Her heart was already heavy with the loss of Logan. This home in all its splendor overwhelmed her senses. She was not in the proper frame of mind to cling to marital vows. Escape sounded all too wonderful, and the thought of being once more in Logan's arms threatened to weaken her decisions and throw herself on her brother's mercy.

She sought to fortify her resolve, but her brother's keen eyes saw through her vain attempt.

"Come here, Rose." He dragged her to an ivory colored settee, pushing down and taking a seat beside her. "I have it on good authority you refused a perfectly good offer of marriage last night."

Her eyes flew wide. "How do you know of Silver Hawk's proposal?"

"Whose words do you think set him to purpose?"

She reared back. "I don't understand."

"Oh, come now, Rose. Did you honestly think I'd let my only sister marry the devil? You marrying Silver Hawk was always my intended goal on this God-forsaken trip. I never thought, in my wildest dreams, you'd be defending Dorchester or wanting to remain his wife. Why can't you ever do the expected? You know, make your poor brother's life a little easier?"

"How...how do you know Silver Hawk?" She could not wrap her addled mind around what Robert was saying.

"Our acquaintance began a while ago," he said, his voice going flat. "Let us just say, like Father, Silver Hawk also has a debt to pay."

"A debt? What sort of debt? A payment owed to you? How is that possible?" She could feel herself losing control of her temper. Logan spoke only of love last night, and she believed him because her feelings were so thoroughly entangled. But the only reason he proposed marriage at all was to cover a debt owed to her brother?

"His debt is one equally shared by me. Thus, the basis for our friendship. A bond forged in blood and death," Robert added bitterly, glancing away.

He spoke this way only when talking about the day the English came to their home, and all the death and suffering that followed.

Had Logan been part of the invasion?

"What debt does Silver Hawk owe you?" she asked, her voice rising.

Robert put a finger to his lips. "It doesn't matter. All that matters is freeing you from Dorchester."

"Free me from Sebastian only to see me bound to a highwayman to pay another debt? Robert, this is nonsense! I am not a horse to be bartered nor sold to the highest bidder. Why should I trade one form of bondage for another?"

"It's not like that, Rose. Silver Hawk genuinely cares for you. And marriage to Sebastian will only bring you pain and more suffering than I fear you can bear."

"You continually mark my husband as a beast, Robert, and I would like to know the reason. He has never been anything but kind and understanding toward me. Even consenting to wait to consummate our marriage until we speak with a physician about my ability to bear children."

"Ah, Rose. You know there is nothing wrong with you. Mother bore the both of us into this world without mishap. It was simply her time to go, nothing more."

"I watched her die in agony, Robert. Whether I can or not, I do not wish to end my life in such pain."

"Well, you can argue for a litter of kittens with Silver Hawk. I certainly don't care either way."

"Fine. But I cannot help but notice you failed to answer my question regarding my husband."

Robert shifted closer; his gaze intense. "He's a predator, Rose. A very clever one. Don't you wonder why a duke—albeit a scarred duke—would marry a colonial girl? Why no other woman would have him? He's a monster. Not just a rake or a libertine, but a man who preys on women for the sheer joy of hurting them—physically and mentally."

She shook her head, not able to credit a word of this nonsense. "No. Robert, you're wrong. I do not see this 'monster.' Sebastian has been loving and kind to me when I deserved far worse treatment. No." She shook her head more forcefully as if to convince herself. "I cannot believe that of him. You're wrong."

"And if I'm not?"

She stared into her brother's somber eyes, seeking truth from madness. A knot formed in her stomach. Her brother believed every word he said, and he would never wish her harm. "If you have a plan, I would hear of it now before I regain sense."

He gathered both her hands in his, holding on tight. "I can spirit you out of this castle and escort you to Silver Hawk. I know where to find him. He would protect you from all harm."

"Because of a debt owed to you," she said, bitterness souring the joy of his memory.

"No, because the man loves you, nitwit." Robert chuckled. "It may have started out as an obligation to balance the scale, but believe me, the man is besotted by you now."

"Truly?"

"Truly." He lowered his voice. "Does that mean you agree to let me kidnap you?"

She blanched. Was this truly where her madness led? The precipice yearned before her, all her choices laid bare, yet nothing to guide her footsteps, nothing beyond instinct and her brother's word that Sebastian was not as he seemed.

Robert squeezed her hand. "I dared to love once. And I lost her. But not a day goes by when I do not wish I could reverse time and hold her in my arms again."

"You loved a woman, Robert? I'm shocked! Who was she?"

"Your best friend, Abby."

"No!" She flinched at the loudness of her voice. "How is it possible I did not know this?" she whispered. Abby had been one of her friends visiting her home the day the English came. She suffered horribly at the hands of soldiers; a violent fate Rose could not save her from.

"We were going to tell you, Rose. We were engaged, but after the attack..." He cleared his throat. "She refused me after what the soldiers did to her, and to my great regret I let her go." He looked up at Rose when she gasped. "Not because of what happened, Rose. I still loved her and wanted her as a wife, but she would not have me. She was ashamed, and I did not fight to keep what we had."

"I'm sorry for your suffering, Robert. Honestly, I am. But my situation is different. You're asking me to abandon a marriage to form a union with another man whom I hardly know."

"Oh aye, hardly know yet love. I saw the two of you together. There was a bond, an attachment my eyes did not miss. Do not deny it."

She sighed. "I do not deny I love him, Robert. Yet for all that, I am reluctant to break Sebastian's heart. I try but fail to see the beast you imagine him to be."

"Imagine?" he scoffed. "I hardly need to stretch my imagination to know his crimes. His victims are proof enough."

She settled back against the cushions, rubbing her temples, fighting the urge to give in to her heart's desire. It seemed a bleak future when considering the passing of years spent as Sebastian's wife, though not because she entertained the notion of his monstrous deeds, but because she loved another man more. And what kind of life was that?

She ought to control her destiny, a thing her father did not care to hear when making plans for this arranged marriage. He bundled her off to England with no more than two weeks' notice, without so much as a by-your-leave.

Resentment simmered until it swept away the last dregs of moral obligation.

"I will go." She sat up; her chin raised. "I'll do it."

His eyes lit up. "You will? Thank God! Now I won't have to worry about how much laudanum I can safely slip in your tea."

"Laudanum? What —"

"Rose." Sebastian strode into the room.

Her heart skipped a beat, wondering if he overheard any part of their conversation. His expression offered no clues to his mood. She rose to greet him, accepting a chaste kiss on her cheek while her brother scowled.

Sebastian took her hands in his. "May I speak to you in private?"

"Of course." She waved to Robert. "Make yourself at home. I'll be back promptly." She gulped, hoping she would be, at any rate.

Sebastian escorted her down the hall and into his study, closing the door behind them. Rose nearly jumped out of her skin at the ominous sound of the latch clicking into place. "What is wrong, Sebastian?"

He turned to her, his expression no longer shuttered, but stormy. "I have to leave for London at once."

Chapter Nine

She took a step back, squelching the sudden burst of relief so he wouldn't see it on her face. "Is something amiss, Sebastian?"

"I do not know." He went to his desk and poured himself a drink from a crystal decanter. He poured another drink, a smaller amount, in another glass and held it out to her. "It's brandy," he said at her askance expression.

"Thank you," she said, accepting the glass. She took a tentative sip and choked. It wasn't quite the same as sherry. "When will you be back?"

He held the glass up to his lips and drank its contents in a single gulp. He put the glass down and rounded the corner of his desk to stand before her. "The Prince of Wales himself calls for me," he said, "and the last time I received such a summons, I was immediately shipped to France to work for our government as a spy."

"I see. So, in other words, you don't know."

His lips flattened into a thin line. "No. And it vexes me." He turned and reached for his decanter and glass, pouring himself another drink, downing it. He sloshed another round into his glass and settled into a plush leather chair, crossing his legs.

She took that as her cue and perched on the edge of a blue chaise lounge, cradling her glass on her lap. "I'll miss you," she said, hoping the words did not sound as false to him as it did to her.

He angled his head toward her. "Will you? I wonder." He sipped his drink this time, eyes reflective. "I was once set to marry a lovely blonde-haired girl named Emily before my country called me to arms. She was an instant success two seasons ago—everyone loved her for her delicate beauty. It was unfortunate she couldn't see past my scars when I returned home to love me in return."

"I'm sorry, Sebastian," she replied, unsure what other condolence to offer.

"Yes," he continued, "when she cried off, I swore I'd spend my remaining days alone and unloved. Then my father found you, and I am at last a husband, but still unloved. And again, called by the crown on some urgent matter. So, I wonder, my dear," he leaned forward, his eyes boring into hers, "if I return home, be it next week or next year, will I find my wife home waiting for me with open arms? Or shall I have to go hunt her down like an errant pup who forgot where her home was?"

Her face drained of blood. Dear God, he had heard. "Of course, I'll be here to welcome you home, S-Sebastian. I'm your w-wife, where else would I be?"

His eyes narrowed. "Where else indeed, madam."

A heavy silence descended upon the room, loaded with tension. Fraught with peril. Because of Robert filling her ears with hearsay and treason, she now navigated dangerous currents alone, far from others to call upon for help.

And alienated her husband with her selfish desires and decisions.

Stiffening her spine, squaring rounded shoulders, she met his cold eyes. "I will be home here at Dorchester Castle, Your Grace."

A cynical smile formed, hardening the ice of a frozen gaze. "Oh, my beautiful pendulum, I know you will be." A leer twisted his lips, hinting at a gathering storm.

Her stomach sank to see such a hard look in her husband's once tender expression. Gone was the gentle kindness he showed her up to now. In its place was cruel hunger, the expression so close to mirroring the soldiers she nearly cast up her accounts on the spot.

The glass of brandy fell from her hands, blanketing the thick carpet with brown that resembled more a crimson red to her panicked mind. She surged to her feet. "I-I don't feel well. I...excuse me."

She stumbled forward with leaden feet, making it halfway across the room before he spoke again.

"No."

She paused, facing the closed door, trembling so she could scarcely speak. "Please, Sebastian."

The cushion of a seat creaked, and the sudden smash of glass greeted her ears. "I said no, madam! I have not excused you from my presence."

Clasping the remains of courage, she whirled. A gasp escaped her compressed lips.

Sebastian held her gaze, slipping his mask off, followed by his frock coat.

Dread curled low in her belly. "Sebastian, what are you doing?"

He loosened his cravat and shouldered out of his waistcoat, discarding it on the floor with his other garments. "Taking the proper precautions to ensure my heir is well underway before I take my leave. Come here."

"No," she said, fisting skirts, fighting the urge to scream the word. "You're angry with me, and I won't let you have me when you're feeling this way."

"*You won't let me?*" His eyes snapped, and a sinister smile formed on his handsome face, causing her stomach to tighten. "Darling," he purred, "when I'm through with you, you're going to beg me to take you. Now, come *here*."

She raised her chin. "No."

"This is your last warning, Rose. Don't make me come over there to get you. You won't like what will happen if I do."

She backed away toward the closed door—her only avenue of escape. With a muttered curse, he stalked after her, and she turned and fled, grasping at the knob with sweaty palms, turning and yanking it wide, only to have it shut in her face.

Sebastian stood behind her, bracing his hands against the door on either side of her head, breathing down her neck. Her pulse hammered. Fear dried her mouth. Robert was not far away, but she dared not scream for him to come charging to the rescue.

"I told you not to run," Sebastian whispered, his lips trailing down her neck.

She shivered when he found a sensitive spot, his lips parting to taste and explore her skin.

What is he doing? What game is he playing now?

Cupping her breasts, his thumbs brushed across her nipples with lazy insolence.

Tension spiraled from her breasts to her core, heightening her awareness of Sebastian's every move and caress. He used his body to cage her in. She was trapped, as a rabbit snared in the jaws of a great beast.

"Look at me, wife."

He spun her around, and she looked up into his fierce blue eyes, scared and aroused at the same time. It was a combination of feelings unknown to her.

He reached for her face, his fingers snaking into her hair, loosening the elaborate hairstyle, sending hairpins falling to the floor. "Do you know why I'm angry with you?"

"Yes." She tried to swallow past a thick tongue, but her body followed her commands no longer. It bowed to Sebastian's mastery, acknowledging his sense of touch held power over her desire to be free of it.

He shifted splayed hands through her heavy tresses, watching her russet strands fall past his fingers. "You are mine, Rose. It doesn't matter how much you think you love another man or fear me to be a monster. I am drawing the line. Here. Now. I am claiming my rights as your husband. You can accept your fate graciously and let me love you, or you can fight, and I will take you forcefully. The choice is yours."

Choice? What choice have I been left to decide? Ravishment by consent or ravishment by surrender? Tears burned her eyes. She longed to slap him, scream her rage to the heavens, or take a quarterstaff to his arrogant face. He wished to punish her then so be it. If she survived an army of English soldiers, she would survive one man who believed himself her master.

"Don't make me do something we'll both regret, Rose. Please do not. Set aside foolish fantasies and embrace a future with me. Please, my darling?"

"Don't you 'darling' me! I am not yours to threaten then sweeten the sting of that bite with fevered kisses and empty promises. You will not bully me into submitting to you!"

Anger clouded his eyes. "Bully? I've begged, pleaded, forgiven every insult and impulsive action of yours. I've tried to be understanding. You know the lay of my heart. You have it for all you seem to care! But I'm not good enough. Oh no. The only man you feel like spreading your thighs for is a bloody thief!"

She slapped his face. Her hand shot out before she could call it back. The sharp crack reverberated around the silent room. They stood regarding each other in anger, but Rose knew she was only now holding onto her rage as a defense to her husband's words. Sebastian was right. She was ruining their marriage. It wasn't him. She needed to let go of Logan. And ignore her brother's opinion of villains and heroes.

But she did not know the road back to her husband. They stood on opposite sides of a great divide, unable to find common ground.

"I'm... I'm sorry, Sebastian." She wrung her hands together. "Though I fear you've made a grave error in assuming I care nothing for you." She braced herself and looked him in the eye. They stood shuttered and cold in her regard. "I've not given you any reason to believe otherwise, but you do matter to me."

"Do I? Forgive me for being skeptical, my dear, but I would have physical proof of this 'caring' you speak of."

Her heart broke with what she knew she'd have to give

Sebastian. It was not her wish, but greater heartache awaited her if she did not yield. He left her with no choice. None. *Ravishment by surrender.* "You once swore to me you'd be gentle in the taking of my innocence. Does your promise still stand?"

"Of course, it does," he scoffed. "I have no desire to hurt you, Rose. I want to love you. I want to show you tenderness and passion if you but open yourself and cease plotting your escape."

"I am tired of fighting," she admitted.

He embraced her. "Then surrender, Rose. Let me be your husband." His face drew near. "Let me love you," he whispered.

She accepted his kiss, allowing him to deepen it. He used the strokes she liked best, and soon she found herself kissing him back. At the first hesitant touch of her tongue, Sebastian tightened his arms, dragging her body against the full length of his. She ordered her muscles to relax, wiggling to mold herself to fit his every curve and contour, yet she felt mismatched no matter how hard she strained against him.

He broke away with a muttered oath, falling to his knees, shoving up her skirts.

"Sebastian? What are you doing?"

He smiled at her with molten blue eyes. "Stay there, love. Just spread your legs a bit for me."

She did as he asked, puzzling over his intent as he tossed her skirts over his head. What was he—?

Oh, my.

His tongue was upon her thigh, lavish in its administrations. Nimble fingers parted short curls and found her center, easing inside the tight passage. She tensed at the invasion before his tongue and mouth took to task where his fingers left off. The sensations of being licked and kissed threatened to melt her bones. What madness was this?

She adjusted her weight, leaning against the closed door, her body burning with a fever Sebastian ignited. Sweat gathered underneath her breasts, which had grown heavy and burdensome. A terrible ache pounded between her legs. She sweated and moaned, not sure if her body meant to fracture or explode.

Slow and calculating, he drew a hardened knot into his mouth, biting down gently.

Rose cried out, tumbling over the edge of a cliff, unaware she'd been dangling so near a precipice all along. Wetness seeped from her pulsing center, her husband lapping it up despite her embarrassed jerky movements to wiggle away from such intimacy.

He chuckled, emerging from underneath her skirts, his mouth

gleaming from her body's juices. "Do you seek to deny me the taste of your first orgasm?"

"I deny you nothing," she breathed, falling against his chest as he kissed her, sharing the musky scent of herself.

He threaded his fingers through her unbound hair, tearing his mouth from hers. He stared at her with eyes that blazed with possession. "You surrendered your body, but your heart is the true prize I crave, Rose. Give it to me. Allow me in, my darling."

Sebastian was binding her to him. One kiss, one gentle touch at a time he created the gilded cage. The prison she would spend the rest of her days languishing in. Her thoughts scattered as puffs of smoke caught in the wind as he masterfully kissed her, urging the intrusive inferno within her body to build again.

Her dress came off with a sharp rending of fabric. The stays quickly followed. Cooling air wafted over her heated skin—nothing could have been more welcome. He eased her chemise aside. Free of clothing and material bonds, she arched into his arms, caught off guard when she met a bare chest. *When had Sebastian rid himself of clothing?*

His skin was hot to the touch and surrounded her in silken heat. "It's time, Rose." Sweeping her up into his arms, he strode to a rug in front of a roaring hearth, lowering her onto the thick, soft fibers, his muscular body covering her from head to toe.

The weight caused an uncomfortable tightness in her chest. Her lungs strained to inhale. Hands clutched her knees, spreading her legs. Visions of red coats and leering faces assailed her, adding to her mounting distress. Riotous laughter. Cold, unfeeling eyes watching her fight to keep from being dishonored.

Her heart fluttered then raced, blind panic fueling the need to fight, seeking escape. She braced her hands on warm stone and pushed. Shoved. Bucked her hips, blind to the face above hers but aware of the body that would soon deprive her of her innocence.

The heavy weight shifted and suddenly she was free, sitting up straddling a male lap on her knees, fingers gentle in their caresses on her cheeks, swiping away moisture. "Shush, my darling. Please do not cry."

Arms came up around her torso, squeezing in a compassionate embrace, urging her face to rest on a rounded shoulder, as she was rocked back and forth as a babe to breast.

The movement was soothing, easing her return to the present, away from nightmares that still haunted her. She closed her eyes, absorbing body heat, finding comfort from unexpected, and undeserved, quarters.

Sebastian's hand moved in slow circles, encompassing the whole of her back, from shoulders to pelvis. After several minutes of his tender administrations, she began to breathe normally, her heart resuming a more sedate pace. Chills and tingles shot up and down her spine, even as a flame sparked to life, igniting a fire in her blood. A frisson of need pierced low in her belly, and she raised her head, seeking answers in knowing blue eyes.

Comfort changed to something else in that moment. It was tangible as both a feeling and a physical awareness of the body hardening beneath her buttocks. Expectation hung heavy in the air. She stilled, scarcely breathing, fearing the delicate noise would shatter the gossamer thread spun between his gaze and hers. A force was driving them forward, on a journey through unknown and dangerous territory, and only God knew where the destination would be. This wasn't the man she envisioned being married to. He was a far kinder soul than she had been led to believe.

She gathered herself with a deep breath, bracing hands on his shoulders, digging into his compact flesh, unable to help her admiration of well-muscles arms.

"I do not know what you would have of me," she admitted, caressing the skin of his chest. He possessed a mat of sparse hair between male nipples she did not mind exploring.

She felt the rumble of his deep voice when she laid a splayed hand on his breastbone.

"I would have you as you are," he said, tucking a strand of her hair behind an ear. "Speaking your mind instead drowning in tears reliving harsh memories."

Ducking her head, she whispered, "I did not mean to cause offense. It was not you."

"Was it not?" The wistfulness in his voice tugged on tender heartstrings. "Have you ever opened a gift and found it to be not of your choosing? Finding greater joy in someone else's present, then falling prey to jealousy when told that particular gift was not meant for you?" His voice had lowered; gaze distant. "Never you."

A shutter over his eyes unhinged, allowing a glimpse of the man. His soul. A hurt not caused by her whispered words of treachery.

She did not know of what he spoke, only that she wished to offer comfort and take away a lingering pain. "My gift may not have been of my choosing, but I find him quite handsome to gaze upon when I am of a mood to look." She smiled when he chuckled, feeling more at ease.

He chucked her chin. "I'm pleased my wife does not find me

wanting."

She shared in his humor, bending to rest her forehead against his. "There is nothing on you I find displeasing to the eye." Touching the ruined side of his cheek, she repeated, "Nothing." She heard his swallow, then started when the tip of his nose bumped back and forth gently against hers.

Her mother used to give kisses in this manner every night upon her bedtime. It was a secret code of theirs, expressing love without saying the words.

She closed her eyes, imprinting this act on her heart. He could not know what the simple gesture meant, and she could not bring herself to whisper of it now. She wanted only to live in this moment, savor the sweet and endearing side of Sebastian, and learn of this bond growing between them, beyond the barriers of physical desires.

Firm lips touched hers, as gentle a caress as the last, but it hinted at a growing storm. Indeed, no sooner had the thought crossed her mind than he bit down on her bottom lip with fleeting pressure, commanding her to open herself to him. She obeyed without hesitation, sinking fingers into thick tufts of golden hair giving in to the demands being asked of her. Soon the kiss was deepening, evolving into something of more substance, another purpose unfolding itself to her.

He was once more easing them on the path toward the marriage act, urging her along this journey with him. Looping arms around his neck, she gave herself over to his tender administrations, arching her spine, tilting her head to the side as he rained wet kisses down her throat, learning her body's dips and curves as she explored him in similar fashion with her hands upon hot flesh.

By the time he reached the valley between her breasts, she found herself making mewling sounds to rival a cat's purr. Her hips were rolling on their own accord, seeking to satisfy a gnawing hunger growing in ever-increasing swells between her thighs. A silken warm staff presented itself to help the annoying itch, and she rubbed herself against it, undulating her hips, grinding harder up and down, side-to-side, trying to find the right angle to ease the damnable pain.

Now her husband whimpered.

She peered into his blue eyes, seeing herself mirrored there. Flushed cheeks, swollen lips, heavy-lidded eyes, her hair a dark brown halo pillowing her face. She did not recognize the face staring back, as she did not know this formidable hunger driving her addled with need. "I hurt, husband."

His nostrils flared, eyes narrowing in his moment of triumph. He cradled her face in both hands, searching her gaze. "I do as well."

"Is there no solution for this madness?"

His generous lips tipped up. "Only one." Placing hands on her hips, he urged her up onto her knees. "Ride me, Rose." He fisted himself, holding his manhood in place. "End this torture for both our sake."

She trembled as he held her, locking her knees from bending. "I'm not sure how."

"Take your time," he soothed. "Instinct will lead once you let go of fear." His head fell forward, assigning his lips to the path they were treading between her breasts, climbing up one ivory peak to the pink nipple at its summit.

Her locked joints wobbled, threatening surrender. Every lick, bite, and tug urged her further down, the ache roaring to life anew from Sebastian's tender assault.

A thick haze enveloped her mind. Thoughts became distant as dreams, and something primal soared through her blood, scorching emotions irrelevant to current desires of the flesh. Moaning, she dipped, spearing herself on silken metal, trying to appease a deeply rooted hunger that all his kisses and nips could not satisfy.

Stretching, filling her core, she descended, hardened flesh made slick from an outpouring of wetness seeping from inside her center.

A barrier prevented further movement. Her lids parted, gaze seeking her husband's. "Why have I stopped?"

Corded muscles stood out from either side of Sebastian's neck. A brow beaded with sweat hung low over probing blue eyes. "It's your maidenhead," he said in harsh, guttural tones. "Take it if desire finds you so moved."

Curiosity warred with hunger. "It is your prize to take, is it not? As man and husband?"

He jerked her flat against his chest, their eyes so close their eyelashes touched. "It's your honor and body. The choice is entirely yours, madam."

Rose blinked, hearing another voice, coming from a memory not yet forgotten. *Your chastity is your gift to give, and I—an unworthy highwayman—am not fit to accept such a priceless treasure.*

Two different men, yet both honorable and wonderful in their own ways. But dear God, it shamed her to the core what she said in reply to Silver Hawk. She shook her head, trying to dislodge the sound of her voice. *I fear my betrothed may not be a man fit to receive it either.*

Sebastian's hands tightened on her biceps. "Rose? What's

wrong?"

This was not the time to have eyes swell with water to rain down on selfish notions and self-centered escape plots. But her body did not heed a broken mind's warning. Glistening eyes met shocked round orbs.

"No," he murmured, withdrawing. "I cannot believe it. You're thinking of him, aren't you?"

Frantic to explain herself, she swiped at her cheeks. "Not as you think. Sebastian, I—"

The fragile bond weaving them closer broke with hard hands ramming her down onto his lap, impaling her to the hilt. She endured the sharp stinging sensation racing north from between her legs, finding it less painful than the accusation and hurt in her husband's eyes.

"Are you well?" he asked in a cold tone.

"Yes, I am fine. Please—"

"Close your eyes," he snapped, "and think of him. I won't take long."

He rolled without warning, sweeping her beneath him, bracing his weight on elbows, his furious face a mere inch from her own. Then he tilted head away, staring at a point beyond her shoulder, and began to thrust with brisk, short pumps between her splayed thighs.

There was no discomfort in this act, but neither was she subjected to it long enough to form a firm opinion. Within mere seconds of starting, Sebastian grunted in her ear, stilling.

A strange warmth filled her lower belly.

She did not complain, but she could not help staring at him in silent question, wondering why he was going back on his word to wait on having children.

He peered at her with a flush hot upon his cheeks. "Do not bloody look at me like that," he said, pulling out.

Standing, he sought his jacket from the floor, then withdrew a handkerchief. Much to her mortification, he moved, kneeling between her legs, avoiding her gaze, as he pressed the silk cloth between her legs, cleaning her with gentle sweeps.

She scooted away as soon as he was finished, wincing when her sore mound rubbed too briskly against the rug fibers.

Sebastian caught her flinch. "Your soreness will fade in a day or two. I took care to ensure I wasn't too rough."

If only you took greater care in the spreading of your seed and promises made!

The thought was uncharitable and unkind. Yet to say nothing would only let a small wound fester when they already faced a mountain of blunders between them.

"You promised to seek a physician's approval before starting a family with me." She clutched at rumpled stays, holding them over her chest, ignoring his incredulous expression. "Why did you spill inside me?"

He took two strides toward her then stopped, clenching hands into fists at his side. "Why?" he repeated, looking furious. "Perhaps I felt a child would help fasten your feet to staying in our home. Honoring your vows."

The savage snarl scythed her heart, but she deserved them. "I hope those reasons will bring you comfort when you find yourself a widower."

"As long as you birth my heir, I shan't grieve your passing overly much."

The tone was harsh, but she didn't believe him for a moment. "I shall offer prayer for a girl, perhaps twin girls since my demise shall be imminent. That way your misery will be all but assured, and I won't have to haunt you in my afterlife."

The corner of his mouth tipped up despite his continued glower. "The devil you say! I'll ban them from the marriage mart and forbid them a coming out so my coffers will not drain beyond reason."

"Ha! Then I shall also pray for a pair of beautiful daughters, so they'll have no need to be paraded around in your marriage mart. Lords will be banging down your door to secure their hands and driving you to distraction."

"If they are cursed with their mother's brash tongue, no dowry will be adequate to entreat men to be their husbands. I'll be stuck with them forever."

"Thus, my punishment shall be complete."

They stared at each other. She with her head held high. Sebastian with a twitchy face. It appeared as though there was a mutiny afoot with his facial muscles. He kept trying to frown, but the corners of his mouth were sporadically pulsing upward.

He was attempting to curve his impulse to smile.

She relaxed with the knowledge. Perhaps all hope was not lost for their marriage. "I don't really seek to punish you," she admitted, casting her gaze to the floor. "The thought of being with child is frightening. I don't know how I'll bear it being alone."

A hiss of breath filled the air, and she started as Sebastian plopped down beside her, sitting shoulder-to-shoulder. "Bearing a child is not a death sentence, Rose. Women do it all the time."

"And perish from the attempt in shocking numbers," she

retaliated.

"I own to not knowing the figures," he admitted, placing a warm hand on her bare knee, "but I promise when your time comes, I will do everything in my power to ensure both you and our child live through the ordeal of child-birthing." He nudged her chin around, gaining her attention. "Do you believe me?"

She wanted to mention his promise not to get her with child in the first place but felt now was not the time to remind him of his failings when he was trying to calm her fears. "I believe you."

"Good." He bent, kissing her closed mouth, then releasing her chin.

They shared a look for long moments.

He was the first to break the heavy silence. "Did you find my touch so lacking in appeal?"

The question was asked without rancor, but it devastated her, nonetheless. The undercurrent of sadness in the eyes imploring her for answers dried her mouth of any moisture. "I found your touch most enjoyable, Sebastian. I swear it."

"Then why were you thinking of *him* for Christ's sake?"

She paused, expecting him to interrupt her yet again, but he only sat quietly, waiting for a reply. "You spoke of my innocence being my gift to give. Silver Hawk spoke similar words to me while I was his captive, and I was lamenting my reply to him."

Sebastian went still. "What did you say?"

She met the gaze bearing down on her with eagle-eyed intensity. "I'm ashamed to say I told Silver Hawk I was not sure my intended was a man fit to receive it either." Breaking, she played with the strings of her stays, twisting them around her fingers, casting her gaze aside. "I didn't know anything about you, Sebastian. I was frightened."

"Silver Hawk was the answer to your prayers?"

She winced, unable to deny the angry words.

A lengthy pause ensued, before a spirited male sigh broke down the barriers erecting themselves between them. Long, aristocratic fingers wrapped her fidgeting hands, giving them a squeeze. "I'm sorry I lost my temper with you."

The apology had her gaze soaring up. "Your sentiment is appreciated, but undeserved. You have been nothing but kind to me, Sebastian. 'Tis I who has played the part of beast and whose manners are sorely lacking."

A look of discomfort skirted across his face. "I'd hardly call myself a saint, Rose." He scrubbed the back of a hand across his mouth as though attempting to rid himself of a foul taste. "I have done things in my past I'm not so proud of too." A cheek indented with a crooked smile. "But it's hard for me to entirely regret my past when you are here with me now."

"I'd judge you to be quite the scoundrel in your youth."

His mouth dipped into a frown. "You make me sound antiquated. I am not as old as that."

"How old are you?"

"Two and thirty, thank you."

She flared her eyes wide in feigned horror. "Upon my word, you're as old as my dear own papa."

"The devil you say!" He shot her a wicked grin, and in that moment of playfulness, she knew her deplorable behavior had truly been forgiven.

Unable to bite back the inevitable question, she asked it, needing to know. "When do you have to leave for London?"

"As soon as I am able."

"What shall I do with myself while you're away?"

He hugged her to his side. "Anything you desire." He stiffened. "So long as it's in the castle or on the grounds of my estate." He shifted to face her. "Rose, I do not wish to restrict you, yet I would see you safe. And I'm afraid the danger is too great for you to travel outside our home."

She understood at once. "You speak of highwaymen."

"Yes." He stared hard at her, and she dropped her gaze, aware of the unspoken message in his eyes. He did not wish her to see Silver Hawk. "I will stay within the castle grounds, Sebastian."

He tilted her chin up. "Thank you," he murmured, kissing her again. He lingered for a moment, then drew away, standing up, before gathering his clothes then putting them back on.

She took that as her cue to dress, fumbling with her torn gown. It sagged open down the front and would remain so until she could flee to her room. She didn't bother with the corset, simply cinching the front of her dress closed with one hand.

She grinned at him as he finished making himself presentable. "I trust you'll show me to my room before you depart, so I do not have to explain my lack of attire to poor Mrs. Brown?"

He chuckled, offering her his arm. "It would be my pleasure to escort you to your chamber, madam." He opened the study door with a flourish, ushering her over the threshold first. She stepped into the hall, smiling until her eyes caught her brother's gaze as he stood a few feet from her.

She inhaled sharply. Robert's gaze dropped, taking in her torn dress. Red rushed up his neck and colored his face, as his lips curled into a snarl of rage.

Sebastian strode over the threshold to stand beside her. "Darling, what's—oh God."

Robert's howl of rage shocked her heart, fastening her feet to the floor.

Sebastian suffered no such hesitation. He pushed her out of the way as Robert tackled him around his torso, sending them both crashing to the floor.

Her brother gained the advantage, straddling Sebastian's body, raining punishing blow after blow to his face, screaming, "You fucking raped her, didn't you, you bloody prick!"

Footmen came running. Sebastian blocked a punch, managing to rotate Robert underneath him. He spit a string of blood upon the marble floor.

She started over to them.

"Stay back," Sebastian snapped, holding her brother down while he yelled and cursed, trying to maneuver his way free from her husband's hold. Sebastian motioned to his footmen, and they each took hold of an arm, keeping Robert in place.

Sebastian swiped the back of his hand across his mouth. "I did not rape your sister, Witherby. Calm yourself and look at her."

Robert glared at him, tugging on his arms. "I don't need to look at her to know you plied her ears with words of love to give herself to you. You knew she wanted to leave you, and you forced yourself on her with pretty compliments and gentle touches! Manipulating her mind, playing on her sense of honor. You knew she loved another man more than she would ever love a whoreson like yourself!"

Sebastian's face went white.

Her mouth fell slack, stunned by her brother's savagery. "Robert, you go too far. Sebastian was only—"

Sebastian held up a hand, and she fell silent. He walked up to Robert with slow, measured steps. Menacing. Controlled. He shucked his jacket to the floor and bunched up the sleeves to his shirt.

Her stomach dropped. She raced to Sebastian's side, grasping his arms. "No, Sebastian—don't. He's my brother! Please!"

He shook off her hands without as much as a glance her way. "Hold him," he commanded of his footmen.

Robert straightened his spine and lifted his chin. Ever the cheeky American.

Panicked, she threw herself in front of her brother, staring down her husband. "You will not touch him," she vowed, her gaze hard upon his face.

He returned her fierce gaze with an insolent smile. "Step aside, Rose."

She squared her shoulders, full of fire. "No."

Swearing, he raked splayed hands through his hair. "I prostrate myself before you just to claim my marital right, and now I'm expected to kneel before your brother and present my ass for *fucking?*" He turned away. "You both mistake me for a fool."

"He loves me, Sebastian. He overstepped, I admit, but you cannot hurt him without hurting me too."

He spun; his eyes full of sorrow instead of indignation. "If any man dared to slander your name or cause you injury, I would erase them from this world without a moment's pause. You're my wife. But I guess the title means more to me in my eyes than the title of husband does in yours." His scornful gaze raked over the footmen. "Let him go. He's not worth the effort."

He took quick strides down the marble hall, rounding a corner falling from sight. The footmen slithering away in his wake.

Alone with her brother, she rounded on him, smacking him in the face.

He gaped at her, his eyes round saucers.

"For every step forward I gain with Sebastian, you are dragging me back two paces. I thought you were being overly protective at first, but now I begin to wonder of perhaps you have someone else's interest at heart more than mine. If that's true, and if that someone else is Silver Hawk, then I must ask you to leave here and never return. Sebastian is my husband and will remain so until death. Neither you, nor Silver Hawk, will change that."

She left Robert with his jaw on the floor, heading deeper into her new home, cursing the day she first heard the name Silver Hawk.

Chapter Ten

It was midnight the following evening when Sebastian and his escort made their way through the cobbled streets of London. Though weary from his long journey, his stomach was in a firm knot. The shod hooves of their horses clattered dully into the quiet air, lined with dark houses clustered closely together on dirty, narrow streets. Eventually, they made their way to the more fashionable part of town—the part of London he was most familiar with. And this side of the city was still teeming with life, the parties and balls just getting started. He pulled his top hat down low over his masked face, praying no former friends would notice him.

They were on Piccadilly, and turning right onto St. James Street, when his escort stopped by an unremarkable brick townhome. Sebastian blinked in surprise. "Why have we stopped here?"

"His Royal Highness is here," replied the servant, swinging down off his horse. "As a guest."

Sebastian declined further comment, willing to let the subject drop. Silently, he urged his aching muscles to dismount and take him up the small flight of stairs to the front door, where his escort waited for him. The door opened promptly at their knock, and a dour-faced butler ushered him inside to an elegant drawing room. His escort did not follow.

"Can I get you anything, Your Grace?" the butler asked.

Sebastian's stomach rumbled. "Aye, a brandy." A bad idea on an empty stomach, but he was parched, and tea would hardly calm his knotted muscles.

"As you wish, Your Grace."

The butler left Sebastian alone with his thoughts, and he wandered around the rectangular sitting room, unable to sit or to calm his nerves. Something was amiss, he could feel it in the heaviness of the air. The taste of dread settled on his tongue like sawdust, and he feared no amount of brandy could rid him of that knowledge.

The Prince of Wales arrived, quiet as a ghost upon the plush carpet. "Dorchester! Thank God you came."

Sebastian turned, bowing in a courtly manner. "Your Highness."

"Posh! It's Prinny to you, as well you know it!" The young, well-dressed man strode forward, extending a hand with a smile, meeting Sebastian's gaze without a single flinch.

Taken aback by the open, friendly face, he grabbed the proffered hand, returning the firm handshake. "Thank you, Your—err, Prinny. It is good to see you again."

"Aye, Dorchester, it's been too long." The prince gave him a measuring look, yet Sebastian could detect no signs of disgust or scorn. It seemed more...calculated. His alarm grew.

"Have a seat, Dorchester." The prince waved to a red velvet settee, and Sebastian sat stiffly, cursing his aching limbs. The butler arrived with a tray loaded with two glasses and a decanter of brandy. "Ah!" Prinny beamed. "You've read my mind, Farnsworth. Set it here, and make sure His Grace and I are left alone."

The butler left the drinks and closed the double doors to the sitting room. It sounded like a tomb closing. Sebastian was getting morbid in his nervous state. He eagerly accepted the glass Prinny held out for him, downing the contents in a single gulp.

"More?" Prinny asked.

"Please," Sebastian replied, extending his glass. Prinny filled it to the top.

Sebastian arched a brow but said nothing as he assumed a casual appearance, relaxing his aching spine into the chair, crossing his legs, this time nursing his drink. It would not do to overindulge before he heard the reason for this visit.

A reason, he had not long to wait for.

The prince set the decanter down, looking at the floor. "You've been well, I hope. I was damn sad to hear about your father's passing."

Sebastian stilled. "Thank you, Your Highness. His death has been a difficult burden to bear." He took a deep breath. "But my new duchess offers much needed comfort."

Prinny's head shot up. "The devil you say! You've married?"

Sebastian grinned. "Only two nights ago."

"Do I know the girl?"

"Unlikely. She's from our old Colony of Virginia, and her name is Rose Witherby."

"A colonial girl? Is she an heiress?"

Sebastian shifted uncomfortably on the settee. "No. My father spared her father's life during the war, and Rose's hand in marriage to me was the reward my father sought."

Understanding dawned in the prince's eyes. "Well, that was bloody shrewd of the old duke, I must say. Capital idea, that." He took a sip of his drink. "And you're happy in this union, are you?"

Sebastian met the prince's steady gaze. "I am." *Mostly.*

"I see."

Prinny's gaze darted to his face and away. He looked troubled now.

Sebastian's alarm escalated. "Your Highness, may I come right to the point and ask why you had me summoned here?"

Prinny smiled, but it never quite reached his eyes. "Call me Prinny, Dorchester, and yes, it's time we got to business." He put his glass down on a side table, now empty, and folded his hands together on his lap, staring at them. "I have a favor to ask you."

He frowned, fearing the favor already. "I am listening— Prinny."

The prince looked up at him, smiling, when he heard his pet name used. "I don't know if you're aware of it, but our countryside is under siege by thugs and murderers."

Sebastian kept strict control of his face, taking care to show only vague interest. "Aye, I am aware of their activity to some degree."

Prinny nodded. "At first, it was here and there. Robbing our aristocrats of jewels and gold, and the like. A nuisance, but a manageable one. Until a few months ago." He stared directly at him. "Our noblemen and women can scarce go out of London anymore without being attacked by these bloody parasites! And lucky they are if the only things they take are their baubles."

"Your Highness?"

"I'm talking about murder and assault, Dorchester! Killing servants and noblemen, and ransoming the women or worst…"

"My God, I had no notion the situation was that dire." Isolated in his estate, he had not heard the news. He all but shunned the outside world. It was purest luck coming upon Robert and Rose's carriage being attacked.

"Nearly every family I know has been affected by this group of pestilent scum, and I want you to find them out, bring them to justice."

Sebastian stiffened. "Me?"

Prinny's keen eyes shone in diabolic glee. "Yes! You're a perfect choice, Dorchester. You're lethal, deadly, and you've done this kind of thing before."

"Yes, but—"

"I want you to infiltrate their network, find out who they are, become one of them. For bloody sake, you already wear the mask. Forgive me, Dorchester, but it's true."

"I am not insulted, but Your Highness—Prinny," Sebastian perched on the edge of his seat, "I am a familiar face. My disfigurement marks me for who I am now. How am I to escape recognition?"

Prinny lounged against his chair, crossing his arms over his chest. "We're going to kill you."

"Come again?"

"I'm going to kill you," Prinny repeated. "Well, not me, but a member of my guard. We will stage a grand spectacle of it. Leave no doubt as to your demise. Then you'll be free to wear a mask and assume a role as England's most feared highwayman. And when the tales of your escapades exceed the current band of criminals, and they come looking for you, we'll bring them to justice."

"No."

"Excuse me?"

"I said no." Sebastian expelled a gusty sigh. "Prinny, for the love of God, I just married! Surely there is someone else who can do this task?"

"Other men yes, but Dorchester, I need *you*."

"Oh please." Sebastian shot to his feet, taking quick strides to the tall windows overlooking James Street. He raked both hands through his hair, locking his fingers together behind his head. "What about my wife? You know it's quite cruel to make someone think you're dead when you're not."

"Yes, but she'll be thankful when she has you back."

Maybe. "But what will become of her in the meantime? I have no male heirs."

The prince grinned. "None that you know of. You did consummate the marriage, did you not, Dorchester?"

"Of course, I did," he retorted. *Once.*

"Well, then," the prince was saying, "your ducal home will not have a new duke until it is certain that your wife is not carrying the next heir, and by then, this whole mess will be over and done, and you can resume your place by her side. We'll dredge up some story about a secret mission, or some such thing. No worries, old chap, everything will be fine."

"No."

"Dorchester…"

Sebastian swung away from the window. "I said no, Prinny. I won't do it. The cost is more than I can bear. I've already done my duty to our country! Now let me in peace and live my life unhindered by royal favors."

Prinny regarded him with thoughtful eyes. "You say this because of your wife—because of Rose?"

"Of course, for her."

"Then come with me." Prinny rose from his padded chair and opened the doors to the sitting room.

Sebastian followed him out into the foyer and up a winding staircase to the second floor. Prinny led him down a short, carpeted hall to another closed door. He paused with a hand on the doorknob.

"Please keep your voice down when you enter," he whispered. He opened the door and stood aside, letting Sebastian go ahead into the darkened bedchamber.

There was a single candle lit by a bed, and as he approached, he could make out the figure of a woman under the covers, her long blonde hair fanned out around the still head on a white pillow. He stopped at her side. His breath caught when he surveyed the damage done to her face. Bruises and scrapes, a crooked, broken nose, and one eye swollen shut.

The floor creaked, and he turned to look at Prinny as he came up beside him by the bed.

"My mistress was beaten and violated by those godless heathens," the prince whispered. "She ventured out for a carriage ride with a friend, hoping to come across this Silver Hawk fellow."

"My God, Prinny, I am sorry."

"Have you heard of him? The worst miscreant of the bunch."

Sebastian suppressed an urge to chuckle. "I've heard tales of his escapades. He's a gentleman thief, though." He swept a hand toward the bed. "This is not his doing."

"No," Prinny agreed, "but he is the lure for many a female, thrusting them toward greater tragedy."

He could find no fault with that statement.

"I would see Silver Hawk brought to justice as well. And in the act, send a message to all those of lower class who think to profit by brute force."

Discomfort twisted his gut. "Prinny, I—"

"This could be your Rose, Dorchester." The prince focused on him. "I fear it will be if the highwaymen are not found and dealt with. It is only a matter of time. You might be there to protect her, but that's a gamble of long odds, isn't it? There's never a guarantee of being forever at your wife's side."

He was right. This had been the prince's last card to play, and he had played it well. Sebastian turned from the bed with a heavy heart, already feeling the weight of a substantial burden upon his shoulders.

Chapter Eleven

Six weeks. Her husband had departed six weeks ago. No letters sent. Nary a word on when he expected to be home. Rose waited on tenterhooks for the man to walk into this castle, and the constant tension was taking its toll on her body.

Exhausted, she slept at odd hours of the day. Food turned to ash in her mouth, causing nausea to swell. She could not recall a single moment in her history where guilt played such havoc with her body's internal functions. She wrote letters to Sebastian, begging his forgiveness, only to shove them into her husband's desk drawer, not knowing where to post them. Her glance skirted over the latest attempt to assuage her soul.

My dearest Sebastian,

I hope this letter finds you well. I am pleased to report your home still stands after six weeks of my occupation. Your staff has been most diligent in their efforts to keep our home clean and comfortable and are a dedicated lot to my health and safety. So much so that the day after I dismissed the cook and prepared a meal, there was a chain and lock on the kitchen door the next morning, barring me reentry. I apologize for letting go a member of your staff, but she tried to kill me with something called haggis. It was dreadful to behold, even worse to eat. The staff disagrees my cooking is any better, though it was sweet of them not to mention the charred worktable and blackened hearth. Did I mention the kitchen repairs are coming along splendidly? The workmen assure me no one will know I started a fire while cooking gingerbread. Mrs. Brown has taken some convincing that I simply like to cook, and I am not trying to kill myself or poison the staff. I would never harm a living soul, Sebastian, yet feel duty bound to inform you the lovely green plant growing in your study is no longer of this world. I seem to have grown a penchant for clumsiness of late.

~~I hope I miss~~ Please come back home soon.

Your faithful wife,
Rose

Satisfied with her newest work, she folded the paper, then tried to tug her letter drawer open. *Drat!* The darn thing was stuck. Bracing her feet, she began to wiggle and jerk, attempting to loosen it from its berth.

It came flying off its tracks, letters and other parchment scattering in all directions. Mumbling curses, she scooted the chair back, falling to the floor, picking up her mess, when one piece of tan vellum caught her attention. She scrambled on hands and knees over to it, picking it up. Casual perusal gave way to a closer inspection after witnessing her name mentioned.

A voice interrupted her thoughts with a polite cough.

She looked up with a jerk, feeling like an errant child caught with a hand in the cookie jar. "Yes, Mr. Harrison?"

"Mr. Witherby and Lord Edgewood have arrived. Should I show them here or would you prefer the salon, Your Grace?"

Her brows knit together, unfamiliar with the lord's name. "The salon I should think. Thank you, Mr. Harrison."

She snatched at the various letters, gathering them into a pile in her arms, dumping them across the neat desktop. There would be time to sort this mess out later. Her guests would not be staying long if she had anything to say about it. Since this was her house, she most certainly did have a say. Pausing by the mirror, smoothing out her hair and wrinkles on her immaculate peach gown, she sailed out of the study as a queen going to meet her unworthy subjects.

Robert greeted her in the hall outside the salon sporting a twitchy smile.

When did he acquire a nervous tick? He must be wary of a beating. "Good day, Robert. Come to take another whack at my marriage? Perhaps there's some dignity left of Sebastian's you haven't stomped on. Or would you care to discuss your plans to slander over tea? And who the devil is Lord Edgewood?" she asked, coming to a halt in front of him. "Mr. Harrison said a Lord Edgewood was here with you."

"So he is, and you will meet him," he said, clasping her arm. "But we should share words before I give an introduction."

Disliking the seriousness of his expression, she disengaged her arm from Robert's grasp. "I'm listening."

"Firstly, let me say Lord Edgewood is a friend. Please keep that in mind when you greet him. I would appreciate it if you would stop yourself from doing or saying anything…foolish."

Oh, Lord! This meeting did not bode well if her idiot brother was issuing *her* dire warnings. This Lord Edgewood must be a base beast indeed. "My dearest brother. When have you ever known me to act with foolish intent?" She blushed, her memory unable to count all the balls, holidays, birthday parties, and such ruined by her temper and brash tongue.

Robert ignored the question. "Remember he's my friend, and I do not offer my friendship lightly to just anyone. Secondly," He tugged on his cravat, fighting with its tight knot. A glistening sheen of sweat dotted his forehead. "Lord Edgewood and Silver Hawk are the same man."

Her gaze snapped to her brother's face. "What? You brought him here? Robert!" She took a step closer, lowering her voice to say, "How could you do such a thing? Was I not clear in my wish to be a faithful wife?"

He flinched. "You were, but circumstances being what they are, we felt family should be here for you in your time of need."

"I need a cold cloth for a growing headache, but I trust my servants to attend me. You and Silver Hawk did not need to trouble yourselves on my account."

Robert narrowed his gaze, scanning her face. "You truly have no notion what has happened, do you?"

"I have a notion of what's going to happen if you two do not leave my home immediately."

Robert opened his mouth to reply, but his stare shifted over her shoulder and his tongue fell silent.

The small hairs on the back of her neck stood on end. Someone was standing directly behind her.

"Greetings, little one."

The deep baritone rolled over her ears, seeping into her mind and filling her heart with pleasure, even as despair followed to tumble her rapidly beating heart. How could she think so highly of her husband, yet respond in such a physical way to Silver Hawk?

Heat clung to her back, signaling the proximity of another body. "Will you give us a moment alone, Robert?"

Robert's gaze sliced her. "I do not think it wise, Logan."

"Perhaps not, but it is necessary."

Rose attempted to swallow, finding it impossible. "Mr. Hawk," she croaked, clearing her throat, trying again. "Please, allow me to escort you to my husband's study. I find myself in need of a drink."

She turned on a heel, not looking in his direction, marching back down the hall from where she came. Boots clacked on the marble floor behind her, causing her heart to flutter faster. By the time she reached Sebastian's study, her nerves were shot, and she did not pause upon crossing the threshold but headed straight to the liquor cabinet. She had not indulged in spirits since the business with her stomach began, but given the current set of circumstances, she needed a tonic to calm her pulse or face the possibility of fainting.

Taking two glasses out, she bypassed the sherry and seized the brandy.

She started to pour a measure out into a glass when she heard the door close and latch.

Her hand trembled so that she was forced to put the decanter down. Facing the cabinet, she asked, "Would you care to join me in a drink?"

"No."

She jumped, the voice coming directly behind her. He was so close—too close. Shutting her eyes, she could hear his breathing, raspy and shallow. Was he nervous?

Thinking of him suffering the same way as she helped to restore her equilibrium. They were being overly silly. He knew she was married and wasn't there to seduce her. Likely he was only paying a call to assure himself of her continued happiness.

You're grasping at stuff and nonsense, Rose! He's a highwayman. He isn't here to discuss England's dismal weather. Of course he means to seduce you!

She closed her eyes, summoning the visage of Sebastian's tender expression, his teasing smile and playful winks.

Iron mettle began to trickle down her back, hardening her spine and bringing her head up with renewed determination.

Taking courage in hand, she spun.

A well-clothed chest met her stare. A deep blue jacket framed a yellow waistcoat, and above that, an expertly tied cravat. Merciful heavens, she couldn't look above the well-formed neckcloth. The highwayman was not wearing a mask. It seemed indecent, as though a naked face was far too intimate a thing for a young woman to view.

"Keep going, little one. While my cravat is of fine quality, I assure you it is not worthy of such determined scrutiny."

A finger nudged her chin up.

The brown eyes were the same but different. Familiar. She stepped back, forgetting the cabinet barred her escape, whacking the small of her back into the unyielding wood. The rigid square jaw, high cheekbones, and long aquiline nose were of pleasing formation, but something about Silver Hawk caused her to shudder, casting an apparition over his appearance.

She had witnessed his likeness before. Somewhere. It loomed just outside of memory.

His gaze in turn roamed over her, in a blatant possessive and intimate manner. "Being a duchess becomes you, little one."

He was still inappropriately close, but instead of taking him to task, she said, "You look familiar to me. Have…have we met before?"

Unease crossed his expression. "Not formally."

"I do not refer to our first meeting when you wanted me for ransom."

"Neither do I."

They were speaking in riddles, dancing around something of greater import. He was familiar. She knew the sensation for what it was, but still could find no answer that satisfied.

A knock rattled the door. "Open up, Edgewood," Robert called. "I changed my mind. I should be chaperoning this reunion."

Logan heaved a sigh, but strode over and unlatched the door, swinging it open.

It was in that moment, looking at Robert and Logan standing together, the dots connected, the puzzle coming together with lightning speed, illuminating the memory as though she stood on the very ground.

In her hands, she saw the bloody tip of her beloved quarterstaff, the snarling bruised faces of the soldiers she fought. Her friends' sharp cries, the tearing of fabric, lewd laughter, and the odd slapping noise of the soldiers' thrusting bodies on her friends' helpless prone forms.

"The officer sitting upon his decorated horse…" Rose whispered.

Tall, broad shoulders, with black hair secured in the back. Brown eyes, flat and cold, watching their plight with nary an expression on his chiseled face as he ordered more soldiers to attack her, to attempt to grind her beneath the heel of the mighty British Empire as her friends so suffered.

Logan and Robert's gazes whipped toward her at her soft disclosure.

Her brother surged forward, holding his hands out in a gesture of entreaty.

"Stand aside Robert." She moved to march around him.

But his hand lashed out, grabbing her arm. "Listen to me, Rose! He's not the demon you believe him to be. He's my friend and—"

Her palm answered his seditious words with a stinging slap across his face. "If you choose to make friends with the devil," she seethed, "that's on your soul. I would not see mine so afflicted."

She swept past her brother, marching across the room, finding the devil's attention riveted to her face as she settled in a wide stance in front of him.

Logan searched for words. "Rose..."

"Did you laugh?" Rose whispered.

He frowned, his brows slashing downward. "Excuse me?"

"At me," she clarified, moving with deliberate steps forward. "When first we met, I sought a kiss from a man whom I believed to value chivalry and honor. I sought a reason to believe in love and desire, instead of raping hordes of men who held no claim to decency and compassion." She stood before him, her hands fisted into the folds of her skirts. "Did you laugh at the poor girl who parted ways with sanity to go seeking a kiss from you?"

His gaze was soft upon her face. "My reply was given in anger, as you well recall, little one."

"Yet you prattled on regarding the value of consent as though the notion held any worth to you!" Jabbing a finger into his chest, she wished it was a sharp blade instead. "And you kissed me, made an offer of marriage, made me..." She blinked back tears, calling back the words before she could embarrass herself with them.

"You and I share an unfortunate past," he said in low tones, "and I know the grievous wounds I inflicted on you. Yet for all that, you and I share a bond not easily severed. A bond I would see strengthened, never to be parted from."

She gazed into eyes burning with purpose. "You and I share nothing but the stench of your treachery and deceit. A stench equally shared by my brother. I wish both of you only to fall from sight, never to darken my home again." She turned to flee, only to find her way out barred by Robert.

He blocked the door. "Be that as it may, Rose, we still need to talk. Sit." He lifted a brow, daring her to defy his order.

"Let me by, Robert. You have no authority to make demands on me." She smiled with false sweetness. "Not that I would heed any command of yours anyway."

"He may not," whispered a voice from behind, "but I do, little one. Now sit."

She spun around. "You will cease calling me by that ridiculous name! I have a title, and I demand you use it, just as I henceforth will address you as Lord Edgewood. And you are not master to this home. I am in my husband's absence, and I bow to no demented demand under my roof."

Lord Edgewood smiled. She noted a feral gleam to that lifting of sensual lips.

"As you are so fond of titles now, *little one*, my name is soon to change. I'm afraid you are addressing the future heir to the Dorchester title and estate."

The walls of the study began to spin. "I beg your pardon. My husband may not be at home, but that does not mean—"

"Sit down," Lord Edgewood repeated in hushed tones. "Your brother and I bear news you may not find to your liking."

"I find both your presences in my home not to my liking. The news you carry will be ill received if I stand or sit, so speak."

"Rose," Robert sighed, "please. For once in your life—"

Lord Edgewood held up a hand. "She's right, Robert." He turned the full force of his brown gaze on her. "We bear sad tidings...of your husband's death."

She staggered. "Sebastian? Dead?" The walls were spinning faster. She shoved the heel of a hand to her forehead. "You lie." She went to collapse on a settee, cradling her throbbing head, closing her eyes as waves of pain lashed at her, body and soul.

The cushion shifted, forced to bear another weight. "I'm sorry, little one, but I do not."

She yanked her pounding head up to give an angry retort, only to clamp her teeth shut as her stomach rolled, ready again to become a geyser. She surged to her feet.

Robert blocked her way. "Rose, I know you're—hey!"

She shoved him aside and stormed past, her gaze spying a vase in a corner. She flung herself toward it and retched, gagging within the now partially filled pottery. Once her stomach settled, she looked up to see a hand with long, slender fingers holding a handkerchief. She accepted it with downcast eyes, dabbing at her mouth while noting the room had turned deathly quiet.

She raised her gaze to find two pairs of eyes studying her. "I beg your pardon, but it's just a vase. Sebastian has them everywhere."

Robert and Lord Edgewood traded poignant looks.

"You two needn't look so concerned," she said. "I'm not sick. It usually only happens in the morning."

Lord Edgewood's face paled.

Robert appeared stricken.

"What is wrong with you both?" she demanded, slapping Lord Edgewood's handkerchief back into his slackened hand. "Have neither of you two nitwits seen a woman retch before?"

Lord Edgewood swallowed hard, the column of his throat moving up and down several times before he murmured, "Excuse me." His gaze flickered toward her and away as he strode from the study.

She frowned at the brief glimpse of pain his look conveyed. What right did he have to look at her that way? She was the aggrieved party here, his actions inflicting a wound she would bear the rest of her life, and he dared look at her as though she inflicted greater injury?

Questions crowded her mind, demanding answers. Lord Edgewood owed her some honest replies, and she would have them if it were the last thing she did on this earth. She took a step to follow, only to find Robert's hand on her arm, once again, restricting her movement.

"Leave him be," he said. "He needs a moment, as do we." He strode past her, flinging himself in the high winged-back chair behind the grand mahogany desk. His mouth opened and closed several times before his expression hardened. "Why did you not tell me you were with child?"

"For heaven's sakes, Robert, I am not with—" Her mind shut down, too busy making calculations, counting the passing of too many days.

Oh, God. Oh God, no. Please, please no.

Tears welled, knotting her tongue. How could she have been so blind and witless to the turmoil of her body? My God, a child! With no father to greet its entry into the world. To love and cherish it when the mother perishes during the birth. *You lied Sebastian! You promised you'd be here and you're not! You took what you wanted with no regard for my feelings, casting me adrift toward an uncertain future!*

She wrapped arms around her middle, aching for another set of limbs to hold her that would never again do so in this life. Her eyes fell upon the letters heaped onto the desk, all the notes she had written to Sebastian in his absence, detailing her existence to a man who never once bothered to write her. Irrational anger seized her thoughts, and before she knew what she was about, she was standing at the desk, tearing the letters up, bundling them in her arms and stomping to the hearth, prepared to toss them all to oblivion in the roaring flames.

Until Robert's arms tackled her to the floor, gently urging her down, spilling the missives on the carpet while he pulled her into a brotherly embrace, nestling her face into the crook of a shoulder.

It went against her better judgement to seek comfort from the enemy, but as there wasn't another soul in England who cared for her, Robert's comfort would have to do. He patted her shoulder, rubbed her back with short, brisk strokes that were less soothing than a bristled brush scouring naked flesh, but some comfort was better than none.

"This has been a day of revelations," he commented, peeling her off his chest. "Why don't you take yourself upstairs and rest? We will talk again when you're feeling better."

A bitter laugh escaped her mouth. "You wish me to find peace while Lord Edgewood yet lurks under my roof? You know I will not."

"He's not a bad man, Rose. He made a horrible mistake, but he's trying to redeem himself."

Another puzzle piece fell into place. She tilted her puffy face up to stare at Robert. "This is the debt you spoke of, isn't it?" She needn't have asked. Robert's flash of guilt was answer enough. She gaped at her sibling. "What insanity possessed you to befriend the man who ordered the raping of your Abby?"

"You think ours was a friendship forged overnight? Hell, Rose." He reclined, bracing his weight on flattened palms on the rug, shaking his head. "You know how we met? I was on the threshold of killing him. I found him casting up his accounts in Mother's prize rose bushes. I was poised above him with a saber, ready to run him through, when he looked up at me with eyes red from weeping and begged me to take his life. He was crying, Rose. He was mad with guilt, demanding to know all your names. I refused to answer any questions and walked away, sparing his life. But he was stubborn. Almost as stubborn as you," he added with a scowl.

She waved a hand. "If you think you're telling me something Mother or Father has not said before you're mistaken, so go on."

Robert's scowl became a smirk. "Indeed. Anyway, he sent several letters after the regiment left our lands, to which I did not reply, until—" His face reddened.

Her alarm escalated. "Robert?"

"You know why Abby disappeared?"

"I assumed she was with child after the assault." A fate her friend Clara had been spared from bearing. Dawning horror slackened her jaw. "Oh God, Robert! I'm sorry, how horrible it must have been for you both."

"Yes," he murmured. "It was horrible. And I unable to help or offer aid. Abby refused to take my name or give her child one. But her parents forced her out with nowhere to go. I wrote to Logan, and he took her in."

"What?" She blinked, unable to fathom such a noble gesture from an English devil.

"That's what Logan does," Robert said. "He helps women, Rose. He shelters the abused, the orphaned. He's never refused a soul that I know of." He gestured toward a wall. "Abby is here in England. Logan took her and gave her a new life. Something she would not have accepted from me."

"Do you mean to tell me Lord Edgewood married Abby?"

"No! Logan's never—well, never mind that." He grinned. "You'll find out someday. Anyway, no. He bought Abby a small cottage and saw her employed with a busy *modiste*."

She claimed no desire to find out what Logan's never done. She sought clarification on another subject. "And what of me? Why did you two plot against me?"

"We didn't plot against you, Rose! We were trying to save you."

"From Sebastian. Yes, I know."

"No, Rose. You don't know." His expression hardened to stone. "Logan told me your husband left a trail of broken bodies throughout England. The former duke raped Logan's mother. Logan is the product of that violent encounter."

"Lord Edgewood is Sebastian's brother!"

"Is it necessary to shout the roof down on my head? Yes. Half-brother. Logan is an acknowledged by-blow of the dead duke—Sebastian's father."

Her head was beginning to spin again.

Robert reached a handout to steady her. "Come Rose. I'll escort you upstairs to rest. You've suffered enough surprises for one day, I think. We can talk later."

She was forced to agree. "Fine. But I can find my way to bed without your assistance."

She climbed to her feet and moved toward the door, pausing before crossing the threshold, looking back over her shoulder. Robert was on his hands and knees cleaning up her spilled parchment, lingering overly long on one paper.

"What is it, Robert?"

His head came up with an audible snap. "What? Err, nothing. Other than an appalling lack of correct grammar."

Bah! One would think by now she would have learned not to ask her brother a question and expect to receive a serious answer. "You're impossible," she huffed, flouncing away, running upstairs to her private set of rooms.

It wasn't until she was curled into a fetal position in bed, alone in her bedchamber that it occurred to her she never asked how Sebastian died.

Chapter Twelve

Robert found him in the stables, lurking in a murky corner of Jupiter's stall. "Does the child change your plans? I wouldn't blame you if it did."

Logan spent the better part of an hour asking himself the very same question. He was ashamed of his answer. "The child changes nothing. I will stay the course."

"I figured you would." Robert lowered on to a bale of hay beside him. "But I know the knowledge hurts all the same. I understand how you feel."

Yes. Robert would understand. "How is she doing?" Logan asked.

"She's overwhelmed. I relayed the story of how we met and the part about you being Sebastian's half-brother."

Logan quirked a brow at that. "Did Rose think my claim as heir an empty boast?"

"My sister did not even ask how her husband died. I'm not sure she's thinking clearly about anything right now."

He grunted his agreement. "Where is she?"

"Sleeping in her chambers. Unaware I locked her in her room."

Logan looked at his friend, questioning the unnecessary constraint.

Robert held up his hands in defense. "My sister strays toward rash actions when upset. I don't want her doing anything to hurt herself or her child."

"You've done no more than shake a hornet's nest, Robert. And she'll blame me for *your* actions. I already have enough on my shoulders."

Robert laughed. "I know she won't thank me for it, but you might one day looking back."

He shared a smile with his friend. "Perhaps." His smile fell sour. "Yet perhaps not." He cast his troubled gaze to the ground. "Robert, I fear my brother may have loved her after all."

"What?" Robert leaned close. "Why do you say such blasphemy?"

He ran Sebastian's visit in his mind, conjuring the scene before him. "Dorchester paid me a visit weeks ago at my London home while I was in residence licking my wounds. To say I was shocked as hell would be a grave understatement. My brother never called on me in life."

"What happened? What did he say?"

"He spoke of his marriage and wished to extract a promise from me—to watch after his wife if anything were to happen to him." He ground his jaw together, forcing words out between clenched teeth. "Sebastian never showed concern for another female in all of his miserable life. But when he talked of Rose, a light glowed from his eyes, his soul breathing life for the first time—I am sure of it."

"So, the devil had a heart," Robert said, his voice going flat. "It changes nothing."

"Doesn't it?" Logan shot to his feet; his conscience burdened beyond his endurance of its weight. "If Sebastian's death proves false as I believe it will, and a confrontation ensues, what right have I to take away a child from his father? A husband from his wife?" He rammed his fingers through his mane of hair. "Will I not stand as evil as Sebastian when the dust settles?"

Robert stood, placing a steady hand on his shoulder. "If you are suffering from a lack of faith in your convictions, then brace yourself." He withdrew two folded pieces of vellum from inside his jacket, holding it up. "God delivered you a reason to see resolve turn to stone in this matter of my sister."

"You do not understand, Robert." He snatched the papers, unfolding them. "I never meant to deprive Sebastian of only his wife. It was his *life* I sought in vengeance for all those he abused and cast aside. Do you understand? I sought out Rose to save her at your request, but it was always my intent to use her to bring Sebastian to his knees, to rid the world of the name Dorchester. Now what in the hell are these?" He scanned one page, then glanced up. "My father's will?"

"Keep reading. You'll find the fifth paragraph of particular interest, I think."

He arched a well-groomed brow but directed his gaze back to the legal document.

His gaze snagged over words that struck a very deep cord within his heart. A roar of denial worked its way up his throat, and Logan choked, working to breathe around it. Staggering, he fell onto the bale of hay, shaken to the core.

Robert crouched in front of him. "Read the other paper."

Shaking hands shifted the parchment, Logan's gaze falling over a hand-written letter from Sebastian to Rose's father in Virginia. "My God." His gaze arched up. "How did you come by these?"

"I was attempting to clean up after Rose and found them in a pile of other paperwork. Fate is favoring you with this gift, Logan. If Sebastian's death does indeed prove false, then you have all the leverage you need against him." He stood. "Without shedding a drop of blood."

Relief flowed through him but ebbed into oblivion. "She hates me, Robert. I no longer hold the sum of her heart."

"How did you envision this afternoon would go? Did you think Rose would greet you with open arms and dewy looks when presented with your identity? You knew she would not."

"Yet I fear her reaction sheds light on my true nature."

"What do you mean?"

"I am the beast in her story, Robert. Not Sebastian. What if my brother is changing into a man redeemed by love? And I am taken to becoming the villain, intent on his destruction?" His lips pressed into a thin line. He hated to be the villain in Rose's story, but no matter how he much he applied reason and logic, it would not change the truth. Nor would a piece of paper.

He was here for revenge's sake.

The truth burned like acid in his mouth. He long to spit, rage, and spew a string of ugly curses to the heavens, but God held the higher ground in this. Logan sold his soul to the devil long ago, and he would have to play his part until the bitter end.

Robert knelt in front of him, cuffing his shoulder to gain his gaze. "You love my sister, Logan, and despite this afternoon's tragic revealing of secrets, I know Rose loves you too. The fact you are here in moral conflict tells me you are far from becoming a soulless monster. You're a man of honor, Logan, and you will always stand as such. You will find a way back to Rose."

He held his friend's stare, grateful for Robert's counsel. He needed a reason to believe in better days. "Thank you, Robert."

"What are friends and a future brother-in-law for? Now," Robert stood up, brushing hay from his breeches. "Let us go see if your hunch was correct. I would see this done while sunlight still burns the sky."

They readied their mounts and made their way to the local church where Sebastian's coffin lay resting until burial.

After a brief confrontation with the local vicar and departing of a rather large sum of coin, Logan stood by Sebastian's coffin, flanked by Robert. Gaslight burned in the tiny room. Logan shivered as a chill sweep through his body. "This is grisly work," he commented, needing to break the quiet. "I never cared much for grave robbing, and this feels exactly like it."

"I agree," Robert replied. "Let's just get it over with, shall we?"

Together, they pried the nails from the coffin, and slowly, lifted the lid.

Robert whistled low. "Your hunch was right. He's not here. And if he's not here…"

"Then he isn't dead," Logan finished.

In his heart, he had known Sebastian wouldn't die so easily. His half-brother was too slippery a predator. Besides, there had been something odd about the way he died. Sebastian had been a recluse after the war, staying only at his country estate. And suddenly, appearing in London the day following his wedding, becoming the toast of society overnight, being in the company of the Prince of Wales? It didn't make sense.

Logan's father, Henry Graham, did not often talk of Sebastian, but Logan always suspected his brother never served his country as he had—as a soldier. Given Sebastian's title and charm, it was reasonable to assume Sebastian served his country in another capacity—say, as a spy. It was not unheard of for titled Englishmen to perform this type of job in French courts in service to the Crown. Was it possible his brother was working as one now?

But toward what point and purpose?

Robert nudged him. "Shall we tell Rose her husband isn't dead?"

"No," Logan said, shaking his head for further emphasis. "Her husband went through a lot of trouble to make his demise public knowledge. And until we know the reason for it, I think it's best if we let Rose believe she is a widow."

"Sounds a little self-serving of you, but I think in this case you may be right. How are we going to find out what Dorchester is up to?"

"I shall make some discreet inquiries, but Silver Hawk might stand a better chance of finding out such secret information." He looked meaningfully at Robert.

Robert nodded. "I will make ready and ride out this very night."

Logan bit back a grin. "Coward."

"A fault I admit to with pleasure." He smirked. "God, Rose is going to hate you when your guests descend upon her home tonight. I am sorry I will have to miss the drama that will ensue."

"They are a necessary evil she will come to be thankful for."

"I hope so." Robert clapped a hand on his shoulder. "But if I were you, I would ride for the castle and hide every saber, pistol, knife, and broom before you let Rose out of her bedchamber. Anything with a point on it. Trust me, I speak from experience."

Logan gulped. His friend may have the right of it. "Report back to me as soon as you find out anything about Dorchester."

"Count on it." Robert turned, striding out of the room, calling over his shoulder, "Good luck!"

A feeling of dread settled into Logan's gut when silence fell. Doubts still plagued his mind, but bright green eyes called to him, filling his blood with a sense of purpose. He swore an oath to protect Rose from harm so he would play the villain. The only role, he feared he'd ever been destined to play.

Chapter Thirteen

Rose awoke to the sounds of crackling fire and a howling wind blowing outside. Darkness shrouded her room, punctuated by flickering flames from the hearth. She rolled to her side, lacking proper motivation to rise from the bed. Too much had happened, too many words said. Her brain felt muddled, her chest heavy with a dull ache when presented with a single question: Whom did her heart grieve for more—the husband lost, or the highwayman torn from her heart? The answer shamed her.

She grieved more for herself because of the child she carried.

She lay a hand to her abdomen, so fearful the tiny life she nursed would one day see her from this world, screaming in agony. Sebastian would no doubt greet her in heaven with a broad smile, perfectly happy his heir robbed her of life. An act of justice for not properly grieving the passing of a husband.

Or loving him as a proper wife should have.

God was punishing her. He listened to desperate prayers regarding her love for a highwayman and found her as lacking in morals as a pirate. And the punishment for such weighty crimes was death by childbearing.

The cruelty of the world did not match the cruelty of God.

Her stomach rumbled its agreement, reminding her the dinner hour was fast approaching.

Turning, she rang for her maid. She had no intention of entertaining a criminal or her brother at the dinner table. She'd dine alone before she played hostess to the pair of them.

A knock sounded on her closed bedchamber door. "Your Grace?"

She frowned. Was her mood so poor her maid feared her presence? "Come in, Milly. I wish to change my dress and have a meal brought up."

The knob rattled. "I can't, Your Grace. The door is locked."

The door was locked? Rose shot up off the bed, pausing a

moment as the room spun before settling, then took quick strides over to the closed door. She tried the knob, twisting it back and forth. Anger, hot and bright, poured into her veins. "That blackguard," she muttered.

"Your pardon, Your Grace?"

"Never mind, Milly. The door is quite stuck. Perhaps you might find Lord Edgewood for the key." Who else would be evil enough to lock her into a room? Surely her brother lacked such boldness of behavior.

"Yes, Your Grace."

Rose turned away, stomping her foot on a surge of temper. Did Lord Edgewood think he could lock her away and forget about her existence? As he forgot about her presence when the soldiers descended upon her like hungry vultures?

Her aching fingers curled into fists at her side. Oh, she was going to teach Lord Edgewood the folly of his thinking.

She marched across the room to a nearby window and pushed it wide open, glancing down and to the side.

There was a narrow ledge offering a slim chance of escape. If she could make her way to another room, freedom would be hers. Falling to her death was also a possibility, but all things considered, it was a risk she must undertake. To do nothing, playing the role of victim, would be a greater crime.

She quickly undid the buttons to her gown and shimmied it down her body. Her corset came off next. In moments she stood clad in nothing more than a chemise and silk stockings, but there was little choice. She couldn't very well wear a gown while making her escape. The hem alone would cause her demise. No, the fewer distractions, the better.

She flattened her palms on the window ledge and pushed herself up. She grabbed the window to gain her feet, then looked down.

That had been her first mistake.

Her second had been her ignorance of the weather. The wind buffeted her poorly clad body as soon as she put a foot on the ledge. Then came the cold rain, soaking her in seconds and making the ledge slippery.

Her third mistake had been wearing the satin slippers on her feet. *Who wears satin slippers on slick stone in a driving rainstorm? Why, the Duchess of Dorchester, of course!*

Inch by precious inch, she made her way along the narrow stone ledge, digging her nails into wet ledge as best she could. Her teeth clattered together hard enough to break themselves. If her eyes weren't frozen, she would have cried. Failing that, the mind turned inward to reflect.

There were times, if one was inclined to reminiscence while facing certain death, that she felt her mother bedded the village idiot to produce her. The lack of wits she possessed was indeed cause for grave concern.

It was sobering to claim kinship to nitwits as she stood immobile on a ledge not fit to bear the weight of a single bird.

The wind howled relentlessly, tearing at her thin clothes. She pressed her face against the rough stone, telling herself liberty was a privilege worth fighting for, no matter the cost. An American euphemism for, *you're going to die a bloody fool*. Sheets of rain mocked her, testing the strength of her resolve beneath a hailstorm of icy water.

Roaring breezes took on a most peculiar voice, forming words accusing her of forgetting the most important reason of all for not risking her life.

The baby. Sebastian's baby. The only remnants of him she had left in this world.

Shame frayed the hard edges of her temper, giving the thunderous gales a louder voice to her berate her foolish behavior.

"My God, woman! Are you trying to kill yourself?"

The tempest morphed into the sound of Lord Edgewood's voice bellowing colorful epitaphs.

Good heavens.

If he was here to play the part of the hero, then she would spare him the embarrassment of assuming a role he knew nothing about. A window loomed only inches from her frozen body. Desperate, she slithered across the ledge and slipped on the wet stone. Gasping, she tethered on the shelf, swinging her arms, unable to regain balance.

At the last possible second, before gravity claimed her, a tree branch slammed into her back, ramming her face against the wall. "Ouch!"

A familiar male voice shouted into her ear, "You could have broken your neck, you reckless little fool! You're lucky a bruised face is all you'll have to show for your foolishness."

A fool was she? Teeth chattering, her body shook as a leaf caught in the wind, but it was hard to tell if the icy, drenching rain or hurricane force winds was the only cause.

She whipped her head to the other side to glare at Lord Edgewood. "I told you to—"

"Be quiet!" he snapped. "And pay attention, or you'll send us both to our deaths!" He snatched her hand, pulling her along the ledge, back to the safety of the bedchamber. Unleashing her briefly to jump from the window, Lord Edgewood spun then clamped his fingers onto her arm.

His palm was hot against her icy, bare skin, and she felt a moment's chagrin to be the only one dying of frostbite.

Lord Edgewood yanked her to the floor, setting her upon frozen feet. She lifted her chin, preparing for a dignified retreat, took one step then fell forward with prompt efficiency. Strong hands shot out, abusing her arms, hauling her upright. It was an odd sensation not to feel the floor under one's feet. Stranger still to have the devil tearing off your clothes, unable to command your own hands to stop him.

"W-what a-are y-you d-doing?" she asked, bringing up shaking arms to cover her breasts, hunching her shoulders forward.

He ignored the question, moving from her side to the bed, ripping the blankets off. Lord Edgewood approached her with quick strides and angry eyes, wrapping her from head to toe in fuzzy warmth. Further ignoring her scowling face, he bent, scooping her up into his arms.

"P-put m-me—" He dropped her in front of the fireplace. "D-down." *Ouch!*

The man had all the genteel manners of a goat. How dare he manhandle her. The warmth of the fire was pleasant, though. She glowered, fixing a frown on her face so the obtuse man wouldn't think her pleased. She needn't have bothered.

He stormed off into a darkened corner of the room, coming back a scarce minute later, lacking wet clothes, and a blanket wrapped around his massive frame. The hearth's fire reflected in his eyes, giving them an unholy glow.

She shrank into her coverlet, not trusting the look in his eyes as he bore down on her.

He didn't break stride until he was a scarce inch away from her face.

She gulped.

"The next time you perform an act of such stupidity," he whispered, "I will personally see you to the dungeon to remain under lock and key until such time I deem you fit to rejoin the civilized world."

"You cannot threaten me in my home! Besides, there is no dungeon here."

"Then I'd see one built just for the privilege of shoving you in it."

"I despise earthen jails. I much prefer ivory towers."

"Of that, I have no doubt." He dragged a chair to the hearth, settling his bulky frame into as though he meant to stay for an extended period. How dare he impose his presence on a naked lady in her private quarters! The man was without proper manners. As well as clothes.

She ordered her gaze to the hearth, refusing to look at the broad expanse of chest his blanket revealed. The patch of dark hair made her numb fingers tingle most unpleasantly.

The silence stretched between them, uncomfortable and filled with questions. Of all the things she wished to say, why now was her tongue so knotted? She waited a long time to demand an answer to a single question, and now as the opportunity presented itself, she shrank in fear of the response.

She sought safe harbor in familiar waters—sarcasm. "Don't you have a village to pillage? Or a coach to rob?"

He slid an amused look her way. "Sacking villages is taxing work. I prefer easier game, the bounty more assured."

She stiffened. "If you think to force yourself on me…"

All humor vanished from his eyes. "I have never forced myself on a woman."

"No, you simply command others to perform the base act and watch as they take their pleasure." Angry tears threatened to burn from angry eyes. "I was too afraid to ask before, too scared to hear your reply. But I must know now. Why did you not stop the attack? You were their commanding officer! You held the power to end our suffering. Why? Why did you sit there and do nothing? Where were your lofty notions on consent then?"

His gaze did not falter. "Do the reasons really matter, Rose?"

"They matter to me," she growled.

Something in his eyes flickered, his shoulders hunching forward. "No answer I give will help heal the scars you bear. I fear it will only rip open old wounds, causing hurt and pain all over again."

"I would make such a determination myself and judge the impact of words on injury."

"You are a stubborn woman, Rose."

"A fault you are no doubt personally familiar with."

"Indeed." Tensing, he scrubbed hands over his face. "The command to attack was given by my father, Rose. I did no more than carry out his orders, much to my shame."

"You could have refused!" she cried, pulling the blanket tighter around her shoulders.

He gave her a look rimmed with sadness. "A soldier cannot refuse a direct order from a superior. To do so would have been at the cost of my life." His voice lowered, deepened as he said, "My father knew this when giving me the directive. It was a test."

Silence answered the whispered tormented words. She did not know what to say. It seemed a man of greater character would have acted to help three women fight for their honor. "We were no soldiers in the war. My friends did not deserve their fate. You should have done *something*, Lord Edgewood."

"You're right, Rose. I should have. Yet I am here now, attempting to right a terrible wrong."

She snorted. "Aye, two years too late."

"Is it?" He bent, reaching forward with a finger.

Her breath hitched when he caught a sodden strand of hair, tucking it behind an ear. "Don't touch me," she barked despising her fluttering pulse.

"I try," he murmured, stroking her cheek, his gaze drifting down below her chin. He fingered the delicate thudding at the base of her neck. "But the force of my attraction is no easy thing to deny. It is a raging thirst, constant in its torment."

She despised the bloom of heat his touch induced. She twisted her face away from his light caresses, scooting back to allow more room between their bodies. "Tell me of my husband," she demanded, changing subjects. "Was it your hands that took him from me?" Though she spoke with icy contempt, such a thought never occurred to her. Sebastian was dead, and to her great shame, she did not think the man sitting beside her responsible for his death. Perhaps Lord Edgewood should commit her to a dungeon for lack of sanity.

"He was killed by an unknown assassin while attending the theatre in London."

"An unknown assailant killed him. That seems rather odd."

"Indeed. Unless you know the man and the crimes he's committed over the years. Then such news causes less confusion and becomes more a cause for celebration."

She inhaled sharply, stunned by his aggressive answer. "How dare you besmirch the character of the man I called husband. I think you should leave."

He raised a brow. "It took you a long time to make such a command of me. Dare I think you enjoyed my company for a moment of time?"

She ground her teeth together. "I do not intend to hold a midnight conversation with my captor without my clothes. Now kindly leave me to grieve in peace, please."

"Don't be silly, Rose. It's barely eight o'clock. In fact, dinner awaits us, so we best get ready." He paused, staring at her. "Are you truly grieving for your husband?"

"Of course, I am! Sebastian was kind and… and…" Her mind floundered for saintly adjectives to describe her husband. "He was my husband," she snapped. "It is proper for a wife to mourn the loss of a spouse."

"Madam, you hardly knew the waste of human flesh you called husband."

Rose sat up straight, clutching her blankets to her in anger. "How dare you speak ill of my husband when he is not yet in his grave!"

Lord Edgewood snorted. "Soothe your feathers, little fool. You have known him for no more than two days, while I, on the other hand, have known him for a lifetime. Of the two of us, I think I am the better judge of character."

"So says the man who allowed an assault to take place on two young women. You're no judge of character, and you're certainly in no position to judge others."

"I suppose you think your husband would have stopped such madness," he murmured. "Gone charging into battle on a white horse to rescue fair damsels in distress?"

"He would have stopped it, yes. He may not have been perfect, but he was far from being a heartless monster, unlike the man who dares insult him now."

"Heartless monster, am I?" His smile took on a sharp, feral gleam. "There is a fine line between hero and villain, Rose, and trust me when I tell you it is too fine a line to tell the difference between the two most of the time."

Uneasiness swept through her at his words. It was a description far too accurate of her current predicament. She feared her husband was no knight of old, charging to a young woman's rescue. Yet neither was he cruel or unpleasant, even when given great cause to be. But now Sebastian was gone, and in his place stood another man. A man who saved her life. A man whose touch caused her body to tremble with anticipation and insatiable need. But a man whose evil deeds would haunt her for the rest of her days. So what did that make him? What measure could she define his character? The line between hero and villain blurred when she thought of Lord Edgewood.

"Did you love him?"

She jerked away, torn from confusing thoughts. "I beg your pardon?"

He quirked a brow. "Your husband—did you love the man?"

"Of course, I did." She turned away, her face burning with guilt at the outright lie. She heard the floor creak, looked up, and willed her heart to slow its rapid beat as Lord Edgewood drew near.

He lowered his face inches away from her own.

She pulled the blanket tighter around her shoulders, tensing, fearing his touch and in equal measure, her response.

He extended a single finger, trailing it down her cheek, circling her chin, lifting it up. Lord Edgewood captured her attention the same way a heart attack claims its victim. Heart squeezing, producing a throbbing ache in the center of a chest.

"Then you were another casualty if you held my brother in such regard, and I am truly very sorry," he whispered. His fingertips continued to graze her cheek.

His attention fell below her eyes. Most assuredly he did not stop to ogle the tip of her nose. Irrational anger seized her, and she clung to the feeling as one would a lifeline. "I am not a victim. I'm a widow, and you will have much cause to be sorry when you'll be without the title of duke!" Her voice fell into a more subdued tone as she said, "My husband deserves to see an heir of his making replace him and continue his line."

Lord Edgewood laughed. "Never fear about that, little one. England is replete with heirs of 'your husband's making,'" he intoned, standing up.

"How dare you imply—"

"Enough!" he roared. "You can defend my brother all you want but know it shall always fall on deaf ears where I am concerned. Now." He picked up his sodden shirt and discarded jacket and rammed his legs into wet breeches. "Ring for your maid and dress for dinner. We have a guest coming I want you to meet."

She gaped at him. "You rob me of my husband and now demand I dance attendance on houseguests? I will not."

"You will," he said, pausing by the connecting door to Sebastian's bedchamber, "because you are duchess here, and there are people who cannot wait for their pleas to be heard after your period of mourning ends. This entire estate sat neglected for far too long, and I will not let it pass another day without some attempt to rectify the wrongs they have endured by my brother's hands. We will both meet with the steward and hear what must be done."

Lord Edgewood's long-winded answer gave her pause. She'd not considered any responsibilities attached to the title of duchess, escape and her lot in life so consumed her. To hear people were suffering because of her ignorance was sobering indeed. "Very well," she agreed.

He looked surprised by her easy capitulation.

"Thank you." He started over the threshold to Sebastian's room.

"Wait!"

He paused, turning back toward her.

She stood. "That's Sebastian's room you go to. The exit to the hall is over there." She nodded at another door across the way.

He smiled, the corners of his mouth lifting in such a way to cause strong knees to weaken. "I know, little one. Unfortunately, close to you is where I prefer to be." He winked, striding from her room, shutting the door.

Curse her knees and curse the bond that saw them weaken from a silly smile from a hardened criminal.

Chapter Fourteen

Dinner was a botched affair, yet Rose's appetite was untarnished by the stilted conversation around the dinner table. Logan watched the woman eat her way through seven courses, the steward watching too, though more circumspect with his attention.

After the second dessert, Logan stood, signaling the end of dinner, afraid his charge would burst at the seams if allowed to continue eating. "Shall we withdraw to the study to look through the accounts?"

She dabbed at the corners of her mouth with a cloth napkin, looking around. "Whatever happened to my brother? It's unlike him to miss a meal."

"An urgent matter called his attention elsewhere for the night." He led the way out of the dining room, with Rose hard upon his heels.

"What urgent matter?"

He gave her a sidelong look without breaking stride. "What urgent matter usually befalls a young man?"

Understanding dawned in her green eyes. "How despicable."

"We all fall victim to baser pleasures, my dear." *Liar.* He stopped at the threshold, holding her arm, urging her aside as the steward preceded them into the room. "Not all men are of violent intent where women are concerned."

Her eyes grew distant and unfocused. "I know, now."

Jealousy clenched his gut. He never witnessed a victim of Sebastian remember her assault with soft eyes, melting at the memory. Rose feared intimacy. It would have taken a great deal of compassion and patience to coax this woman into the marriage bed. Virtues he never suspected his brother capable of possessing. God, how he had wanted to be the man to teach Rose the wonders of physical intimacy. Standing on the outside, watching as she remembered a tender touch not received from him, was a painful experience.

Resentment hardened his voice. "I can see you do."

He pushed away, cutting a path to the liquor cabinet. He poured three drinks, giving one to the steward, the other to Rose. The steward lifted a brow but downed the offering all the same. It probably went against some social rule to not drink with the servants, but to hell with that. A man should not drink alone.

Logan waved a hand at the mountain of paperwork already spread out on the giant mahogany desk. "Shall we?"

~ * ~

Two hours later, and Rose wanted to scream. It was clear Sebastian ran his people into the ground. His coffers overflowed with money, but it was a price paid in blood. The farming accidents, the poor conditions of cottages and barns. The families were starving to death to pay their taxes. This could not stand.

She sat and listened to Lord Edgewood and the steward discuss farming techniques and repairs to buildings. Lord Edgewood proved highly competent and knowledgeable about such things. All she offered was a few sneezes and the occasional horrified gasp.

Appalling. She sat in luxury while children starved to death not feet from her front door. Why had Sebastian let this happen to his people? What purpose of his was served by this contemptible act?

She sneezed again, feeling a headache coming on.

Lord Edgewood looked up from across the desk. "Rose, it's getting late. Why don't you turn in? Sebastian's burial will be in the morning. You need your rest. I can finish up here."

Sebastian's burial. Drat!

An occasion she was not ready to deal with. She stood from the chair she'd been gracing with her presence. "Very well, Lord Edgewood." She started from the room when the buzz of many voices reached her ears. Halting, tilting her head, she said, "Do my ears deceive, or is there a ruckus coming from the direction of the front door?"

"A ruckus?" Lord Edgewood stood, taking quick strides to the study door, peering out. His face paled. "Bloody hell. I forgot about them."

Forgot about them?

She crept up behind him, straining to see around his big, brawny body. She counted five, ten, no! Twenty females of various ages and children.

Was this a planned revolt? Had Sebastian's tenants run Mr. Harrison through with an ax and now lay siege to her home to sack and pillage?

Rose brought a hand up to her throat. Would her demise come by chopping block or noose?

"What are you thinking rubbing your neck like that?" Lord Edgewood stared down at her with a quirked brow.

"I think Mr. Townsend comes too late to help. The revolt is already upon me."

"The revolt?" Comprehension lit his eyes. Laughter bubbled out from his lips. "You're daft."

"Easy words for you to say. You're a thief. They probably hail you as their hero, reaping laurels upon your head."

He sobered. "I am no one's hero, nor would I want to be." He waved at the chaos amassing in the front foyer. "Come, let us greet our new arrivals."

"You want me to embrace this madness and welcome it to my home?" She gave him a look that threatened violence should he force this issue. "If they are not here to revolt their poor treatment, then I assume they are here at your request. In that event, I suggest you go and greet them yourself and leave me—Logan!"

He gripped her arm, dragging her down the hall with him. He stopped when she called out his Christian name. "Yes?"

She tried to shake him off her extremity. "What are you doing? Have I not suffered enough surprises today?"

"You have suffered," he acknowledged with a nod. "Yet there is one more thing I would ask you to bear before taking to your bed. One you will not thank me for but must be done."

"I do wish you'd straighten your tongue and stop talking riddles. I have a headache."

"I will see you to bed soon," he promised, resuming his forced march. He reached the foyer, dropping her arm, cupping his hands around his mouth, shouting, "I thank you all for coming. Your bedchambers are ready, and footmen await to help you to your rooms. But first," he turned to her, "may I introduce you to Rose Graham, the Duchess of Dorchester."

She smiled at the female congregation, all staring in rapt attention at her, but found her smile wilting as a male child stepped forward. His likeness she'd seen before. Somewhere. The hair coloring as summer wheat, the deep blue eyes staring at her with a familiar glint.

A lead cannonball sunk into her stomach. Her gaze darted to another child. A girl, with different coloring in hair but the face, the proud tilt of the chin and nose was unmistakable.

Rose took an involuntary step back, putting her hand to her mouth. Her brain registered the complete lack of noise in the hall. All eyes were upon her. Waiting. Watching.

She took another step back, then another, her body smacking

the wall. Lord Edgewood was at her side. "Who are these people?" she whispered. "Why did you invite them here?"

He lowered his face to hers. "They are known to your husband. And I invited them here to prove a point of gravest concern."

She stared at the male child, feeling herself come undone in front of them. "Send them away," she ordered in soft tones. "I do not want them in my home."

Fisting her skirts, she turned tail and ran, further into the house, finding the library and shutting herself inside. It was blessedly devoid of people. She threw herself into an armchair, clutching at the cushioned arms. Her life was unraveling faster than she could draw breath and see it mended. What did Lord Edgewood want from her? What was the purpose of bringing those women here?

The soft clicking of a door latch brought her head up from her hands.

Lord Edgewood stood at the door. "May I come in?"

"No."

He slipped inside and closed the door. "Thank you." He cut a path to stand directly in front of her. "Come here, Rose." He yanked her up by her hand, pulling her into his embrace.

She made a half-hearted attempt to struggle but lost the spirit to fight. The sturdy pair of arms holding her felt too wonderful. Laying her head on Lord Edgewood's chest, she closed her eyes as she listened to the steady pounding of his heartbeat. It was traitorous of her to be seeking comfort from enemy quarters, but she had no one else. Mrs. Brown would surely faint if she sought her ample bosom to pour her tears on.

Lord Edgewood rubbed Rose's back in long, soothing strokes, his lips at her ear. "I am sorry for all you have suffered today."

"Are you?" She sniffed. "You think slandering my husband's name will elevate yours? I understand he was not a good man, but what difference does it make now? What use is it to hurt me with his mistresses? He's gone from this world. I do not care to know how many fallen women he kept for his pleasure. They matter little now. Unless," she withdrew from his arms, "unless you brought them here to seek retribution from me." She waved a hand. "Give them whatever funds they deem themselves worthy of and see them from my house."

He stiffened, eyes snapping with anger. "You do not possess enough wealth to see their misery slackened or to compensate their losses. I've toiled for years to see such a day hastened, yet for all that, there is only one thing they desire." He shoved his face in hers. "They have all sworn oath to never let another of their gender fall victim to

Sebastian Graham, Duke of Dorchester. That is their purpose here."

"Victim?" She flung a hand toward the door. "There are no victims in this house, save for me. Only women light of skirt and short on morals crowd my home."

His smile sent chills down her spine. She stepped away, but he was having none of that.

Lord Edgewood snatched her hand. "Come with me." He dragged her back toward the melee of running children and gossiping women, pointing a finger at them. "Go on, little one. Tell me which face in this sea is the mistress, the light skirt, or the victim."

Rose locked her jaw, eyeing the women. Their clothes were simple frocks, the necklines modest, displaying bodies that were slender, while others were curvy. None of them claimed haughty airs or downcast faces, complaining of their lot in life.

She shook her head, unclenching her jaw. "You know I cannot."

"Aye, I do." He turned to her, staring hard into her eyes. "The same applies to men. You cannot see a murderer or a thief, nor a duke who applies intimidation to rob a woman of virtue or rapes them for his amusement."

Her chest began to ache anew. "Sebastian, he did that?"

"He did that and more."

Lord Edgewood's face flushed red in his fury. He believed what he said.

She stared at the women with fresh eyes, trying to see them from Logan's point of view. "No, no. I cannot believe that of him. He was gentle. He cared, he…"

The little boy with golden brown hair approached her with a flower, staring at her with Sebastian's eyes. Her heart crashed. A wall within her crumbled, and on the heels of its destruction, one lone tear escaped. Was this child born of such a violent union? Such a sweet, angelic face the product of a monster?

She knelt before the child, taking the offering, kissing his cheek, unable to break words. She stood and fled, past all the faces eyeing her with sympathy instead of righteous anger. Past Lord Edgewood who let her go unhindered. And past the servants who stared at the floor, their guilty faces downcast.

Everyone knew of Sebastian's nature but her. She had let herself be led astray by a silver tongue and a handsome face, never realizing a predator toyed with her emotions, making ready to pounce.

Running to her bedchamber, she slammed the door and bolted it. She ran to the connecting door to Sebastian's room, locking that as well. Lord Edgewood would not be bothering her again tonight.

She sneezed, her entire body now aching along with her heart. Climbing into bed fully clothed, she gathered blankets around her to ward off a chill. Yet no amount of covering could thaw a heart turning to ice, doomed to lay forever frozen.

~ * ~

Sebastian's corner of the inn was dark, but it afforded him an unobstructed view of the comings and goings of the other patrons in this fine establishment.

His first night on assignment was off to a brilliant start. He was three sheets to the wind, and it was barely midnight. Must be the outfit. The somber attire required of a highwayman hardly helped to lift his flagging spirits.

By now Silver Hawk must be at the castle, having received his blessing to visit. What had Sebastian been thinking, inviting the wolf into his home? It was a moment of weakness that sealed the fate of his marriage. An insanity he was only now lamenting.

Surely Rose must have been informed of his demise. It killed him not knowing how she was faring, or precisely how much 'comfort' his brother was providing. The dishonorable dog would no doubt be wooing her and planning an elaborate honeymoon. Picking the names of their parcel of children they would sire together.

Children.

Off his duchess, no less.

A roar of denial nearly fell from Sebastian, but he swallowed it back with gulps of ale, washing away the bitter taste of betrayal and heartache. His gaze fell to the collection of empty tankards on the table. By his impaired judgement, he'd spent a small fortune washing away various grievances, yet still they lingered. Taking on different forms but all tormenting him with wicked thoughts he could not silence. No, the drink would not satisfy or cleanse him of his pain.

He loved a woman who loved another, and no tonic on earth would help him.

A commotion from another table sought his attention with its growing melee of strident voices. The tones hinted at anger, but that's not what held his regard.

Robert was sprawled out in a chair, looking similarly out of sorts, facing two large men with an ax to grind. *Were they accusing Robert of sitting in their spot?*

Rubbish. The gents were spoiling for a fight, but Robert seemed unwilling to accommodate them, slumping onto the table with a fist balled into his cheek, his eyes vacant, seeing something of more importance.

The expression touched a familiar chord in Sebastian to such extent his feet found the floor and pushed. Swaying, he sauntered over, his hand patting the area on his hip where his rapier ought to be. He frowned, feeling only bone and cloth. Turning, he looked back toward his seat.

God's teeth! The rapier was still resting across the top of the bloody table.

He picked the wrong night to get foxed.

Stomping back, he secured his weapon, spun then marched across the room to perform a hero's duty.

He paused halfway to Robert's table, wrestling a thought from the haze of his mind. He was supposed to be dead, was he not? He couldn't simply run to rescue family. Particularly family he didn't like. Scratching at the beard he'd been working on growing the past several weeks, he shrugged, then caught his breath.

One of the bullies unsheathed a blade and was waving it in front of Robert's vacant stare.

Devil take it!

Charging to the rescue, Sebastian took three strides, tripped over a chair, then fell face down onto Robert's table, flipping the top so it banged Robert in the chin, knocking him back away from the knife onto the floor.

There! A proper rescue for a nitwit in distress.

Ambling to his feet, Sebastian drew forth his rapier, waving it in a wide, wild arch in front of the barbarians. "Now see here," he slurred, "this happens to be my spot. You curs will have to move on."

The twin mountains of evil turned to the other and grinned.

Sebastian tightened his grip on the hilt, prepared to defend the pile of rotten wood that dared call itself a piece of furniture.

He was waxing on rather poetically about broken splinters of timber.

Must be the bonds of marriage making him addled. His mind never wandered in such a serpentine manner before. Was that a fist flying toward his face?

Ouch!

The floor rushed up to greet his falling body for the second time. He might as well embrace it to his bosom and call it home for the night.

A face appeared above his, a hand waving in front of his eyes back and forth. "Are you alive?" Robert asked.

Sebastian laughed, finding morbid humor in his brother-in-law's question. "To my regret, yes." He shoved Robert away, sitting up. "Where did the nitwits go? I wasn't finished with them."

Robert collapsed beside him on the floor. "They moved on to more sober companions." He nodded, indicating the pair of tavern wenches draped over the brutes.

Sebastian grunted. "Who said there's no justice in the world? They give me a black eye and in return they receive the dubious gift of syphilis."

Breaking out into rough guffaws, Robert eyed him. "Spirits make you a tolerable soul, Dorchester."

"Recognize me, do you?"

"It's the voice mostly. An arrogance I would know anywhere. And the eyes."

"You notice my eyes?" Sounded damn intimate.

"Only because they're so cold. They remind me of a sunny March day in Virginia. The sky may be blue when you look at it from inside the comfort of your home, but it's a siren's lure, for as soon as you take a step outside, you freeze. The sunlight is deceptive, offering the promise of warmth then laughs as you writhe in torment from frigid winds."

The observation stung. Why Robert's opinion mattered baffled the mind, but it irked like a splinter underneath his skin. "You've a fanciful mind with a keen eye for seeing only what you wish to see. It's a common talent and hardly impressive."

"What are your talents in this world? My sister bowed to your demands for her maidenhead, so I would guess them to be considerable."

He stiffened. "I didn't rape her, Witherby. I assure you she succumbed to my advances of her own free will."

"I know."

"You know?" He roared that loud enough to cause a moment of silence in the tap room. "You know?" he repeated in a lower tone, leaning forward. "Then why—"

"Because I was angry, I failed to protect something for a friend," Robert said, giving a helpless shrug. "I make vows only to see them turn to ash. It's my curse. Another talent I've acquired in recent years. Rose's curse and talent is knowing how to fight. She's not afraid to defend her honor. Emerging from your study that day, the glow of happiness suffusing her face, I knew at once you had not forced yourself between her thighs."

A knot loosened in Sebastian's chest, a tightness restraining the taking of a full breath. "Thank you, Robert. Your news offers much comfort. I worried my actions might have turned her from me." He played with a sliver of broken wood. "Were you present when she received news of my death?"

Robert hesitated, then said, "Yes. Edgewood and I rode to your estate together."

Sebastian's brows shot upward. "She learned the true identity of Silver Hawk and my demise within the span of a single day?" At Robert's nod, he fell silent. He would not have wished Rose to be burdened in this way. The matter of Silver Hawk's identity was a necessary evil, but to have received both news together must have been crushing. "How did she handle it?"

Robert pursed his lips, scrunching his face. "She raged at Logan, but when told of your death, she cast up her accounts."

He brightened. "Did she?"

"Yes. I'm sorry, but why are you dead? I don't recall your reason."

Sebastian patted Robert's knee. "I'm feeling rather magnanimous at the moment, so why don't we get our arses up off the floor and I'll tell you over a round of ale."

Robert hesitated, peering up at him. "Logan knows of your deception. He saw your father's will."

Ice congealed in his veins. "I did not expect him to remain ignorant of my deeds for long. Besides, he would have acted to regain her favor in any event, regardless of our father's will." He swallowed over a painful lump. "He's in love with her, and she with him. When I was forced into this farce of a life, I left fate to God. It seems He has chosen." He laughed, a self-depreciating sound. "In truth, I never expected any other conclusion to this tale."

Robert wobbled to his feet, frowning. "I do not understand. You knew who Silver Hawk was, what he meant to Rose, and still you sent him to your home?" He stared, baffled. "Why would you do such a thing?"

Sebastian shrugged, striding unevenly toward his abandoned table, throwing himself into a chair. He heaved a tankard up to his lips, pausing when Robert joined him. "You may not believe it of me, Robert, but I do hold your sister close to heart. I care very much for her welfare."

"Then why—"

"Because I committed a grievous act on my part, robbing her of a choice, as you are no doubt aware by now. If you loved a woman and did wrong by her, would you not do all in your power to reverse the grievance?"

Robert paled. "You need not say more. I understand. Perfectly." He shoved to his feet abruptly, stumbling to find a serving wench, bellowing for more ale.

Sebastian reclined, folding his arms, watching. He struck a nerve with his brother-in-law. How curious. He meant to strike at the minuscule nugget that called itself a mind, but it would appear as though he dealt an unintentional fatal blow.

Chapter Fifteen

"You're sick."

"I am not. I am grief-stricken and mourning the loss of my husband." She swallowed a bite of toast, smiling weakly at Lord Edgewood from across the breakfast table as the muscles in her throat worked the bread down to her protesting stomach.

She knew her forehead was hot enough to boil a kettle of tea. And a heaviness saturated her lungs, but it was damn indelicate to speak of it to her. Why the devil couldn't he leave her alone to grieve Sebastian in peace? The man acted as though he were her husband, constantly hovering all the time, behaving much too protective for a sister-in-law. The only good thing about Lord Edgewood's consistent badgering was that it left her precious little time to dwell on Sebastian's mistresses.

She'd been another conquest to her husband. Her brother tried to warn her, as well as Lord Edgewood, but she had been so sure of Sebastian's intent, she never stopped to give her brother or Lord Edgewood's objections proper consideration.

She had been played for a fool.

"I knew you would catch your death after that stunt you pulled last night," Lord Edgewood muttered, shoving a forkful of egg into his mouth. "After the burial service, you are to go straight back to bed."

She stared at him, simmering. "Who are you to give such an order to me? You are not my husband or father. You cannot tell me what to do."

He glared, pushing away his half-eaten breakfast plate. "Are you willing to die just to spite me?"

"What would you care if I did?" She tossed her hair back, her nose in the air. "Then you would be the duke, uncontested by me. A good solution to your problem."

"You are not my problem!"

"Ah ha!" Rose slapped the table with her open palm, cursing the loud ricochet as it set off a headache. "Now we come to the point of this madness. I am not your problem or responsibility, and you will cease treating me as one of your charity cases for Sebastian's victims!"

Lord Edgewood took a deep breath. "I didn't mean it that way."

"Excuse me."

"What?" they both barked in unison, turning together toward the intruder.

A young woman Rose had not seen before stood at the doorway of the dining room. She was long of limb, willowy, and possessed an abundance of pale, flaxen hair.

And she was pregnant.

Her budding headache soared to new heights.

"May I join you?" the woman asked, her voice lilting and light.

Lord Edgewood smiled and stood, holding out a chair for the woman to sit.

An astonishing emotion seized Rose's innards as she was forced to listen to the two of them exchange pleasantries.

Jealousy.

She snorted out loud, unable to credit the feeling. Both Lord Edgewood and the young woman turned to look at her. She shrugged, offering no apologies for her behavior.

Lord Edgewood frowned. "Lady Emily, may I introduce you to Her Grace, Rose Graham, Duchess of Dorchester. Your Grace, this is Lady Emily Harwood—Sebastian's former betrothed."

Lady Emily paled. "Oh dear, I am sorry for the intrusion, Your Grace. This must all seem so improper to you."

Rose smiled over gritted teeth, aiming a withering glare at Lord Edgewood. "On the contrary, Lady Emily. I am learning the words 'improper' and 'Lord Edgewood' go together in nearly every sentence I have uttered since his untimely arrival on my doorstep." She buttered more toast simply for something to do. "Speaking of untimely arrivals, has my brother made an appearance yet?"

Lord Edgewood tugged on his immaculately tied cravat. "I have not seen him." He looked at Lady Emily, changing subjects. "How was your journey here?"

Lady Emily nibbled on toast, her lips twitching upward. "Uncomfortable and long."

Lord Edgewood shot Lady Emily an aggrieved look. "Then why attempt the journey in your condition? You could have declined my invitation."

"A pressing concern," she said, her gaze flitting between her and Lord Edgewood. "One I would speak to you about when you have a moment to spare, Logan."

Rose listened to their discourse, her ire quickly rising at Lady Emily's use of Lord Edgewood's Christian name. What was the nature of their relationship? And how lovely to not be included in their conversation. It would make her escape so much easier.

Dabbing at her mouth, Rose stood then swept away from the table with her head high. The lack of manners exhibited in this house was already inflated beyond bearing. Neither of those two lovebirds would dare voice their objections to her rudeness.

Rose hurried outside, noting the brisk wind tearing at her bound hair and gown, but the fever kept her warm. And her temper. *Devil take the lot of them!* She forged onward, heading into the dead garden. Spying a stone bench near a gazebo, well away from prying eyes, she collapsed, rubbing her temples, unable to come to terms with all that had transpired in her life. Indeed, between two men and a mountain of various grievances, she didn't know who to start cursing at first. If only it would help. It wasn't possible to rant at the dead and receive a reply that proved a healing balm to an open wound.

And Lord Edge—Logan, telling her she alone could boast of having the privilege of knowing his first name. What rubbish. Men were all deceitful, lying whoresons.

Yet why did seeing Lady Emily and Logan together hurt so bloody much?

Rose refused to acknowledge the dreadful answer. Logan was a man no better than her husband, and in many ways, was the worst offender out of the two. So why could her heart not sever their bond? Claim a mistake and move on to adopting kittens, lavishing on them love and devotion?

Her hands fell to clasp her stomach, a darkening shadow on her horizon. Alone and with child. What was she going to do?

Considering the options, she stroked her flat belly. Since marrying Lord Edgewood was not a choice, what position did she stand in the eyes of English law? Certainly, Lord Edgewood could not inherit until Sebastian's child was born and the sex of the baby known. She had time yet to think of her future. If she lived through child-birthing. It would not do to get ahead of herself.

"Must you always run off when presented with a situation not of your liking?"

She straightened in her stone seat. "Must you always come to my rescue? I don't need you."

"Thank God." Lord Edgewood plunked down beside her, uninvited. "Being a hero is exhausting work. Always rushing here or there to rescue women is work for younger men."

Rose rounded on him to give a lecture on the dangers of soliciting unwanted advice but caught the teasing light in his eyes.

"Thank you," he murmured. "I despaired of ever seeing your beautiful eyes on me again after I witnessed you storming away."

She cursed her fluttering heart. "I did not leave in such a manner. I arose as quiet as a church mouse and left the castle the same."

Brown eyes widened in feigned horror. "I thought an earthquake was tearing down the castle when you slammed the front door shut."

"I am certain you were too occupied with Lady Emily to notice a stone roof falling on your hard head."

"Ah ha!" A smile emerged. "The reason for your hasty departure at last revealed."

"I hate you. I do not care whom you fawn over or sing love sonnets to in your free time."

"My relationship with Lady Emily isn't like that." He crowded her space, his expression earnest. "And you don't hate me."

"Really, Lord Edgewood. Do you carry a crystal ball upon your person to know the lay of my thoughts? I don't care what your relationship to the woman is."

"The hell you don't."

Fine. She did care, but not in the way he assumed. She thought herself special, cared for by the men who made her promises. But they all lied! Twisted the truth to suit their own needs. Even her own father abandoned her to pay a debt.

Anger brewed and simmered, waiting to ignite into a fury. She wanted vengeance.

But for now, she would take simply Lord Edgewood giving her room to breathe. "Do you mind?" she snapped. "It's hard enough work to draw breath without having to share it first with you."

Lord Edgewood scowled.

She scowled back.

He slapped a hand against her forehead. "I knew it. You're burning up with fever." Lord Edgewood stood, pointing an imperious finger toward the castle. "You're going back to bed this instant."

"I have a funeral to attend."

His eyes narrowed, anger darkening his brow. "God, my brother must have played the role of loving husband to perfection to command such love and loyalty—even in death." He looked away, clenching his jaw.

She lifted her chin, feeling her back and forehead bead with sweat. Her fever was gaining ground. "We all have roles to play in life, and I will play mine until the end." She managed to stagger to her feet, blessedly unassisted by her hulking male chaperone.

"Perhaps you are right," Lord Edgewood said, grinding the words out. "I was a fool to think you'd be willing to assume another title if requested of you."

She snorted. "I would caution asking anything of me. I am not in the mood to be granting favors." Dear heavens! That was a rather ribald, suggestive thing to say. Still, the words were out, and could not be retracted. "Excuse me," she mumbled, slipping around Lord Edgewood's glowering face.

"Oh, Your Highness?"

She stopped, refusing to whirl around toward him. "What now?"

"The burial service is in the other direction."

"I know that," she huffed, squaring her shoulders, adjusting her course.

He smirked. "You didn't even know your husband long enough for a tour of his estate, did you?"

She marched past him, ignoring his grinning face. *Men!* A racking cough seized her, and she stopped, doubled over, trying to catch her breath.

Lord Edgewood was at her side when she finished. "You need a doctor," he growled.

"Cease pretending you care!" she cried. "I find the pretense of your caring to be nothing more than hollow ash." She folded at the waist with another coughing fit, fighting for breath.

He gripped her elbow, frowning. "Come, let me escort you back to—"

She ripped her elbow free from his hold. "Stop touching me. I can take care of myself without your assistance in the matter."

She moved past him, blindly walking, not knowing where the burial ground was on the estate. She stopped; her chest weighted by a loadstone. But it would be a cold day in hell before she would ask Lord Edgewood for directions.

Besides, she didn't feel like mourning her husband. She was angry. So angry she feared she might throw herself on the coffin in a fit of rage. That would never do. She clutched her skirts, looking down. In fact, she wasn't going to wear black either. She detested the color.

Turning, she headed back toward the castle, skirting Lord Edgewood, averting her face from his. She was walking back and forth like an idiot.

"Rose," he called.

Hearing her name spoken in tender tones broke her restraint. Shoulders sagged, though her eyes remained dry. Strong arms wrapped themselves around her middle, pulling her against a familiar broad chest.

"I'm sorry, Rose," he sighed. "Sometimes I get so caught up in our arguments I forget you're mourning the loss of someone you loved." He stroked her hair with long, light movements of his hand. "I do care about you. I never stopped, and I shall prove it to you one day."

She sniffed, knowing she should pull away, yet unable to perform the simple task. Rose could not explain why, but for some reason, his presence—indeed his arms—offered her greater comfort from her tremulous thoughts than anything else. She didn't want to think of the reasons why she should pull away and didn't want to consider the possibility of staying.

Lord Edgewood did not release her from his arms, nor did she ask. In fact, she pressed her cheek against his chest, inhaling his scent. *Sandalwood.* Sebastian's clothes smelled similar, but the man himself carried another scent altogether different than Lord Edgewood. An elusive aroma of man and spice, a smell forever now denied her.

The knowledge was crushing, erasing the sudden appeal of Lord Edgewood. Anger was a shallow disguise to deeper emotions. Something was working itself free from within, and it had precious little to do with her lung's offering of phlegm.

Lord Edgewood must have sensed her withdrawal. He extracted himself, taking a step away to search her face.

"Good morning," called a pleasant female voice.

Rose cringed.

Please, dear God, let this not be another pretty young woman.

Breathing hard, ignoring the whistle in her breathing now, Rose looked to see an older lady with black hair walking toward them. She uttered a silent prayer of thanks that the woman wasn't young or with child.

She approached Lord Edgewood and kissed his cheek.

"Mother," he said, raising a brow. "May I introduce you to Her Grace? Rose, this is my mother, Lady Delphine."

Rose nodded but had to force herself not to wince when the older woman's gaze sharpened on her face.

"My child, you are not well. You should be in bed." She turned to Lord Edgewood. "Logan, shame on you for trying to kiss this child when she has a fever and needs medical attention."

He blushed, but his smile was unrepentant.

Rose thought he looked charming, standing there beneath his mother's withering gaze, solid and steadfast, but still coloring as though he were in the school room.

"Mother, I did try."

"Indeed," she chimed in, blinking at the husky sound of her voice. She wasn't usually this deep. "But I am a stubborn woman not easily persuaded."

Lady Delphine's eyes twinkled. "Back in my day, when a young woman did not fall to command, she was hoisted up over her husband's shoulders and carried away to private quarters where her husband corrected her behavior."

Rose laughed. "Allow me to guess the rest—her bottom was then blistered or kissing ensued to bring the young woman to such heights she would lose her senses." She chuckled. "Lady Delphine, I am too old to believe in such nonsense. There is never a moment where a woman can lose such command of her mind. A man's kiss is not that poignant."

Logan stared at her with that dark, wild gaze of his, and her heart jumped in response.

His mother simply smiled. "Well," she said, "it was a long time ago when men behaved as brutes. Time has moved on from such behaviors, perhaps." She looked at Logan and winked. "I am heading to the service, my dear. Please take care of your charge." Lady Delphine walked away, her blue gown buffeting her body from a sudden breeze.

Rose glanced aside to Lord Edgewood, then performed a double take. She backed away. "I am not your charge," she warned him, "neither am I your wife. You cannot take your mother's advice to heart."

He stalked forward as she retreated, but her strength quickly waned, and she stopped, choosing to face whatever he planned. A beating might be just the thing to expel the mucus from her lungs. She hoped in vain.

Cupping her face, he said, "After the service, you are going straight back to bed."

"You're not going to kiss me senseless?"

His eyes darkened. "Would you like me to?"

"Yes. I spit in your breakfast repeatedly this morning, but the plague hasn't hit you yet. Perhaps a kiss will hasten it along."

Groaning, he took her elbow, escorting her in the direction his mother selected. "Your manners are terrible. How did my brother stomach your bold tongue?"

Remembering better times, she smiled. "He found my tongue to his liking as I recall."

Stiffening, Lord Edgewood dropped the subject, not daring to utter another word.

There were few people at the service; not even Sebastian's loyal servants attended. She found herself clinging to Lord Edgewood's arm as the vicar droned on. Lord Edgewood did not push her away to a more proper distance, and she was thankful. Knowing her husband's body was so close, and not being able to see him, was unbearably hard. More so than she wanted to admit. His absence was beginning to hit home, and she cared not for the emptiness gauging her soul. She touched her stomach, catching an errant emotion new to her. It was fleeting, but devastating, nonetheless.

She tucked the thought away, to give it closer inspection when she was alone. Beads of sweat rolled down her back and moistened her brow, despite the brisk wind in the air.

The service ended, and Lord Edgewood turned at once to her. "As you promised, young lady, go back to bed."

"Is that what you say to all your charges? They await your pleasure as you command?"

He blinked before anger took over his surprised expression. "My *charges,* as you call them, can follow my command without question—a sign of trust and respect. Traits I have yet to earn from you, I know. But Rose," he glanced at his mother, approaching them, and leaned his mouth close to her ear, "I will earn it, and you will fall to my command one day soon. And may even come to love me."

She gasped. "Lord Edgewood, you are too bold!" Rose turned on her heels and fled. On a scale of one to ten, she daresay Lord Edgewood's vow ranked somewhere between the most arrogant and the most preposterous words ever uttered by a man. Pssh! *Fall to command* as if she were a well-heeled dog.

She stopped, considering, and changed direction. She needed time alone and doubted the odious man would give her a second of it to call her own. There could be little harm in indulging in a quick ride to gain a measure of space. She'd not go far, just far enough.

Chapter Sixteen

"What do you mean he's not dead?" Lady Delphine cried. "Yet you dally with his wife? It's unlike you to do something so dishonorable, Logan!"

Despite the early hour of the day, Logan sipped a brandy. "My intentions toward young Rose have always been honorable," he argued, "I have treated her as a sister." He refrained from flinching at his outright lie, but his mother was no fool.

She wagged a finger at him. "I may be an old woman, but I know passion when I see it in a man's eye, and you Logan Sandhurst are far removed from brotherly affection. That was not what I witnessed when watching the two of you together. That was not you with another one of Sebastian's victims. You treat those girls with brotherly affection, but that is not what lights your eyes when Rose is by your side."

"Is it so wrong to want a wife and family of my own?" he snapped.

"Rose already has those things," his mother stated in a firm voice. "I love you Logan, but your quest for revenge will bring her nothing save for grief. Why would you be responsible for such a thing if you love Rose? Do you think she will view you as a hero for killing her husband?" She shook her head. "I tell you she will not see it as a kindness, as so many of us would. I have watched Rose, and I do not believe Sebastian roughly used her. No, you cannot kill Sebastian and keep Rose too. She would never forgive you, and you would lose her, son."

"Don't you think I know that?" He prayed every day for a solution to this mess, but no deity with a crystal ball was forthcoming. "He doesn't deserve that woman, Mother. I'm not sure I do, either, but damn it! I want the chance to try. After all I've done to help others, can I not reward myself? Must every dream I have be forever out of reach?"

"Logan," Lady Delphine dabbed her eyes, "not every dream dreamt is meant to come true. There are times when we must accept what is not meant to be. This might be one of those times for you."

Logan stared at his drink, wrestling with the remnants of a conscience, weighing the consequence of listening to his mother's words.

Lady Delphine stood from her chair. "At the very least, I suggest you cease parading all of Sebastian's victims in front of Rose and let them go back home. She knows her husband was a libertine."

"I will make arrangements," he promised, eager despite himself for a reprieve from the chaos. "But for now, I am going upstairs to check on Rose."

"Oh no, you don't." His eyes widened as his mother glared him back into a sitting position on the settee. "She is married still by your admission, and you will treat her as a gentleman should. I will see to her needs."

Amused, Logan watched his mother stalk out of the salon. He had no intention of letting his mother keep him away from Rose, but for now, he would concede the battle. She'd figure out sooner or later his bedchamber was adjoined to Rose's. He'd have hell to pay when that day came. But he was not moving her so far away. If for no other reason, then he needed to watch over her—keep her safe from Sebastian, in case he should appear in the castle.

Just the very thought of his half-brother on top of Rose boiled his blood beyond endurance. But Logan forced it back with a quick swallow of liquor. He could not change the past. But he'd be damned if Sebastian got the upper hand on him again. He was not a man who made the same mistake twice.

The rapid patter of feet reached his ears, and he stiffened, wondering what disaster had befallen one of the children or women now. But it was his mother who barreled into the salon, red of face and out of breath.

Logan shot up from his chair, knocking his glass to the floor. "What has happened?"

"Rose," she panted, "is gone."

A cold, hard fist clutched his heart, but on its heels, came raw fury. "Search the house," he snapped. "Grab everyone and set them to the task. I will search the grounds." He took quick, angry strides out of the salon and down the hall to the front doors. His mind worked furiously, thinking where Rose might have gone. What would he do if he was grieving and heartbroken?

I'd take a long ride on Jupiter.

Praying he was wrong, he cut a path to the stable. He pushed the massive barn doors aside, his gaze falling on the stable boy. "You there," he called. "Did Her Grace come by here recently?"

The boy's head bobbed. "Yes, My Lord. She took Greta for a ride about half hour ago."

"Which direction did she ride," he growled. "Toward the village?"

The youth shook his head. "West," he said. "To the forest."

Of course, she did. Why did he think Rose would merely go to market? No, she would pick the most dangerous route to go for a ride.

"Saddle my stallion," he commanded, his eyes narrowing. "And be quick about it."

Turning on his heel, he rushed back inside the castle to grab his pistols, stomping upstairs to his bedchamber. The words *Rose* and *trouble* were fast becoming nigh inseparable in a sentence. How Robert managed to bring his sister to England in one piece was a bloody mystery to him.

On that note, Logan reached inside his chest and grabbed a knife for his boot, a rapier for the belt on his waist, in addition to three more pistols.

He passed Lady Emily heading out the door, glancing her way only when the sound of a giggle escaped her lips. "What?" he snapped over his shoulder, pausing at the door's threshold.

She bit her lip to stifle the amusement he saw shining in her eyes. "Forgive me, Lord Edgewood. You appear armed to lay siege to a castle or small army."

"I'm going after Rose," he bit out.

"Ah." Her expression softened. "Going after the woman you love. That does explain the unnecessary armory."

"Unnecessary?" He snorted. "Forgive me, Lady Emily, but you do not know the woman who bears the title of duchess in this house. She is willful, spiteful, stubborn, and witless—"

"Lord Edgewood?" she interrupted with a smile.

He was forced to pause from listing Rose's finer points. He raised a brow.

Lady Emily made shooing motions with her hands. "I understand, now go rescue your love and bring her back home."

His love. Home.

He swallowed back the tide of strong emotion pushing at his heart. What he wouldn't give to have those words be true. He nodded and turned, unsure if he was setting himself on the path of villain or hero in this rescue attempt.

Whatever the role he chose to play, one thing was dead certain—Rose was coming home with him. Willing or not.

~ * ~

An hour on horseback never left Rose feeling more aware of every aching body part than it did at that moment. Vengeance was a notion for the healthy to embrace. She had no business riding in the cold, with nary a cloak, or proper clothing. At least her fever kept her warm. And delusional. Was that a man in black clothes and mask riding across an open field toward her? Was the whole of England besieged by highwaymen?

She had no quarterstaff or purse to satisfy this thief's lust. If he was of a mind to roughly use her body, at least he would die of whatever plague she was being affected by.

Too sick to run or fight, Rose pulled her horse to a stop and waited.

The man nudged his horse into a canter, slowing to a halt about a hundred yards away. "Good day, my lady."

The deep baritone sounded familiar to her ears. She focused her attention on his appearance. A black mask hid his face, but deep blue eyes stared back at her with open interest, boarding on affection. A wild growth of hair covered the lower jaw, and dark golden hair was cropped close around the ears and neck.

With exception to the beard, his resemblance to Sebastian was uncanny.

And she found herself growing agitated in his presence.

"Let us dispense with frivolous conversation and get down to business," she said, her voice hoarse and raspy.

The highwayman's gaze sharpened on her face. "You are sick."

A horrible racking cough delayed a witty, intelligent reply consisting of two words: I know. When at last she gained breath, the highwayman stood beside her on his horse.

He tugged a glove off, touching a hand to her cheek. His gaze jerked to her face. "You are very sick, madam. Come here. You are in no condition to be riding alone."

The tone of command was as familiar to her as the voice, but it could not be. She just buried her husband. This man was very much alive. The fever was confusing her mind.

She offered no resistance when the highwayman heaved her from the saddle, into his arms, settling her limp body in his lap. "If you think to ravish me now," she warned, "you'll die of the plague."

His laughter boomed. Chucking her chin, he grinned. "Then I better behave myself." He nudged the horse forward, his arms cradling her with gentle pressure.

Rose's face jostled against a warm chest, and she nearly wept for the comfort of it. "Where do you take me?" she asked. The man's actions and attitude did not seem of violent intent. "What about my horse?"

"I am bringing you back home first, then your horse."

"You do not know where I live."

"I am a highwayman. I make it my business to know everything about everyone in this county."

"Of course." She was dubious, but who was she to argue with her warm blanket. "Then you must know the vexing Lord Edgewood. He has set himself upon me in the most terrible fashion."

The highwayman wrenched his back upright so fast it cracked in three places. "Lord Edgewood *set* himself upon you?"

She yawned, wondering at the rapidly beating heart beneath her warm cheek. "Oh yes! He thinks I'm with child, and he is always pestering me to stay in bed, or eat my food, or stay off the ledge in the rain and dark of night. Things that sorely test my temper."

A finger nudged her chin up, and she found herself staring into a familiar tender gaze. "Madam, are you with child?"

She ignored the question, too caught up in the familiarity of this masked thief to Sebastian. The last time a pair of blue eyes looked this way was when Sebastian was making love to her for the first time, attempting to calm her fears of the marriage act.

Unbidden, the face of the little boy who gave her the flower surged to mind.

How many other women had her husband treated to the same view? How many had he charmed and seduced, leaving them with broken hearts and filled wombs?

Grief and anger pushed her over the edge. "Put. Me. Down."

The highwayman blinked, the affection melting from his eyes. "Excuse me?"

She began to struggle within his arms, desperate to be free of his touch. "You're too much like him. Leave me be. Leave me—"

Twin vices locked around her torso, throwing her up against a boulder for a chest. "Cease your mad tantrum, woman, and start talking sense before you hurt yourself or the…the baby."

His throat moved with his swallow, as though he were overcome with deep emotion, acting as though he were the father.

It was the last straw.

Sobs squeezed out from her closed mouth, choking the breath from her lungs. A dam had burst within her heart, from an injury she did not know she'd been bearing.

"Christ." The highwayman halted the horse, swinging from the saddle with her in his arms, cradling her as he carried her to a sprawling oak tree, sitting beneath it on the sparse grass. "Madam, would you care to unburden yourself before you drown in tears?" He eased her head away from his chest, smiling into her eyes. "I can't swim, but I'd be happy to listen."

His teasing smile made her cry harder.

He groaned at the new flood, rubbing her back in rough, tight circles. "I'm terrible at calming females, not having much practice at it. What can I do to help?"

A wild, mad thought claimed her mind. This thief was unusually accommodating, so perhaps he wouldn't mind her asking a strange favor. "You look like my husband, sir."

His muscles tensed beneath her. "Do I?"

"Yes, and I buried him today."

"Are those the reasons for your tears?" He brushed at the lingering wetness on her cheeks with bare fingers. "I'm sorry for your loss. You must have cared for him," he added in a whisper.

She grabbed his fingers, pulling them from her face. "Yes, I cared, but more than that, I didn't get to say goodbye."

"I see."

With reckless courage strengthening her resolve, she stood, ignoring the world as it spun in circles. "I would ask a favor, sir. Since you bear an uncanny resemblance to my husband, would you pretend to be him so I can say a proper goodbye?"

The highwayman stood, bowing. "It would be my honor, madam." He straightened and stepped closer, arms at his side.

Taking a deep, rattling breath, her hand lashed out.

Then smacked him across his masked cheek.

"That's for not waiting to see a doctor."

His booted foot met the heel of her slippers.

"That's for getting me with child when you knew how I feared having baby."

Next she pummeled his broad chest.

"That's for dying and leaving me alone with child."

Thumping his chest again, she swayed. "And that's for..."

She couldn't bring herself to mention Sebastian's mistresses, or victims, as Logan believed. It was too embarrassing a detail to share. Letting the sentence go unfinished she sank to the ground, exhausted by her outburst. Sweat mingled with tears on her face.

The highwayman cautiously sank to the earth beside her.

Rose focused on the dying grass. "I was eight and ten when told I would have to marry a stranger and go live in a country I'd never been to, without family or friends to offer company or solace. Can you imagine, thief, what it is like to not be able to control your life, but be made victim of it? I trusted my father, and he betrayed me."

He reached for her hand, threading his fingers through hers. "I understand."

Surprised at his answer, she inclined her head to the side, only to find his gaze on the horizon in the direction of her home.

"I'm sure it is always a defining moment when a girl realizes there are no heroes in life," he said. "And the only rescues guaranteed are the ones forged by her own hands."

"Yes!"

He smiled. "I am of a similar mind. Even if chivalry does not exist outside the pages of a fairytale, men do. And what are we? Not angels of God, surely, or Lucifer in all his frightening glory. No, men are beasts locked between good and evil, and women suffer for it. I know they do. Men suffer too, from broken dreams and hearts that will not mend."

She squeezed his hand. "Who wounded you?"

"My mother," he said without delay. "Father was a cruel man, infatuated with himself and the power his title afforded him. He used to beat my mother and made me watch, telling me it would make me a better man. Eventually, she died, leaving me alone with the monster. The monster groomed me well, but even as I tried to please him, there was always one who pleased him more. My half-brother."

"Did he treat women as badly as your father?"

"God no. He honored them. Elevated them above his own welfare. He lived by his own code of honor, and my father respected him for it. Made him a member of the peerage. Brought him into our home and paraded him around in front of me."

"Was your father so proud of him then?"

He frowned. "No. Rather the opposite. But I made the mistake of letting my father know how much my half-brother's perfection bothered me. It became a means of torture then to the old man. So, I left home. Bought a commission in the army."

"You were a soldier? How dreadful."

"It didn't last long. By the time I arrived back home…"

She laid a comforting hand on his slackened arm. "Your father did not welcome you back?"

He shuddered, then pulled himself together, smiling down at her. "My father found other pursuits while I was away. I was no more than an afterthought to him."

She peered into the guarded expression, experiencing a feeling of one who has heard a story before but not being able to place it right away. "Your life sounds dismal. I hope you achieved a measure of happiness for yourself."

He chortled. "Indeed, I did." He sobered. "For a time. In a marriage to a beautiful, brave young woman."

"Did you love her?"

The highwayman stared hard into her eyes. "Yes."

A moment of silence passed between them, and it was hard to ignore the poignant pain consuming her chest. "Then why are you a criminal, working outside the law? I thought your father was titled?"

He glanced away. "We do what we must, so those we love may have a better life."

Feeling a kinship with him, she leaned over and kissed his masked cheek. "A better life for a woman shall always include having the man she loves by her side."

Surprise slackened her jaw when tears glistened in the thief's eyes.

"I know," he said, "but I cannot let go. And a child changes everything."

"There are other ways for a poor man to support his family. Surely there must be honest work out there for you."

He laughed an unhappy sound. "As I said, there are no heroes here. Only lofty dreams and stark reality."

A horse whinnied in the distance, entering the open glen where Rose sat with her wayward highwayman. She caught sight of a familiar form astride a black stallion. Logan.

"I have to go," she said, whirling to address the highwayman. "Thank you for—"

His lips rushed up to grind against hers.

She pushed, and he released her, his eyes somber and forlorn.

"I don't want you to go," he whispered, "but neither can I ask you to stay." His gaze drifted to Logan. "There would be a conflict."

Unsure of the thief's motives when he had a wife he loved; she could only nod her agreement. "Yes, Lord Edgewood is very protective of me."

Blue eyes sliced her. "As well he should be with a pregnant widow in his care." He jerked his head in Logan's direction. "Go then. Before he finds me."

She stood and hurried away across the open field as best her wobbly legs could carry her. It was a blessing to find this strange highwayman. Talking to him did, in fact, make her feel better, as though she truly had been given a chance to say goodbye to her husband.

But it was not long before the highwayman called out to her from behind. "Get down!" he ordered, lunging to the ground.

Rose followed suit without question, but with less dramatic flair, and more of a disjointed belly flop.

"Careful." He tossed a look of disapproval her way before directing his attention toward Logan.

"Fear not, strange thief. I may have eaten poorly this morning, but I assure you there's enough fat on my body to properly cushion a growing babe. Now what pray tell are we on the ground staring at?"

Smirking, the highwayman's gaze trailed from her head down to her toes and back up, meeting her stare. "I guess I'll have to take your word on that. As for your Lord Edgewood," he pointed, "there's two men approaching him from the east. They don't look to be in the talking mood, if you get my point."

She didn't, but she nodded, nonetheless, not wanting the stranger to know he was being humored. Logan slowed his mount, his attention riveted on the impromptu visitors. They approached Jupiter with slow steps, their hands out in front of them, acting cautious. His expression was ominous. No one likes surprise visitors even in the best of moods.

"I do not understand," she finally confessed after a few minutes. "This all seems harmless to me."

The highwayman's gaze was stuck fast on the trio. "No. This is a setup. The men are a decoy."

Rose propped her chin in a palm. "How do you know that?"

"Because there's a third man coming up behind Lord Edgewood unnoticed. They're thieves."

"Acquaintances of yours?"

Blue eyes rolled. "Hardly. Madam, just because I'm a highwayman, does not mean I am personally familiar with all criminals."

"You knew what the men were up to. It implies familiarity."

"It implies experience. You know," the highwayman turned to scowl at her, "you jump to conclusions much too swiftly. I suppose if a man steals a loaf of bread under your watchful eye, he must be nothing more than a degenerate thief. Do you never look beyond a man's actions and have a deeper thought? Such as what motivated the man to steal in the first place? A hungry family, perhaps?"

Rose dropped the supporting hand from her chin. "Are you accusing me of being naive?"

"Maybe. Young and immature, to be sure."

"Well you're a man. I'm surprised your eyes have stayed on my face the entirety of your tedious lecture. Surely your hands must be itching to hike up the hem to my frock by now."

"Quite frankly yes. I'm entertaining fantasies of blistering that porcelain round ass of yours with the palm of my hand. Now be quiet."

"Ha! My backside is pockmarked and square as a nail head. And I never plead for pardons from men. Just ask my father."

The highwayman shifted to look at her. "Excuse me?"

"He tried to curtail my willful ways more than once in my childhood by using a strap. Let me say only that I'm a slow learner."

The highwayman regarded her for a full minute without blinking, then inched forward, his masked head close enough for Rose to make out her reflection in his clear blue eyes. Raspy breathing hitched. *No! No, it cannot be. Sebastian is dead!*

"Madam," came a husky murmur, "should the day ever come where my hand finds your backside, I promise you it will be for your pleasure only." Pupils dilated; a silent promise made.

She gaped, unable to rip her gaze away from an invisible tether, bound to her and held by the masked man, as he reeled her closer still by the sheer force of his gaze. Her lips parted. A word emerged. "Sebastian," she sighed, raising her chin, touching her lips to his.

The man stilled, his lips frozen shut. Not a rustle of air passed from his nose.

She grew uncertain in her convictions. Confused, she began to pull away...

Only to be tugged into a familiar embrace by loving arms and rolled underneath a lithe body, as a firm mouth claimed her lips in a searing kiss, wiping away any doubts. "Rose," Sebastian's ragged voice groaned. "Oh God, love, I've missed you so." His touch grew gentle, the fire in his eyes mellowing into something softer, but no less fierce.

If only Logan had let her eyes remain closed to her husband's past, what a happy reunion this might have been. But the wounds were too fresh. The women and children still resided inside her and Sebastian's home, filling her ears with sounds and eyes with sights not to be forgotten.

Wiggling her hands in between their touching bodies, she pushed, gaining release. Tears gathered, threatening to become deep pools. "Why, Sebastian?" She meant the women.

He brushed away the wetness, trying in vain to stem its flow. "Darling, I can explain in time. I'm sorry."

The simple apology was no more effective than putting a thin strip of linen over a gaping wound. Her husband likely thought he was acknowledging the mockery of his supposed death. She wished with all her shrinking heart that lie was his only crime.

The clamor of male voices raised in anger diverted both their attention from the other.

Sebastian jerked his head up, rising above the grass. "What the *hell?"*

Gun shots and two sharp whistles from Logan halted further words.

Rose gasped, breaking free from Sebastian, lurching upward. Logan shot the two men talking to him, while Jupiter kicked out with his hind legs, bringing down the third man approaching from Logan's rear position.

Her head spun, her mind reeling from the violence and suddenness of Logan's attack.

Sebastian was not so affected. "Christ! He's heading this way. Get down!" He drew Rose underneath his body without hesitation, taking care not to smother her with his weight. "Be very quiet," he whispered into her ear. "Hopefully the grass will hide us, and Edgewood will pass us without incident."

She waited, clinging to Sebastian, listening to the sound of rustling grass, and the dull thud of hooves striking earth. He was tense, his fear bleeding through to her, confusing her thoughts. Logan would not hurt her, would he?

Uncertainty kept her quiet, her mind twisting upon itself as she sought an explanation for her silent tongue. Sebastian's weight, albeit light, was becoming too much for her labored lungs to endure. The urge to cough was of paramount concern.

"Greta?" Logan's voice carried on the wind, laced with anxiety. "Is that you? Oh God. Rose! Rose! Can you hear me?"

The fear in his voice caused more tears to prick Rose's eyes, blurring Sebastian's face. "Let go!" she muttered, twisting her head to hack into the dirt. "Logan must think those men harmed me," she rasped. "I can't let him think that!"

Sebastian pressed upon her with more weight. *"Logan must think those men harmed you?"*

Oh dear.

"Rose! Darling, where are you?"

Sebastian tensed at Logan's endearment. *"Darling?"* he snarled, his body fast becoming a mass of trembles and spasms. "Over my dead body!" Blue flames leaped from eyes promising more brimstone and death than Armageddon.

I'm going to die.

Rose opened her mouth to scream, or to make an observation, she wasn't quite certain. Certainly, no inane comment on the weather could work at a time like this. An apology would be the worst offense. Her husband was no fool. Yes, not only was her husband not dead or an idiot, but spent his youth attempting to populate the whole of England. And he dares to place himself on a moral pedestal and look down on her?

He slapped a hand over her open mouth, digging gloved fingers into the hollow of her cheeks. "Don't say one word," he growled. "Not one. Your precious Silver Hawk is heading away from us. I want to keep it that way."

"Mmmph an arghugh."

Sebastian lowered his lips to her ear, giving her lobe a gentle brush. "Quiet, woman."

The goosebumps raised at his slight touch sank back into oblivion. Arrogant ducal commands were not as arousing as one might think. She considered her options. When dealing with a strong husband with a rock for a body, there was only one path available.

Her knee shot up between her husband's legs, connecting with a part of him most assuredly not made of stone.

The bluster fell from his face. A howl wrenched free from his compressed lips as he surged off her, clutching at himself.

"Rose?" Logan called from a much further distance away.

She rolled onto her side, propping her head against a closed fist, watching Sebastian writhe. "Quiet husband, you mustn't say a word. Not one. We wouldn't want your beloved brother to find us." She frowned. "What makes you think Lord Edgewood is Silver Hawk?"

He cast her a glare to make a lesser woman cower. "You're not protecting him, Rose. I've always known Silver Hawk's identity. Why do you think I sent him to you in my absence?"

Her mouth fell open. She stared hard at the masked face, searching for any hint of a jest. "You…you sent Lord Edgewood to me, knowing he was the highwayman I—" She caught herself before uttering a word that would hurt her husband. She glanced away, ashamed.

Sebastian grunted as he shifted into a sitting position. He caught her staring and offered a sardonic smile. "By all means wife, finish you sentence." When nothing but silence answered his taunt, he supplied his own reply. "Love? Was my *wife* admitting to loving another man? What ho!" He laughed, an unhappy, derisive sound. "I thought when I sent Lord Edgewood to you and you discovered Silver Hawk's true identity, your infatuation would evaporate, not gain in

148

enthusiasm."

"I do *not* love Lord Edgewood."

Sebastian stared hard and long into her eyes before shaking his head. "I do not know what you two share but it is not a bond of hatred. And it is something I am not a part of."

"Don't be silly. We share no tether to the other."

"Once more, Duchess, you are proving your youth and inexperience." He winced, getting to his knees. "It's a simple enough dilemma, though I cannot figure out which of the two you are most affected by."

"Really, Sebastian. My mood does not favor a game of riddles at this moment."

"Love or lust, Rose. That's what I'm referring to."

"I do *not* love or want —"

"You do, Duchess," he interrupted with quiet dignity. "I think you're experiencing one more than the other. I just wished to hell I knew which it was."

Her right eye was beginning to twitch. "You're not listening to me. Why in heaven's name would I love or lust after the man who ordered a company of soldiers to attack three innocent young women?"

"If I knew the answer to that question, Rose, I'd be a happier husband."

She was grinding her teeth to pebbles. "The answer is irrelevant, anyway. You're not dead. I'm still married. However else I feel, it matters naught. I am your wife."

"My *faithful* wife?" A hard edge crept into his deep voice.

"'Tis your child filling my womb, is it not?"

"Is it?" he shot back, gaining his feet, towering over her.

Anger blossomed, a welcome friend to evict her guilt. She stared him down as she stood, yearning for a mounting block or tree stump so she could use the height to her advantage. "I wish I could claim to be the village light-skirt, but sadly, I cannot! Mrs. Brown can vouch for me if my word is no longer to be trusted. I was a solitary, pathetic figure gracing the halls of your home for over a month while you fretted and whiled away your time in London, dancing attendance on ladies more suited to your station."

His mouth now fell open. "Is that what you think I did while away? Attend balls and house parties flirting with widows and debutantes?"

Her chin sailed up, daring him to lie.

Full lips pressed together into a thin line, while blue daggers took aim at her face. His hand shot up, ripping his mask off. "Have you forgotten what your husband looks like?" he snarled. "Well, I can assure you, the *ton* have not, and no woman, young or old, would dare associate with the monster of Dorchester Castle!" His bellow echoed around the clearing.

Letting the silence hover, she stepped up to him, staring into a shuttered, wintry gaze. She placed a hand on his heaving chest, feeling the rapid patter of his heart. "My dearest husband," she whispered, "I do believe some women dared. I've seen their faces, met their children—or should I say *your* children." Her hand dropped away. "Your by-blows, are they not?" She cursed her thickening voice. "Have you even met them? Know of their existence? Their names? Anything?" She babbled as tears ran in fat rivulets down her cheeks. "There's Thomas, a dear boy with your hair color and eyes. And Mary, a shy girl with a penchant for sweets. And oh! Charles of course…"

Her voice stuck in her throat, and she turned, feeling herself fall apart, bewildered by the sharp pain in her chest.

Gloved hands gripped her shoulders, bruising tender flesh. Hot breath blew across an ear. "A pitiful act, from a poor actress. I should know. I bedded enough of them. Being heir to one of the richest duchy's in England had benefits up until recent years."

His harsh laughter ripped open another wound, scarring an organ tender and new to emotional havoc. She shrugged his touch from her person, stepping away. "Was one of those benefits bedding women who did not consent to your touch?" She stared ahead, too much of a coward to face him. Her back tingled in awareness as warmth touched her back, radiating from the closeness of another body.

"The only woman I've ever bedded who did not beg for my touch was my *wife*."

The low voice was laced with venom. Accusation. Hurt.

Hurt?

She couldn't injure him. He spoke of her as a possession. Something he owned, not someone he loved. She was a token bestowed on him. A gift from her father for sparing their home from being plundered, their land looted and left barren of livestock or food. She was nothing and was bartered away with nary a thought toward her wishes or desires. Why would she mean anything to him? He didn't even know her. She could not hurt a boulder with a scoff of her foot, no more than she could pierce the heart of the Duke of Dorchester after only being married six weeks.

He had no right to sound as though she caused him pain.

She may have elevated Logan beyond his worthiness, but at least she kept to her marriage vows. She was nothing if not a loyal possession. She coughed into her arm. A plague-ridden possession.

Spinning around, she said, "I may not be the loyal prize you wanted," jabbing a forefinger into his sizable pectoral muscles, "but if you had given my tongue a rest that day in your study, I would have told you your touch was wanted and I would have begged for it."

That sounded remarkably like a compliment. *Drat!* She meant to cause grave insult. She tried again, wiping her face. It was hot out for an October day, was it not?

She redoubled her efforts to slander. "What I…err…meant to say was you surpassed all my expectations of the marriage bed duties."

God's blood! Did another flattering remark pass her lips? At least her husband stopped scowling at her. Though who could tell the lay of his thoughts beneath that beard? Goodness, its length would have made a French fur trapper proud. What possessed him to grow such a wild wealth of hair on his handsome face? It's not as though he had need of further adornment.

He narrowed his eyes. "Rose, you're sweating."

She offered her husband praise, and he retaliated by making ungracious comments on her perspiration habits. How dare he! "It's unseasonably warm out," she snapped.

Flurries peppered their faces with wet kisses.

Sebastian stepped forward.

She retreated, trying to keep a fair amount of grass between them.

He was beside her in two quick strides. He clamped both bare hands on either side of her face, squishing her cheeks together so her mouth was forced to pucker like a fish.

"Your face could fry an egg," he grumbled, releasing her. "Stay here. Now that Silver Hawk is gone, we can go." He marched toward his tethered mount.

"Go? But where?" she called to his fleeing backside. "You're dead, playing the part of highwayman, rescuing damsels in distress. Avoiding your wife in favor of other women. And I'm a widowed duchess doomed to die by childbirth or plague. You've committed yourself to this new life, and I believe I should seek out Lord Edgewood and leave you to it."

He whirled. "You are my wife," he bellowed. "You will do as I command!"

"I am a woman!" she shouted back, wishing her voice did not sound so hoarse. "With a mind and will of her own. You," she pointed at his tall figure, "shall soon know the bitter truth of it."

She fisted her skirts, launching herself toward Greta, though the dratted horse kept splitting into two images. Cursing assaulted her ears in loud, ringing tones. The perfect background music to her mad dash to freedom.

But the run was cut short.

Another man on a giant black stallion arrived on the opposite end of the field.

Lord Edgewood. Naturally he heard a female yelling and came racing to help the poor addled woman from all manner of villainy. The man even came prepared, carrying a veritable armory in his clothing. Weapons of all shapes and sizes littered his person as a street hawker might be so encumbered selling his wares in a village square.

Rose halted; taken back by the black look he was directing behind her back. Toward Sebastian. Logan's eyes promised death and blood.

She turned, noting she now stood directly in between the two men. Her husband was mounted, returning Logan's silent message with one of his own—*stay away from my wife.*

Her parched throat convulsed, fear swelling fast and swift. A confrontation was imminent. Logan was well-armed. This must have been the reason Sebastian hid her in the grass.

Thinking only of her husband, she flung herself at Greta, jumping up into the saddle with more gusto than her body seemed capable of, spurring her gentle beast into a gallop then heading for the forest.

She caught the sound of her name carried on a breeze, and she risked a look behind. Jupiter's long strides were eating the distance between their two mounts.

Sebastian was closing on her position from the side, swinging in at an arc.

Sweat beaded her forehead, her breathing as labored as Greta's. She leaned over the horse's neck, patting a lathered coat. Her dear companion needed a rest. And a nap sounded wonderful if she were being truthful. Her strength was fast waning. A choice was needing to be made.

She snorted. It wasn't much of a decision.

If the men were occupied with chasing her, then they wouldn't be fighting with each other. She must keep the game going.

Nearing the tree line, she urged Greta faster, crossing the threshold into the dense shrubbery. Prickly branches tore at her face and hair, before a trail came into view. She directed Greta there, spying the answer to her dilemma dead ahead.

She hadn't done this trick since her skirts were lowered. And she had been in much better health. But this was for a good cause—keeping her husband alive.

Standing in the stirrups, she dropped the reins, balancing, then stretching her arms overhead. As she approached the tree, she ducked her head, said a prayer and grasped the rough bark as it whacked into her hand. Latching on, Rose felt her feet leave the stirrups, and Greta raced on without her.

Rose sighed. That was the easy part.

Swinging her legs back and forth like a pendulum, she gained enough momentum to haul herself up onto the long, mercifully sturdy oak branch. Gathering her skirts around her feet, she pressed back against the trunk, as the sound of galloping hooves neared.

Holding her breath, she looked down.

Without slowing, Logan raced past.

At the pounding of a second set of hooves, Rose quickly gripped the branch, casting herself over the side to the ground below.

Sebastian swore, yanking on his mount's reins, causing his horse to rear, pawing at air.

She crashed on the dirt path as a tangled mass of limbs and fabric, while her husband got his steed under control. Virulent cursing assaulted her ears. She would guess her husband would not be offering praise for getting them out of a potentially dangerous situation. Indeed, had it been her father glaring at her from atop his horse in such a manner, she would wager a strap to her backside would be in her immediate future.

She didn't care to receive a beating in her current condition. Exhaustion and a wheezing sound were punishment enough for her foolish behavior.

Blinking, she jumped to find Sebastian beside her, hoisting her into his arms.

"I don't know how you managed that in your condition," he said, leaping up into the saddle while managing not to tumble her from her perch, "and I'm not going to ask."

"I stood up in the stirrups while Greta was running and grabbed the tree branch while she kept going."

Sebastian swore underneath his breath, settling her in front of him, cradling her as a babe to a mother's breast. He turned the horse around, taking them in the opposite direction of Logan. "Did it not occur to you that you're a mother and should behave with respect to your new title?"

"Am I not also a wife with a duty to protect her husband?"

"You're confusing my vows with yours. You agreed to obey

your husband. It's *my* job to protect *you*." He kissed her forehead, placing a cheek against her hot skin. "In sickness and in hell." Touching his heels to the horse, he directed their flight through the cold winter air, eyes intent on the countryside as it blurred by.

He jerked when she placed a hand on his unmasked face, commanding his attention.

"I could not bury you twice in one day," she murmured, holding his incredulous gaze. "Once was quite enough."

She cuddled against his chest when he fell silent, his heart thudding in a rapid staccato beneath her cheek, belying the impression that her words meant nothing to him.

Chapter Seventeen

Hours came and went, marked by the pounding of hooves striking earth. Rose opened her eyes after a long blink and found the world a darkened place, the sun having long since departed.

She yawned. "Where are we?"

Sebastian reined the horse. "Home."

"Home?"

"Well," he nodded, indicating a small thatched roof cottage, "a smaller, less grand version of our home, to be sure. Come." He gathered her into his arms, dismounting, before carrying her across the threshold of the simple dwelling.

A surprise greeted her upon entering—Robert.

Her brother was bent over a pot hung over a fire in the hearth, tasting something pale and pasty. He dropped the wooden spoon, hastening over. "Rose? What has happened?"

Sebastian laid her on a lumpy bed, pushing covers back. "She escaped her chaperone to join us for dinner, Witherby." He winked at her. "Please go see to my horse before he wanders away in want for a real shelter."

"But—"

"Now, Witherby."

To her shock, her brother pressed his lips together and did as her husband asked, no smart remark uttered.

"What did you do to him?" she asked, confounded. "Haunt him in your afterlife? Place a witch's curse upon his mortal soul? Why is he here? Logan said he was out bedding wenches or some such thing."

Sebastian urged her into a sitting position, turning her around so he could unbutton her gown. "He went to pay call on a young woman who did not favor his company, then decided to get foxed at an inn, where I saved him from a beating and sobered him up. In short, he now owes his life to me."

"I should like to hear the details." She coughed into an arm as her corset was loosened.

Sebastian eased her clothes off a layer at a time, leaving nothing but her chemise and stockings on. "Another time. Under the blankets, wife, before your brother comes back." He tucked the blankets up to her chin, propping pillows underneath her back.

"Thank you. I feel better without the corset alone." *Almost better.*

There was a lump in the bedding digging into her hip. With Sebastian busying himself over the black cauldron hanging above the fire in the hearth, she set to work freeing the hard, oblong object from its hiding place. She lifted her hips and yanked, pulling it up and out from beneath the blanket.

A book.

The cover was black and titled *A Treatise on the Theory and Practice of Midwifery.* She flipped through the pages, gasping at the pictures. When a throat cleared itself above her, she lifted her gaze, holding up the book. "Is this yours?"

Sebastian set a bowl on the wood planked floor, then lowered himself beside her. His face was as red as a summer cherry. "You weren't supposed to see that."

"You...you were reading a book about...this?" She placed a hand on her abdomen, touched in a way she had never felt before. "But why?"

He grimaced, not meeting her eyes. "You feared child birthing, and I wished to slay your dragons," his voice lowered, "and mine as well."

"Your dragons?" Entirely off-center, she could not grasp his meaning.

"I may have felt guilty about spilling my seed without a doctor's approval. If anything happened to you because of my loss of temper," his Adam's apple bobbed once; twice before his gaze fell to a point on the floor, "then that would make me a man no better than my father." He picked up the bowl, handing it to her without looking in her direction.

She took it from his hands, watching him, fighting a sliding warmth in her chest. It lapped over her as soothing as bathwater. The sensation was curious—unusual and conflicting. If she was to give the feeling a name, could she call it love?

Logan stirred something similar in her, but it was more of a physical awareness. It shamed her to have those feelings. He awakened her senses to what a man's touch could be—shocking. Exhilarating.

Sebastian was awakening something else within her, and it was by far a more poignant emotion with little to do with physical appearances or desire as she knew it. There was nothing physical about this buoyant joy filling her breast.

Perhaps it was only mucus consuming her lungs and ability to breathe, but somehow, she did not think it was entirely the plague.

She touched Sebastian's jacket sleeve, waiting for his gaze to find hers. When they did, she smiled. "I do not care what the reasons are that finds this book to your hands. You are the only man of my acquaintance who has tried to alleviate my worry." Her smile widened into a grin. "Or slay my dragons. Some might say such consideration falls under the guidelines of a hero."

He made a choking sound that sounded like a cross between a bark of laughter and a derisive snort. "I told you once there were no heroes here, and certainly none stand so honored in this room."

Robert burst through the door, slamming it shut, throwing his weight against the back. "We have a visitor!"

Sebastian surged to his feet as the front door crashed open, throwing Robert to the floor.

Logan filled the doorway with his enormous presence. He raised a pistol, aiming at Sebastian, before ramming back the hammer. "Where is she?" he bellowed.

She flinched underneath her covers, drawing the blanket up to her eyes. This was the first time she cowered before any man, but Logan's expression threatened a kind of wrath she'd never witnessed before now.

Sebastian stood his ground, placing himself in a protective stance in front of her. "In here, you dolt. Now come in and shut the door. She's sick, and you're letting in a chill."

Logan stomped further into the room, still holding his pistol on Sebastian, before locking eyes on her. When their gaze collided, all the bluster went out of his face. He whirled, stalking to the door, slamming it shut.

The rigid outline of Sebastian's shoulders relaxed. "Thank you. Our father told me you were raised in a barn. I am relieved to find your manners better than what he implied."

Logan took two strides, putting himself directly in front of Sebastian. It was shocking to see them nose to nose. They really were equal in height, but Logan's shoulders were a bit broader. Sebastian was more compact, as one would expect of stone.

"Do not mistake my capitulation for acceptance of this situation. The only reason your forehead does not bear the mark of a lead ball is because I do not want to appear the brute to Rose."

"That would belie all those fine stories of your heroic acts,"

Sebastian agreed with a humorless smile. "Let it never be said the infamous Silver Hawk acted in anything less than perfect chivalry."

Logan growled, then turned to Robert, offering a hand. "Allow me to assist, Arnold."

Robert grabbed the offered hand, letting Logan pull him upright. "I'm sure I'll regret asking, but who's Arnold?"

"Benedict Arnold. A traitor famous in your country, is he not?" Logan arched a brow. "Though I admit that hardly seems fair. He betrayed millions, while you only betrayed one. I'm guessing that makes you more a Judas than an Arnold."

Robert drew himself up, chin lifted. "I didn't run to my brother-in-law, whispering of your plans to him. As it turns out, Logan, not everything in life has to do with you and your desires."

"Really," he drawled in a terrible voice. "I shall remember that the next time you write me a letter for help."

"Enough!" Sebastian snapped. "We are all adults here and should be able to comport ourselves in a manner worthy of our respective titles. Not a word, Witherby."

Robert shot Sebastian a cheeky grin, throwing his hands up.

"Now," Sebastian marched to the rough-hewn table, hauling out a chair. "May I suggest we sit down and discuss our situation?"

"Fine." Logan strolled over, reaching inside his jacket, withdrawing a sheath of parchment. He slapped it down on the table. "I *suggest* we begin our discussion with our father's will."

Alarm crossed Sebastian's face. His gaze rocketed to her. "No," he murmured. "Not here. Not now."

Rose sat a bit straighter in her bed, making sure to keep the blanket up around her chin. "Sebastian?"

"It's all right, wife." He delivered a chilling stare to Logan. "My I speak to you in private?"

Logan smirked. "Nervous?" His amusement fell flat. "You should be."

"Bloody hell, Edgewood. 'You should be?' Are all heroes this unimaginative in their threats? You're boring me to tears. There. How's that for trite conversation?"

An odd look crossed Logan's face. "I am *not* a hero."

"At last, a thing we agree upon." Sebastian stormed across the room to the door, wrenching it open. "Shall we?"

~ * ~

"You cannot tell Rose about our father's will," Sebastian said, trying in vain to stem his sense of panic. "Not in her current condition," he added when his brother opened his mouth to refuse him. "It would only add to her misery and may impede her ability to fight whatever is ailing her."

Logan hesitated, frowning. "She has a right to know the truth."

"She will, as soon as she is strong enough to hear it." He fought the urge to plead and beg. Not behavior worthy of a duke.

Logan inched his face closer, his gaze impenetrable. "Good. Because I wouldn't want it to be a shock when she suddenly finds her marriage annulled."

"You know of course I'll fight you. Being a duke is not without its advantages."

"I'll take those risks." Logan turned to go, dismissing him.

"You know you can't marry her," Sebastian called out, balling his hands into fists, fighting an overwhelming urge to beat his giant of a brother. "Even if you do succeed in proving our union a fraud and the court annuls our marriage, the law prevents you from marrying her as well."

Logan whirled. "Those laws only pertain to ceremonies here in England. There are no laws barring us from marriage in France. Or even America, should she wish it."

Sebastian swallowed over a lump in his throat. "Our child?"

The severity of Logan's face eased, compassion rising to the surface in his fathomless eyes, if only for a moment. "I will claim the babe as my own. It will never know the bitter title I held throughout my childhood."

"What if she loves me?" He nearly laughed at his question. It was probable, just not possible. "What will you do then?"

Logan retraced his steps, again putting himself face-to-face with his estranged brother. "You sent me to her for a reason. You knew I was Silver Hawk. Our attachment to the other was obvious the night you stole her from me, was it not?"

Sebastian rocked his jaw together. "It was."

"So, you knew of our mutual attraction and still you asked me to be at her side. Why?"

"Need you ask?" Sebastian scoffed. "Because I knew what atrocity you committed against her, and she would hate you once your identity became known. It was a desperate bid for self-preservation."

"But you could have told her all this. There was no need to send me to your estate."

The lie was becoming harder to hide. Was there really any point anymore? His brother was not going to be moved from his latest rescue campaign. No, Sebastian had a strong suspicion Edgewood would be staying the night, possibly the next several nights, in the cabin alongside Robert and Rose.

At this rate, he would be adding an addition to this ramshackle hut. "You're right," Sebastian struck a defensive pose, jutting out a hip and crossing his arms. "I did have an ulterior motive."

Logan waited on tender-hooks, as evident by his unblinking death stare. "That would be?" he prodded when the silence dragged out too long.

Sebastian cleared his throat. "I wanted her to have a choice."

"Why?"

"Why what?" A less intelligent reply had yet to grace his lips, but Sebastian was growing tired of innuendos.

"Why go through all the trouble of blackmail if you were always going to give her a choice?"

"It wasn't *always* my intention to give Rose a choice on who she wanted for a husband," he said. "Do you think me a fool?"

Confusion marred Logan's brow. "Then why—"

"Because I fell in love! God's teeth, must I spell it out for you?"

"You're a Dorchester." Logan made the statement in a flat voice. "You're not capable of love."

"Am I not? Thank heavens. It must be Rose's plague, then." He closed his eyes briefly, digging for patience and finding none. "How many times must I tell you I am not my father? I'm in possession of a fully functioning heart, complete with all the trimmings. In fact, I have been known to experience emotions quite frequently—like now, for instance. I'm fighting against a rather visceral urge to bash your face in with my fists."

Logan almost cracked a smile. The corner of his mouth twitched. "Then what stays your hand from acting upon such desires? *Love?*" He sneered the word. "You love women the same way as our father did—by forcing yourself between their thighs!"

"This argument grows tiresome, Edgewood. I'll not have it again. I'm going back inside to see to *my* wife."

"*Your wife* can see to herself," said a hoarse voice from the open door of the cottage. "And would have you stay to finish this discussion." Accusation and hurt screamed from Rose's rigid posture and overly bright eyes. She shivered, wrapped from head to toe in a blanket.

"How long have you been standing there?" Sebastian asked, fear knotting his stomach.

She shook her head. "Not long enough. I was hoping to catch a confession or two from you, but as always, my temper reared its head and interrupted what I wanted most to hear." Her direct gaze had the effect of a lead cannon ball striking his gut. "Is it true? What Lord Edgewood said? Did you... Did you...r- rape those young women in our home and leave them with child?"

His eyes popped open. "Excuse me. Did you say those young women are in our *home?*" He curled a lip in Logan's direction, baring his teeth, before turning back to his wife. "Hell no. Rose, I—it wasn't like that."

"Oh Sebastian, do be serious. I'm not an innocent. Some of those children look exactly like you."

Enraged by the position his brother was putting him, he found himself marching up to Rose, only to have his path blocked by Logan, as his brother struck a protective position in front of his wife.

Rose peeked at him over the top of Logan's shoulders, but made no move to come forward. He glowered at Logan, attempting to wrestle his temper back under control, forcing himself to focus on Rose's pale, determined face. "I am serious, Rose. I know they resemble me. Fortunately, I think you will find they resemble my father a little bit more."

"Your *father* assaulted those women?"

A crooked smiled emerged. "If you never met the late Henry Graham, consider it a mercy. I had every portrait of him removed from the castle after his death. I'm sorry I cannot prove my words."

"Don't listen to him, Rose," Logan interjected, "he's lying to you."

"Maybe they were lying to you," Sebastian barked, rounding on Logan. "Have you ever considered that, Edgewood? Or did you take their stories at face value, not caring to know the truth so long as they served your purpose?"

Logan folded arms over his chest. "Why would they lie to me?"

"Money. Protection. Those charlatans wanted to be taken care of and that's what you do, Edgewood. The entire peerage knows it, as well as the crooks. I helped them too but was far less noble about it. I didn't deplete my estate to take care of them like you. Nor seek a life of crime to earn the funds. I helped them the only way I could—by going to the source and seeing justice done."

Logan's stare was filled with wariness. "Justice? What manner of retribution did you deliver while locked away in your castle?"

"The only kind that matters. What you tried to do the night you held up our father's carriage."

"My intent was to divest him of funds. Not of life."

"No? Well I suppose you're right. You always played the part of the hero and liked it. To be a real villain you need a depth of character good men always seem to lack. Thank God my soul is damned to hell. Otherwise, Henry Graham may still be of this world."

"Sebastian," Rose cut in, a quiet voice in the condemning silence. "Did you *murder* your father?"

He was burning his bridges. Her eyes held a kind of stupefied horror that mirrored Logan and Robert's gazes.

Sebastian pinched the bridge of his nose, closing his eyes, breathing deep. When he opened weary lids, it was to find three pairs of eyes on him, displaying varying degrees of shock. The entirety of his family faced him, judging his actions from lofty perches, as those with loving childhoods often do.

Something fragile broke within him in that moment. A madness to unburden his soul. To destroy all the happy tomorrows he spent the past weeks praying and hoping for. Logan was determined to make his life hell and here he stood at the very threshold.

He took the plunge.

The fall into eternal suffering was always inevitable. He was a fool to think acquiring a wife would end his misery. Staring at Rose was like viewing heaven. Something to be admired but never touched, knowing your sins placed you in a cage of your making, dooming you to question the decisions and actions you've taken, hoping to find some measure of comfort in a life that was many things but never kind.

He hated all the faces staring at him in that single moment.

"Yes, Rose. Your husband murdered his father. Is it really so shocking? The man was a dark blight upon humanity. If he had been of low birth, he would have faced death long before the heel of my boot met his throat."

Logan shifted his weight to the side, making way for Rose to move a step forward.

Even in the dark Sebastian could see the deep green hue to her eyes and the pain she could not disguise from him. His wife was a guileless, open young woman. Too young to understand the depths of depravity men will sink to in desperation.

"I cannot believe it," her rough raspy voice said. "You're not a murderer, Sebastian."

He met her direct gaze as he imagined a man might meet a hangman's noose. False bravado, pretending his heart wasn't a battering ram against his ribs. "We are all many things in this life that God never meant us to be. I'm sorry I cannot be standing here as you would have me—an honorable husband in possession of a strict moral center. I sold my soul for vengeance. God helps those that help themselves, but there is price to be paid in the end upon seizing such opportunity."

"You lie," Logan whispered. "You didn't kill him." His gaze flickered to Rose, then back at him. "I did. I know I did, though it was never my intent. The horses took a fright. I watched father's carriage run away, slipping, falling over an embankment down a steep cliff. No one could have survived such a fall."

"The old man was pinned beneath a carriage wheel, still clinging to life when I found him," Sebastian said. "Still coherent and in possession of all his senses, to which I profess made me grateful."

Rose swayed, and Logan was there, wrapping an arm around her shoulders. He ruthlessly choked down the savage anger rearing its ugly head the moment his half-brother dared to lay a hand on his wife. If Logan had his way, she would not be his to claim much longer. The court would take away all his rights as a husband. He'd be left with nothing but this possessive, impotent rage filling his breast. Alone with his demons once more. The promise of love and family ripped from his grasp before his fingers even began to close into a fist to fight in this tug-of-war battle.

Rose's face was so pale, her scarlet cheeks appearing far more blood-stained. "Why were you grateful, Sebastian?" She didn't so much as move a muscle away from Logan's body.

Sebastian scarcely heard the question asked of him. *Shift, lean, gesture, do something that tells me all hope is not lost!* But she did none of those things.

In fact, she leaned with greater weight into Logan's side.

A knife stabbed through Sebastian's chest, spearing his heart. Nothing could hurt as much as his wife's defection did at that moment. But how could he blame her? He was the tyrant who forced her from her home, who laid claim to her body, knowing full well she feared child-birthing. He was the bastard who did not care how she felt so long as he was the one to lay waste to her maidenhead. Now he was confessing to murdering his parent.

"I was grateful," he forced out of a rigid mouth, "because I wanted Father awake and aware. His body was being ground into dust by an enormous wooden wheel, and he was alive for every minute of that agony. I imagine that's how the little girl felt when I stumbled upon him raping a mere child in his study. Bones snapped beneath my father's formidable weight. Do you know the force needed to snap a bone in half, Rose?"

She paled, clinging to Edgewood.

Sebastian continued without mercy to her delicate condition, needing her to understand how evil his sire had been in life. "He was breaking a child from pelvis to shoulder. Her cries of help were ridiculed by the tyrant, even as they excited him." He spat on the ground, needing to rid himself of the foul taste of this gruesome tale, then looked his wife dead in the eye. "I would rather be condemned as a murderer than a rapist. I see that sweet child's face in my every nightmare. I will never forget her agony. And I made damn sure my father knew something of that child's pain before I let him leave this world."

Silence descended on the four of them as a heavy cloak.

"All this time I thought his death was my burden to bear," Logan murmured, the first to break the awful quiet. Shaking his head, he pierced Sebastian with a penetrating gaze. "Why did you not tell me the truth?"

Sebastian snorted. "If memory serves, you never gave me the chance, Edgewood. You condemned my soul along with my father's without ever speaking a word to me." He crossed his arms. "I'm surprised you rescued me from the villagers if you believed me responsible for the child's condition."

"I did not think it at the time," Logan confessed, looking grim. "I didn't even know it was you, if I'm being honest."

Sebastian cursed underneath his breath. It explained why his half-brother rescued him.

"All I saw was a man being held down by a mob, being tortured for a crime I did not know of," Logan continued, oblivious to Sebastian's growing ire.

Rose gave a small gasp, putting a hand to her mouth. "Your face, your scars? You did not receive your injury from Americans during the war? You…you lied?"

He smiled without humor. "It was a war of sorts, and some of the villagers may have been American. Who knows?"

"Sebastian be serious! I want to know what happened to you."

He sighed, scrutinizing the ground, scuffing dirt with a booted toe. "After I rescued the child, I brought her back into the village, searching for her home and family." His voice lowered with remembered pain. "They found me first. Believed me the one responsible for her condition." He glanced up. "My face bears the mark of their rage."

She pushed away from Edgewood; her gaze hard on his unmasked face. "What else have you not told me, Sebastian?"

He shared a look with Edgewood, begging him with silent,

raised brows to spare Rose certain details of her arranged marriage. His wife had endured enough secrets for one day. He would not have this out in the open as well.

Robert caught the hidden communication between the two men. He rushed to her side, glaring his displeasure at them both. "My sister is in no condition to stand around all night and listen to further confessions. Have you both lost your wits?" He shook his head, ushering Rose back inside.

Sebastian prowled up beside Logan. "I don't know about you, but I lost mine the moment I first saw her face, staring in utter rapture toward you."

Logan swiveled his head, taking his measure. "I believe your study bears the mark of my bad temper upon learning Rose was always meant to be mine."

"Then we agree we're bastards."

"We are at that."

They considered each other. Logan cleared his throat. "It does not mean I'm giving Rose up without a fight."

Despair threatened to knock the wind from his lungs. "There's not going to be a skirmish to claim Rose's heart. I could see tonight nothing has changed. I've confessed to murdering my parent. I've frightened her away, Edgewood. She'll want nothing more to do with me." He moved to go inside the cottage, but a hand on his arm fixed his feet to the ground.

Logan stared at him, compassion sneaking out behind a cool facade. "You're wrong," he said in soft tones, "The time you spent with her was few in hours, but enough to ensure a place in her heart. How exactly you accomplished this feat I do not know, but I believe the manner in which you claimed your rights as a husband may have had much to do with it."

"What are you saying, Edgewood?"

"I'm saying, I know you're not Henry Graham." Logan proceeded into the small hutch, leaving him gaping in his wake.

Had the almighty Silver Hawk spoken an apology of sorts?

Perhaps this night was not without the promise of miracles after all.

Chapter Eighteen

Rose dug a spoon into the bowl, eating the porridge without taking any pleasure in it. It was unsweetened and tasteless, and the undercurrent of depression in the atmosphere didn't enhance the flavor.

She had been sent back to bed, while the men sat around the table, picking at their bowls. Like a condemned man, Sebastian donned his mask and wasn't meeting anyone's eyes. Logan was scowling at the wood surface as though the furnishing had grown a mouth and insulted his mother. And Robert eyed a bottle of liquor on a sideboard.

They were a sad group indeed.

She wanted to ask Sebastian more questions, like what he and Robert were doing out there to begin with but feared the revealing of more secrets this night. Some dolt said ignorance was bliss, and for tonight, she agreed. If her husband had been pulled into service for the crown, and was working on a secret agenda, she did not wish to know of it at this moment. She did wish for a moment alone with her husband, though. She needed to make it clear she did not condone killing as a way of solving problems but was glad he did it. Henry Graham was a duke who thought himself above the law. Untouchable. Soiling women with no regard to the consequences or the lives he ruined by his savagery. Such a man deserved his fate, and she was not sorry Sebastian claimed the title of avenging angel.

In a way, his brand of rough justice was a healing balm for her. And Clara. And Abby. For she knew it was Henry Graham who ordered Logan to send the soldiers to attack them.

If only she could get Sebastian alone to offer her gratitude. She observed him again, poking at his bowl of food, morose and sad. She would not have it so.

Grinning, she asked, "Have we any pickles?"

Three male heads bobbed up.

"No, Duchess," Sebastian said. "You'll have to make do tonight with what you have." He barely glanced in her direction, resuming his sullen contemplation of his bowl of gruel.

Undaunted, she asked, "How about fruit or honey? 'Tis rather plain to eat."

This time his eyes met hers. "Is that the colonial way of expressing gratitude? Because in my country we say, 'thank you' when someone does something nice for someone else." He took a spoonful, shoving it in his mouth, chewing.

Rose dropped her gaze, seeking something more interesting in her food than the set of male lips wrapping itself around a spoon, pulling a sticky substance into an unsmiling, generous mouth. "My apologies. Thank you, Sebastian. I'm certain it was quite taxing on your mind to have to cook a pot of gruel. Tell me, is it a Graham family recipe? Thin and grainy porridge for the poor demented duchess?"

Logan choked, spitting out his mouthful of porridge, his shoulders shaking in mirth.

One of Robert's cheeks was indented, as though he were biting the inside flesh to keep from smiling.

Sebastian slammed his utensil down onto the table. "Are you inferring that eating something I prepared is a form of punishment?"

"Now husband, that doesn't sound like me at all."

"I'm starting to see the wisdom of the type of discipline your father doled out."

"It didn't help him, nor will it benefit you."

His eyes glittered, the irises of both eyes merging with dilated pupils. "Depends on your point of view, Duchess."

"Stop calling me that. I have a name."

"I used to call you 'darling' but that endearment has been stolen." He leveled a glare at Logan.

"I cannot help what other men call me," she said, fearing her playful banter turning into a shouting match.

It was just as well. Nature was calling, and she could not ignore the pain of a full bladder any longer. She stood, dragging her blanket up to cover her body. When the edge slipped off a bare shoulder, she found two sets of male eyes glued to her person.

Sebastian noticed the direction of Logan's stare. His eyes flashed a dire warning. "What are you doing, Rose?"

She shrugged the blanket back up, cinching it closed underneath her chin. "I need a moment of privacy."

"Privacy?" Sebastian growled. "For what purpose?"

She stared pointedly at him.

"Ah." He waved a hand toward the door. "Do not tarry. I'll expect you back shortly."

She started for the exit when Logan spoke up.

"Aren't you going with her?" he asked, disapproval lacing his voice.

Sebastian's glare turned uglier. "No. Rose is fully grown. She does not require a nursemaid."

Logan edged forward, scowling back. "She should not be outside alone without one of us to watch out for her."

Rose held her breath, waiting by the door. Logan's protectiveness really bordered on obsessive. It was fast becoming tedious.

Sebastian barked a laugh. "Edgewood, Rose defended herself quite well against His Majesty's soldiers without your help in the endeavor. I am certain she is more than capable of relieving herself without our assistance. But if it makes you feel any better," he stood, striding to her side, "here, Duchess." Sebastian handed her a pistol. "If you see anything moving in the darkness you do not care for, shoot it."

Pleasure suffused her at his trust. She straightened beneath his regard, smiling into his eyes. "Thank you."

His scrutiny dipped to her lips. "You're welcome," he murmured, dragging a heavy-lidded gaze up to caress her face.

Invisible fingers touched the skin of her cheeks and chin, danced across her fevered forehead. A fire burst low in her belly, reacting to the phantom caress.

The intensity of these new feelings was alarming. Was it so long ago she found his kiss unremarkable? Dreaded the joining of their lips?

The heat emanating from Sebastian's body enveloped her through the layers of blanket, he stood so close. Reaching up, she brushed her fingertips against the wiry hair of his beard. "You've a handsome face. Why do you cover it?" she asked, blurting it out, quite without thinking. She inhaled, shooting a glance at his eyes.

He laughed, low and warm, chucking her under the chin. "Imp. Go on with yourself and see to your needs before I assign myself the duties of nursemaid."

They shared another smile, long and slow, before her hand found the doorknob, freeing her from an invisible cord.

She shut the door and leaned against it, overheated and out of breath without knowing the reason for it. Very confusing, indeed. Doubtless it was the plague wreaking havoc with her body's failing internal temperature. But what did the illness have to do with an unrelenting throb and moisture in between her thighs?

The skin was fairly oozing with some kind of heavy dampness she's never experienced before now.

Good God in heaven, had she wet herself without realizing it?

Mortified, she dragged a hand along the rough-grained wood searching for the door handle, twisting it when found until the latch gave way. She pushed, forming a crack wide enough for her head to slip through. Thrusting her neck out, she peeked around the corner.

Three pairs of male eyes stared back at her.

She gulped, looking down, not finding a wet spot on the floor, then glanced up, smiling. "I mistook the cottage for a tree. It's bloody dark out here. Excuse me, gentlemen." She slammed the door shut then bolted, gathering the ends of the blanket up, dropping the pistol in the process.

Damn and blast!

Well she wasn't going back for it.

Striding with haste, she scanned the dark foliage for a spot to attend business but caught the sound of babbling brook instead. She made a beeline for it, finding herself in desperate need of a good washing beneath her cotton shift.

She was still oozing.

A sudden fear reared up, stopping her. Was it the baby? She never leaked so down her legs before she became with child.

She dropped her blankets, putting a hand between her legs, reaching a finger up to probe inside herself. Wrenching her hand up, she squinted at her finger. No blood stained her pale digit, but a goo of sorts was sticking to her skin.

She must be defective as a woman.

Good God, she leaked like a bucket of water with a hole in it.

"What are you doing?" A tall form emerged from the shadows.

Gasping, she spun, facing the intruder. "Who goes there?"

"Who goes there indeed," answered an annoyed male voice. Sebastian stepped into the scarce moonlight. "Your husband, madam. Who else were you expecting? Silver Hawk, perhaps?"

She sagged, relief sending her heart pounding. She sank to the ground, sitting upon the discarded blankets. "No. I wasn't expecting any callers, Your Grace."

"Are you going to answer my question? Because from my point of view, it appeared rather like you were…ah…devil take it! Woman, you were touching yourself."

She slanted a look up at him. "Why do you sound angry? It is my body, is it not? I touch it quite frequently." She coughed, slapping a hand across her mouth, wrestling with her lungs to form deeper breaths.

"That's not what I meant, and you damn well know it." He plopped down beside her, pulling a corner of blanket over her bare legs.

"It's freezing out here, Rose. Stay covered." He gave her a hard look. "In all seriousness, what were you doing?"

She gathered her courage. "You have a defective wife, Sebastian. I'm sorry."

His hand blanketed hers, warm and reassuring. "Before I agree or disagree, I think I might need some more information." When she didn't answer the verbal nudge, he sighed. "You're going to make me drag this out of you, aren't you?"

She took a raspy breath. "Perhaps it is the baby; I do not know. I've never encountered this amount of moisture before. It is so odd."

"Baby? Moisture? Rose, I'm not following any of this nonsense. Darling," he turned her chin around so he could look into her downcast eyes, "please tell me what is troubling you. I promise I will do everything I can to help."

She stared into his tender gaze, ashamed. "Sebastian, I…I…"

"Just say it, Rose."

"I leak!"

He blinked. "You *leak*?"

She closed her eyelids, too afraid of seeing the disgust in his beautiful eyes. "Yes, it's true. Your wife dribbles with abandon when you get close to her. I do not know what harm has befallen my body to make it act in such a manner. I've carried on a great many conversations in my life and never once has such a flood stormed down my legs."

"I see."

"You see? Is that all you have to say to me?" Annoyed, she turned to face Sebastian, only to find his masked face devoid of all expression.

Before dissolving into helpless peals of laughter.

Bemused and annoyed at the same time, she watched the man hoot and holler. Was he addled? She confessed to a fatal hole in her person, and her husband carried on as though it were some ghastly jest. At least he wasn't sulking anymore. No, not only was he not depressed, but he was also no longer wearing his mask. The dratted man swiped it off his neck and was using it to blot the tears from his eyes.

"Are you quite finished?"

He brought a hand to his chest, gulping air. "My apologies, Duchess. It's just—when you said, 'dribbles with abandon.'" He lost his voice again, giving her a helpless shrug before hiding his face in cloth, the sounds of high amusement now muffled.

"Vulgar cad."

In a huff she stood, seeking a bush to relieve herself while her husband curled into a fetal position on her blankets, holding his stomach.

When she emerged from the shrubbery, he was standing again, holding her blankets out with the most tender look in his eye. "Come here," he bade.

She stood her ground, obstinate as a mule. "I'd sooner freeze." Much to her chagrin, the refusal only inflated his smile. "Why are you grinning at me in such a manner?"

Folding the blankets over his arm, he sauntered closer. "It would appear I know something you do not."

She backed away warily. "This is cause for joy?"

He stopped. "Yes. Along with a fair amount of satisfaction too, I might add."

"Sebastian?"

"Yes, darling?"

She tilted forward so he could see the seriousness of her expression. "I do not wish to alarm you, but you're proving to be defective too."

"Is that so?"

"Aye. I'm noticing a few cavities where it ought to be solid body." She pointed to her skull.

He guffawed, holding his ribs. "Oh God, I haven't laughed this much in well, ever." Affection, along with some deeper emotion, softened the lines around his mouth and eyes. "I wonder, is this what marriage to you will be like? Silliness of all sorts? Filling our days with laughter and nonsense?"

His eyes enchanted, the curious light within those glowing orbs casting spells. That mysterious sensation arose within her heart again. Warmth. Connection. The invisible rope between them binding her tighter, filling her soul with knowledge. No longer did her body tremble for fear of embarrassment standing before her husband. Indeed, if her body was truly broken, it no longer signified. Rather, it filled her breast with strength where none had existed before. She cleared her throat, seeking equilibrium in a tilting world. "I believe that the only days' worth living for are the ones spent in never-ending hilarity of some nature."

"I've never known such bliss as what you described." His hands found her waist, and he inched her forward. Allowing her time to resist. Pull away. Utter grievances.

The Earth dipped some more as her head reclined, the rope strengthening to become a vice from which she could not escape, the universe narrowing to a blue point looming closer on her horizon.

Sebastian's forehead rested against hers, eyelashes batting her skin as light as butterfly wings. "I knew when first we met, you would own my heart." He brushed a light kiss across her nose. "You are my warrior goddess," he whispered, his lips trailing across her cheek, hovering over her mouth, "and I the scarred beast in need of saving." He brought their lips together in a soft kiss, whispering in a rough voice, "I love you, Rose."

His gentle affirmations proved a heady magic, one that left her craving more, furthering a growing need for intimacy. She wiggled closer, arms winding up to loop around his shoulders, encouraging his attentions.

The invitation to deepen their kiss went unanswered. He continued his assault on her senses using only the softest of touches, light sweeps of firm lips, feather-like caresses with his fingertips. Passion was tempered into something far more poignant in this embrace.

Was this love?

The darkened forest was quiet, the lack of wind a mercy. There was no cold, no chilled ground beneath her slippered feet. Her senses filled with Sebastian. He exhaled, and she inhaled the same air, tasting the scant of brandy on the back of her tongue. Ears caught even breathing, the imagined rumble of a strong heartbeat. Eyes filled his golden hair, a face blending perfect unblemished flesh and ruined, pink scars. The warmth of his body heat, the silky texture of thick locks, curling around her fingers.

Her heart pounded. The world where she now resided was a shared space with another soul, desiring the same things as she, living with an unbearable ache only the other could fill. She raised heavy lidded eyes.

Sebastian brushed a lock of hair behind her ear, the action slow and lingering. "At last," he murmured, "I see an invitation in those green eyes." His lips swooped in, pausing before laying claim. "If this is a dream," he murmured in a deepened tone, the blankets dropping to the ground, "then I pray to never awaken." Seizing her face with rough hands, his mouth took hers in hunger, as a man who's been starved for too long without nourishment.

Limbs intertwined and strained, seeking a unity impossible to satisfy with clothes enforcing unwanted barriers.

Rose melted. Burst into flames. And dribbled.

She clenched her legs together. "I'm wet."

A male groan vibrated through a heaving chest. "How wet, my darling? Tell me." He rained kisses down her throat.

"My thighs are slick with moisture," she admitted, feeling less ashamed about her defects inside his embrace.

He pulled away, smiling. "Haven't you figured out the reason for your leaking?"

"I know only it has something to do with you."

"I thank God for it." He kissed her deeply, before finding her ear to mutter, "Though I confess to wondering why. What reasons are driving you to such a state while the man of your dreams lurks nearby?"

Her questing fingers froze while attempting to wiggle through his unruly beard. "The dreams of my childhood never included a man."

"Oh, come now, Rose. Every young woman dreams of a handsome man, brimming with love sonnets to sing and flowery compliments dripping from his tongue. Edgewood fits the arch-type of hero perfectly." His hands dropped from her face, fisting at his side. "While I reside with the depraved and wicked, cast among the evil souls because of my choices and decisions. Are you saying you're proud to be married to a murderer? The villain?"

A hundred different replies battled for consideration, but only one word escaped her lips. "Yes."

He regarded her, eyes flashing, narrowing. "Do you trust me?"

"Yes." The word left her lips without thought or hesitation. Yet her lack of consideration made it no less true. That knowledge left her reeling, but now was no time to panic.

Sebastian was staring her down. The air suddenly cumbersome and heavy, as though a wet blanket shrouded them.

Fighting for breath, she inhaled in short, shallow pants, her heart beating much too fast for simply standing still.

"Rose!"

Logan's sharp cry from the cabin did little to penetrate her world. Twin blue stars illuminated a path to heaven. Like the North Star, the lights urged her home, beckoning to her with a brilliance no fire or candle could match.

"Rose, where are you?" Logan called.

Her husband took a step forward.

She retreated one step. "Logan sounds worried. I should go back."

Sebastian advanced without pause or words, steady in pace, unrelenting in his scrutiny of her face.

The rough bark of a tree trunk halted her backward fumbling. She gripped the base with both hands, seeking something of substance in a world suddenly gone from grasp.

"Rose!"

The voice was no closer, but strident in tone. Logan was becoming anxious.

She moved to go around her husband. "I should—"

His hand lashed out, catching her wrist. "Don't."

Pausing by his side, heart thumping, she risked a peek at his face.

Sebastian's gaze was stuck to the earth, unsmiling. But the grip around the delicate bones of her wrist was fierce. "Don't go," he said. "I'll not say please, nor will I beg." His voice lowered to a whisper as he said, "Neither will I command as your husband. I ask as a man—" He canted his head, turning to face her. "—in love with you." Taking a harsh breath, he growled, "Don't go."

"Rose!"

The vulnerable, open look scythed her heart. "He'll come after me if I do not show."

"Let him." His arms opened.

Sebastian, what are you doing to me? She rushed forward with a cry, not questioning the impulse that led her to jump, wrapping slender legs around a trim torso.

Surprise flared in his eyes, before a grin bunched his cheeks into twin apples. Twisting, he twirled them around, bringing her back up against sturdy bark. "Is this my wife who despises intimacy?" His hips surged forward until her legs gave way, allowing the press of a hard ridge to her moist center. "Are you not afraid?"

Rose caught the silent need in his eyes. "I do not fear your touch, Sebastian. Quite the opposite, in fact." She licked her lips, the movement drawing his regard. "I confess I've missed it. Longed for it when I was alone and cold in my bed."

'I wish so much to believe you." He groaned, placing urgent kisses along her jaw, underneath, trailing down the slim column of her throat. "I find I am the one afraid, fearing the depths I'll sink to should you turn to another with your heart and body."

She clung to bunching muscles of broad shoulders as weight was shifted. One of his hands disappeared beneath her chemise. A furious melee of tugging ensued underneath her bottom.

Biting her lower lip to keep from giggling, she asked, "Do you require assistance?"

A disgruntled grunt answered back. "I believe my breeches acquired a new opening not intended by my tailor."

Her amusement faded as a rounded head found the entrance awaiting its presence, clenching with an urgency she did not understand.

He brought their lips together as his hips pressed forward, stretching and filling her passage as tenderly and patiently as he had the first time he'd taken her.

Thin, corded muscles stood out in his neck. Harsh breathing assaulted her ears. It was clear he was in control.

But she would not have it so.

Her world was splintering apart, fracturing at the seams. Lost in a void of ever-changing emotions and circumstances. There was no anchor in this melee of desire, doubt and need. Was she falling or flying? There was no direction.

Only Sebastian.

Lost with her in the tumbling waves of an ocean without end.

"Find me," she gasped, "bring me home." Idiotic nonsense and random words from a soul gone astray.

Yet her husband understood.

Nostrils flared, eyelids hooded, he yanked her tight against him, thrusting inside her to the hilt with one hard jerk. "Always," he ground out, beginning a fast, driving tempo that robbed them both of further speech.

The movement of pelvis meeting hips was savage. His large hands gripped underneath the rounded globes of her ass, holding her in place to a ravishment that demanded everything she held dear—soul, heart and mind. Sanity was stripped away to be replaced with primal urges so strong she heard herself growl, fisting his hair, demanding deeper, faster strokes.

Throwing back his head, he laughed, the sound both lusty and maniacal. "As my duchess demands." Turning again, he dropped them to the harden ground, yanking her legs atop his shoulders.

The result was a lascivious position that set her teeth on edge as it fired the blood.

Sebastian nudged her chin up. "Trust me?"

Looping arms around his neck, she replied, "Always."

With a rush he filled her. To the womb. Snapping his hips, back and forth, faster. Violent yet tender. Unrelenting in a fast rhythm that wouldn't allow her the privilege of catching a breath.

But she rode the storm. A hurricane gaining force within her heart, swirling winds to a vortex leading to her aching center. They were mutual points in the same cyclone, spinning together with a force she could not see or control.

Destructive swirls gathered in fury; the path laid bare before her.

A precipice yearned.

He drove. Driving hips moved and commanded, urging her to let go. "Come with me," her husband growled, moving deeper. Faster.

Pain and pleasure crested to a great swell, sweeping her over the edge.

Screaming aloud, she unraveled. Fell.

Arms gathered around her body, catching and guiding her descent back to Earth. The anchor pulled her home, to blue eyes staring back at her in love. Sebastian eased her legs from his shoulders, scooting down to place a loving kiss on her flat abdomen.

"Your mother's dribbling is going to be the death of me," he whispered, rubbing the tip of his nose across her smooth skin.

Her uneven breathing hitched.

He placed another tender kiss on her belly. "Welcome to the world, little one." Wrapping her in arms that trembled, he laid his cheek to her abdomen.

The ensuing silence was heavy, despite the quiet, filled with sated appetites and a profound sense of peace that was equally powerful as it was moving. Waves no longer swelled but lay placid and calm, allowing a glimpse of the treasure hidden in their murky depths.

Her heart was yielding toward the sun, allowing itself to thaw and beat for something greater than herself. The acknowledgement was her undoing. Yet it didn't feel mad, rather it felt right. Like a piece of a puzzle that finally slipped into place without force or coercion.

A sudden motion from the corner of her eye caught her attention. She gasped, tensing.

Sebastian yawned against her belly, replete. "Sod off, Edgewood. You're interrupting a private family moment."

Logan stepped forward, a tall black giant against the silver light of the moon. "I heard a scream. I came only to—"

"Rose," Sebastian cut in, anger tainting his voice, "tell your brother-in-law you gave yourself willingly to the monster of Dorchester Castle, so he'll leave us alone."

She trembled, her peace of a few moments ago turning to ash. Tension boiled the air. "I am well, Logan. Truly. I'm sorry if I caused you alarm."

"Don't be sorry," Sebastian snapped, sitting up. He slid the hem of her chemise down, slapping blankets over her exposed form. "You're my wife, and you're allowed to be as vocal as you wish when riding my—"

"Sebastian!"

"What?" He stood her up, giving her a scowl.

Her gaze darted to Logan and back. "Must you be so crude?"

"That wasn't crude, that was blunt."

"You know what I meant!" she cried. Wrapping her blankets around her as a queen would wear a cloak, she took off in a huff, plowing past Logan without looking at him, running to the safety of the cabin.

She nearly plowed into her brother upon crossing the threshold.

Robert's gaze swept from her tousled tresses to her dirt-stained toes. He opened his mouth to speak. "Rose —"

"Please do not treat me to any of your brotherly wisdom tonight, Robert," she interrupted. "I've had enough of men. I want to go home."

"Home? It's too dangerous to ride back to the castle in the dark. Highwaymen will be out in full force, I'm sure."

"I care not. 'Tis far more dangerous to stay another moment here."

"You're not going anywhere, Duchess," boomed a commanding voice from the doorway.

She whirled.

Sebastian fixed a hard stare on her. "I've decided my afterlife was not miserable enough and needed company. In other words, make yourself at home, because you're not going anywhere else for the foreseeable future."

~ * ~

Sebastian lay on his bedroll with an arm flung over his head, listening to the crackling of fire. Logan and Robert snored, and his wife tossed and turned in bed, coughing at intervals. She was uncomfortable and not able to sleep, despite the illusion of privacy he had insisted upon, hanging a sheet up around the parameter of her bed.

Sebastian doubted her reason for lack of slumber had to do with unrequited needs, but still her restlessness was a needed excuse to go check on her.

Slipping from his coverlet, he padded barefoot across the floor. He tossed back the linen barrier hiding her from view She lay curled on her side with closed lids, but her chest rose and fell too rapidly to believe she slept.

"Rose," he called.

She rolled onto her back, fixing him with a stare filled with misery.

Concerned, he stepped forward, letting the curtain fall back into place, lowering himself on the bed beside her. He smoothed heavy locks of auburn hair away from a warm face. "How are you feeling?"

he asked.

"A little queasy," she admitted. "I have the oddest urge for pickles and hard-boiled eggs."

"Surely you jest."

"I never jest about food."

Reaching down, he kissed her forehead. "Very well." He stood, making to leave, when her small voice called to him.

"Sebastian?"

He turned.

Rose pushed herself up onto an elbow. "Where are you going?"

"Pickle hunting for my duchess. Never let it be said I let my wife expire from hunger." He bowed, lifting his head to wink, only to see the glitter of tears in her eyes. His heart quickened at the sight, sending him back to her side in a rush of stumbling feet. "Rose, what's wrong?"

She swiped her glistening cheeks. "Nothing of import. I'm afraid I'm as quick to temper as I am to cry lately. I swear my constitution never suffered so before marriage."

"It's the baby," he soothed, taking her into his arms. "According to my reading, this is quite normal and is to be expected."

"It is? Thank heavens." She snuggled into his side, and he made himself comfortable, leaning back on the pillows, tugging her closer. Pickle hunting could wait a few more minutes.

He breathed in her scent, floral and sunlight. Light and airy. Comforting. He allowed his head to rest on top of hers. If he closed his eyes and pretended hard enough, he could imagine them in his giant four-poster bed at home, without his brother-in-law and Silver Hawk asleep on the floor not five feet from their position. How had his life come to this confusing pass?

Still, he was grateful it was he and not Silver Hawk in this bed tonight.

"Sebastian?"

"Yes?"

"May I ask you a question without causing insult?"

"Of course." *Oh God.*

She turned her face into his chest. "What is the difference between love and lust?"

He stiffened, unable to curb the impulse. His wife was lounging comfortably in his arms and was thinking of Silver Hawk. She must be to ask such a question. It was either the oaf himself or his memory constantly driving a wedge between them. Intolerable.

But not unexpected.

Ordering himself to relax, his spine resumed its casual slumped curvature. He gently pushed Rose away so he could scrutinize her face. Beseeching green eyes drilled a hole through his chest, taking aim at his heart. She was an excellent marksman. He was as vulnerable and open as a deer standing in a clearing without shelter. He didn't want to have this conversation now. Crawling into a corner and curling into a fetal position nursing a bottle of brandy was vastly more appealing.

Still, his wife had asked him an important question, and he must devise an intelligent answer that didn't sound belligerent or jealous. He wanted to encourage trust between them, which was best accomplished by listening to her feelings and thoughts in an unbiased manner.

He knew the answer his father would have provided: *slap the chit silly and send her to bed wailing over the unfairness of the world.*

That was not a viable option.

But what in the hell was he going to say? Lust was an easy enough explanation, but love? He was still puzzling out the intricacies for himself.

Reaching for her hands, he enclosed slender fingers between his large, calloused ones. It was a marvel what these delicate digits accomplished. She fought an army to defy his father and must have impressed the old man to some degree as he made a betrothal contract for a son—albeit an illegitimate one. His wife was a force of nature his father would never been able to beat into submission.

Nature. Flowers. Rose.

That was the angle he was looking for! "Flowers," he blurted out. *Brilliant, Dorchester. Look at your wife's forehead wrinkling. She thinks you're a bloody idiot! Try it again.*

"Let me finish," he shifted his weight on the hard mattress, resting his elbows on his thighs. He stared into an emerald abyss, willing her to understand. "Flowers are the most beautiful in full bloom, are they not?" At her nod, he continued, "But their beauty fades in time. Sometimes it dies prematurely from lack of sunlight or food." *You're butchering the hell out of this!* "Rose, what I'm trying to say is lust is like the petals of a flower. It's short-lived. It attracts bees, I suppose, but in this case, I mean men. I'm actually not sure what I mean anymore."

Her eyes laughed, but the smile she bestowed on him was filled with an emotion he dared not identify.

"I think I understand lust. What about love?" She removed a hand from his grasp and caressed his scarred cheek, as though she preferred the grotesque facade of skin to the unblemished side of his face.

What about love indeed? "It's the roots to the flower," he whispered, losing himself in twin mirrors, seeing himself reflected there: sweaty, pale and scared witless. *You're the perfect ducal image, Dorchester! Get yourself together!* "Providing the flower with life. Unmovable. Something to depend on no matter what storm the flower must weather."

Rose's eyes went glassy.

He struck a nerve. Thank God his inane rambling made sense to somebody.

"Even as beauty fades and bees no longer hover," he continued, catching one lone tear from Rose's cheek. "The roots continue to take care of its charge. Until death parts the roots from the flower."

"That was lovely." She sniffed, smiling. "You have a poet's heart."

"I'm no Shakespeare to be sure." He settled back against the pillows, holding out his arms, smiling.

Rose fell forward, allowing him to pull her up against his chest for a good cuddling. It felt incredibly satisfying having her snuggle into his side as though she belonged. Better yet, as though she wanted to be there.

Drawing covers up over them both, he yawned. Scouring the countryside for pickles would have to wait until daybreak. "Did I solve your dilemma, or should I try to mutilate another simile?"

She wrapped an arm around his torso, squeezing. "I understand. I just needed to hear it from another point of view."

He wanted so badly to ask if it was him she loved, but he couldn't force such a confession. His wife would tell him what was in her heart when she was ready.

He thought admitting his sins would push Rose away. Bury their future before it even had a chance to flourish. But it was a worry without foundation. She never once looked at him with condemnation or reproach.

Killing his father would surely send him to hell one day, but not now. God had granted a reprieve in the form of marriage and a family. Blessings he never allowed himself to dream or hope to have.

If he could remain patient but for a little while longer.

And keep Edgewood the hell away.

Chapter Nineteen

Knowing what he would find, Logan ripped the curtain back.

He needed to see it with his own eyes.

Sebastian and Rose lay curled together spoon-fashion, back to chest, sleeping. The arm wrapped around her was tight with possession, even in deepest slumber.

Logan was intruding once more on an intimate moment and all the wishing in the world would not change what his eyes told him.

His Rose was finding love in another man's arms. And the brother he thought a devil, was falling in love in return. Their unity was more than evident last night.

How could this be so? He'd been so certain Rose was the one for him. Was every instinct wrong when it came to the female gender? How could he trust his heart when his body seemed to lead his mind, claiming his thoughts, producing nothing more than illusions for him to see?

Kicking the side of the bed, he barked, "Good morning."

Sebastian stirred. "Milly, go ask a footman to tend the fire. It's cold in here."

So, his brother thought him the lady's maid, did he? With a hard smile, Logan grabbed Sebastian's bare foot, yanking him from his warm bed onto the floor.

"Hey!" He sat up, blinking like an owl. "What was that for?"

For stealing my woman! For ripping my heart from my chest! "Build your own bloody fire," he snarled, stomping away, wrenching the front door open.

"I will," Sebastian said, standing up, scowling. "Leaving before breaking your fast?"

Logan paused at the threshold. "I'm riding out for a doctor. Rose's coughing kept me up damn near most of the night."

"I daresay not the entire night judging by your immense snores."

Shooting a black look over his shoulder, Logan slammed the

door shut. It took most of the day to locate the busy physician, then ride with him back to the cabin, his mood growing fouler the closer they got.

He dreaded what intimate setting he'd be stumbling upon returning to this snake infested den of debauchery.

Motioning for the doctor to wait, Logan dismounted, entering the cabin without knocking. He was pleasantly surprised to find Rose sleeping in bed and Sebastian sitting in a chair beside her, reading.

Logan gestured to the door. "The doctor is just outside." He eyed Sebastian. "Should you don a mask? I assume you wish to keep your identity a secret since you're supposed to be dead."

Sebastian snapped the book shut. "Was that a jab?"

"If it was an insult, you'd know it."

"Forgive me, but your sarcasm is a bit vague for my liking." He stood, glancing over Rose's prone form in a protective manner. "Yes. As it happens, I do wish to continue with my charade." He strode to his trunk, finding his needed accessory, then placing it on.

"Toward what purpose, may I ask?"

"Because the crown wants you and your raping brethren eliminated. Prinny volunteered my services to capture you and bring the highwaymen to justice."

"You had to die to accomplish this?"

Sebastian shrugged. "Prinny thought my distinctive scar would prohibit me from joining your ranks, thus making a public spectacle of my death a necessary evil. Personally, I think the mask alone would have covered needed ground, but I was overruled."

"What are your intentions now, dare I ask?" His attention was on Rose, who miraculously aroused herself from slumber and was listening to this discussion.

Her eyes naturally were only for her husband.

God's blood! Was it only yesterday Logan held her as she sobbed in the decaying garden? Seemed a lifetime ago now. With the passing of the sun, his mission in life had changed as well. He could not find it within himself to hold Sebastian accountable for the crimes committed by the father.

His life since coming home from America had been one led in vengeance. Now what was he to do?

Sebastian's growl pierced his musings, bringing him back to the present.

"Are you done ogling my wife?"

A weary sigh hissed from his lips. "Yes."

"Thank you. As I was saying, I have not forgotten my debt to you. Silver Hawk's identity will always be safe as far as I'm concerned. Unless," Sebastian scowled, "you cannot keep your hands to yourself. In that case all sworn alliances will suffer."

Anger exploded, the day's events reaching a boiling point. Logan turned so Rose could not see or hear him speaking. He took three steps, placing him directly in front of his brother's ear. "You think you've won because you fucked her?" he whispered.

He stepped away at Sebastian's quick inhale of breath. Sure enough, his brother's face turned an ugly shade of red. A right hook came for his chin before Logan could blink or think to block the punch.

The blow staggered him back, but he fell to the floor in feigned injury when Rose's screech filled the air.

She rushed to his side, shooting glares at her husband. "Sebastian Graham! Is that anyway to treat your brother?" She fussed over Logan's split bottom lip.

He aimed a pleased look over her shoulder.

"Half-brother," Sebastian growled. "The bastard half."

"A rather large extension of that family branch, I daresay," Rose muttered, patting his lip with the hem of her sprigged muslin gown, surrounding him with her light floral scent.

"What was that, Duchess?"

"I said are you going to ask the doctor to come in or do you intend to wait for the butler?"

Sebastian grinned. "Edgewood, in case you're wondering, that is how sarcasm is done properly. Do you see the difference?"

Rubbing his sore jaw, Logan stood. "I'll go get Dr. Wilson. You'll scare him away before he gets to see the patient." He put a hand down, helping Rose to her feet, allowing his hands to linger with hers.

Sebastian's grin fell flat.

Logan enjoyed taking the smile off that face more than he was willing to admit. "I'll be right back."

~ * ~

Rose jerked her brows up, rounding on her husband as soon as Logan was out the door. "Why are you glaring at me like that?"

"You let him touch you!"

"Logan helped me into a standing position. He was being a gentleman. Ask your furry friend what the word means if you find yourself unfamiliar with it."

Sebastian's finely arched brows caved inward with his frown. "What in hell is that supposed to mean? What furry friend?"

"The one that crawled up on your face and died while you were sleeping."

Drawing himself up, he snapped, "It's called a beard, Duchess. It's part of my disguise."

"It looks like something you slapped on without aid of a looking glass or sound judgement."

The door opened, admitting Logan, guiding an elderly gentleman. She recognized him from the first day she met Silver Hawk and Sebastian. How blind she had been to her highwayman, and how she loathed her future husband for reclaiming her.

It only proved how little she knew of life.

Sebastian strode to a far corner, fading into the shadows with one last glare in her direction. Their fight would continue another time. He was becoming insufferable whenever Logan talked to her or came near her for any reason.

The wizened gentleman ambled to her side, sitting in a chair by the bed, putting a black bag on the floor. "Your Grace?" He darted a look at Logan for confirmation.

Logan hesitated, before nodding. "Forgive me. Dr. Wilson, this is Rose Graham, Duchess of Dorchester. Your Grace, Dr. Wilson of Dorset."

It was startling to hear Logan call her by a title, when he refused to acknowledge her new status as duchess before. She sat on the edge of the bed, extending her hand.

The old man grasped it, inclining his head. "Your Grace. May I offer my condolences on your husband's recent passing."

"Thank you." She frowned when her hand was not released promptly.

"Hmm," the doctor said, "very warm indeed." He turned to Logan. "May Her Grace and I have a private moment to speak?" His fingers moved to her wrist.

Logan glanced at the corner. "I do not mind."

Sebastian emerged from the dark. "I do. It's bloody indecent for a physician to do an exam without a chaperone present. She's a duchess, not a common peasant."

Dr. Wilson's keen gaze glanced from her face to Sebastian's, his fingers still on her wrist. "And you are, sir?"

Sebastian crossed his arms. "No one to be trifled with." His eyes narrowed. "Or defied."

Displeasure unfurled in her stomach at Sebastian's protective words and stance. *Hell and damnation! Not this again.*

Logan rolled his eyes. "For God's sake, he's a—"

"I know what he is!" Sebastian interrupted with a snap. He nudged the doctor's black bag with the tip of a boot. "Pray tell, what is hidden in here? A jar of leeches, perhaps?" He loomed over the doctor; a frightening masked man dressed in somber shades of black. "If I see one leech go near this woman, or blade intent on letting blood, I will end your wicked life this very day. In fact, you shall not touch her without first seeking consent from me. Is that clear, Dr. Wilson?"

Logan stared slack-jawed at Sebastian.

The doctor laughed, slapping his knee. "By Jove! Well done, sir. You remind me of your father. You're the spitting image of him, right down to the ducal tone of command." He cackled, spittle flying from his mouth. Withdrawing a handkerchief from inside his puce-colored jacket, he coughed into it. "Ah me, well done indeed. Brings back the years when I was heartier in health."

"You forget yourself, doctor." Sebastian said. "I am not a duke. Only a man."

Dr. Wilson harrumphed. "I may be old, Your Grace, but I am not blind or deaf yet. Fear not, your secret is safe with me, as Silver Hawk's has been for these two years past."

"I am not afraid." Sebastian did not move, but his tone of voice deepened, taking on a more menacing quality, blanketing the air with a dangerous undercurrent as he said, "But I shall keep my mask on if it's all the same, as I do not wish to make *you* feel uncomfortable by the revealing of my face."

A tense silence followed his statement. Rose thought the doctor would ignore Sebastian's insinuation, but to her shock, he did not.

Turning fully in his chair, facing Sebastian, staring at him dead in the eye, he said, "Your Grace, I have long believed a grave injustice was done to you that night. I was not there, I did not witness your attack, but I never believed the child I brought into this world was capable of the same atrocities of the father. You were always too much like your mother. A respect for life in all its forms."

Shock crossed Sebastian's eyes. "Y-you knew of me as a child?"

"Did no one ever tell you? I was the family physician for the Dorchester family for two generations. Until your father sacked me for trying to help your mother escape."

"Escape?" Sebastian staggered back a step, all the bluster falling from his posture. He sought out another chair, falling into it. "From my father?"

"Yes. It was the only viable option for her once she knew she was with child." He angled a curious look at him. "I beg your pardon, Your Grace. I thought you knew the reason for your mother's death.

Forgive me, but your father was always a tyrant. I daresay no one blames your mother at all for finding love in other man's arms."

Sebastian's jaw locked, and a muscle ticked in his cheek as if the furry animal on his face regenerated and gained a heartbeat.

Oh dear.

Placing a hand on the doctor's sleeve, Rose gained his attention. "Perhaps it's best if we allow my husband some time to think while we talk."

"Err, yes of course, Your Grace." He dutifully turned his focus on her face. "You obviously have quite the fever raging. And by the sound of your voice, are you feeling a heaviness when you breathe?"

She nodded.

"Some malady of the lungs is affecting you, Your Grace. I would not—"

"Hold a moment, Doctor," Sebastian interrupted, finding his voice as he surged to his feet. "Did you say my wife is suffering from *some malady of the lungs?* Did one of your leeches whisper that idiotic nonsense into your ear?" Slapping a hand onto the table, he bellowed, "By George, I could have made such a proclamation! Pray tell, Dr. Wilson, is *some malady of the lungs* a course of study at the University of This n' That?"

"Enough!" Logan roared, grabbing Sebastian's arm, pushing him toward the door. "I didn't drag the poor man from his house to be insulted by you all day. Out!" With an impressive display of strength, he shoved Sebastian out the opening, following him into the sunlight, shutting the door with a loud bang, rattling the windows.

In the sudden quiet, Dr. Wilson guffawed. "University of This n' That, indeed." He chuckled. He hooked a thumb toward the doorway. "That young man is quite taken with you."

Rose smiled, relieved the doctor was not insulted. "And I with him." She blinked, the words flowing from her tongue as natural as you please. But were they true?

"I can well see such sentiment returned. Now then," he picked up his bag and stood, "I best find myself your door before your husband comes in demanding satisfaction for your honor." He winked before shuffling to the door.

"Dr. Wilson."

He turned.

"Thank you." She wanted to elaborate but didn't know how to thank a man for saying an unintended compliment.

Dr. Wilson nodded. "You seem of good stock to me, Your

Grace. You'll be good for him; I have no doubt. It's about time something wonderful happened to that young man. He has suffered much of late, to my regret. Terrible incident that robbed him of having a whole face." He let himself out the door.

~ * ~

"What is wrong with you?" Logan shoved Sebastian away from him. "The man is a fine physician and is a friend. You've no right to act in such boorish and rude manner. I'll not have it."

"The man all but called my mother a whore."

"He did no such thing. Have you always had this annoying habit of hearing only what you choose to hear?"

"If you ever bothered to come down from your high horse and gotten to know me, you'd know the answer to that question."

"Touché."

"A 'malady of the lungs', Logan? I've heard more relevant mutterings from Robert regarding the weather. My wife is sick and in delicate condition. She needs—"

"Rest, Your Grace." Dr. Wilson walked with a limp to where the two men stood arguing. "Her body is fighting an infection and nothing in this world helps the body more than a good night's sleep. Although I admit I didn't know she was breeding."

Sebastian stiffened. "Does it matter?"

"It shouldn't, Your Grace."

"That does it." Sebastian held out a hand. "Edgewood, give me your gloves."

Logan fought the urge to roll his eyes with every fiber of his being. "What for, dare I ask?"

"To throw them down. I'm calling out this imbecile physician. I've had enough."

Logan caught himself attempting to smile. "You've a sense of humor similar to Robert. I did not know."

"There's no need to be insulting, Edgewood. I'm not afraid to call you out either." Sebastian turned the full force of his formidable glower on the doctor. "What did you mean it shouldn't matter?"

"Your Grace, there is a reason why it is called a 'delicate condition.' Many things can go wrong within the first months of conception. But," he held up a hand to halt Sebastian from speaking, "if you can get your wife to stay in bed and rest, there is every reason to believe the pregnancy will proceed as it should. I will stop by the apothecary on my way home and leave a list of items you may pick up in the morning that may help Her Grace rest more comfortably, but beyond that, it's in God's hands."

"God's hands? I fear I'll have as much success praying for a divine miracle as I will attempting to get my wife to stay in bed. Excuse me, gentlemen." Sebastian stormed off, going back inside the cottage.

Logan was forced to agree with his brother. "Rose can be stubborn and willful," he explained in Sebastian's wake, "and would try the patience of a saint. Dealing with her tends to leave a man ill-tempered."

Dr. Wilson smiled, waving away his apology. "His Grace is in love. Such an affliction affects men in different ways, as I have learned throughout the years. It is heartening to witness His Grace acting as a woman's protector, is it not? So much shame and dishonor has befallen this family's name, and it wasn't always so. When I brought Sebastian into this world, I had hope. After tonight, I do again. That young lady is just what this duchy needs to restore it to its proper place among the peerage."

Logan felt the uncomfortable pull of a conscience again. Damn, the more time he spent among Dorchester and Rose, the more he felt the villain. If he hadn't witnessed the two of them together, he would not have believed it. To his shame, he had not walked away after coming upon them in the forest. He stayed, telling himself it was only to make sure Rose wasn't being taken against her will, but that wasn't the only reason. Seeing her face contort in ecstasy, then wonder as Sebastian talked to the babe in her womb, confirmed his worst fears.

Rose was turning from him. Falling in love with the enemy.

Chapter Twenty

Rose opened the cabin's front door, peering out.

The coast was clear. The men gone doing whatever it was men do on a sunny day. Not a note had been left informing her of plans, so she felt inclined to return the favor. Slipping free from the confines of her prison, she hugged a towel and bar of soap to her bosom and took off for the creek behind the cottage.

The walk was so refreshing she nearly skipped in sheer delight, but the tightness in her lungs had not quite vanished, and she had no wish for more tonics to be shoved down her throat in the name of healing.

Hearing the happy sounds of a babbling brook, she soon spied the narrow stream. After taking off her dress, shoes and stockings, she waded into the cold depths with only her chemise on for modesty's sake. Strays hadn't graced her body since the first night in her confinement.

The water was jarringly cold, so she made quick work of washing her hair and body, thoroughly soaking her thin chemise in the process. It was of no importance though. She had a towel awaiting her onshore and—

Drat!

She'd been followed.

Logan stood on the bank, holding her towel out to her with a frown. "Have you no care for your safety, madam?"

She rolled her eyes so far back the orbs ached from the abuse. Presenting him with her back, she called out, "Close your eyes, Logan! I'll not come for the towel with you watching me, for heaven's sake." Hearing a disgruntled snort, she peeked over a shoulder.

He still held the towel up, but his eyelids were closed.

Satisfied, she emerged from the stream, dripping wet, crossing her arms over her chest. She paused before reaching out for her cover to acknowledge a powerful tenderness in her breasts. This ache was new. And uncomfortable.

"Are you coming for this towel or have you left me standing here like an idiot?" He opened his eyes.

His gaze stuck fast to her breasts where she was rubbing them.

"They hurt," she bit out, snatching the towel from his slackened hands, wrapping herself up tight. "Why are you here?"

"T-the cabin was empty," he stuttered. He rammed a splayed hand through his thick mane of hair. "God's blood." He turned, stomped three paces away, turned on his heel, then took four strides back, wrenching her up against his body in a rough embrace, his lips claiming hers in a carnal kiss.

Shock held her immobile for precious seconds, before she found her tongue, or rather, Logan did. She struggled. Squirmed. The word 'no' was sucked from her mouth along with her breath.

To her mounting frustration, Logan did not release her.

He squished her against his massive chest, as if bruising her back and ribs would ignite a fire in her body. His tongue lashed in punishing blows. This wasn't Silver Hawk! Where was the man who never put a wrong foot forward, but treated all women with respect and courtesy?

Managing to get her hands up between their bodies, she pushed, gaining just enough space to soundly slap his face.

He released her with a curse.

She ran for the cabin, not bothering to grab the towel, or her dress. Making it unmolested, she barreled through the front door, slamming the bolt home to lock it. Panting, she rested her forehead against the frame, going over the humiliating last few moments.

Hard hands whirled her around.

Sebastian's face whitened as his gaze swept down her near nude state, her quaking limbs. His scrutiny snagged on her swollen lips. "I'll kill him," he vowed in a soft voice, his color rising along with his voice. "I'll fucking kill the bastard!"

Robert came up beside her, adverting his gaze as he held out a blanket.

She took it, embarrassed and frightened. Not for herself, but Logan of all people. "N-no, Sebastian, please. It's my fault."

Incredulity widened his eyes. "The devil you say!"

"It's true," she insisted, trying hard to compose herself. "I slipped in the brook, and Logan dove in to catch me."

"I don't believe you." He regarded her for long moments, before barking to Robert, "Leave us."

Alone they faced each other.

"Did he rape you?" Sebastian asked in a flat tone, his sculpted body rigid.

Holding his gaze, she muttered, "No. It was nothing like that."

"Then what—"

"He kissed me," she blurted out. Mortified, she shook once more within the blanket. She wanted privacy to unravel, to hide her shame, but what bothered her so much she couldn't say.

Sebastian wrapped his arms around her, his heart a frantic patter against her cheek. "Talk to me, Rose. Tell me what happened."

Like a child, she drew comfort from the embrace, a knot unwinding in her belly. "I'm being silly. It was just a kiss." *That I didn't want or desire!*

Sebastian rubbed her back. "Did you..." He swallowed. "Did you consent?"

"No." She wanted to bury her face and forget a broken trust, but her husband would not allow her cowardly behavior.

Tilting her chin up, he asked in a deceptively quiet voice, "You told him no?"

"I fought him, but he did not seem to care." Tears brimmed. "I thought I could trust him, but he betrayed that confidence." Anger roiled through her now. The real reason for her state coming to light. "He made me feel helpless and afraid. I trusted him."

Sebastian swept tendrils of hair away from her face. "Such a betrayal should be dealt with the harshest retribution."

"You cannot kill family, Sebastian." She gasped, throwing her hands over her mouth. "I'm sorry. I meant to say you cannot kill all your family. Drat! That was poorly done of me. What I really meant to say was—"

"Enough!" He barked, striding around her toward the sideboard, taking something out behind it.

A stick.

No, not a stick.

She lifted wide eyes to her husband. "Is that a quarterstaff?

Holding it out to her, he shrugged. "I had one made for you today in the village. A wedding present, if you will."

She took the long wooden staff in hand, testing the balance. It felt good.

"Rose," his expression was somber, "I am your husband. Your battles are my battles. I will always defend your honor without hesitation or questions. I hope you know that by now."

Nodding, she bit her bottom lip, doing her best not to melt into a puddle on the floor. His words washed over her as soothing as bath water, stirring an ache in her breast that was fast becoming difficult to hide.

He flashed a grim smile. "But there are some battles that should be fought by the victim." He opened the door. "It's the only way to regain what was ripped from you. The only way to move past a terrible action. Now, get dressed." He exited.

Finding a simple peach-colored day dress from her meager wardrobe, she followed her husband, considering his words, watching the proud expanse of shoulders move as he led a forced march of sorts back to the scene of the crime.

Logan stood by the stream where she left him, joined by Robert. The two men were conversing, pausing when Sebastian came down the path. Logan's eyes widened for a fraction of a second, before knowledge filled those dark orbs when he saw her striding toward him with staff in hand. He understood the punishment to be dealt. Separating himself from Robert, he faced her, eyes full of silent apologies.

Sebastian took a position on the side by her brother, folding his arms across his chest, a feral smile gracing his face, his gaze expectant.

He reminded Rose of a spectator in Roman times, waiting for the lions to eat the Christians. The bloodlust in his gaze was at such a fevered pitch, it gave her pause on the beating she was about to dole out.

She wanted Logan to know the error of his actions, not trounce him within an inch of his life.

Her stare raked over him, his hulking form approaching her, his hands fanned out in a gesture of peace, an entreaty in those chocolate brown eyes.

She held the staff before her, shifting her weight, prepared to defend the offense against her person.

He fell to his knees before her.

She hadn't been prepared for that.

His gaze sought hers, wild in self-inflicted misery and pain. "Rose," he said in a voice that scraped over her sensitive skin, "I'm so sorry. I have no excuse for my base behavior."

She gripped the staff, strangling her stick. "I trusted you, Logan. I thought you of all people would never force me into action of a carnal nature."

His eyes closed, the column of his throat moving. "I know."

"You betrayed my confidence."

Eyelids lifted. "Yes."

They stared at each other in silence, and Rose's anger dissolved as water hitting sand. It was difficult to work up a satisfying anger against a target who would not fight or argue back but took full responsibility for his actions. What was she to do now?

Sebastian, for his part, stood on the sidelines looking flummoxed. "Aren't you going to beat him?"

She returned the bewildered expression. "No. He apologized, and I've decided to forgive him this one offense."

"What?" Sebastian bellowed, his voice echoing through the trees. He hooked a thumb at himself. "I get you with child, and you make an attempt at turning me into a eunuch. Edgewood makes you a victim of physical assault, and he receives a slap on the hand with the proverbial 'don't do that again?' What sort of nonsense is this? Beat the man, for Christ's sake!"

She jumped at the boom of his voice, stepping back from his wrathful expression.

Logan ambled to his feet, putting himself in a protective stance in front of her.

This entire situation was escalating to towering heights of insanity. Sebastian was right. Why was she more upset with her husband for his offenses than at Logan who committed a worse blunder?

The answer presented itself in stunning white light with trumpets blaring.

"It's my fault," she murmured.

Logan whirled. Sebastian rolled his eyes to the heavens and they never came back.

"It's true," she insisted at Logan's astonished look. "If I hadn't encouraged your attentions that first day together, you would have never tried to kiss me just now."

There was a moment of silence, then Sebastian quite loudly snapped, "Rubbish." Stalking forward, he held out his hand. "Give me your quarterstaff."

She surrendered her wedding present, eyeing her husband with misgiving.

He waved her back, not satisfied until she stood a good ten feet away. Pointing the quarterstaff at her, he narrowed his eyes. "Pay attention, Rose. I'll not repeat this lesson." He jerked a finger at Logan. "*He* is the violator. Of what, you ask?" Sebastian swung his damning finger in her direction. "Of *your* body and *your* trust. *You*," he took several stomps toward her, "told him no." He pointed back to Logan. "*He* ignored your wishes and took what he wanted." His voice lowered into a tone more suited to eardrums. "Logan knew what he was doing, and that's his burden to bear. It's not yours, Rose. You established boundaries. He ignored them. Do you understand?" Blue eyes searched her face.

Nodding her understanding, the quarterstaff was again placed in her hands.

"Now let us try this again," Sebastian said, striding away, resuming his place beside Robert. He swept a hand toward Logan.

Gripping her staff, Rose walked with measured steps, swinging the quarterstaff up high, her eyes hard upon Logan's inert body.

He stiffened, bracing himself, hands down at his sides.

She decided to make this short and sweet. "Do not touch me again, Logan." Swinging the quarterstaff in a single short blow, she walloped her opponent across the temple, bringing him to his knees. Spinning, she performed the same maneuver, knocking him flat with the force of her swing.

She panted, the exertion tiring her limbs. Warmth clung to her side. She looked up.

Sebastian no longer appeared the avenging God. While Logan lay on the ground, shaking his head, her husband slipped an arm around her waist, hauling her up against him, kissing her soundly on the mouth.

"That," he proclaimed in between kisses, "was a proper pummeling. Well done, wife."

Logan started to rise from the ground.

Sebastian kicked him in his back, sending Logan sprawling back in the dirt as he led her back to the cabin.

~ * ~

Several nights later Sebastian sat drinking coffee, watching his wife dart about the cabin, cleaning up from supper. Logan and Robert left to run some fool's errand, expecting not to be back until the morning. Sebastian highly suspected the errand had something to do with highwaymen. If his priorities had been in order, he would have asked questions or donned a disguise to follow them. That would have been the logical thing to do. Instead he shaved the hairy beast Rose named Wilbur from his face and was enjoying a quiet evening at home with his wife.

Home.

God help him, this tiny cottage was becoming more endearing to his heart than the giant hundred room monstrosity he spent most of his life residing in. What's more, his wife didn't seem to mind the meager interior. Even coerced him into buying table linens and other paltry sundries for the place.

It now resembled a cozy love nest for a pauper.

He really ought to send her home. She was a distraction to his plan of wallowing in self-pity. Instead of fantasizing about his brother romancing his wife, he could view the spectacle in person. Perhaps take notes so the next time he decided to steal another man's bride he'd be better prepared.

Yet for all of Logan's persistent attention, Rose did not treat him any differently. No lustful eye stared below his waist. Not a breath of wind escaped her lips in a wanton sigh whenever the crafty devil came in dripping wet and bare-chested from bathing in the creek. Hell no. Instead she scolded him for mucking up clean floors and ran after him with shirts insisting he wear them.

It gave Sebastian a measure of confidence he wasn't used to feeling. Indeed, with his meddling brother gone, perhaps now was a good time to ruffle Rose's feathers and see where it led. He eyed the neatly made bed, picturing rumpled white sheets and his wife splayed out before him in a lascivious sprawl, her glorious auburn hair fanned across the plump pillows.

He sighed into his coffee, creating bubbles.

Rose wiped her hands on an apron and sauntered over to the table, plopping down in a chair beside him. "I'm glad we have this night alone together."

Hope swelled in his breast. "You are?" Casually his took a gulp, bringing the rim of the cup up over his eyes so he could cheer in private. Lowering the shield, he assumed a nonplussed look. "Whatever for?" His dratted heart raced. He started to take another sip.

She gave him a winsome smile.

The roar of blood going to his head and cock at once nearly felled him.

"I think we should discuss repairing your reputation with the villagers."

He spit a stream of brown liquid across the table. "What?"

"Your reputation." Oblivious to his growing ire, she continued spewing verbal nonsense the likes of which had not been heard since some fool decided to raise the tea tax in America. "Logan and I met with your solicitor, and I must confess to feeling quite horrified over the rent system you have in place. It exceeds all bounds of decency, Sebastian."

"Better that than having them dragged off to the Tower of London for assaulting a duke." He couldn't believe they were having this conversation. Their first moment alone since their wedding night and she wanted to talk about peasants with a penchant for maiming dukes?

"Would you please stop fisting your hair into unruly spikes and listen to me?"

He wondered why his scalp was tingling in an unpleasant manner. Assuming an air of indifference, he dropped his hands to the table. "I'd wrangle Wilbur, but I disposed of him this morning."

"I noticed." Her gaze scanned his face, breathing life back into a snuffed-out flame.

He straightened. "You did?"

"Aye. Now about your tenants—"

Jumping to his feet, upending the chair, he shouted, "Hang the tenants! Get over here, wife."

"Have you noticed you have a tendency to shout when conversing with me?"

He stomped over to her, bent, then swooped her up into his arms. "Wife, I never had tendencies until I married you. You drive me to the brink of madness."

Coiling her arms around his neck, she smiled, slow and saucy. "You seem impatient for some reason. Could our sudden bout of privacy have something to do with it?"

He halted by the bed, trying to decide if he should lay her down with tenderness, gentle force or a bellowing blackguard. Would she trust him if he took her fast and hard? Or would she scream and declare him an uncouth barbarian? He settled for a compromise.

Bracing a knee on the mattress, he plunked her down, watching in satisfaction as she bounced, her mouth making a small o. Her attention was riveted to him now.

A seductive promise glittered in his eye. Or a demented gleam. Without aid of a looking glass, he suspected it was the latter. Either way, he prayed the message was clear: take off your clothes. "Yes, my darling. A night to ourselves has everything to do with my current mood." Reaching behind, he grabbed a fistful of shirt, dragging it up, only to get it stuck on his head.

He forgot to untie the bloody cravat first.

Cursing he released the garment, made short work of the neckcloth, then dragged the shirt off.

His wife was in stitches by the time he wrestled the garment to the floor.

This bumbling inept attempt at seduction was becoming rather comical. Was there ever a time when he was debonair about the whole affair of lovemaking? He used to charm and enchant the ladies of London with the best of them. Now he had all the grace and aplomb of a two-year-old, hopping on one foot to get a boot off, attempting to cope on his own with buttons of all sizes.

Rose appeared before him, a goddess with nimble fingers, wordlessly offering her assistance. She worked him free of his mangled attire, stopping to place a hand on his bare chest, over his pounding heart.

Their gazes collided.

His rioting thoughts and emotions calmed. Staring into an endless expanse of green framed by lush black lashes, he found his center. His world.

The only face reflected in that innocent wide gaze was his. All the troubles and doubts and heartache faded to the distant. There was only here and now.

In this she looked at him differently than Logan. Carnal knowledge of the other was a barrier Edgewood couldn't breach. Of course, why would he when he owned her heart?

Black, ugly emotions stole the glory from this moment, twisting Sebastian's innards as effectively as any knife. Tonight was a reprieve, nothing more. A taste of heaven for a starving man, pining for the fullness and weight of a meal to fill an empty belly.

Where was her heart this night? With him in this cottage? Or with the highwayman out somewhere on the road assaulting villains in the name of decency?

Jealousy was a sharp blade without mercy for its victim. It plunged, and he found his mouth forming words to a question that held the power to destroy him. "Do you love me?"

Black lashes flared wide, touching a finely arched brow. "I… I…"

Pain lashed his insides, crumpling heaven in favor of hell. "Never mind, Rose. I shouldn't have asked."

"Sebastian, I—"

"I said never mind!" he snapped, turning, seeking his discarded clothing, jamming them back on. "You love him, Rose. I understand. I'm the fool who mistakenly thought I too was worming a way into that ironclad heart of yours."

Shoving his arms into a jacket, he stormed to the front door, turning to her, fighting a visceral urge to toss her over a table and plow his way into her body. The only path to her heart he knew to take. Perhaps his father had the right of it all these years, forcing himself between thighs. Easier to scale flesh than lay siege to unyielding stone.

The ugly thoughts gutted him, leaving him reeling with self-disgust. Without another word he vanished into the night, going for his horse and saddling him, riding the animal hard and fast, wanting to encounter highwaymen in this current mood so he could burn out this white-hot anger burning his insides.

But no masked criminals assaulted him during his journey, and eventually, he found himself back home, worn out, body and soul.

Dismounting, he stabled his steed, and sought the cottage door, finding it locked as it should be. He fumbled in a pocket for a key, rammed it in the lock and turned, easing the door open.

A fire burned low in the hearth, but even in the low flickering light, he saw his wife. Curled up on her side with…

Hell.

She had one of his shirts pressed against her face while she slept, her pallor still blotchy as though she cried herself to sleep. Disrobing, he climbed between the sheets next to her, dragging her up against his frame. Laying a kiss on her hair, he murmured, "I'm sorry."

Sniffing, she rolled to face him. "I am too."

Smoothing hair back, he acknowledged the truth. "You have nothing to be sorry for. I did this to myself." Lowering his head, he caught salty lips, kissing them clean, pressing her soft yielding body back upon the pillows.

He made love to her with gentle fervor, banishing the insidious commands inside his head.

His father's voice was a phantom forever branded into his mind, but he vowed to vanquish the demon once and for all.

Starting in the morning. Devising a new rent scale for his struggling tenants.

Chapter Twenty-One

"Tell me again why we're traveling to see Dr. Wilson?" Sebastian tugged on his cravat, appearing green around the collar. "Your health, and dare I say your appetite, have been improved for weeks. We have no further need for his services."

Rose chewed, not allowing her husband's dour attitude to spoil a brilliant luncheon of pickles, hard-boiled eggs and pig's feet.

Sebastian and Robert stared at her while she stuffed her face. They had food of their own getting cold. Both men seemed to prefer their pints of ale in the inn they had stopped at while Logan had a shoe replaced on Jupiter at the blacksmith.

She licked her fingers. "Because he wanted to check on the babe. Can you pass the strawberry preserves?"

The other patrons gave them a wide berth. At first, she thought it was because of Sebastian's mask and fierce scowl, but their attention, like Sebastian and Robert's, was focused solely on her plate of food.

Robert passed the small glass jar containing the fruit, waving a hand in front of his nose. "By the saints, that is a foul odor. I wonder if it will smell better when she throws it up."

Sebastian's complexion went gray. "It can't smell any worse than this morning's offering of blueberry jam and chicken liver. I had to throw away a perfectly good pair of Hessian boots."

Robert snickered. "You have more. I'm sure you won't miss them."

"I know of one cheeky American I won't miss when he sails back to that infested—"

"Gentlemen," Rose interrupted. "Behave. For me."

"This is behaving." Sebastian snorted. "This is also tolerating. And patronizing. And indulging. I'm keeping myself well-managed, thank you."

"Indeed, sister. Have you ever heard me be more congenial in all my life? A little gratitude, if you please."

She rubbed her temples, pushing away her plate. "I need a

moment." She stood, and the men jumped up as well. "To myself," she snapped. "To take care of certain needs."

"There's a latrine in the back," Robert called out.

Sebastian covered his mouth with a cloth napkin, but it failed to hide his quaking shoulders.

She marched through the dining room thinking unkind thoughts regarding the men in her life, crossed the threshold to a cold winter's day, then continued her march around the backside of the building. She did not see a latrine but there was a small girl staring up at a tree with fat tears rolling down her cheeks.

Rose sidled up to the child, looking around for parents. "I say, dearest, what seems to be the matter?"

She pointed up, and Rose followed the small index finger, raising her gaze. In the middle of a branch, high up in a sprawling oak tree, sat a tiny black kitten.

"Oh dear! Is that your pet, sweet one?"

The little girl squinted at her. "He won't come down. It's stuck. Can you help it?"

Rose began to say yes but thought twice. She promised Sebastian she would start thinking like a mother. Surely a woman with child would not dare to climb a tree. After a defenseless baby kitten.

The baby gave a short, high-pitch cry and every promise she made to her husband flew out of her head. When he scolded her later, she would claim a mother's protective instinct overcame her good senses.

"Fear not, dear child. I shall have your pet to you in a trice." Rose stepped up to the trunk, reaching overhead for a branch. She got a good grip and lifted a foot off the ground. Strong hands wrapped around her waist. Her head fell back to see Sebastian standing behind her.

He blinked at her from behind his mask. "Rose, what is your middle name?"

She sighed. "Marie."

"Thank you." He yanked her feet to the ground, twisting her around to face him. "Rose Marie Graham, what in hell do you think you're doing?"

"Climbing a tree to rescue a kitten."

A small crowd of men, woman and children were gathering.

"Climbing a tree to rescue a kitten," he repeated. He looked to the heavens, moving his lips, uttering silent words.

It looked to Rose like he was counting. She waited until he reached ten before adding, "I had to, Sebastian. The baby is stuck up there!"

"So, my pregnant wife once again decides to take matters into her own hands."

She smiled, tilting her head to a saucy angle. "I daresay it's all a woman can do when there's no man around to come barreling to the rescue."

A ripple of amusement passed through the crowd.

Sebastian remained ignorant to the attention their little spat was creating. "No man born would risk his neck for a scrawny feline who can claw his way up a tree but not know the slightest thing about how to get back down. It's called common sense, and all men have it."

Deep murmurs of approval echoed.

Rose crossed her arms. "In my country, men of common sense toe the mark with cowards. If you are too scared to climb up a tree, then stand aside to let those with more valor do the rescuing. Men make terrible heroes at any rate. It's the women folk who truly get the job done."

A round of applause broke out, and Sebastian jerked around, scowling at the crowd. "What the devil?" He turned back to her. "You're making a public spectacle out of me, so I'll rescue that mangy feline, aren't you?"

"Please, Sebastian?" she murmured, hoping he would accept the gauntlet.

He surrendered with a curse and a sigh. "Very well, Duchess. Stand aside."

Rose moved out of the way, watching with the rest of the interested onlookers while Sebastian pulled himself up into the tree. When he gained the same branch of the kitten, he glanced down.

Rose gave him an encouraging smile, but it faltered when her husband looked away. The branch he was putting his weight on swayed alarmingly to and fro, the kitten clinging with a slinky tail.

Sebastian stretch out on his stomach, slithering forward. He reached the middle of the branch, snatching the kitten to the applause of the crowd, grinned and then it happened.

A loud crack ripped through the air.

He had just enough time to utter a ribald metaphor before plummeting to the ground below.

Rose raced forward as soon as he hit the grass. "My darling, are you hurt?" She snatched the kitten, fussing over every inch of fur, petting the baby while her husband moaned, holding his ribs. She glanced down. "Sebastian, it was good of you not to land on the baby. Must have been common sense that prevented that tragedy." She gave him a simpering smile.

He glared at her, shooting invisible daggers, then his eyes widened. He patted his face and looked up. His mask was hanging by a tree branch.

The sudden silence was deafening.

Thinking swiftly, Rose sank to her knees, hugging her husband about his neck, hiding his face in her skirts. "I was wrong," she said loud enough for William the Conquer to hear from his grave, "when given the opportunity, men do indeed astound and amaze by the largeness of their hearts. Thank you, fearless stranger!"

"Rose," Sebastian gasped, "I can't breathe."

She loosened her stronghold around his windpipe, then felt tiny claws prick their way up her arm. The fuzzy kitten perched itself on Sebastian's shoulder, giving him several earnest licks to his ear.

A man dressed in simple clothes stepped forward, doffing his cap. "Pardon me, Your Grace, but we heard you was dead."

Sebastian grimaced, sitting up. "Am I not? This looks like hell to me." He glanced at the kitten still sitting on his shoulder. "Has all the makings of eternal suffering."

The kitten licked his nose.

"My husband's demise was a mere rumor," Rose supplied, speaking to the growing crowd of villagers.

Sebastian ambled to his feet.

"A misunderstanding. He... He..." she looked at her husband for help.

He lifted a sardonic brow back at her.

Pointing a finger at his wrinkled forehead, she shouted, "Lower that brow at once, sir! You can hurt someone with that if you're not careful."

Sebastian stared at her as though she were a candidate for Bedlam.

She might be by the end of the day, but she was desperate to have these villagers not fear her husband. He was misunderstood and condemned for crimes he didn't commit. Let the people see his wife was not afraid of him. That he could smile and be charming. Certainly, rescuing a kitten helped her new cause.

"That's better," she announced, turning a pleased smile upon her captive audience. "As I was saying, my very loving, heroic, undead husband and I were simply having a honeymoon of sorts, but he felt it would be safer to travel in disguise given the current highwaymen situation and," she shrugged, keeping her insipid smile in place, "I was eager to meet the people who worked the land for us and to see the estate and meet all you lovely villagers."

She stepped toward a well-endowed older woman, wearing a stained apron, thrusting out a hand. "My name is Rose Graham. I'm an American, by the way." *And a babbling idiot when nervous, but please don't hold that against me!*

The older woman took her hand but cast a frightened gaze over Rose's shoulder.

A heavy silence stole over the assembly, all attention on the tall, brooding gentleman sporting a kitten perched on one shoulder.

She turned. "My darling, won't you introduce me properly?"

There was a message in those blue depths she could not decipher. The creased forehead and dark glower seemed to herald a warning, but any man wearing a kitten on his person was hard to take too seriously. Dukes were no exception.

Sebastian finally stepped forward, putting an arm around her waist, bowing his head toward the woman whose hand Rose still held. "Mary McGregor, are you not? The butcher's wife?"

She curtsied. "Why yes, Your Grace." Her eyes widened in surprise.

"Mrs. McGregor, please allow me the pleasure of introducing you to my wife, Rose Graham, formerly of Virginia."

Mrs. McGregor curtsied again. "A pleasure, Your Grace."

Rose placed her hands over Sebastian's, still lingering on her abdomen. "Thank you." She beamed up at her husband. "Darling, should we announce the coming of the babe now or later?"

A murmur rose within the group of men and women.

He frowned down at her. "Later. We must be going, Duchess."

"But Sebastian—"

He cut her a look that had her bottom stinging. It was similar to her father's that went along the lines of: *one more word out of you and you're going to regret it.*

Rose wilted, defeated for the moment.

Sebastian lifted his head, speaking for the first time to the crowd. "Ladies and gentlemen, my apologies, but my wife and I must be going. Excuse us, please."

He touched her elbow, steering her through the departing crowd with all the haste of a man with his pants on fire, but a shrill voice halted his retreat.

"Wait!"

Rose spun, immediately finding herself holding the little girl.

"Thank you for saving the kitty," she said, beaming at them both, not shrinking away from Sebastian's scowling face.

"Well aren't you going to take him?" Sebastian asked.

"Oh no, it ain't mine. Me mum would skin me alive for bringing home an animal. I didn't want it hurt." The girl grinned, backing away and disappearing with the crowd.

"We've been suckered by a ten-year-old gutter snipe," he muttered.

Rose agreed. "But it was good to let the people see you playing the role of hero. Perhaps they'll change their regard where you're concerned."

"Is that what you were about with all this nonsense?" He ripped the kitten from his shoulder, handing it back to her. "My dear, your efforts are noble, and I'm flattered, but it will take more than one act of charity on my part to win over my tenants. The history of their suffering runs long and deep. I thank you for trying." He managed a crooked smile that resembled more a snarl, then turned on his heel then strode for the front of the inn.

She petted her baby, thinking. More than one act of charity…

Hell and damnation. She should have thought of this notion sooner while in her sickbed. She ran, catching up with her husband as he rounded the corner of the establishment.

Robert was leaning against their horses, watching them approach with a grin splitting his face from ear to ear. He nodded to Rose. "What have we there? The newest member of the Graham family?"

Sebastian looped his hands, boosting her up onto their shared horse. "Hell no. We're not keeping that filthy animal!"

"Sebastian, please?"

He mounted behind her, wedging himself against her with more force than necessary. "I said no, Rose. I am the head of this household, I make the rules, and I say this thing is not coming with us!"

~ * ~

"I can't believe it's coming with us." Sebastian looked to the heavens for answers while his wife was busy casting up her accounts alongside the road, with Logan standing in her shadow offering comfort. He supposed as his wife, bearing his child, the duties of offering comfort should be dealt with by him, but as God as his witness, he needed a break. This morning's regurgitated repast of chicken liver almost had him retching beside his wife.

The kitten was sound asleep, sunning itself on the saddle. "Every time I turn around, our family has gained another member. God's teeth! I made myself quite clear on the issue, did I not?"

"I heard you tell Rose 'no' several times," Robert replied.

"Thank you. At least some heard me speaking."

"Then what happened?"

"I have absolutely no notion. That's the hell of it. One minute, we're having a spirited debate on pet ownership, then the next thing I know, we're having a spirited debate about naming the animal."

"What did you decide to name it?"

"Nutmeg. But I honestly can't see a Nutmeg running around the castle, can you?"

Robert burst out laughing. "I can, actually."

"Why the hell are you laughing? I find nothing humorous about a woman who cannot take care of herself, to trust with taking care of a baby kitten. Rose is unpredictable and—"

"She has you wrapped around her little finger," Robert said, interrupting a promising rant. "I saw what happened from my horse, Dorchester. Yes, you told her no, then she turned to you, batted some eyelashes, you stopped speaking and stared at her like a love-struck boy, then wondered aloud what you were talking about."

"That's not true." Sebastian drew himself upright, intent on giving his witless brother-in-law a dressing down when something crawled onto his shoulder, meowing in his ear. He despised being at the beck and call of a tiny ball of fur. He was a duke. Not a footman.

"If you're hungry, you'll have to wait for your mistress."

"Meow!"

"I heard you the first time, but I am not—"

"Meeeeeooooow."

Sebastian picked up the yowling rodent by the scruff of his neck with his thumb and forefinger, bringing it around to stare at it eye-level. "I don't think you quite understand your precarious situation here. Your existence in this witless family is entirely dependent on my good nature, and right now my mood is as sour as those rotten pickles your mistress keeps eating."

Robert roared with laughter, holding his stomach.

Sebastian ignored him, determined to make one soul in his growing household recognize him as a source of authority. "Good. Now, as I was saying, you'll have to be patient."

The kitten hung there, blinking at him.

Robert wiped tears from his eyes. "And lo, how the mighty have fallen." He chuckled. "Give it here. Nutmeg is simply hungry, oh wise leader."

Sebastian handed the hairball over to more capable hands, watching Robert dig through a saddlebag. "It's never too early to teach manners to children."

Robert snickered, pouring milk from a flask into a tin plate. "I am eager to see you tackle the role of fatherhood with such noble thoughts. I wager within the first day of their existence you'll be reduced to jelly, unable to remember your name the first time you lay eyes on your son or daughter." He set the kitten by the plate, petting its tiny black head.

A curious warmth swept through Sebastian's chest, staring at the kitten, thinking of holding his child for the first time. Was he going to have a son or daughter? He wanted both with a desperation that weakened his resolve to see Rose have her choice. Hope was a seedling newly planted in his heart, but it was growing. The past few days were bloody encouraging.

"I fear you may be right," Sebastian admitted, "I'm not very good at keeping a thought when your sister smiles at me, I can only imagine the power my children will one day wield." His gaze caught sight of a cart and a man coming down the road when a great splintering noise ripped through the quiet. "Bloody hell let's get out of here! That man's cart just hit a rut and broke a wheel. Rose will insist I help if she sees—"

"Oh sir! May we help you?"

"—him." Sebastian rolled his eyes upward, mouthing silent epitaphs to an unforgiving God.

"She's just trying to help your image with the people," Robert offered, standing up.

"It's madness," Sebastian countered. "One afternoon of manual labor is not enough to rid a man of a lifetime of wicked deeds. Those villagers will only view me in one light—a sinister red one. If I'm being honest, I'm not too fond of them myself."

"You may not be fond of them," Logan said, striding up, watching Rose like an overbearing nursemaid while she talked with the stranger, "but they are fond of Rose. She's accomplishing something I never thought I'd witness in my lifetime."

Irked, Sebastian turned to his half-brother, raising brows in a sardonic arch, until Nutmeg climbed up his person, perching himself on his shoulder and starting gnawing on his earlobe. The arrogant stance was ruined to the point of laughable, but Sebastian clung to his dignity, crossing his arms, ignoring the kitten using his earlobe as a nipple. He'd gone from duke, to indentured servant, to wet nurse in a span of one day. "What's that Edgewood?"

Edgewood wiped the back of his hand across his mouth, trying and failing to hide a growing smile. "Rose is making you, a Dorchester, approachable for the first time in your family's history." He sobered, casting his gaze again at her. "She's warm. Endearing."

"And daft as hell," Sebastian added, fighting and failing to follow the direction of Edgewood's stare.

His gaze took in her lush, hour-glass figure, before his attention was arrested by the tinkling sounds of female laughter. The pull on his heart was undeniable. He shot a quick look at Edgewood.

The barbarian's eyes were equally besotted.

The expression gutted him, turning the blade to a knife firmly lodged in his heart. It was beyond bearing thinking of his wife in Edgewood's arms, but his half-brother looked no less smitten now than he did when he first stole Rose away from him months ago.

His rage and jealousy were bitter monsters waiting to strike, the battle to keep them at bay exhausting his control. Fear, ugly and bright, tried to overtake his senses, but he was ruthless, pushing it aside. "I better go and make sure my duchess understands I am not available to play the part of wheelwright today." He strode to his wife, ignoring the wet sucking noises Nutmeg was still making on his ear.

Edgewood fell into step beside him. "Nonsense. There's always time to help another soul or learn a new trade."

Sebastian had only time enough to shoot his brother a glare before Rose turned the full force of her smile on him. And Edgewood. Though her smile widened at Sebastian when she caught Nutmeg mutilating his flesh.

She cooed at the kitten, taking the animal from his shoulder, her eyes brimming with laughter. "Sebastian, you're too kind to our baby."

His heart skipped a beat. And damn if his mouth didn't dry out at the choice of words.

Edgewood's complexion turned a shade gray.

Suddenly in a generous mood, Sebastian gestured toward the stranger. "Whom do we have the pleasure of meeting this fine day?"

The man doffed his cap, eyes downcast. "Me name is Hartford, Your Grace. William Hartford."

Rose stepped back, standing closer to the wagon bed. "Mr. Hartford was just telling me his daughter is getting married tomorrow morning."

"Poor blighter," Sebastian said beneath his breath, earning him an elbow in the ribcage from Edgewood. "That's wonderful," he proclaimed out loud, rubbing his side.

Rose was trying to catch his eye, nodding toward the back of the wagon.

He prowled over at the pretense of looking over the broken

wheel axle. He glanced where Rose indicated. Some food stuff littered the back. The man went to town shopping for the bridal breakfast. What was the import of that?

"They're having a large gathering of friends and family. Most of which are your tenants," Rose whispered, staring at him in silent expectation.

Sebastian eyed the meager fare again, understanding what his duchess was hinting at. Fighting the urge to sigh, roll his eyes and declare himself the village idiot, he did the only thing he could do.

"Edgewood," he called, "why don't you assist Mr. Hartford with his wagon?"

Suspicion rolled across Logan's face. "What about you? Have you hurt your arms today after wrestling with a hog in the mud, Your Grace?"

He glowered, straightening to his full height. "No. I feel a pressing need to head back into town and drain the remnants of my purse."

Understanding flashed in Edgewood's eyes, followed by a smile of approval. "There may be hope for you after all, Your Grace."

Scoffing, he departed the trio, only to hear Rose call his name. "Sebastian!"

Whirling, he saw Nutmeg charging down the road to him, a furious whirl of black heading toward his pant leg. He braced, and Nutmeg climbed, reasserting himself as master of his domain—the top of Sebastian's shoulder.

Hands to her ample breasts, Rose's full mouth formed an O-ring. "Our baby loves you!"

The wench sounded surprised. *At least someone loves me.* The thought was uncharitable but not without cause. He scratched Nutmeg on his head, watching his wife turn her smile upon the highwayman, her attention riveted to whatever drivel was spilling from his mouth.

Robert laughed behind him. "I had no notion the infamous monster of Dorchester Castle could look so forlorn." Coming up on his side, he took Nutmeg from his shoulder. "I do not know how you English go about courting, but back home, we don't show our underbellies to the competition." He shot a pensive look at him. "We fight, Dorchester. Why aren't you fighting?"

Caught in a vulnerable moment, Sebastian turned away without answering, striding toward his horse, uncomfortable with the tightness clawing at his chest. He was playing a very dangerous game. One without rules or boundaries, except those he made up as he went along.

How could he explain to Witherby that lines were blurring?

Right and wrong were notions with grey smudges, borrowing from the other, mixing in the pit of his stomach along with self-respect and honor.

Bloody hell. He was liking Edgewood. For the first time, he felt more a sibling than a rival. He craved that connection. The bond of family and friendship.

But he hungered for Rose more.

Alas, she was the dream denied him. The promise of a child brightened his once bleak future. He swore on his honor that he would give Rose a choice, but the cost of offering his wife freedom was becoming more than he could bear.

He couldn't lose her.

And he disliked the notion of making an enemy of Logan.

If that wasn't enough to sour a man's appetite, there was also Prinny waiting in London for word of Silver Hawk's capture.

Yes indeed. A damn pickle of a situation.

He started when the warmth and weight of a hand met his unoccupied shoulder. He jerked his head around, meeting Robert's concerned hazel eyes.

"You didn't answer my question."

Irritable, he shrugged off Witherby's touch. "You know why. I'm keeping my distance to give your sister room to explore her feelings toward Edgewood." He suppressed the urge to flinch, for the words torn from him cut to the quick. A physical, real wound that would never heal should his wife find love in another man's arms.

Witherby regarded him with an open, frank gaze. "I think I'm the only soul in this traveling party who is noticing something strange."

"Other than a kitten sucking on my earlobe with abandon? Or my pregnant wife acquiring a penchant for all things pickled? Or my highwayman half-brother who fawns obsessively over her? No, Witherby, I haven't noticed anything of import of late I'd label as strange."

"Are you done?"

"For the moment."

"Thank God. As I was going to say, I have noticed the look she once reserved for Silver Hawk, is now being bestowed on you whenever she looks your way—which is quite often, I must admit."

"Stop it, Witherby." He gripped the reins, telling himself to mount and ride away. This conversation was pursuing dangerous ground. It was feeding the seedling. He couldn't afford to listen. "I was no doubt standing in the way of her supper. There's nothing she loves more right now than filling her stomach."

"True."

He cut Witherby a curled lip, put a foot in the stirrup, then glanced at his wife, unable to resist the temptation.

She stood beside Edgewood speaking with Mr. Hartford when she doubled over with a coughing fit.

Edgewood wrapped an arm around her waist, dragging her into his side.

The world erupted in red hues to rival hell itself.

Snarling, Sebastian withdrew a pouch from inside his jacket, shoving it against Witherby's chest. "Go back to the village and buy a wagon, horse and enough food to fill the man's home for a year."

"Where are you going?"

"To fight."

He mounted his mare, heading straight to his wife with murder in his eyes.

Edgewood glanced up from patting Rose's back, cursing virulently. "What the—" He dove to the side, missing the business end of a pair of hooves by inches.

Sebastian jumped down, grinning at his prostate brother.

Rose gathered her breath, gaping at him. "Are you daft? You could have hurt Logan!"

"Lord Edgewood," he corrected, drawing his wife close, whispering, "I cannot tolerate listening to you speak of my half-brother as though the two of you are on intimate terms. Please have mercy on my sanity, madam."

To his shock, Rose's expression became contrite. "I'm sorry, Sebastian. You're right."

"No, he's not," Logan barked, sitting up, wiping mud from his eyes. "We are family and need not necessarily stand on formality if I have granted permission to use my Christian name." He stood. "Which I have, long before she met you."

Sebastian bristled at the reminder of the time Rose spent in his company as a captive of Silver Hawk. He touched his wife's arm with gentle hands, pushing her away with care, before stepping up toe-to-toe with Edgewood.

A good deal of glowering ensued along with silent promises of retribution. Sebastian longed for the day when he could land a punch on Edgewood, but that time was not now. Not with Rose ready to leap in the middle of their fisticuffs should he throw the first fist.

He backed off slow, holding Edgewood's gaze. "Do not touch her like that again," he murmured with as much vehemence as he could in a whisper. "She's still my wife."

A considering look passed through Edgewood's eyes. He lowered his lids, guarding his expression. "You're right. I'm sorry, Dorchester."

It was Sebastian's turn to gape. An apology from his brother was the least thing he would have expected. Unsettled, he turned his back, focusing his attention on Rose.

She stared back at him with a guilty expression.

He jerked his head toward the horse. "Come, Rose. Edgewood and Witherby will help Mr. Hartford. We must continue to the doctor's home."

Chapter Twenty-Two

She was back at the place this twisted tale started. But in the arms of another masked man. One she swore she'd never love—or bear his children.

How ignorant she was of her dreams and desires. She knew a handsome face could hide a dark soul. But evil takes many forms and not all are so easily distinguishable to the naked eye. She would give the world to reverse the sun and be the proper wife Sebastian deserved. Never in her mind would she have counted herself as the problem, bending in whichever direction the wind was blowing.

It was a wonder her husband still wanted her. The man possessed a deep well of patience to rival God Himself. She could only imagine how far Henry Graham must have pushed his son. Sebastian was a master of control as far as she could see. She knew the decision to kill a parent could not have been an easy one.

Nor his current decision to keep himself from touching her while riding behind her in the saddle. Her husband was currently straining his spine to the utmost, attempting to keep his posture stiff and straight as an arrow. As a result, there remained a good gap between their two bodies. She did not know where his thoughts lingered, but it must be someplace unpleasant. He had been sullen and quiet for much of the ride.

Her nerves were being stretched thin by the silence. But idle conversation would not drip from her tongue for once. All she could do was endure the ride and pray for the strength to get through.

This was her happily ever after, and she was ready to fight for it.

In another hour the doctor's cabin came into view, a familiar clearing in the woods opening before them. So little had changed. The thatched roof cottage stood tidy but small. A grassy yard separated the home from the barn. Smoke spiraled from the chimney, hinting at warmth and a meal.

Sebastian dismounted, dutifully plucking her from the saddle, but letting her go as soon as her feet hit the ground. "I'll stable the horse and meet you inside." Without waiting for an answer, he walked the animal to the barn, disappearing into the darkened interior.

Shaking her head at his stubborn refusal to meet her eyes, she strode to the cottage, opening the door, knowing the home to be deserted. Smiling, she viewed the handiwork of the doctor's wife. Her attention to detail was brilliant.

Eager to rejoin her husband, Rose nearly skipped across the grass, smiling to herself. All would be well soon enough. Sebastian was moody and rightly so. He yearned for something he thought another man held, and she would prove to him tonight all his fears were unfounded.

She had long believed words were easy, and actions were for the bold.

Crossing the threshold of the barn, she paused, laying a hand on a wood beam, remembering a man and words spoken a lifetime ago. How Silver Hawk had captured her imagination, fulfilling her girlish dreams of what a hero should be.

How foolish and naive she had been of men back then.

Not long ago she stood there seeking peace from a stranger she knew only by rumor, his image forged by gossip. Common sense hadn't stood a chance against a pair of deep chocolate eyes promising her to make love to her if she consented to the act someday.

But fate had intervened, throwing another masked man across her path. One she had no foreknowledge of, whose looks rivaled her dear highwayman's, but whose demeanor at first seemed formal and austere.

She was again in this barn, facing temptation. Life was coming full circle, offering second chances to an unworthy soul. To a masked man she loved without fear or hesitation.

She removed her hair pins, sending the mass tumbling over one shoulder. Shoring her courage, she rounded the corner, entering a stall on quiet feet.

Sebastian had his back to her, brushing down his horse with quick, efficient strokes.

Stepping up behind him, she laid a gentle hand on his shoulder.

He stiffened without turning. "Don't."

She recoiled at the sharp rebuke. "Sebastian?"

His hands clenched around the handle of the brush so tightly his knuckles whitened. "Don't touch me while you're thinking of *him*." He went back to grooming, not bothering to look at her.

His comment stung. But was it unfair?

The answer saddened her. She approached him again, this time wrapping her arms around his torso, resting her cheek against the bunching muscles of his back. "Sebastian, you're wrong."

Tensing, he stopped, his hands locked on the flanks of the mare. "Do you think me the fool? I know it is not me in your thoughts here. At this place. How could they be? I was little more than the monster you were fleeing from in fear."

"I'm not afraid now, Sebastian."

"Are you not?" He whirled. "You don't know me or the things I've done. My confessions of the other night were the tip of the iceberg." His eyes flashed a warning. *Stay away.*

She decided to take that as an invitation. She had to, there was no alternative. "I know something of your deeds."

"Do you know why your father sent you to England to marry me?"

His expression was so forlorn, she ached for the heavy burden he kept shouldered.

"The betrothal contract," she said.

"Yes. There was a contract, but it was between you and Edgewood."

Her smile never faltered. "I know, Sebastian."

His gaze turned incredulous. He took one step away, colliding with the horse. "You know? How—*Edgewood.*" The name was said as a growl.

Not wishing to crowd her husband, she stood her ground. "Yes. Lord Edgewood told me all about your father's will and about the letter of blackmail you sent my family. I know all of that, but not why you wrote it."

She sought the memory in her mind, going over every detail. Her father sought her out among the apple trees where she'd often go to be alone. His face had been much like Sebastian's was now—resolute, unyielding. He told her of the agreement with the duke and declared she had two weeks to get her trousseau together, for she'd be sailing for England with Robert to marry his son, Sebastian Graham. All the tears and begging in the world did not move her father or seem to faze him in the least. He made his announcement and left her crying in a heap in the grass.

Sebastian regarded her in pain and sorrow, slouching the proud breadth of his shoulders. "You were a gift for a by-blow who didn't deserve you. My father petitioned the crown to give Edgewood the title of viscount, worked out a betrothal contract for a wife, gave him an estate to make into his own for a family he would one day have. For me? Henry Graham gifted his rightful son with no more than his due as heir—a title with no honor, tenants who despised the name Dorchester and the legacy of assault it stood for. I was alone, and my father did everything within his power while alive to ensure I would stay that way!" He stepped away, putting himself in a far corner of the stall, thrusting splayed fingers through his thick hair. "I was beyond rational thought after the solicitor read my father's will. All I wanted was given to another man, and I went mad with jealousy."

"Sebastian, you were the rightful heir." Taking slow steps, she closed the distance between them, touching his face gently, urging him to look at her. "Your scars are not so disfiguring as to render the female population speechless with horror."

He smiled at that, cupping his hand over hers, leaning into her palm. "You're wonderful, Rose, but so ignorant of the world I live in." He kissed the inside of her wrist, releasing her. "I told you once I was engaged. Do you remember?"

She nodded. "Yes, Lady Emily. I met her just the other day."

"Of course, you did." His head shook back and forth. "Edgewood would leave no stone unturned in his pursuit of slander."

"She was lovely. I can see why you would like her."

He gave her an odd look. "I was betrothed to her since birth. Whether I liked her or not had very little to do with our relationship."

She didn't want to discuss Lady Emily. "Then why—"

"It was never about my face! I lied to you. I broke our engagement after I healed from the villagers' attack, because I knew, from the moment I caught my father raping a child, that my wife, and daughters, should I be blessed to have them, would always be at risk from the man."

Stunned, Rose stared, sorrow creeping in, as her husband's words began to make sense.

Glistening pools gathered in Sebastian's eyes. "I would always live in fear for their safety with my father near. Then I killed him, to spare the world one less monster. Only to find the beast I long feared resides in me."

She moved to embrace him, whispering, "Sebastian."

He jumped back, snapping, "Let me finish!" He swiped at his eyes, refocusing on her. "Our first night together at the inn I nearly raped you. I was already so infatuated with your beauty, filled with a kind of possessiveness I've never felt before, and when you whispered Silver Hawk's name, I nearly lost all control. You have no notion what it took for me not to throw you down on the floor and take your maidenhead by brute force."

"But you didn't, Sebastian." She spread her hands out,

imploringly. "You forced nothing between us, staying your hand from abuse as well as your mouth from speaking out of anger. You did have control. Can't you see that?"

He closed his eyes, the muscles lining his throat rippling up and down. "And in my study? I had no restraint to cling to after overhearing your plans to leave. I forced you then."

"You gave me a choice." She could feel his pain, was desperate to rid him of it. "It was I who robbed you of alternatives, whose selfishness backed you into a corner not of your choosing."

"Do not make excuses for my actions," he barked, slicing her with a glare. "It only makes it worse. I knew better. You were the puppet, dancing to a story created by others with power. I should have been sympathetic toward your feelings. No, instead I gave full rein to the beast and took your innocence on the floor." His face went white. "In the same room as my father tortured a young girl." His face crumpled in grief, his revelation wiping away the rest of his composure in a wave of tears.

With his defenses down, Rose jumped toward him, embracing him around the torso, hugging as tightly as her arms could hold him. "Sebastian, please don't do this to yourself."

He returned her hug, his breath hot upon her neck, wetness slicking her skin. "I must face what I am, Rose. Every time Edgewood looks at you, touches you in any manner, I am forced to the same conclusion time and again."

She trembled in his arms, not liking the bleakness to his tone. She drew back, staring into a face devoid of emotion. It frightened her. "Sebastian?"

He stroked her cheek with the pad of a thumb. "Thank you for every laugh. Your smiles and kisses. You gave me the only happiness in two and thirty years of living. I'll treasure you for the rest of my life. I promise."

"Stop this," she said, backing away. "Wherever your thoughts now reside, stop. I will not countenance this sort of discussion." She swallowed over a hard lump in her throat. "Please."

He walked toward her as she retreated. "Never say 'please' to Edgewood, my love. It gives him power over you. Allow no man that privilege."

She stumbled, quickly righting herself. "W-why do you say such things? Logan is not my husband and bears no responsibility toward me other than the ones he imagines."

Sebastian smiled at that, but it never reached his eyes. "He will be your husband, Rose. If I were you, I'd set the tone now for a happy marriage."

She halted. "I'm not marrying Logan. I'm already a wife."

He stood before her, shaking his head. "No. You were a coveted prize. One without choice or consent in the matter. I'm annulling our marriage, Rose."

She stared at him, unable to comprehend. "Is this a test? Are you punishing me for having feelings toward Lord Edgewood at one time? I'm sorry I hurt you! I never wanted—"

"I know," he said, cutting in. "I want this, Rose. It's the only way to come back from the journey I set myself on. I can't be my father. I'd rather be alone than live as a reflection of his image."

She shook her head like a simpleton, unable to grasp the reason for this madness. "You can't annul our marriage. It's been consummated." Her tone hardened. "We have a child."

"As Edgewood will confirm, I can petition the court for an annulment on the grounds of fraud. Between the betrothal contract and my blackmail letter the dissolution of our marriage will be all but assured." He closed his eyes, his throat working for a full minute, before whispering, "He'll take responsibility for our child, giving you both a name." His eyes opened, regretful and stricken. "He'll take you back home to Virginia to live if you wish it."

"I don't wish it," she snapped. "I won't marry him."

"Rose." His cheeks dried, but bitterness still clouded his eyes. "Must you be stubborn about everything?"

"It is my nature to be contrary. Logan will never stomach it. We won't suit."

Sebastian scowled. "You admitted to having feelings for him! Are you daft? I'm giving you your wish! Stepping aside, bowing out. Returning the life I stole from you both!"

She folded her arms. "So, I should trade one gilded cage for another? Is that what you would have of me?"

A muscle twitched on the side of his jaw. "You're angry with him," he said. "You'd rather run away, stay married to the wrong man, than face my half-brother and work out your feelings—be they anger, grief or pain. You cannot bottle up your emotions and pretend you do not have them. You've more courage than that, my dear."

"It not about courage!" she shouted back, thrusting fingers through her hair, tempted to rip it out by the roots. "It's about vows spoken! It's about the babe growing within my womb! It's about," her voice faltered, becoming a whisper. "Love."

He snorted. "Love?" Laying hands on her shoulders, he whirled her around, sinking hands into her hair, holding her head in place, while staring deep into her eyes. "When you look at me," he whispered, "there is another face you see. No," he growled, "do not bother denying it. I know there's a vacancy in your eyes I do not fill. I stare into a void empty of emotion. Yes, you discovered passion and desire in my arms, despite my forcing your surrender, but I never reached your heart. We share lust between us, not love. Edgewood stole your heart before I had the chance, and I fear it was always fated so. You are clinging to marriage vows only to spare yourself the pain of confronting Logan. I won't let you. The uncertainty of your regard is driving me to depths I swore I would never sink to. This has to end. For my sake, Rose. Please."

Pain crushed her chest, giving her voice a rough edge. "You speak of courage with a coward's tongue. I did confront the devil from my nightmares," she spat, wrenching herself away, brushing aside useless tears, hardening herself against the urge to weep, cower or beg. "And I did it for you. For us. 'Tis why we are here now, Sebastian. Dr. Wilson didn't ask for my presence at his home because he wished to check my recovery. I asked to come here to start anew with you."

Shaking his head, Sebastian smashed any remaining hope. "I don't believe you, Rose. I know the depth of your affection for my brother."

Her chin nudged up, along with her spine, stiffening into a straight, proud line. "You know nothing, Your Grace."

She withdrew from the stall with a flip of her hair, striding from the barn. Her throat worked over a burning lump, but she refused to shed tears. Turning, she sought the darkened road, desiring quiet and solitude, even though she knew the cottage to be empty. But it was filled with potent expectations that would never be filled this night. Sebastian had decided it was not to be. There was nothing in that cabin that would change his mind, not if he didn't believe what was in her heart.

The truly sad part of this macabre affair was that Sebastian had every reason not to trust in what she said. She was the human pendulum, swinging back and forth, believing in hearsay and rumors about a legendary gentleman thief, and quivering in fear over an unknown man she would have to wed. Holding on to that ridiculous infatuation, even when wed, just because the thief made her feel desire for the first time during a kiss.

Ridiculous!

Yes, she was, but not anymore. Her heart lay firmly with Sebastian and the physical havoc his touch stirred within her blood.

A gunshot exploded, and she jerked to a stop.

Oh no! How far away from the cottage did I walk?
~ * ~

Sebastian flung the brush into a bale of hay with a sharp flick of his wrist. Damn his wife! He wanted so badly to believe in her fairytales it took every ounce of control to keep from running after her.

God, is she right? Am I only proposing this annulment because I'm a coward?

Spearing fingers through his hair, he collapsed onto a bale of hay. The bitter, horrible truth was eating a hole straight through his gut. Rose was never a good liar. Why hadn't he just kept his mouth closed and listened with his heart?

Because you're a coward and a bastard, Dorchester! Now get up and go after your wife!

The inner voice was right. Once again, he let jealous thoughts control his tongue and actions. And crushed a young woman's attempt at opening her heart to him.

Jumping to his feet, he ran from the stall, out of the barn then across the small area of grass to the cottage's door. Not bothering to knock, he opened the door, flinging it wide.

Oh God. It was just as he feared.

Candles wavered in a flickering dance around the small room, along with a roaring fire in a hearth. A bounty fit for a king lay spread on a table covered a white cloth, with two place settings already arranged.

Stepping inside, he closed the door. This was a single room cottage, a simple dwelling for a doctor and his wife, but he knew the rents were high, because he was the one to set the price.

In one corner of the rectangular room stood a bed, and his gaze snagged on the furniture. Walking over, he picked up a slinky, red silk material, holding it in his hands

A negligee.

Next to it, lay a brown wrapped package with his name scrawled over the top.

Throat working, he released the piece of silk and attacked the package, discarding the paper and eyed the unmarked white box laying before him. Lifting the lid, he stepped back, his heart skipping.

His father's will. And a copy of his blackmail letter.

Looking closer, he saw a folded sheet of parchment. He took it, unfolded it, catching his breath as he read.

Dorchester,

You won her heart. Please be careful with it. I shall trust you to destroy the evidence so I'll not be tempted to change my mind.

Edgewood

Oh God, what had he done?

Glancing around, hoping for a dark corner he might have missed in his singular inspection, Sebastian called out, "Rose?"

Silence met his inquiry.

He strode to the door, wrenching it open. "Rose?" He hurried around the entire perimeter of the home, bellowing, "Rose!"

She was either not here or not responding.

He'd bet his entire fortune the daft woman went off on her own. Well, she couldn't have gotten far without a horse or carriage.

Reassuring himself with those thoughts, he struck out for the barn to saddle his horse.

Halfway there a gunshot echoed in the distance, stopping Sebastian in his tracks.

Terror iced his veins, and he ran. Tearing open the barn doors he readied his mount in record time, flinging himself into the saddle, heart racing as he touched his heels to the flanks of his horse.

Please God let me not arrive too late!

~ * ~

Six men on horseback emerged from the night. Dark of dress, their faces masked. They surrounded her in a tight circle, their pistols drawn. "Ho there," called a male voice dead ahead. "We are looking for the Duchess of Dorchester."

Rose's heart tripled its beat when the man speaking urged his mount closer, his hard gaze relentless on her face. She had no weapon to defend herself. Meeting his gaze, bunching her trembling hands into fists, she asked, "Why do you seek the duchess?" Chills raced down her spine when he smiled.

Dismounting, he stalked forward.

She fought for even breath, working past the knot of fear twisting her stomach. She had to think past the savage need to scream and flee. Find a weapon, look for an avenue of escape. Be alert.

The highwayman extended a gloved hand, touching the hollow of her cheek. "My, Your Grace, what is this? A man allowed to touch your skin without feeling the sting of your staff beat him down?"

She bit her lip to withhold a gasp. Fear coiled its tentacles around her throat, squeezing. Panicked. "You—you were on my family's farm? You—" She couldn't say anymore. This was her nightmare coming back to haunt her.

His smile turned to a leer. "Yes, Your Grace. I know your face, but not your body. And here we are blessed again in each other's company." He inched closer. "With no staff to come between us."

She could see the measure of the man before her in his flat gaze. He meant to force himself on her.

"Christ, Lincoln! Just take the wench! We are not here for this tonight."

"Silence!" the man barked, never breaking his reptilian gaze from her. "The duchess and I have unfinished business, and I would see it brought to its proper conclusion before riding out."

She shifted her weight to the balls of her feet, retreating as he advanced. "My husband will kill you," she vowed, knowing at least that much was true.

"Many husbands have tried to defend their wives' honor, but all have failed." He slithered forward, assured of his victory because of his strength and arrogance as a man.

How thankful she was to be taught to fight by a woman.

She allowed a token of the fear she felt to show in her eyes, pleading, "Please don't do this. His Grace is a wealthy man and can pay any price you demand."

"We know this. Why else do you think we picked you for ransom, Your Grace?" His smile would have made the dead roll and twist in agony. "A wife bearing a future heir is twice as valuable, is she not?"

Cursing erupted behind her. One of the other highwaymen. "Bloody hell, Lincoln! That's precisely why ye shouldn't be touching her! The man won't pay as much if ye kill the babe."

"I won't be overly rough." Lincoln's cold smile promised otherwise.

Rose draped herself in the garb of a damsel in distress, knowing the stench of fear and helplessness would be a potent lure for a predator. She scanned the darkness in practiced frantic movements, finding what she needed without alerting her pursuer. She led a backward race, pretending to trip on a rock when the moment was right.

The highwayman pounced as she knew he would when presented with opportunity.

Turning, she brought her elbow up and rammed it back, hearing a very satisfying crunch and sharp howl of pain. Spinning smoothly, she struck with a leg, taking the feet out from her attacker.

He landed flat on his back to the laughter of his accomplices.

Finding the rock, she gripped it in stable hands, bringing it crashing over the writhing man's head. Two dull thunks later, and the man was unconscious.

Silence met Rose as she straightened and looked at the other five men still astride their mounts. "Which one of you blighters would like to be next?" Movement on the ground caught her eye. A tiny black shadow running through the grass, taking aim at her legs. *Nutmeg?* Overjoyed, she looked all around, but found no other shadows.

A low whistle sounded. "Your Grace, we are impressed. A feat not easily accomplished. For this we will promise not to dishonor you as Lincoln surely would have." He pointed his pistol dead center on her chest. "But you will come now, Your Grace, or you will suffer other forms of pain."

"I can't tell you how pleased I am to have the promises of a highwayman. I surely will sleep so much better tonight." She braced as tiny claws climbed up her dress.

Nutmeg perched himself on her shoulder, hissing and ears laid flat on his skull.

Smiling with new confidence, she said, "Unfortunately, I regret to inform you my kitten just whispered into my ear that we have a previous engagement and will not be coming with you this night or any other night."

The click of a hammer was loud in her ears. "Don't be foolish. There are five of us, and you are quite alone."

"She is not alone," called a new voice, riding astride a giant black stallion, followed by another silhouette of a man on a smaller mount. "But quite correct in stating she will not be enjoying your company for the remainder of this night."

A loud crack echoed in the air, and the highwayman wielding the pistol, gasped, holding his empty hand. "Get them!" he bellowed.

Chaos erupted with a stampede of hooves and hoarse shouts, pistols firing. A general crush of villainy ensued, and she ducked behind a tree to keep from being trampled or shot, viewing the battle in case her rescuers needed help or a distraction.

Until a hand closed around her mouth, and hot breath warmed the back of her neck.

Nutmeg purred and rubbed against the blighter's fingers, the traitor.

"Rose Graham, I'm going to beat your backside until you can't sit for a week."

She relaxed against her husband's stiff body. "Harrrrmp annn fouu."

The hand lifted, only to grip her hips, turning her around. "What was that, madam?"

She stared into the most welcome sight in the world—her husband's cheek twitching in time to the muscle spasm of his eye. He was furious. "I said I'm happy you're here."

"I'm going to thrash you," he promised, ignoring her declaration of joy in favor of briskly running his hands up and down her person.

"What are you doing?"

"Assuring myself you are uninjured," he bit out, growling in frustration when she tried to squirm away. "Hold still!"

She allowed the rough hand inspection until she recalled the reason for her reckless walk. She jerked away. "You're being terribly forward with a woman you intend to cast aside. In fact, I should not be allowing this intimacy. Logan will be put out that his wife is—"

A visceral growl swelled from a deep chest. "You're *my* wife, and I'll damn well touch you if I—"

She raised a brow.

"—if you let me." His fingers sank into silky tresses, anchoring to her skull, tilting her head back. "Tell me you forgive your foolish, jealous husband who loves you so damn much it hurts."

"I don't know. I wouldn't want to be accused of you turning into a hideous beast every time my brother-in-law tries to converse with me."

"Your husband promises not to rage and snarl his way between you two."

"Lord Edgewood will be an uncle to our child, after all."

"Make him the godparent for all I care."

"I may smile at him on occasion."

"As long as you smile at me more."

They stared at each other, searching. Building courage. The future yearned before them, a bright ball of happy tomorrows filled with love and laughter.

Until an eclipse of the sun started, claiming Rose's attention. As if time elapsed in slow motion, she watched Lincoln rise from the ground, his pistol coming up, taking aim on Sebastian's back.

"No!" Reacting without thinking, she lunged at Sebastian, pushing him to the ground as two sharp reports collided with the other.

A searing pain ran across her temple, and darkness chased away the sound of Sebastian's frantic voice, echoing in her ears.

~ * ~

"Logan!"

Sebastian scrambled onto his feet; his focus glued to the still form of his wife lying face down in the dirt. "Logan!" he bellowed, lurching toward her, his heart in his throat. A terrible sick feeling clawing at his innards.

He grabbed her, gingerly flipping her around face up.

Oh God, no! No, no, no!

Blood.

Her head.

A wound.

His brother was beside him, far more efficient in thoughts and actions. "Robert," Logan shouted, taking off his jacket, wrapping it around Rose's head to staunch the bleeding. "Get Jupiter over here. Hurry! Sebastian..." He grabbed a black fur ball from Rose's head, putting it aside, glancing at him.

Then he smacked him across the face. "Get yourself together," Logan snapped, bundling Rose in his arms and lifting her.

Sebastian mentally shook himself, rocketing to his feet, holding his arms out to receive his wife. "I'll take her; I'm all right."

Logan peered at him for a heartbeat, then nodded, apparently satisfied by whatever he saw. "Take her to the inn in the village," he advised, handing Rose over. "Dr. Wilson and his wife took a room there." He held Jupiter's reins, nodding for Sebastian to ride him. "Robert and I will take care of this rubbish. Go!"

Sebastian didn't hesitate. With Rose as a dead weight in his arms he mounted, moving through the dark countryside with the woman he loved.

Racing time. Death.

No. He couldn't think that and keep his sanity.

He looked down. The red was a bright contrast to her pale, bloodless face.

She saved his life. His worthless, misbegotten life. It wasn't worth her soul to save his, but she didn't hesitate. The final expression he would always remember was one of profound tenderness and determination.

She sacrificed herself for him when he had less than an hour ago proclaimed he didn't want her. If she died now...

Tightening his arms, crushing her to his chest, he urged Jupiter faster.

Chapter Twenty-Three

Sebastian's hands, still tainted by Rose's blood, scrubbed his face. Her head lay wrapped in a bandage, crimson spotting the area over the wound. Sitting in a chair by her bed, watching her sleep, he felt the weight of a hand touch his shoulder. He glanced up at Dr. Wilson.

"'Tis just a flesh wound, Your Grace. She'll be right as rain in a week."

Sebastian couldn't bring himself to ask the question that haunted him. He stared, opening his mouth and closing it several times, trying in vain to speak around the burning knot in his throat. "The baby?" he managed in a voice twice deeper than usual.

Dr. Wilson's gaze was frank and honest. "I'll not lie, Your Grace. She lost a lot of blood. The little one's health is in God's hands now. All we can do is let her rest. And pray."

He nodded, hearing the doctor take his leave.

All alone, Sebastian clutched Rose's hand, cradling it in his larger one.

The door opened, the sound of boots scraping the floor reaching his ears.

Suddenly Logan and Robert were there with him, each man looking grim.

Sebastian couldn't bear it, but neither could he bring himself to ask them to leave.

Logan tore his gaze away and settled it on Sebastian. Walking over, Logan grabbed a chair from the corner of the room and slapped it down next to his. "She's going to be fine," he said, putting a hand on his arm, waiting for his attention.

Sebastian's eyes were burning along with his throat. He turned his head away, attempting to hide this weakness. "This is my fault," he ground out, unable to stop the flow of tears from leaking any more than he could halt the Thames River from flowing into the sea. "I pushed her away out of spite and jealousy when all she wanted to do was show me she loved me." A terrible wound shredded his heart, the kind no doctor or surgeon could fix. "Why didn't I accept her confession? What devil rode my shoulder to denounce her and her love?"

Robert came to his other side, hunching down beside him. "Sebastian, you cannot torture yourself with what if's and why. Rose loves you. There was nothing in this world capable of halting her from protecting you. It's her nature to fight. She's been doing it in some form or fashion all her life. And she was ready to fight for you. I'm sure she didn't walk away with a broken heart after your quarrel. She was probably out looking for a stick to go back and beat some sense into you."

Logan chuckled.

Sebastian managed a smile. He could picture Rose doing that very thing.

Robert nudged his knee with a hand, standing up. "My sister has made peace with her past. I think it's time you did the same." He looked meaningfully at Logan, walking around the bed, striding from the room, closing the door.

They sat regarding the other with blank faces.

Clearing his throat, Sebastian stuck out his hand. "Thank you, brother, for saving my wife's life. And, granting your blessing, as it were." He didn't elaborate.

By the size of Logan's grin, he didn't need to.

"You're welcome, brother," Logan said, grabbing his hand in solidarity, shaking it, sobering. "I won't intrude on your life with Rose. I promise to respect your privacy and will make every effort to—"

"Save your breath, Logan. She already has plans to ask you to be a godparent, for heaven's sake. She wants you around as a member of our family." He gazed at his brother. "As I do."

Logan's face lit with hope. "She does? You do?"

He sighed. "Yes." Then frowned in good humor. "Though mind you're not around too much. I already have a feeling Robert is going to be living with us, and a man has his limits."

They looked down in unison. Their hands were still clasped.

Yanking them apart, they scooted their chairs away another few inches, clearing their throats in sudden discomfort.

Logan settled back in his seat, crossing his arms. "So, I shall be an uncle and a godparent?"

"If she doesn't lose the baby," Sebastian said, resuming his troubled thoughts.

Logan nudged his shoulder with his. "Do not borrow trouble, Sebastian. Have faith. In fact," he reached out, dragging him to the floor, bringing them both to their knees. "Let's say a prayer while we're waiting for a miracle."

"A prayer? You must be jesting."

"Would you rather play with Nutmeg instead?"

Sebastian grumbled, but stayed on his knees, nonetheless. It couldn't hurt.

An hour later, a knock sounded. Robert let himself in. "The magistrate is here wanting to know what should be done with the highwaymen."

Sebastian knew exactly what to do. "Tell the man to ship them to London to the care of the Prince of Wales, courtesy of the Duke of Dorchester. And tell him," he smirked at Logan, "tell him the dead one is Silver Hawk."

Logan peered at him with a brow arched. "Do you think he'll believe that?"

Sebastian shrugged. "I don't care what he believes, but last I checked, being a trusted patriot to the crown is not without advantages."

Robert laughed, exiting the room to carry out his orders.

Sebastian smiled, despite himself. "You realize that Silver Hawk cannot ride pillaging the rich purses of the peerage, don't you?"

Logan glared. "Yes. I'm not stupid, thank you."

"I'll give you whatever funds those women and children need. You can settle down and see to your own life now." He slid a sly look his brother's way. "Attend a Season. Find a wife."

Logan shuttered. "I shall consider it. Right after I see to Lady Emily's dilemma."

"My ex-fiancée? What trouble has she found?"

"Nothing of note. Something to do with her sister."

Appeased, Sebastian let the subject go. His wife's condition was of more import now. Logan sat vigil with him. He didn't talk a great deal, but still Sebastian was surprised to find his brother's constant presence an unexpected comfort.

Twelve hours later, Rose deigned to open her eyes. Sebastian was at her side before her eyelids finished ascending. "Darling." He laid his hands on either side of her face, waiting for her to come further awake.

Logan discreetly exited the room to give them privacy.

Her eyelashes fluttered. A moan escaped her dry lips. "Thirsty," she croaked.

Sebastian fetched a glass of water from the side table, placing a hand underneath her head, lifting as he brought the glass to her mouth.

She drank greedily, spilling as much liquid down her chin as she ingested. Sated, she turned her head. "Thank you," she rasped.

"How do you feel?" he asked, lowering himself beside her on the bed.

"Headache. You?"

"Fit as a fiddle." He leaned close, brushing away limp strands of her glorious hair. "Thanks to you," he whispered. "My love, you saved my life. I have no words for your sacrifices."

Her eyes swelled when he mentioned sacrifice. "The babe." She clutched her stomach. "Am I still—?"

"Yes," he rushed to reassure her. "You suffered nothing more than a minor head wound. As far as Dr. Wilson can tell, you are still with child. No miscarriage has occurred." He smiled for her, not wanting to disclose the possibility of one still existing.

She calmed herself, swiping her face, sniffing. "I suppose I'm in trouble for not acting like a mother."

"Yes. And the punishment for such ill behavior is a lifetime with me as your husband.

"Let the punishment fit the crime?"

He chuckled. "Indeed."

She stared at him with such tenderness he ached to do more than hold her.

"I can live with that," she murmured, closing her eyes. "I love you, Sebastian."

The words he waited so long to hear wrapped themselves around his heart, suffusing his body with warmth. "I love you, Rose."

He watched her drift back to sleep, confident for the first time of what his future would hold.

Chapter Twenty-Four

A few months later...

"Sebastian!" Rose waddled into the study, irate with the world and all its inhabitants. Sebastian was seated at his desk, talking with Logan. When she shuffled in, both men came immediately to their feet.

She pointed a damning finger at her husband. "You hid them, didn't you?"

Sebastian raised his brows. "You're going to have to be more specific, darling."

"Don't you 'darling' me! I'm pregnant, not addled! Where are they?"

He feigned ignorance. His only defense. "I'm sure if you just settle down—"

"They're in his liquor cabinet," Logan supplied with a laugh.

Sebastian shot him a glare. "Traitor."

Rose glowered at both men, wiggling her way across the room like a fat cow. She rummaged through the contents of the cabinet, saying, "It's bad enough having to endure my confinement with you two nitwits and my brother, but hiding my pickles and pigs feet?" She found both jars, tucking them in her arms. "Bloody hell, Sebastian, that goes beyond the pale!"

Sebastian rushed over to take the jars from her. "Now, darling, I know the last month has been stressful on you, but—"

She yanked the pickle jar back. "But nothing! You cannot comprehend stress until you carry around eight pounds of baby in your body."

He tugged the jar back. "Not even Nutmeg will sleep with you anymore. Your obsession with all things pickled has to stop."

Reaching for the jar again, she gasped at the wetness gushing down her dress. "Sebastian, you leaked pickle juice down my dress. Do you realize how long it took Milly to get me into this frock? Now I'll have to change."

He wrinkled his nose, eyeing the glass container. "Darling, this glass is fully closed. It isn't pickle juice."

"Husband, I'm dribbling all over the place. You haven't touched me." She glanced at Logan shyly. "In that way," she whispered.

"Well, if you're dribbling then I must be too, because my boots are all wet."

Logan jumped to his feet. "It's not pickle juice. Rose, your water broke."

All manner of hell broke loose after that statement. A doctor was summoned, jars of pickles and pigs feet went back into the liquor cabinet under lock and key and Sebastian rushed her up to their bedchamber as though she announced a willingness to procreate again.

The first cramp hit as he was sitting her down on their massive four-poster bed. "Oh dear." She stiffened, quite unprepared.

He blanched. "The book suggested breathing deeply when in pain." He sat on the bed, unlacing her gown, then assisting her into a clean nightgown. As a second wave of pain left her reeling, he held the covers aloft, whisking her back to bed.

"I'm dying."

"Don't be dramatic. The birthing process is just getting underway. From what I've read upon the subject, these things can take days and the pain will increase with each cramp."

"Sebastian?"

"Yes, darling?"

"Sod off."

He drew himself up, offended. "Is that anyway to talk to the love of your life?"

Her stomach clenched, arching her back in misery, ripping a groan from her mouth.

Sebastian went white, attacking her back with short, abrasive strokes. "I'm an ass. I don't know how anyone puts up with me. I'll be quiet, darling."

She was certain he meant this massage as a soothing balm, but it was more like an abrasive punishment for a crime she couldn't recall committing.

An hour into her pummeling, a knock sounded, and she collapsed against pillows in relief when Sebastian stopped raining blows along her spine.

Dr. Wilson arrived, striding through the bedchamber door with sunlight streaming behind him, creating an angelic glow about his short body.

Was it her imagination or were there cherubs playing harps as her savior strolled up to the bedside, smiling in good humor?

Until her sadistic torturer noticed his arrival, ceasing the battering and thumping movements. "What are you doing here?" he demanded, jumping to his feet. "Have you come to inform us that my wife is suffering from some malady of the womb? Or perhaps you're here to deliver something or other? Tell me, Dr. Wilson, do you remember from your training which end to smack once my heir is born?" Sebastian was working himself into a quite a state.

The poor doctor simply stared in mute horror at her husband. It was all a man could do when faced with a temper tantrum.

Speaking through gritted teeth, Rose said, "My apologies, Dr. Wilson. My husband is distraught."

He patted her shoulder. "Most new fathers are, Your Grace." Shifting his attention to the addled duke, Dr. Wilson said, "There is a woman from the village who asked to deliver your babe into this world, Your Grace. She's a midwife. A very good one."

That news shut Sebastian's mouth.

It was a precious second of quiet Rose enjoyed until another cramp hit, and she was lost to pain and suffering.

"Why does she wish to assist my wife in this birth?" he asked, his tone suspicious.

"Because of the life you once saved," an authoritative female voice answered from the doorway.

All eyes zipped to the portal of her chamber.

A sturdy, well-endowed woman stood before them, her gaze direct but friendly, her dress a serviceable brown wool. "My daughter," she clarified, entering the room. "You saved her life, bringing her back to me, paying a terrible price to do so." Her gaze stayed on Sebastian. "I've wanted to thank you for a long time, but I was too ashamed of what kin and neighbors did in vengeance."

"I-I am not sure what to say," he admitted, looking to Rose for help.

She took his hand, smiling at the woman. "We would be honored to have you help with this birthing." Another shot of pain rolled deep in her belly, and Rose bit her lip, drawing blood to keep from crying out.

As soon as the woman saw her pain, she assumed command of the bedchamber.

Dr. Wilson was ordered out. Sebastian was evicted seconds later with minimal fuss.

Whoever this woman was, Rose was so grateful she began to cry.

And was shortly ordered to get herself together.

Rose loved her at once.

~ * ~

Unable to sit still, Sebastian prowled the halls of his castle. He'd been walking for hours waiting on news of Rose. His stomach hurt, his thoughts a jumbled mess. So exhausting to be in this state of anxiety for hours upon hours.

He could only imagine how his Rose was enduring.

God, he hoped she was coping. He was barely coping.

Running his fingers through his mussed hair for the hundredth time, he decided he'd reached rock bottom. Desperate times, irrational measures, something along those lines.

Damned if he could think a straight thought.

And when a man couldn't reason or ponder with any sort of clarity, there was only one thing for him to do.

Seek out family for company and cheer.

He stalked into his study, calling for Logan and Robert. He regretted the hasty decision within two minutes of their arrival.

"I heard screaming twenty minutes ago followed by maniacal laughter when I walked past your bedchamber," Robert teased, puffing on a cigar.

Sebastian longed to ram it down his throat.

"Robert," Logan chastised, sitting in a leather chair, petting Nutmeg as the older kitten snuggled in his arms, "don't be so unkind." He grinned. "I snuck by not long ago and heard the most fluent cursing coming from a young woman's mouth. Something about cutting off male appendages."

Sebastian went for the sideboard, pouring himself a brandy. He didn't offer any to the nitwits. He endured their company and humor for another two hours before a knock sounded.

"Enter!" he barked, nearly dropping his glass in a sudden fit of nerves.

Mrs. Brown opened the door. "Your Grace," she beamed, "the midwife asked for your presence."

The housekeeper hadn't finished talking before Sebastian was running out the door, taking the stairs to the second floor three at a time, his heart pounding. Racing down the halls, he saw the door to his suite of rooms he shared with Rose.

A high-pitched cry rendered him motionless.

Joy crashed into him so fiercely he whooped out loud, not caring if staff or family overheard the very outlandish behavior. Bursting into the room, he took in the scene.

Rose, pale and sweaty, hair plastered to her skull and face.

He stepped closer; his eyes glued to the tiny bundle wrapped in his wife's arms.

"There you are, Your Grace." The midwife approached him.

Sebastian went weak in the knees.

The midwife stretched out another tiny bundle to him, smiling from ear to ear. "Your heir, Your Grace."

He accepted his son, cradling him within his arms, utterly spellbound. A riot of auburn hair framed his face. He'd expire on the spot if his son sported green eyes like his mother.

Tears swelled from some depth of himself he did not know existed, and he walked as if in a trance to his wife, lifting his glistening eyes to her. "Darling, he's beautiful. Thank you."

"You mean *they* are beautiful," Rose corrected, folding back the tuft of blanket. "Meet your daughter, Your Grace."

Sebastian sank onto the bed, without words for the blessings in this room. "My God, twins." He snuggled next to Rose, looking at her truly for the first time. "You are well?"

She smiled, stroking her daughter's cheek with a forefinger while she suckled. "Surprisingly, I am." Her gaze lifted, finding his. "Everything I fought against and feared for all my life was for naught." She shook her head. Tears glittered. "My youth I wasted on silly notions."

Sebastian put an arm around her, seeking comfort as well as providing it. "Nonsense. I am grateful for your tribulations, for they brought you to me. And I find you perfect, just the way you are."

"I could use a pickle or two. I'm famished."

"Nearly perfect," he amended, earning an elbow to the rib. "Better than Robert, to be sure." He kissed her cheek. "And miles better than Silver Hawk."

"We promised each other not to say that name aloud again."

"'Tis the last time my lips shall utter it," he vowed, winking.

"Though I confess, Silver Graham has a nice ring, does it not?"

"Over my dead body!" he barked, startling both babies into crying. He heaved his son to a shoulder, glaring at the woman he loved more than life itself.

She smiled sweetly, urging her nipple back in their daughter's questing mouth. "It was just a thought, Sebastian." Winking, she added, "I love you."

Swearing virulently, he found himself returning the smile, his anger melting away as winter snow. Rose angered him as much as she amused and delighted him, but in one respect, they were of similar mind—their love for each other was unmatched, and he knew it always would be.

About the Author

I am a proud wife, overworked mom, and wicked stepmother to a lovely blended family. I hail from Upstate NY, but currently reside in southern Pennsylvania, while dreaming of someday putting down roots in Virginia.

My favorite things in life include how to use the weather to cover awkward silent moments, avoiding housework, pretending laundry doesn't exist, chocolate for breakfast, and cats.

Faith loves to hear from her readers. You can find and connect with her at the links below.

Website/Blog: http://www.faithcameron.com
Twitter: https://twitter.com/F_CameronAuthor

~ * ~

We hope you loved *No Hero Here* as much as we did. If you did, please write a review and tell your friends. Looking for something else to read? Check out the other terrific offerings at Champagne Book Group.

Author Acknowledgement

For their support and encouragement, I thank my husband Jamie Potter, friends, family, my editor Kelli Keith, Cassiel Knight, Pandora, and my favorite pair of earbuds.

Yes, thank you earbuds for blocking out the noise of one snoring husband, four rowdy children, five shameless cats, and one needy husky.

~ * ~

Now turn the page for a peak into *Eliza* by Joyce Proell, a historical romance where a young woman fleeing an abusive marriage finds a new life…and love.

Eliza
Joyce Proell

Posing as a widow, Eliza Danton flees an abusive marriage determined to live a solitary life on the Minnesota frontier. When she finds herself homeless, her livelihood threatened and her safety compromised, she must rely on a man who stirs a forbidden longing and jars her well-laid plans. As her world shrinks with lies and deception, the only way out is the truth, but the truth may strike a deadly price.

Haunted by a tragic past Will Heaton vows never to love again. But a chance encounter with a mysterious widow awakens painful memories and a yearning he can't ignore. When she's harassed by the same man he believes killed his wife, he grabs at a chance to resolve past mistakes and possibly find love and redemption in the process.

As Eliza and Will struggle to trust again, the past returns with a renewed vengeance, testing them in unimaginable ways.

EXCERPT

Elizabeth Douglas couldn't think of a better incentive than a husband who wanted her dead. Thus inspired, she'd packed a bag, changed her name and now gripped the handrail of the *Northstar* as it shimmied up the Ohio. Despite the warm air, she shivered. Abe would look for her as certain as the glistening blades of the paddlewheel churned the muddied water. When a man loses his greatest possession, he himself becomes possessed.

'*If you ever leave me, I'll kill you,*' he'd promised. She didn't intend to die. At least, not yet.

"Mrs. Danton."

Startled to hear someone call her new name, she spun toward the voice. She brushed a hand over the black fabric of her widow's weeds, loathing the dress and the deception.

Against a backdrop of Pittsburgh's receding factories, Reverend Vernon Deeds minced around the thinning crowd on the ship's deck. One arm clutched a chubby baby to his chest, the other hand tugged a small lad behind him. Flushed, Vernon dropped the boy's hand and pulled a crisply folded handkerchief from his coat pocket. He mopped his beaded brow. "Who would have thought June could be so muggy?"

"Zaza," the baby chirped then jammed a pudgy fist back into her mouth.

"Hello, my sweet," Eliza cooed. She'd known little Ada only a few days and already she'd bonded with her as if she were her own.

"The children were asking for you," Vernon said, tucking the hankie back into a pocket. "Mrs. Deeds was saying this morning how blessed we are to have you along to watch after the children."

"I consider myself blessed to have heard of your need." She smiled at the freckle-faced boy staring up at her.

"Yes, well." Vernon thrust his pointy chin forward. "It's never a good idea for a woman to travel alone. Too unprotected, you see. Anything might happen." He rocked back on feet too small for his wide frame. "I admit I thought it too soon for a widow to travel."

His opinions made her bristle. Until a few days ago, she was a stranger to him. Did he now think to presume what was best for her?

"Fortunately, Mrs. Danton, your desire to get to High Bluff coincided with our need to have a companion for the children."

"Then it is lucky, indeed, we are both getting our needs met." She grazed a hand across her forehead as though it might soothe her ruffled feathers.

He opened his mouth, preparing to speak then hesitated with a frown. Apprehension fluttered in her stomach. Was he about to voice some criticism of her? Had she acted too happy and not enough like the grieving widow? Did he suspect her ruse?

"So it seems," he agreed with a dismissive shrug. He dropped a look at the boy whose sun-kissed face reflected both wonder and excitement.

"Would you unpack some toys for the children? Then perhaps a tour of the boat before lunch."

Eliza opened her mouth with a ready reply but he rushed on. "And you'll help with the English lessons today?" He smiled expansively, seeming confident of her agreement and thrust the baby at her.

His bossy manner irked, and she recognized in it Abe's domineering behavior. How pitiful that even in his absence, Abe's controlling ways loomed as forbidding as the gunmetal clouds clustering over the tree- shrouded horizon.

"And, of course, the children will need a rest this afternoon," he said, his brow furrowed as though compiling the list of her many duties boggled his mind.

Despite his overbearing manner, Reverend Vernon Deeds was a whirlwind of good intentions. How could Eliza complain if some of his good deeds involved her? She was happy to care for the children and help the German-speaking passengers with their English skills.

She clamped her mouth to keep from saying something brash or imprudent. Hadn't Abe always complained she lacked obedience and humility requiring him to take her down a peg or two? She forced a pleasant smile.

Vernon patted his pockets in a primping fashion. "Till lunch then," he said, and he shuffled off. "Papa, wait!"

Vernon spun about and chuckled. "Forgive me, son." A dusty blush deepened his ruddy complexion. "I promised Chet a trip to the pilot house. Come along then, boy."

Grinning, Chet skipped after Vernon whose shoulders drooped slightly as if weighted by the humid air.

Eliza brushed aside any disquieting thoughts, vowing to stop thinking of the past. Instead, she focused on the giant paddlewheel shooting hundreds of creamy droplets into the air.

"Let's wave goodbye, shall we?" She lifted Ada's plump hand and shook it at the smoke stacks and brick factories lining the shore. Before long, the landscape flattened, and the acrid smell of burning coal no longer filled her senses. A new future lay bright before her. She intended to seize its possibilities.

When the shrill whistles and bells of the busy harbor fell silent behind her, she mouthed a final goodbye. Turning, she surveyed the unfamiliar river ahead. With a little luck and well-laid plans, all would be well, she prayed.

Sighing, Eliza looked at the curly-headed girl. "Well, what say you to a walk, young lady?"

Ada gurgled and jutted a wet, glistening finger in the air.

"I'll take that for a yes," Eliza said and smiled with a sense of hope and belief absent these past brutal months.

They meandered once around the busy promenade deck thick with excited passengers and uniformed deckhands. They climbed two flights of stairs to the upper deck. From this vantage point, Eliza could see for miles. When Ada grew heavy, they dropped below to the boiler deck and settled into a wooden lounge chair painted a glossy white.

Ada cooed and babbled. Eliza cooed and babbled in return, delighted with their game of patty-cake. A couple strolled the lengthy exterior deck, a tasseled parasol slung over the woman's shoulder as a barrier to the brilliant sun. As they neared, a small child popped out from behind them and stopped to scramble onto a deck chair. In no time, the curious boy bent recklessly over the water.

Eliza let out a strangled cry. "Chet! No!"

She flew from the chair like a panicked pheasant and glanced about wildly. A man in an ivory suit leaned against the nearby wall.

"Will you help?"

His eyes flared in surprise, but instantly he reached for the baby.

Thinking only of Chet, Eliza sprinted off. "Get down," she shrieked.

Chet's head swiveled in her direction, his eyes startled and confused. She eased her steps, containing her panic so as not to alarm him further. In his fear, he might topple over. The thought made her quiver. Beating a steady path to him, she prayed.

Don't fall. Don't fall.

In the few seconds it took to reach him, she could have sworn day turned into night.

"Chet," she breathed and swallowed him in a big bear hug. She clung to him, wondering whose heart pounded the loudest. Setting his feet on the sturdy planks, she dropped to her knees, her fingers clasped about his thin shoulders. "Whatever were you doing?" A silly question, she knew.

"You scaredid me," he accused in a muffle. His mouth and nose pressed against her shoulder while his chest rattled in her arms accompanied by a sniffling noise.

She leaned back, trembling and studied his face, her grip on him still firm. Innocent blue eyes sparkled with unshed tears.

"Oh, Chet."

Fear left her shaken. She hugged him tight again, smelling the sweet heat of his bony little body. "I was scared, too."

The boy shouldn't have been alone. "Where's your father?" she asked, her tone clipped with anger.

Slowly, his skinny arm lifted, pointing some fifteen feet away. Through the windows of the promenade parlor, Eliza recognized the back of Vernon's head, his golden hair cresting the dark collar of his jacket. Scattered around him were three men engaged in a serious discussion. Her mouth pursed with scorn biting back the scolding words for now.

Inhaling deeply, she leaned back on her haunches and gave Chet her best mock, stern look. "Don't ever do that again. Chairs are to sit in, not for climbing."

He stared at his boots, pink flushing his cheeks. She lifted his chin and caught his eye. "You are not to hang over the railing. Understand?" At his nod, she stood and offered him her hand.

"Now, let's go get..."

Her gaze covered the length of the deck to the chair where she'd been sitting only minutes ago. Her chest constricted. Where in blazes was Ada? And where was the lanky stranger?

"There you are little man." Vernon hurried toward them with a distracted air.

"Papa!" The boy dropped her hand and scampered to greet his father. Eliza scurried away, calling over her shoulder, "I'll be right back."

Fear pealed in her voice as noisy as a clanging church bell. "Ada?"

Terrifying thoughts about where and why he might have taken her raced through her mind.

"Ada!"

A deep, composed voice broke through her panic. "Your child, ma'am?"

She whirled around, her pulse fluttering like the wings of a hummingbird. Ada dangled over his forearm like a carelessly draped bath towel. A breath of relief whooshed from Eliza's lips. As she gaped at the bizarre tableau, an urge to both laugh and cry overcame her. Ada's chubby legs and arms spun like a windmill. Despite the man's shortcoming in proper toddler control, she looked none the worse, appearing content and drooling happily. He, on the other hand, did not.

A muscle twitched in irritation at the side of his wide mouth. He glared down his long, straight nose at Eliza. The broad rim of his Panama hat shaded his face and added to his fierceness. It sliced like a knife to the heart. In protection, her hand dropped to her chest.

"The child crawls as fast as a centipede," he drawled.

Eliza envisioned Ada scooting over the stained planks on rounded knees, her ivy sprigged smock and lacy bonnet fluttering around her. Biting back a nervous smile, Eliza stepped forward to ease him of his bundle of energy.

The man stood a good head taller. She tipped back her head and stared up into his eyes. Cool, appraising eyes stared back. His penetrating gaze went beyond the bones and skin of her face and right to the center of her shame. Did he think her negligent, a foolish woman who couldn't keep track of her children?

"Thank you," she murmured stiffly with outstretched arms.

"You mind your mama now, little lady," he said handing Ada to her. "I'm not her mother." She glanced away with a trace of embarrassment she didn't understand. "I'm traveling with her. Helping the parents."

At the sound of footsteps, Eliza turned. Chet skipped toward her singing a little ditty.

"Is everything all right? You ran off." Vernon drew near wearing a worried look.

Heat rose into her cheeks. "Everything's fine." She didn't want to explain in front of this stranger whose probing stare set her heart racing. She jiggled Ada on her hip and said, instead, "The children belong to the Reverend Vernon Deeds."

Vernon stretched out a hand.

"William Heaton," the man said and grasped Vernon's with a hearty shake.

"I can't stay to talk," Vernon explained with a hurried air. "A man has collapsed minutes ago. My services are required, you see." He inclined his head in Chet's direction. "You don't mind, do you, Mrs. Danton?"

"No, of course not." She laid a hand on Chet's shoulder. "Sorry to rush off. Perhaps we'll meet again."

The somber gentlemen watched Vernon scurry away. "Busy man."

"Yes, he is."

She felt tongue-tied. Surely, from his stiff expression, he judged her harshly. "You must think me quite incapable of minding children." She cringed, wishing she hadn't revealed this insecurity. Biting her lip, she glanced at Ada's mop of golden curls then chanced to look at him again.

He shrugged broad shoulders that seemed as wide as a doorway. "I wouldn't know. I don't have children. They'll keep you running though. You were fast on your feet saving the boy. I take it he was in the care of the Reverend at the time?"

"Yes. How did you know?"

For a moment, he didn't say anything. "I saw you come down the stairs with the girl and head over to the deck chair. The boy wasn't with you."

He'd been watching her. But why? Abe used to complain that men gawked at her and said she was too pretty for her own good. To avoid stoking his anger, she always wore simple yet tasteful clothes; dresses that were plain and forgettable. She wiped her hand against her black bombazine skirt, realizing her hand was slick with sweat. Chet tugged at her other hand.

"Goodness. Where are my manners?" she blubbered flicking her head back and forth from boy to man. "I'd like you to meet Master Chester Deeds." The small boy puffed out his chest at the grownup introduction.

To her surprise, the man whipped off his hat, revealing thick hair as glossy as a black cat's fur. Resting the hat against his thigh, he bent from the waist bringing himself as low to the boy's height as possible. He held out a hand graced with tapered fingers, not the hands of a journeyman or someone who works the earth for a living. "How do you do, Chester. My name is William Heaton, but you may call me Will."

Sheepish, Chet inched partway behind Eliza's wide skirt. "He won't bite. You can shake his hand," she prompted.

Chet chewed his upper lip a moment before shoving out his stubby hand. The man pumped it triggering Chet's ear-to-ear grin.

"And this is Miss Ada Deeds," Eliza offered, shifting her charge to her other hip. The baby puckered her lips.

The well-dressed man straightened. As he watched Ada blow bubbles through her stout fingers, his stern face relaxed and touched something pleasant inside Eliza. "We've already met though not formally." His voice droned as smooth as molasses in July. Then white, even teeth flashed in a grin so captivating it seemed the sun sliced through the storm clouds and graced them all in rays of warmth.

"Indeed," she muttered, incapable of further words. Threads of gold sparked in his green irises and ignited feelings fallow and long forgotten. Want and desire flared inside, and she reared back, horrified and overcome by the intensity of her need.

Inky brows lifted in studied consideration, as if he sensed her turmoil.

Blinking nervously, she fought against the attraction. Not once as she planned her journey did the thought of a man, or her response to one, enter her mind. Now, as the sweat beaded on her forehead, she silently cursed her betraying body. Attractions, such as this, had no place in her life.

"You haven't mentioned your name, ma'am?"

Leg muscles twitched in an urge to run. Her throat grew thick, and she swallowed a fortifying gulp. "I'm Mrs. Eliza Danton."

She struck her chin in the air defying him to question her while inside she quivered. Like a guilty prisoner standing before a judge, she felt his unwavering, doubtful gaze. Suddenly, she wanted to proclaim the truth, stop the lying and plead forgiveness. Yet to do so would be insanity. Nobody could know her secret.

"I'm a widow." At the lie, her cheeks burned. "My husband died a month ago." The urge to babble on, to ply him with details of Abe's phony demise tugged at her. She held her tongue.

When he remained silent and his eyes shined with a constant question, her uncertainty mounted. Did he know she lied? But how could he? She turned and stared at the dark water afraid her face might reveal too much. Inhaling deeply, she noted the subtle scent of cloves and pepper that clung to his clothes.

An eternity passed before he broke the silence. "Sorry to hear about your husband."

She faked a mournful sigh and gave a helpless shrug. What could she do or say when none of it was real? But he already knew that, didn't he? Aware of his sharp looks of disbelief, she hadn't fooled him for a moment. Would he make an issue of her lying; press her for truthful answers she couldn't give?

She picked at her top button, her breathing shallow and forced herself to look deep into his eyes. A flinty cleverness stared back. A perceptive man had his dangers. He might use his knowledge of her deception to wield some power over her for his own gain. She had no reason to trust him. With his threat heavy like a stone in her chest, she grabbed Chet's hand and backed away.

"I haven't thanked you yet for keeping an eye on Ada. So thank you." Reeling about, she marched briskly away towing Chet behind her.

Later, she would think it incredible how quickly one's security could vanish. Her safety had evaporated quicker than the tiny drops of river water settled on the ship's outer deck.

Damnation. Only hours into her journey and now there was another man she hoped never to see again.

~ * ~

With mounting curiosity, Will watched the young widow bolt. But from whom or what did she flee? Surely she had nothing to fear from him?

Leaning back against the railing, arms crossed, he pondered the matter.

Eliza Danton was something all right although he wasn't certain what. Feisty and full of fire one moment, shy and uncertain the next. But most of all, she seemed afraid.

He'd lost a wife, murdered some five years ago. All too familiar with the pain and still burdened by her loss, he lived with a constant regret and a loneliness he kept to himself. But during all those rough passages he couldn't remember any fear. So what made Eliza Danton so fearful? It didn't make sense and that bothered him.

Logical and levelheaded, facts were the bedrock of Will's life. When a woman's fear yowled louder than a pack of coyotes he wanted to know why. Was there someone she feared? If only some sign of danger had been as notable prior to his wife's demise, he might have prevented the tragedy. And despite his desire to find the answer, her distress tugged at his conscience in some idiotic way he fought to ignore.

That she'd lied to him, he didn't doubt. She lacked the artifice to deaden her expressive eyes. And her body had bristled with the discomfort of her untruths.

But what did she hide?

He snorted, annoyed he should care. Yet he loved puzzles of all kinds, mathematical, structural, mystical and human. They ensnared him like a fish in a net. Once snagged, he'd see the question through to the end. And Eliza Danton posed a big question which begged to be solved. But was he foolish enough to plow into her life to find the answers?

His interest in her had nothing to do with her looks, or so he tried to tell himself. Her beauty was so fresh he couldn't stop staring at her. Instead he blamed the boredom of ship travel which undoubtedly enhanced her air of mystery and added to her allure. None of this would be worth consideration at home in High Bluff with his busy law practice and the mill to keep him busy. And he might yet walk away from this enigma if he knew what was good for him. The woman smelled of trouble.

But seven days on a paddlewheel was a long, long time.

Find *Eliza* at all major retailers.

~ * ~

Interested in getting advance notice of great new books, author contests and giveaways, and only-to-subscriber goodies? Join https://www.facebook.com/groups/ChampagneBookClub/.